ALL THE MARBLES

Dusty Rainbolt

All the Marbles
Dusty Rainbolt
First Edition Copyright © Dusty Rainbolt, 2003

Published by Yard Dog Press at Create Space

This is a work of fiction. All the characters and events portrayed in this book are fictitious, and any resemblance to real people is purely coincidental.

ISBN: 1-893687-34-1
ISBN-13: 978-1-893687-34-9

Yard Dog Press
710 W. Redbud Lane
Alma, AR 72921-7247

http://www.yarddogpress.com

Edited by Selina Rosen
Technical Editor Lynn Rosen
Cover art by David Lee Anderson

Second Edition June 15, 2018
First Edition August 1, 2003
Printed in the United States of America
0 9 8 7 6 5 4 3 2

Dedication

To my Dad, the original phone company communications engineer; my husband, Weems Hutto, who turned out to be my Wright in shining armor; and my mentor, Lee Killough, cuz she's a redhead with a wicked sense of humor.

Chapter One

Alone. This time Chandra was *really* alone. In a sleazy deep space port bar, she sat among the scum and the runners. How the hell did she get here?

As she stared into her drink, Chandra Solomon ran a trembling finger along the lip of her glass. She took a deep breath and gulped down the last of the acrid Leonian brandy. Sure, it tasted like antimatter coolant, but it was cheap. Not that it mattered, since she was so broke her wallet needed traction.

How could he have done this to her? How could he leave her alone in the worst town in this sector of the galaxy?

Damn you, Tyrus! Why'd you have to get yourself killed?

He'd stranded her here in the town of Bitter with no money, no friends, no hope and worst of all, no phone. Bitter! Not only was she *bitter*, she was *pissed.*

The dimly lit bar reeked with the collective odors of unwashed aliens, smelling like a cross between the Ecto-Super locker room and a sewage treatment plant. Every few minutes a light germicidal mist sprayed from vents to kill all lifeforms too small to carry a credit chip. It also vented a deodorizer to keep the patrons from passing out from the collective stench. In the background, some band played a cacophony of musical flatulence, a less than graceful performance that also contributed to the interior air pollution. The atmosphere in the bar and the music reflected her mood.

Chandra had never been particularly fatalistic; when she looked at it, the brandy snifter had always been half full. But on this backwater planet that the phone company hierarchy unaffectionately nicknamed "Distress," she quickly learned that the glass was not only completely empty, she owed money on it as well.

One lesson that she'd learned from her late partner: If everything seems to be okay, then you simply do not understand the situation.

Her hand, unsteady after too many brandies, brushed through her untamed teak hair, a nervous habit she'd acquired through the years trying to buy time during heated exchanges with Tyrus. Small wonder she took to drinking. But now she'd give anything just to let him verbally trounce her—just one more time.

She stared at her old phone company-issue titanium hard hat on the table next to her glass. Her hand ran across its ridges. Its cool surface gave Chandra a comfortable, though somewhat unwarranted, feeling of protection. Her fingers found the slight dent on the right side just above her ear. The headgear had saved her when a metal beam snapped loose and slammed against her head. Although she heard ringing in her ears for days, she spent only one night in the infirmary. Somehow, even after years of abuse, the Mother Bell insignia, a bell with nine planets orbiting it, escaped disfigurement.

The same company logo was displayed proudly over the left breast of her shimmering silver kevlon flight suit. A gold braid that identified her as a senior field engineer of InterGalactic Bell—communications conglomerate extraordinaire—encircled it. The flight suit fit snugly against her trim frame without betraying too many fine details. Between the logo and all her phone company gizmos dangling from the tool belt, Distress natives never needed to ask her planet of origin or for whom she worked.

The locals had viewed Tyrus and her as objects of curiosity; those wacky humans, who spent megabucks on watered-down booze and would someday build a communications complex that would transform their slovenly little planet into the showcase of the galaxy. They would be disappointed, maybe even hostile, to learn that for now there'd be no massive new inflow of IGB dollars. She didn't want to be around when the word leaked out, if it hadn't already.

She emptied her glass, making sure she drained every drop. As that last sip of cheap booze reached its final destination, it seared the pit of her stomach. Even if she could afford a meal, she wouldn't be able to hold down real food for a week. But something besides the brandy made her uncomfortable. She finally realized it was that horrid feeling of being watched. Chandra gazed down at the trio of mouse-sized quell squirming around in the bottom of the snack basket.

Talisman's Bar generously provided the salted snacks to encourage prolonged consumption of their over-priced booze. No, it couldn't be them; quell didn't have eyes.

She stole a glance about the bar at the assortment of patrons. There were representatives of just about every race she'd ever met and a few she hadn't. None of them looked to be a member of the bourgeois of their planets. From what she learned of Talisman's, most creatures that drank here either had a price on their heads or were conducting an illegal transaction. Everyone but her, that is. She simply had no place else to go.

She saw a Corvian web flyer that she'd failed to notice before—quite a feat considering he was almost as big as her speedster. He must have been staring at her since the moment she entered the bar. In Talisman's subdued light the Corvian's semi-transparent lime-gelatin skin glistened. His armor plating strained to accommodate a spongy body as wide as it was tall. He had trapped her in the fixed gaze of those vacuous amber eyes; his reptilian mouth curled in lecherous anticipation.

Chandra shuddered and tried to dodge the web flyer's stare by reaching into the snack basket of tidbits. At her touch, the live crunchies wriggled to the edge of the basket, momentarily escaping their fate. Chandra frowned and withdrew her hand. Even starving, she could not bring herself to eat anything that wasn't at least eligible for last rites.

He rose like a green tsunami. Picking up his drink, he swaggered over to her table and plopped down beside her. He flagged the waiter. "Now give Earther intoxicant." His garbled accent made the words almost unintelligible.

"No, I just want to be alone," Chandra said.

He held up her empty glass. By the shapeless splotches of crusty crud caked on it the glass had never been entirely clean, perhaps even when it was new. "Bring whatever this," he told the barkeep.

He set the glass down next to the snack basket. Absently he reached for one of the quell, eyeing it for a moment before taking a bite. It squeaked, but Green Face popped the rest of it into his mouth, chewed heartily and swallowed. "Good quell."

Chandra drew up her face and turned away. "Take off. I'm hoping to meet something a little closer to the top of the food chain."

Not easily discouraged, the Corvian eased closer. He

grabbed her chin between two phlegmish fingers and pulled her toward his face. Chandra cringed from his breath. She'd sooner spend a day on a methane planet without an oxygen mask than to sit this close to him. She tried pulling loose, but he only tightened his grip.

"Come, my sludgedove. You want see real ship?" He leered. "Show you—laser cannon."

"Here." The barkeep slammed down the glasses, managing to slosh only half of the drinks on the table.

Grabbing the Corvian's glass, Chandra pitched its contents into his face. Old Green Face straightened his back, a feat nearly impossible for something that resembled a six-foot tall slug. He blinked a few times and growled at her, probably the most in-depth conversation he'd had in months. Sulfur-colored liquid collected in tiny drops and hung at the base of his chin, undulating and shimmering each time the creature moved his head.

From behind the Corvian, a small voice said, "Move on."

The Corvian staggered around; his complexion flared to chartreuse as he stared down into the gaunt face of a three-foot Pictorian trader. The little creature was barely large enough to survive the aerosol germicide. Snarling, Green Face smashed a fist down on the Pictorian's head, sending him stumbling onto a table occupied by a guy sharing his drink with a cat. The cat and his guest continued to drink as if this happened every day. The trader's head jarred back as he slid to the ground, unnoticed by most in the bar except Chandra, the Corvian, the man and his cat, and a woman with the looks and build of an Erosian warrior sitting alone in a poorly-lit corner of the pub. Picking himself up, the Pictorian brushed the floor's filth from his costly hand-woven robe. As he hobbled back to his own table, he paused to nod across the room at the ebony-skinned woman. Nodding in return, she settled even further into the darkness of her corner.

Green Face turned back to Chandra. "Die him later. What you say, huggie? I make your night."

She struggled, scratching and kicking, but she might as well have been fighting the undertow during the noontime deluge at the Bitter sewage treatment plant. Nor would calling for help do any good here in Talisman's. During these romantic interludes, the bar's patrons conveniently turned deaf and blind. He twisted her arm. Any more torque and she feared her elbow would shatter. She considered her options as he dragged her toward the door. She could either go along or lose her arm, and she *had* grown rather attached to that arm.

Suddenly, Green Face released his grip, slapped at the back of his neck and groaned. A small metal bug dislodged from his skin and fell to the stone floor with a faint ping. He and Chandra stared at the floor. He was lucky, Chandra thought. It could have been a swamp wasp. Now, *that* would really have hurt. They like to hang out in bars and didn't respond to the sprays.

While the Corvian grabbed at his neck, Chandra inched away. He *had* stunk before, but not this bad. His dead-and-rotting-in-the-gutter aroma had grown even more unbearable.

Nearby, the cat hissed, jumped down from the table and headed for the door. The man followed—a few paces behind—with his hand covering his nose.

Something else had changed. The Corvian seemed to be shrinking, or maybe she had grown taller. She had always wanted to be taller.

She covered her nose. "Righteous Sapiens."

An oozy green chunk of Corvian flesh slid to the filthy floor, followed by another and then another. Soon, nothing remained but a putrid puddle of curdling goo oozing from under the battered plates of armor.

Like Chandra, other nearby patrons backed away. As the odor expanded, they parted like the Red Sea and headed for the exit. She moved through the exodus back to her table.

Slugging down the drink that Puddles-of-Goo had kindly paid for, she leaned back in the pub's off-balanced chair. What a shame she hadn't ordered something more expensive and easier to swallow.

With a deep breath she yelled, "Barman!" The dreaded moment had arrived. She couldn't begin to pay the exorbitant tab she had run up over the course of the afternoon. She wondered what penalties she'd suffer for stealing drinks in this province. It didn't matter. If they arrested her, she'd at least have a place to spend the night. They might even feed her. Of course, the chance existed that she could wind up being some other prisoner's food. But, that would *certainly* take care of her housing problem.

"That brandy tasted like swamp water," she complained.

He picked up the empty glass and held it upside down. Not

even a drop remained. "This drink was made from the finest embalming fluid."

"Look at this mess!" She pointed at the puddle undulating on the floor. A small cloud of steam hung grayly above it. "What kind of a low-life dive is this? That is the most disgusting thing I've ever seen."

The waiter eyed the offensive pool.

"Not only am I going to contact InterGalactic Bell and inform them that this pit isn't fit to serve any more of their personnel; I'm going to call the health inspector!"

The waiter rolled his weary eyes. "If you don't like the service in this low-life joint, there's a bunch more down the street, only they're not as nice. As for the health inspector, he works here after hours to pay for his wife's tongue electrolysis. Is that the best excuse you can dream up for not paying your tab?" His forehead furrowed in an expression that said he'd heard it all.

Chandra slumped into her chair and tapped her fingers on her hard hat. *Now what?*

The waiter's lip curled. "I'm disappointed. I thought you might have some imagination. But I shouldn't have expected much from a phone company bimbo. And don't get your thermals in wad. Your tab's already been paid."

"It has?" Apprehension erased her comfort. Worse beings than the Corvian frequented the bar. "By who?"

"That Pictorian." The waiter picked up her glasses and the empty quell basket.

She glared in the direction of her benefactor's table, half-expecting to see the little man preening his ears. But he'd already departed, leaving behind him a litter of empty glasses, half-smoked fire logs, and scattered crumbs. A nearby horde of Wiathaleans and their stale-smelling dates watched as a waiter cleared the clutter so they could commandeer the table.

Without another word she rose, grabbed her hardhat and tool belt, and eased toward the door.

"Here." She flipped the waiter a coin as she passed him. The waiter's reflexes, sluggish from a long day of too many rude patrons and too much cheap booze himself, didn't kick in fast enough. The coin flew past his fingers and clanked as it bounced on the floor and into the puddle of Corvian goo.

Let him scramble for it. She smiled at the mental image of him sifting through the viscid Corvian remains, only to find a coin that would not admit him to an outdoor potty.

"My Harbinger," she told the doorman, holding her hand out.

He left his station and came back with a battle-scarred light pistol in a well-worn holster.

Her green eyes narrowed. "That's not mine! What are you trying to pull?"

"All right, all right." He left and returned again, this time with a new Harbinger light pistol encased in a finely tooled Rigelian lizard holster.

She snatched it out of his hand. As she stomped out the door, she slung the holster over her shoulder, pelting herself hard in the back. "Share the tip with Smiley over there. Should be enough for both of you."

With that kind of gratuity she dared not show her face in Talisman's again, not that she had any inclination to frequent this fusty dive in the near, or for that matter, the distant future. As she walked past a phone outside the bar, she stopped, stuck a finger in the coin return slot and retrieved a deci. *All right! Solvent again!* Only that nearly worthless coin stood between her and absolute destitution.

A week ago her partner, Tyrus, had helped himself to InterGalactic Bell's more-than-generous per diem and the rest of her travel expenses. As always, he had every good intention of paying her back with his first winning hand at Cryptic. After Tyrus won a one-way trip to the morgue, the manager of Bitter's only two-and-a-half star hotel rousted her out of bed and tossed Chandra and her tool belt into the street. Her company credit chip was not only depleted, but overdrawn as well.

Now she was broke, empty broke as the locals called it, referring to the hunger that inevitably accompanied such total poverty. She found herself the sociological equal of squeegee people, who cleaned speedster windows at traffic control stations and then stuck blasters in the face of the drivers to encourage generous compensation for a job well done. Later they slept in wallows lining the muddy streets of Bitter. The scene actually looked very similar to one she had just left in Talisman's Bar. Even the air outside smelled of brine, beer and piss.

What a miserable planet!

Why couldn't Tyrus have stranded her on, say, Mercy or

Orion 3? She remembered such luxuriant, green landscapes. The towns and countrysides, immaculate beyond reasonable imagination, permitted a person to fall asleep beside a babbling stream with no worry about what would happen to them in the night. Tomorrow, she would probably wake up next to a babbling alcho.

No, Tyrus picked this civility-forsaken planet to die on. He left her here among the thieves and the freighter pilots, who were nothing but thieves with a pilot's license. A few military men and some cops hung out on Distress, and a whole boatload of attorneys practiced sordid variations of their trade, but none of these were any better than the scum.

Now, she's stuck on this planet where the air smells like the inside of a dumpster and on a clear day a light baby-blue haze hung in the atmosphere. Despite the ecological squalor, wildlife abounded. The birds may have developed an additional leg growing out of their backs, but they thrived nevertheless.

It wasn't the mutated animals that worried her.

As a precaution, she strapped on her holster and checked the weapon. It held a full charge, enough firepower to last her through a small war at close range. She'd never owned a nicer piece. Knowing Tyrus, he probably stole it from someone, or more likely, he won it gambling. It never ceased to amaze her the things guys risked in a wager.

Several years ago Tyrus won a wife. It did not take him long to find out why the Betan so quickly bet his own mate, including an extensive dowry. She possessed the disposition of a grizzle beast in heat and the bulk of a megabison. Two hours later, Tyrus found another game on the other side of town and squandered everything he had just to make sure he lost his new Betan life partner, too. Chandra guessed that somewhere across the solar system, a poor slob still counts his intentionally diminishing funds, shakes his head and says, "Take my wife."

But Tyrus never bet his gun.

Chandra stepped off of Talisman's porch and headed down the road that led out of town. At least she could go be with Tyrus. She edged toward Bitter's outskirts. Exhausted, the pangs of hunger and hangover eroded her belly like a flood of sulfuric acid.

In tipploriums across the galaxy, Chandra had discovered the Law of Alcohol Relativity, which proved that the effect of any liquor lasted in direct proportion to how much it cost. Needless to say, the intoxicating power of the Leonian brandy did not last much past the steps of the tavern.

Too soon, the warm tingling drained away, replaced with cold fatigue. So overpowering was her hunger, that Chandra, had she the money, would have even eaten at McDonald-Douglas—the worst fast food chain in the galaxy—where the food tasted like charred road-kill sandwiched between heat resistant tiles, and was almost as nutritious. But today even a bargain Big Doug was out of her price range.

Without money or credit chips, staying in town was impossible.

Tomorrow she would walk to Bedlam. Although travel books described it as dirty and disgusting, she could put her engineering talents to work and soon make enough to reach the closest ultra-long distance phone. But the long trek on foot was one she simply could not make tonight.

Shadows had already begun to lengthen.

As she strode down the street, Chandra's phone company training took over. She focused her senses on the subtleties around her. She must be cautious. Each sound, the crackling of dead leaves beneath her feet, the rustling of the wind chasing the naked branches of the trees, and the chinking of metal behind her, filled her mind with dreadful images.

She stopped often, listening. Behind her, she heard the gentle rustling of fabric and a soft *ca-chink, ca-chink.*

Wright Aulweighs climbed in the left seat of his speedster, and studied the lines of Talisman's Bar. From an architectural perspective it would make a first class outhouse—just a filthy hole—except it didn't smell even that good.

Beside Wright, the cat, Ivan the Terrible, stared at his humanoid chauffeur with unblinking amber eyes. Dinnertime was rapidly approaching, but it didn't look like his companion was in any hurry to return to the ship to feed him. If something didn't happen soon, the cat would have to take desperate action. A polite tap to the arm served as a first request. This usually did the trick. When Wright failed to respond, the gentle patting escalated to tapping with the claws and eventually an insistent slap with claws fully extended.

Most of the time that worked, but Wright ignored his feline companion and continued to watch the door to the bar.

The mass exodus of drinkers into the street continued. Some left the bar in a hurry. Others stumbled down the steps. A few minutes later, the woman wearing the hard hat and silvery flight suit strode down the stairs. She adjusted her holster.

Wright watched her until she walked out of sight. He wanted to follow her but figured she was smart enough to know that the speedster was tailing her. Every few moments he'd ease forward barely keeping her in view. That's when he realized he wasn't the only one shadowing her.

He'd have to make his move later...if she lived. For now, Wright had to go feed Ivan...that is, if *he* wanted to live.

Chapter Two

Chandra picked up her pace. As if in echo, the trailing sounds also moved faster. Several someones shadowed each step. She stopped, turned around and stared into the dusky void. The *ca-chink* stopped.

Chandra unsnapped the holster and slipped her fingers around the Harbinger. The cool smoothness of the barrel felt comforting, like a protective big brother. She slid the safety off, but before she could pull her weapon from its sheath, she found herself on the ground, held down by a Totgarian officer and his enlisted henchmen. Their bejeweled uniforms glistened with medals for all occasions.

Corruption, greed, and a great looking profile...all attributes considered desirable by this bizarre race whose sole ambition in life consisted of making the most noise when walking. What egos! They often threw their considerable weight around to impress the natives of whatever underdeveloped planet they happen to be harassing. If the planetary inhabitants amassed more bulk than the Totgars, or could kick their massive butts to a mushy pulp, the Totgars had a tendency to quietly slip into a pub and behave themselves.

Years back she did a stint on Totgara. Many of those in the military fancied themselves great bounty hunters. However, tracking games while wearing their noisy medals and ribbons was like trying to sneak up on a deer while ringing a cowbell. The phone company security manuals classified them as harmless. These guys didn't look harmless.

The officer's face drew closer to hers. His cologne smelled strong but not unpleasant, a combination of spices and fruit.

"Still. Still, little lineman," the one with the most medals said softly as if soothing a frightened animal.

A second officer peered over his shoulder and removed her Harbinger from her holster. "No need this," he said. He held up the light pistol that his superior officer just handed him. "No pain you much. We talk. Right BossCom?"

BossCom stuck his milky face next to hers. "You know we want."

Chandra mentally nodded her head. *Sex, of course.*

He pointed at his palm. "Give it. We give you something for trouble."

She stopped struggling. They wanted it *that* bad? "Enough to get me off of this rock?"

"Certainly. Enjoy killing, but we –uh—do compassion," he said struggling with his words. The other officer nodded his head in agreement.

"You want me to strip right here in the middle of the street?"

"Treasure there?"

Chandra's eyebrow rose to an arch.

These guys sure have a lot to learn about human anatomy. Either that or...

Her hand stopped. "Exactly what is it you want? Could you tell me in terms even a human could understand?"

His lips curled up. "What partner gave. Worthless to dead Earther."

"Dead?" Without thinking, she zipped her suit up. "But you have the Harbinger. The cops told me he lost everything else in the Cryptic game."

Chandra crossed her arms.

BossCom looked at her with disgust. "It hid," BossCom told his sidekick. "Rigmar, look tool belt. If not there, break – uh—arm."

Chandra struggled while Rigmar tugged at her utility belt.

"Nothing here," he said. "Nothing but phone company junk."

Chandra managed to dart out of BossCom's clutches, but the other Totgarian grabbed her as she streaked past. Clutching her flight suit collar he dragged her down the main thoroughfare to Bitter's outskirts.

She screamed to casual passersby who stopped to watch, grew bored and then left, complaining that nothing exciting ever happened in Bitter.

Rigmar hauled her through disrepaired streets into an adjoining alley and pulled her to her feet. Chandra's hands groped for release, but none came. Her hard hat tumbled from her head and rolled behind her as he dragged her to a halt at the end of the alley. Frantic gurgles, wheezes and gasps froze in her throat. With her strength slowly sapping away, her finger's grip around his hands weakened. She would have told them, if she had any idea what in Sapien's universe they were talking about. As millions of tiny black spots clouded her vision, the Totgarian's words faded into the distance.

The commander stomped impatiently around them. "Rigmar, don't play with your food. Don't kill it; just maim it real good. It can't talk if it's dead." One stomp too many and his ampleness slid up to his knee into the opening of a damaged manhole cover with a loud and final ca-chink. He tried to pull free, but his leg stuck fast.

"Rigmar, forget that block-minded Earther and get me free."

Rigmar looked up at BossCom's predicament. "I can't let it go. It might get away." His voice sounded hopeful. "I guess I can break its legs or something."

The commander hissed through his teeth. "Oh, all right. Go ahead and kill it. Just hurry up."

Rigmar turned back to Chandra.

"It's...it's..." she gasped.

He released the pressure from her throat, allowing her head to slam against the street.

"What'd it say?" BossCom asked.

"It said, 'It's...'"

"It's what?" demanded BossCom.

"It's there..." Chandra wheezed.

"Where?"

"There in my hard hat."

Rigmar scowled. "Couldn't be."

"Rigmar, you mother's disappointment!" BossCom yelled. "Do something with the snag and get me free!"

Chandra gasped for air. "It's not actually in the hard hat itself. But Tyrus left me an infochip map that pinpoints its location. I'll show you." Rigmar held Chandra fast by the collar as she took the half dozen steps to retrieve her lost helmet. She picked up the hard hat by the small bill and looked inside. "Good. It's still there. I thought it might have fallen out while you rat parasites were introducing my teeth to all of Bitter's potholes."

Rigmar tried to peer over her shoulder.

"Nuh-uh." She pulled her hat against her chest. "You said you'd pay me. You think I'm stupid enough to just give you the chip for nothing. Wake up and smell the acid rain, fellas."

"The blood's stopped circulating," BossCom moaned. "Leg

will drop off if my future dead subordinate doesn't free me—now!"

Rigmar ignored his superior. He clung to her collar and held his hand out in wild expectation.

Suddenly, Chandra doubled over, clutching her chest. "Oh, Sapiens!" she screamed. "It hurts so bad."

Alarmed, Rigmar bent over her at the same moment Chandra swung her hard hat into his groin. The Totgarian fell back holding his crotch, and rolled into a big ball, bobbling around like an irregular marble.

Leaping up, Chandra placed her hard hat on her head and grabbed her utility belt and her Harbinger. "Bye, guys. It was fun."

She charged down a deserted alley desperately seeking a safe escape. Empty shipping boxes and stacks of trash, piled nearly to the tops of the buildings, blocked her way.

Yep, ma'am, you just put yersef in a right nice corral. Too bad you didn't bring yer horses.

She turned around, crossed the street, then dashed down the alley in the opposite direction.

Rigmar staggered over to BossCom. He tugged, but the commander remained wedged fast in the hole. Rigmar pulled out his own blaster, taking careful but wobbly aim at the manhole cover.

"Hold that thing still," BossCom yelled.

Still? He stood as still as he could, although his legs were unsteady and the ground felt as firm as a river running rapids.

Finally, Rigmar pulled the trigger. The blast missed the manhole cover entirely, hitting BossCom's leg right above the knee. Totgarian flesh flew everywhere in a spray of white tissue. The air smelled like fried piña colada.

BossCom moaned.

"What's going on here, yet?" boomed the voice of one of Bitter's finest. "Clean up this mess." The cop handed one citation to Rigmar for destruction of public property and one to BossCom for littering with formerly organic matter.

"Hey, I'm not dead!" the commander exclaimed.

"Close enough. Now, clean up this mess."

Chandra's eyes quickly grew accustomed to the murky darkness. The shadows felt comforting. Every few hundred meters bare trees and deteriorated buildings allowed a few rays of light to filter into the seldom-used byway. She dove behind a pile of garbage. While she waited, she watched a large dog-like brugo beast in search of his evening meal crawl into a garbage chute and disappear, never to be seen again.

Large-fanged rodents scurried about while bugs of all shapes and sizes traveled on self-made super-highways of trash. In all, an uplifting scene.

Shortly, Rigmar ambled through the alley rummaging through the piles of trash.

Soon, the Erosian warrior Chandra had seen at the pub also wandered into the alley. With all this foot traffic, whoever owned that stretch of alley should start charging a toll fee. The warrior jogged from pile to pile, searching each heap as if she, too, had lost something valuable.

Chandra ducked deeper beneath her pile of trash, not unlike ones she and Tyrus had cleared from their ultra-long lines installations. Mainly nondescript rubble interlaced with petron cables, twisted parts from a rec-cruiser engine complete with E-pistons, and worn carpeting from one of the local pubs, stained with drink and Sapiens only knew what else. The E-pistons provided a cranny large enough for her to slide into, but because of that, her stalker would look there first.

She slipped into the comfort of the shadows, taking slow easy steps until she found one of the many vacuum chutes lacing through Bitter's elaborate underground network. Most of them sent garbage to underground storage dumps; however, merchants and businessmen used other chutes for about every conceivable purpose from cross-province banking to area-wide smuggling. This one must have been a refuse chute for large objects. Certainly, she could fit into the thing.

One dark notion nagged at her. Was the chute a way out of the blaze or just a short cut to another frying pan?

The Erosian made her way down the alley, closing in on Chandra's haven.

"Solomon," the warrior called. She kicked over a food storage drum too large to drop down the chute.

Chandra clutched the fabric of her own flight suit, which had been kindly provided by her employer. Mother Bell assured her that its impervious metallic fabric would protect her from a hostile environment, but they never said anything about hostile natives.

"Solomon, Tyrus sent me. My name is Bosson. I can help

you." The woman's words sounded inviting, but her face and voice lacked sincerity. Her ominous form closed in on Chandra's refuse refuge. A black hand pulled a roll of cable from the heap.

Chandra froze, afraid to even breathe.

"The little snag must be here," she muttered as she tossed the four hundred-pound spool across the alley as easily as Chandra could toss a spool of thermo-lite line.

The hell with it, Chandra thought, and slipped her legs into the meter-wide tubing mounted into the side of the dimly lit building. Suddenly, the whine of servos and a violent rush of wind deafened her. Following the hurricane of sound, Chandra's ears exploded and the vacuum sucked the breath from her lungs. Strength drained from her hands and in moments her grip failed.

Chandra fell and bounced against the dark unknown.

Chapter Three

As abruptly as the darkness had overtaken her, bright lights and white walls blinded her. Chandra slid to a stop at the end of the pneumo-tube to find herself at the conjunction of six corridors. The hallways, all identical, appeared endless, disappearing into gently curved angles. With no reference of scale, the visible corridors could have gone on for miles. She supposed one direction was as good as the other.

A strident yak-call alarm echoed from speakers down each of the corridors. Soon, but not soon enough, a nasal male voice replaced it, "Napul, grade, verify and off-load unlabeled slab—tube D." She suspected that she stood in tube D and *she* was the unlabeled slab.

White seemed a damned odd color to paint a garbage dump when the rest of the planet looked so dirty and dingy. How did they keep it so clean? From the look of the place, and the disgusting chemical odors, she concluded that she had somehow slid into a hospital. However, while the odors smelled chemical and medicinal, they still lacked many other hospital smells. But, characteristic of *all* hospitals, robocarts, the workhorse of programmable autowagons, lined the walls.

Another message boomed out of the public address, this time more insistent. "Napul, I'm busy. Now, drag your lazy ass down there and pick up that load!"

Immediately following the announcement, footsteps approached.

Chandra picked up her hard hat, checked her utility belt and weapon, and headed down the hallway. She took strides as long as she could without making the normal amount of noise her flight safety boots made, while she muted the customary chink of her utility belt with her hand.

"Aw, bloggin' fell," echoed a whining masculine voice at the tube drop. "We lost another one."

Chandra hiked for kilometers, or so it seemed. She resigned herself to the fact that she would probably starve to death in this alabaster prison. In eons to come, some archaeologist would run across her spindly skeleton and determine that this human female died as result of some natural catastrophe, starvation being a disaster to her. Her remains would be moved to some museum to be gawked at by aliens who would consider a creature with only two arms, two legs and one head a primitively developed creature in the first place. And to end it all, her bones would probably end up as a snack for the curator's famished brugo-beast that someone accidentally locked up in the museum one weekend.

Again she heard footfalls. Rounding the corner, she ran into one of the few native Distressites she had seen since she landed on the planet. He wore no clothing, only a belt around his middle to cover his navel. The reason remained a mystery, since a thick coat of fur covered his entire body.

"I'm a little lost," she said.

"You must be the load from tube D." He eyed her, toe to head and then back again.

"I must be."

"We've been looking for you."

"Can you show me the way out?"

"Down the end of the corridor." He pointed. "Last door on the left. It's marked 'exit'."

"Thanks."

When Chandra left, the technician ran over to the intercom. "Hey, Napul, load D heading your way. I'd say she weighs about fifty-two kilos on the foot. She's certainly not choice. Maybe a grade 'B' at best."

Navigation had never been one of Chandra's strengths. Back on Earth, her manager at Mother Bell touted her engineering skills as unsurpassed. She had set up communications pubs so complex that they boggled the average engineer's mind. But reading a map and following road directions put her at a loss. Realizing her weakness, Chandra's regional supervisor teamed her with Tyrus.

"Let Tyrus be your guide," Gerkin said. "You're my best engineer, Solomon. But you couldn't find your ass with both hands and a map."

That day, at the corporate office under a rainy St. Louis sky, her supervisor sealed Chandra's fate. She spent the next four years in a veritable purgatory. But at least with Tyrus, she knew where in purgatory she was.

Now, lost again. "Last hall on the left and the second door on the right?"

Suddenly, the scent of chemicals reached down her nose and pulled out her lungs through her eyes. It came from a door labeled in bright red letters: "Preparation."

She kept walking. Maybe she could find somebody in one of these rooms to give her directions again.

"Cold Storage" tagged the next door, a slightly more interesting prospect. Almost no odor came from this door. Chandra triggered the laser eye on the cold storage room and entered at the opening door's invitation. This time an icy blast greeted her arrival.

She turned the thermostat in her flight suit to "warm."

Like the rest of the building, this room stretched out stark and bare. A number of large steel tables stood along the wall. On one of the tables lay a tissue bag with "Napul" scribbled on it in indelible ink.

Chandra smiled as she lunged for the sack. Someone's lunch! Not much of one, granted, but even the Borian mammoth hand pie would help appease the gnaw in her belly. The piecrust tasted a little dry, but she inhaled the aroma of the meat, smoked and tender. Add a snifter of ale and a romantic fire and the scene would have been perfect.

As she slowly savored Napul's lunch, she leaned back against the wall and again turned up her thermostat.

What now?

For the first time in days, she felt hope. She would find the exit, and tomorrow, head for Bedlam, if she could find it. And the way she felt now, she could find anything!

Standing up, she spotted a lever on the side of one of the tables. On impulse, Chandra pulled it. A low hydraulic hum ensued, followed by the tabletop lifting up. It rotated until it slid invisibly beneath the table. It turned out to be not a table after all, but storage compartment, more like a large steel bathtub. She peered inside.

"Sapiens!" She leapt straight backward.

Inside the hold lay the badly mutilated body of a Bulivarian pilot. Beneath the cuts and bruises on his bronzed face, he wore an expression of anger and surprise.

She shuddered. "A morgue! This is a morgue."

She looked back at the pilot with his broken bones and massive gashes. Poor man. Either an accident killed him or he owed someone money. It could have been a traffic accident. Those freighter pilots flew like madmen when confined to the inter-planetary traffic.

Chandra cringed. For a morgue, something still seemed strange here. A purplish mark showed on the man's thigh. She peered more closely, but could not quite make it out. She never learned to read the native language on Distress very well.

Chandra pulled her translator from her utility belt. She punched in the symbols on the man's leg. It answered in English with the words: "OK - prime choice, number 17."

Prime choice? Prime choice?

"Sapiens. Prime choice. That's a cut of meat." She jumped back from the cart. "This isn't a morgue. It's a bloody packing plant!"

A shudder ran down her spine as she threw the sandwich down on the spotless floor.

"Sapiens, Tyrus," she said to herself. "You're lucky I claimed your body so quickly or you might've wound up on someone's dinner plate."

Hiss. The door opened and in walked a jabbering technician. "Come on, Commander," he said to the corpse. "It's time to get you down to processing."

"Excuse me," Chandra said.

Startled, he peered into the cart. "Yes."

"No. Over here."

He turned around to find Chandra huddled in the corner, the crumpled bag in her hand hidden behind her.

"Can you tell me how to get out of here?" she asked.

The hairy technician gave an understanding yellow smile and repeated the directions to the door marked "Exit."

She triggered the electronic beam and left.

"Hey, Napul," the hairy guy said into the intercom. "On the foot, headed your way. Oh, by the way, she just ate your lunch."

Finally, Chandra found it, the door label "Exit."

Exhaling a deep breath of relief and chemicals too numerous to name, she triggered the eye and wandered through the door to safety and freedom...she thought.

But instead of a poorly lit alley at dusk, she found yet

another room with more colorless walls. Soft, contemporary Earth music fed through the intercom. In the center of the room stood a thickly padded table sporting two speakers at the head, and heavy straps and an IV bottle.

"You're late." Napul, the Distressite frowned. "I picked the music just for you. You like it?"

Chandra nodded silently.

"Great. Now, why don't you lie down and we'll get on with it? It doesn't hurt, you know. You'll feel great when the drug hits you and then you'll just go to sleep."

"Uh—it's nice-but-uh-I'm not supposed to be here." Chandra eyed the table with a shiver. "There's been a mistake."

He gave her an understanding smile. "I know you're having second thoughts. Most of them do by the time they get here."

Chandra stepped back. "No, there's been a *big* mistake. I was just trying to escape."

"I know you were," he said. "This is the most common form of escape on Distress. That's why we have conveniently located tubes all over town. You know we have more branches than the local banks?"

"No, I don't mean *that* kind of escape."

Napul placed one of his three arms on his hairy hip. "Look. I've got a job to do and a quota to fill. You came down the chute voluntarily, and *that* constitutes a contract. If you didn't want to terminate, you shouldn't have jumped in the tube."

"When I got into that tube I thought I was going to the bank," she lied.

"Yeah. That's what gets us through the slow periods. You know, when the economy is good and everyone feels like they've just got to go on living another day," he said. "It's been a little slow around here lately expect for a couple of speedster crashes and a few murders."

"Do you really package people for food?"

He scratched his chin with his upper arm. "Sure. I'm told most humans taste like chicken. Corvians taste more like that green stuff you find in old forgotten containers in the cryo units. We get more per pound for humanoids and humans." He looked her up and down mentally weighing her with his eyes. "Oh yes, humans are a premium."

Her stomach churned. "Sapiens! Do you eat this meat?"

"Are you kidding? I know what you humanoids eat. You think I'd put something that filthy in my mouth? No, I eat tubers...Now, why don't you climb up here and I'll just get you started."

Chandra looked at the intravenous bottle. It contained an opaque pink liquid.

"What is that?" She pointed at the bottle.

"That? It's called Benther Dunthit. It helps you relax. After you're unconscious it starts the decomposition process, or if you prefer—aging process, but it stops before the tissue gets too spongy. It's hard to sell the meat if it's either too chewy or too gooey. The Benther controls that."

"That's a huge needle."

"Everyone says that. It's not so bad. Just a little stick then you won't feel anything *ever*."

"Look. I've decided I don't want to do this. I don't think the contract is legal, because there wasn't full disclosure. So why don't you show me the way out and I'll leave you to your next case?"

He took a couple of steps toward her. "Our attorneys said the action of climbing in our tubes is a perfectly legal contract and is thoroughly binding to the death. After you're dead, if you still want to leave, you can." He took another couple of steps toward her.

Chandra ran to the door, but it was completely flush with the walls—no knob or handle to grab, no buttons to push. She pushed it, but vaguely recalled that it had pushed inward when she entered the room.

He came a little closer to her. "Now, you will lie down peacefully, or do I have to stun you?" He pulled out his people prod.

Earlier today, if someone had told her things could be worse, she wouldn't have believed it possible. Now here she was at the OK Packing Plant and some jerk wanted to inject her with hallucinogenic meat tenderizer for her own good.

"Drop dead!" She pulled out her Harbinger and pointed it at the termination technician. "If anyone goes out feet first, it's not going to be me. Now. Just tell me how to get out of this place and nobody will get hurt, especially you."

Napul clutched the prod with more avid determination and shook his head. "If I stun you, you'll miss out on all those wonderful sensations you get from the drugs. You wouldn't want to do that, would you?"

Chandra clinched her own jaw with matched resolution

aiming her blaster. "Are you going to let me out of here or are we going to have the stun fight at the OK Corral?" She pulled the trigger, but nothing happened.

Napul continued to stand scratching his chin and occasionally his hairy rear end. "That won't work in here. Magnets in the wall disable all of your equipment. I just love my job," he said pressing the stunner to her shoulder.

Chandra slumped to the floor conscious, but unable to move.

He picked her up and carried her to the gurney. "See, you humans just make too big a fuss about stuff. You should learn a lesson from us." He laid her down, taking time to straighten her legs and place her head on the pillow.

Napul cranked up the music just a little and started moving around the table doing something a little like the samba, except with an extra arm and all the additional finger-snapping action.

Although she still couldn't move, Chandra could feel a slight tingling sensation in the tips of her fingers and toes.

Napul continued to samba, as he messed with the IV set. He tried to roll up her sleeve but the protective kevlon would not allow him to open the cuff.

"You humans are so much trouble," he complained. He left her bedside for a few moments. By this time the effect of the stun was wearing off and Chandra could feel her knees and elbows.

The Distressite returned to her with a giant knife, probably the kind used to gut the carcasses once the subject was dead. He tried to cut the sleeve, but a mild static shock traveled up the metal blade into his hand. He stumbled back a few feet, looking from the knife to Chandra and then back again.

By this time Chandra could actually wiggle her toes and could feel her back against the cushy gurney.

"This is going to take more work than I thought." Again he left her side to check out the assortment of instruments he had laid out to finish the process.

When he returned, he found her upright with the gutting blade in her hands. Although he was larger than she was, with the knife against his belly she backed him up against the wall. She sliced downward, cutting his belt with a swift motion. It clinked to the floor.

"Now what are you going to do?" he asked. "You can't leave this room."

From the door there erupted a noise. Standing at the entrance was a Dolomite, his ash gray face filled with desperation.

Chandra backed away from Napul and ran to the door.

Napul slammed down the instrument in his hand. "All right, be a bad sport. You probably would've been tough anyway."

She patted the Dolomite on the shoulder. "Good luck," she told him.

Leaving Napul's deceptive "Exit" behind, Chandra finally found a door labeled, "Termination."

"This must be it," she said and opening the door, she took a deep breath of Bitter's polluted air, and sighed. Nothing had ever smelled as sweet.

Chapter Four

The dirt road to Tyrus's grave twisted and turned in a most precarious manner. Few beings used the pathway, mostly Distress's economically challenged residents. Weeds and grasses had overgrown the trail making it invisible to all but the keenest of eyes. Sometimes the dense overgrowth of fescue covered large holes, creating natural traps.

At least it's not raining, she thought.

Off in the distance, thunder rumbled. *Great! Now my life is complete.*

On most planets, rain served as a cleanser for all of nature, but not here! Scientists who manufacture chemical weapons often visited Distress to monitor the poison levels of the rain with unconcealed envy. Gene Kelly would have needed bunker gear to dance in this rain. No one with any amount of intelligence dared stay out in a rainstorm on Distress without special corrosion-resistant rainwear.

Before long, large drops of rain pelted the ground, drenching every part of her body not shielded by her protective kevlon flight suit. Her hair was plastered against her face and throat. By then, drops of rain trickled down the suit through the neck and wrist openings. The rain that seeped into her mouth tasted like an uncoated antibiotic pill. It pounded against her unprotected face and eyes like liquid fire ants.

The shower turned to downpour and then became a deluge. She had to find shelter soon or she'd wind up with some nasty acid burns on her face and hands.

When the rain did slacken a bit, she caught a glimpse of a lighted neon structure far ahead. Mechanically, she trudged toward the light. As the flickering of the phantom lights became more pronounced she recognized the name of the drinking establishment, The Tippolium. The lewd sign outside depicted several mostly naked women committing obscene acts, some of them involving vegetables and household appliances.

They had found Tyrus' body not far from there. He'd

probably gambled away both the transport and his life at this very dive.

She ducked down into the thick grass. As a speedster flashed overhead, the heated blast from the engines hit her, slapping her in the face with her own wet hair. It felt like someone belted her in the face with a red-hot rag.

Chandra peered around the corner into the underground parking garage. A small ocean of water flowed down the ramps and collected in pools around the parked speedsters. "Those twits." She cursed the incompetent architects and mentally revised the blueprints to include proper drainage and security.

She walked down the ramp and slogged through the two-foot deep sludge lake, looking for an appropriate vehicle—appropriate meaning unlocked and full of fuel.

Most of them proved to be third-rate speedsters, held together with rust and ventilation tape. In this rain, they would last about five minutes. None of those speedsters met her criteria. She temporarily abandoned her quest.

At least she found a water faucet. One drop at a time she collected the water in her hands. It smelled funny, foul but at least it rinsed the acid from her skin. It took quite a while but she finally washed the rain out her hair. Maybe it wasn't burned so badly that it would fall out. She'd just have to wait and see.

The rainfall trickled to a stop, and when the sky showed signs of clearing, she left the safety of the garage and headed down the path to spend a last night with Tyrus.

Chapter Five

Several kilos away, Chandra found the place. Near the road, beneath a leaf-bare Termagant tree, lay Tyrus' grave, marked only by a mound of newly disturbed dirt and his hard hat.

After the cops had finished their fifteen-minute investigation, they released the body to Chandra where it was found. She buried him only meters away from where officials said he had been tortured. Someday she would come back with a headstone shaped like a giant playing card, a three of clubs. Either that or someone from the phone company would come to Distress and take him back to Earth. His family would probably honor his wishes by having him interred under the marble floor of his favorite casino.

Sitting down and leaning against the tree, she picked up a clod of soil and rolled it around in her hand.

"Damn you, Tyrus. How could you do this to me?" She threw the chunk onto the mound. "You drag me half-way across the galaxy for nothing. Now you're gone. You couldn't even wait till we set up the ultra-long lines here. No, you had to get yourself killed just after we landed, when no one will be expecting to hear from us for another four months. I can't go home and I can't do my job because I don't have a ship. No food. No money. Nothing.

"I should have listened to Mom, I should have married that Sirian proctologist. They make lots of money, you know. Sirians have three assholes. That keeps their proctologists real busy.

"But, now I'm here and you're there. I'm just guessing but you're probably a lot warmer than I am, you royal asshole. You don't have any problems. I should've known you'd take the easy way out, you botcher's apprentice!"

She stared at the mound half-expecting Tyrus to magically appear through the dirt, laughing about the great joke he had pulled and begin groveling for forgiveness. Of course, nothing happened.

Her long walk out of town had made her hungrier than ever and the pleasurable effects of the Leonian brandy had long since passed. The more Chandra thought about her hunger, the more ravenous she grew. Even the small grasshopper-like insect, which played around at her feet, started looking tasty. As Chandra grew hungrier, Tyrus's status slipped from a fun-loving-kind-of-jerk to the biggest son-of-a-bitch in the galaxy.

Before long she found her eyelids weighted with titanium bricks. Chandra leaned back against the tree. She unsheathed her Harbinger, laid it across her knees, and readjusted the temperature on her flight suit to a more comfortable setting. Maybe a little sleep would help her think more clearly.

Her head rested against the knurled bark of the tree and she sighed deeply.

Suddenly, an odd sensation overtook her. Movements became surreal, as if under water. Strange thoughts ran through her mind and dreamy images seemed to form around her. She heard the sounds of a party, laughter, glasses clinking and the dull roar of muffled conversation.

Tyrus stood in front of her. He looked transparently the same as he always had, yet opaquely different. Built like the progeny of a mating between a military tank and a grizzle beast. In death his taste in attire had taken a dramatic turn. Instead of his IGB flight suit, he wore a tuxedo. He almost looked sharp.

"Hi, Chani."

She waved back at him. "Hi, Ty."

"No, Chani, I didn't mean "hi.' I meant I want to get high. Got anything to drink? I can't drink here."

"All out. You took it to the game. Remember?"

"Oh, yeah. Sorry 'bout that. Never mind. I just wanted to come by and say a last good-bye, you know, for old time's sake."

"You insincere rat hunter. Have you seen what you've done to me, you no good, foul breath—"

"Now, now, now...Is that any way to talk to the dead?"

"Why not? It's the way I talked to you when you were alive. If all of a sudden I got nice, you'd think I hated you or something, now wouldn't you?"

The strangely glowing figure thought about it, and then nodded his head in agreement. "Good. I'm glad you're not pissed about the speedster and all."

"I didn't say I wasn't pissed! I'm going to die on this deplorable hole in space!" she yelled. "And then I'm going to come and get you, you bastard!"

Odd. The dream possessed a strange quality about it. Too realistic.

"Hey, kid, you'll be okay. Have I ever let you down before?"

"Yes, Tyrus Ratsall, you let me down all the time."

He thought about it. "You're right. I guess I have. Not this time, though."

"Not this time?" She slammed her hands against her thighs so hard they stung. "You've got to be kidding! Some slimy pig-faced Corvian bought my drink a little while ago...I had to eat dinner with a corpse..."

"Yeah, he really enjoyed it, too."

"Huh?" she said. "Why, I swear, Tyrus, you hourly promise-breaker, if you weren't already dead, I'd kill you! What do you want from me, Tyrus? Don't you think destroying my life was enough?"

From out of nowhere a woman asked for another drink. "What was that?" Chandra asked.

Nervously he looked around. "Nothing. Chani, I'm running out of time."

"And I'm not?" Despair trickled through her.

"Chani, they let me make only one three-minute call and you're it. You remember our ship?"

"You mean the ship you sold without telling me? That ship? Yeah, I remember it. Why?"

"Honestly, I didn't sell it."

"You didn't? You mean I have a way off of this rock?"

"No. I just mean I didn't sell it. I lost it playing Cryptic. I couldn't lose. Three aces. Three aces. Nothing beats three aces...except four kings. Don't worry though. I know where it is."

"How do you know?"

He looked smug. "Cuz its debris is scattered half way across the province."

"You wrecked our transport? That's phone company property! How could you? Tyrus, as project engineer I was responsible for that piece of equipment and everything in it. What am I supposed to tell the long line supervisor...that my partner wrecked it in a drunken stupor then conveniently got himself killed?"

"I didn't trash it. The chump who won it from me did. I forgot to tell him about those bad brakes. Serves him right for skinning me at Cryptic."

She had to laugh. "I bet you pissed him off."

"Yeah. He's not speaking to me, either. But he thinks you're cute."

"Huh? What do you mean?" she asked.

"You had lunch with him. Don't you remember Ranknard?"

Chandra thought for a moment. "Oh, Sapiens, Tyrus. Are you talking about that corpse in the packing plant?"

"That's him. He says, 'hi'. He said he liked you, and that's kind of why I'm here," Tyrus said. "Now, shut up and listen. This is real important and I'm just about out of time."

"Important? That's what you said about the three hundred credits you borrowed from me to impress that exotic dancer on Phad."

"Chani," he said in a grim voice that sounded as if he suffered from something between hemorrhoids and a paper cut, "I'm not kidding. You need to find the van. In the cockpit under the instrument panel, you'll find a glass thing. My friend wants you to have it. It's your ticket to anywhere in the universe."

"I don't understand."

"You don't have to understand. I don't even understand. All I know is that you need to get it to the third planet in the Fomalhaut system before the Festival of the Fat Bore. That's nine days. If you don't...well, I don't know what will happen, but it will be awful. Chani, this is for all the marbles."

"Hell, Tyrus, I'm living 'awful' right now."

"I know it'll be really bad for a lot of people, not just you. Maybe everybody."

"This is what they're trying to kill me for, isn't it?"

Tyrus nodded sadly. "Be real careful, Chani, and don't let anyone else get that rock. Oh, yeah," he added as an afterthought. He reached forward and placed something in her hand. "Keep this with you. Now, don't lose it. You'll need it."

The muffled conversation grew slightly louder then fell quiet following the sound of breaking glass. An angry voice called Tyrus's name.

"I gotta go." Tyrus's image began to fade.

Clutching the object, Chandra said, "Ty, help me."

"Chani, you were the best bloody engineer I ever worked with. Don't worry, kid. You'll be okay."

"Tyrus!" Chandra woke with a start. A thin film of sweat covered her.

What a strange dream, she thought until she felt something cold in her hand. She opened her hand and found the object Tyrus had given her in the dream, an eight-sided azure crystal shard glowing in the darkness.

Chapter Six

Chandra trudged down the abandoned road in search of the mangled phone company transport. Hay-colored weeds hid the once heavily traveled path. She opened the pouch on her tool belt and pulled out the crystal Tyrus had given her. In the faint light of the overcast sky, it looked like nothing more than a piece of crystal: clear azure with eight equal sides and uneven, broken ends.

Off in the distance, Chandra heard the whine of a speedster approaching from the south. She ducked behind some scrub brush long since denuded of leaves. *Maybe they won't see me.* As the speedster shot past her, its high-pitched turbine engines screamed at ice-pick-in-the-ear levels. *What I wouldn't give for a speedster right now!*

She climbed out of the bushes and continued the jaunt toward her objective.

"Ty, this better be good or I'll...I'll..." Chandra stopped and laughed aloud when she couldn't think of anything she could threaten a dead man with.

Is this all really happening? She accepted the word of a hallucination, who in life lied habitually, of the value of this allegedly existing glass thing. She took the crystal out of her belt. No, the crystal in her hand *was* real.

Just this once, she would have to go on faith. She shuddered. *Faith in Ty? Faith in the man who told me the universe is just a big party and we're going to crash it?*

We're not the only ones who crash things, she thought as she walked past a few twisted pieces of metal. Ahead of her, equipment, personal effects and debris littered the clearing. One fragment was etched with the same IGB logo as her flight suit, but the insignia on the wreckage looked as if someone had taken a giant bite out of it. A few steps later, she happened upon the remains of her high-density material boring vaporizer...utterly useless now. Not far from it lay some remnants of the power source incident radio.

As she continued to walk, she came across more and larger pieces of debris until finally she found what remained of their phone company issue speedi-van. Its once clean, white body and aerodynamic lines had accordioned and wrapped halfway around a large tree as if the pilot couldn't make up his mind on which side of the tree he wanted to pass. The transport was twisted into a pitiful mass of metal, and the tree had not fared very well, either. What a horrible fate for such a faithful piece of machinery. She even felt sympathy for Tyrus' Bulivarian partner in crime. What was his name? Oh, yeah, Ranknard.

Chandra found debris scattered everywhere. She combed through each scrap of metal, hoping to find a functioning com-unit or some credit chips that might have been lost between the seat cushions. She found some long steel bars that belonged with some of their testing equipment, her phone company ID, and a quartz light bar. She pocketed the ID. Nothing else was of any use.

The touch-tone pad on the back door of the van looked undamaged, but when she punched in her security code nothing happened—not even the annoying series of tones followed by prompts complaining about invalid codes. She tried prying the door open with one of the testing bars she found, but the fuselage was too badly warped to budge the hatch even a millimeter.

Instead, she took the bar to the cockpit, and, using the blunt end, smashed the already broken windscreen into thousands of tiny transparent squares. She pushed away the shattered glass fragments and poked her head and shoulders through the hole. Tears in the crinkled upholstery exposed lining and super-safe, heavy-duty, mega-soft panel filler. Ant-like insects, which had just begun relocating to the console liner as they claimed their new home, filed in and out of the hole. She would have given anything to have her own custom work gloves—so thin she could feel a human hair through them, yet tough enough to protect her from almost anything. They had been molded to fit her hands. But they were hidden somewhere inside that small-scale disaster area under heaps of shattered equipment with Tyrus' mismatched off-duty clothes. She reached in and probed through the hole in the console. The insects crawled across her hand and up the arm of her flight suit. She ignored the crawling sensation and probed further. Nothing! Inserting the bar, she tore the panel apart. She eased her hand into the opening and felt around. Her fingers found only the cottony touch of padding; probably just the ants' new den. Her fingers continued probing...and finally encountered something cool and smooth, perfectly round.

That must be it!

She wrapped her fingers around it and pulled it from the hole.

Opening her hand she found a glass ball...beautiful, perfectly spherical, and flawlessly clear. Smaller, yet surprisingly similar to the crystal balls fortunetellers used back on Earth, about the diameter of an old fifty-cent piece in her antique coin collection.

With that part of her mission accomplished, she decided to retrieve what valuables she could.

Chandra climbed on top of the wreckage. It looked like the aftermath of a tornado. There seemed to be no way into the cockpit only a large tear in the fuselage to look through. Her personal items and test equipment were scattered everywhere, some broken, some torn, others smashed. One tripod leg had hit the back of the transport with such force that the pole penetrated the hull that had earlier in the month been certified as space worthy.

The long-range relativistic direction finder and distance measure appeared virtually unscathed, but it packed too much bulk to be of any value to her. And the cybernetic module that interfaced with the hyperspace interline computer, her only possibility of planet side communication with Mother, had warped with the frame of the transport, rending that sensitive device useless as an icemaker on Neptune.

Across the cabin she spied a hologram of her folks, her baby brother Jeffrey, who now stood a strapping six foot two, and her cat, Ree-u. The sunlight peeked through the leaves and waved and bobbed through the crevice, making it hard at times to make out the images. Her dad, the perfect picture of a phone company engineer, himself: strong, straight and a little tired. Mom's silvering hair in a freshly coifed do, Jeffrey with the mischievous expression he would never outgrow and, of course, old Ree-u, her old black and white cat from adolescence, who used to steal the food right off of her plate. Time had dimmed his eyes, but his picture would follow her always.

"I can't leave them behind."

Chandra grabbed one of the longest beams lying twisted and bent outside the wreck. She removed the laser hand welder from her belt and heated the metal until it started to sag, creating a small cup. After it cooled, she stuck it through the hole and fished for the holo until it slipped into the jerry-rigged receptacle. Very carefully, she drew the treasure-laden rod out.

She twisted the ring encircling the holo, and it came alive. Mother's familiar voice said, "Now, Chandra Marie, I want you to take care of yourself while you're out there. Keep away from that navigator's no-good friends and watch your back. Call us when you can, collect, of course."

Dad stood there with a big grin across his lightly creasing face and said, "We love you, baby, and we're proud of you. Your old supervisor told me a few days ago that you were the best damn field engineer he has. Doesn't surprise me a bit. See you in a few years, honey."

Jeffrey, on Mom's left, looked at Chandra with mischievous hazel eyes. "I hope you do real good out there, Chani. Mom made me say that. By the way, Mom says I can have *your* old room so you can stay out there as long as you want." He paused and added with a grin, "I'll pack up what's left of your stuff. Oh, yeah, don't worry. I won't read your diary." He smiled. "At least not while the camera is on."

Chandra smiled back. Ages ago she planted a fake diary at the house. She had waited years for him to find it and learn about all her fictitious exploits.

Between them, Old Ree-u pawed at the camera and meowed. He blinked at her with amber eyes.

She watched the holo over and over again and finally placed it next to her face. When did everything become so complicated? A little over a week ago, she just wanted to ferry out of the transport ship and start on the new installation. *How quickly things change!*

She slipped the holograph in her belt and peered back into the cabin. Maybe she could find something else useful in there.

Using her pole, Chandra fished out a micro materials assayer, her Personal Protector, a weapon usually concealed up the sleeve, and extra power chips, and a non-specific account credit chip with a significant balance. On the floor she spied her hand-held transept and mini material replicator in tiny fragments.

Then, peeking out from under some shredded upholstery she thought she saw the glint of the soft metallic packaging of emergency rations. She caught it by the edge of the freshness-assured wrapper with the tip of the pole. Food. *Food!* She moved it a few centimeters then it slipped out from under the grasp of her pole. She tried again and gained a few more centimeters. Finally, she dragged the pouch within arm's reach.

Hardtack never tasted so good. It wasn't much more than an imitation meat flavored nutrition bar, but it tasted like sirloin steak to her. She tried to savor the bar, but she simply couldn't resist and nearly inhaled it.

She managed to fish out a couple more packs of the sealed rations.

She took one last look at the shattered replicator. *That's just how I feel*, she thought as she walked away.

As Chandra left the wreckage behind and started walking the long journey toward Bedlam, the sun sank down to touch the horizon. She secured her newly recovered Personal Protector around her wrist and armed the trigger connection to her thumb. The farther from Tyrus' eternal resting-place she moved, the more uneasy she felt. Somewhere out there, other interested parties waited for her. She popped a chunk of unreconstituted tuna casserole in her mouth and chewed...for a long time.

When she stopped for a rest she tested the ball on her materials analyzer. Crystalline silica—glass. All this ruckus was over a lousy ball of glass!

How could glass be her ticket to any place in the galaxy? Not an obscure, but highly desirable, this jewel. Not even marginally valuable like the Centaurian blaze crystal Tyrus had handed her, or perhaps even Pegasus apples. No unique conductive characteristics...glass! Maybe it was an antique. She would have to talk to someone who knew about rare gems. Not on this planet, though.

Chandra heard a speedster approach. For a moment she thought about jumping into the bushes. *What's the point? The sphere is worthless.* Besides, hiding from every passing vehicle looked suspicious itself. Some wacko might rob her just because she acted as if she had something valuable.

The speedster shot past her, completely oblivious to her presence.

Sometime later, a new set of blinking lights appeared over the horizon. She smiled with a confident air, but that cockiness quickly faded. This time as the speedster approached her, it slowed.

Chandra unbuckled her utility belt and tossed it in the bushes, taking mental notes of the nearby rocks and trees without breaking her stride. The lights grew brighter, almost blinding. It so illuminated the path that she could make out the strange hexagonal shapes of the grass beneath her feet.

The speedster slowed to a full stop beside her.

Chandra stopped, too.

Her hand rested on her light pistol and she turned to face the driver of the Chariot.

"Need a ride?" a raspy disembodied voice asked. It sounded like a cross between a coyote's howl and public address feedback.

Her eyes narrowed and she stared warily into the darkened speedster. "No, thanks. Just stretching my legs." She walked on.

The vehicle matched her speed. "Not safe."

"It's a dangerous place for anyone." Her hand patted the Harbinger's grip. "I would hate to put you in jeopardy, friend, so why don't you just fly on?"

The mysterious creature gave an admiring smile within the darkness. "You take chances."

Her fingers slowly crept around the stock of her pistol. Easing the weapon out of the holster, she thumbed the safety to the 'armed' position. Chandra held the gun loosely at her side ready for this fool to make his move.

"I insist," he said.

She brought her weapon to bear on the stranger's window and made her voice sound fierce. "So do I."

Screw fair play. Her jaw tensed as her finger squeezed the trigger. For a moment everything lit up with an eerie iridescent glow. It faded, leaving behind a dark night sky, a frightened woman, and a healthy stranger in a really nice speedster.

That wasn't supposed to happen! The beam should have penetrated the windshield, frying the creature on the other side.

The Chariot's canopy lifted and he emerged, a towering figure in black robes, black as hell. From within the chariot, she heard his bone-chilling voice. "You have no choice." She had concentrated her attention so much on the windshield she neglected the Chariot's internal defense system. For a moment, the ground lit up again, but this time the Chariot emitted the beam source.

Chandra's head jerked forward as the speedster hit some turbulence. She opened her eyes to find herself in a darkened Chariot with a really great sound system. Soft music flowed from hundreds of speakers throughout the vessel. Each instrument had its own speaker and it sounded to Chandra as if she had awakened in the middle of a symphony orchestra with a poor sense of rhythm. The whine of the speedster engines droned on, barely audible above the background. But even over the melodious cadence and the whine of the engines, the creature's breathing made the same labored sound her dad did when he cut logs with a hand saw for the exercise. Inhale, forward. Exhale, back. Inhale, forward. Exhale, back.

"What do you want?" she asked.

"You don't know?"

She shook her head and closed her eyes.

"Your dead friend had something *I* want."

Damn. Chandra raised her head very carefully and peered at the creature. A black hood hid most of his face and the shroud of darkness concealed what little was visible. Shadows in the faint blue light of the instrument panel accentuated the knobs on his face. His thin snake lips forced him to struggle with each word of English he spoke. He fixed Chandra with an impenetrable stare.

"Nothing would please me more than to give you whatever it is that you want. But, I don't have it. I never saw Tyrus again after he left for the game, and the only thing the cops gave me was his Harbinger. If I were you, I'd question them."

"I did."

She sighed. "Tyrus left me at the Bitter land office. He was supposed to play a few hands and come back for me. That's how he recruited laborers for our construction projects. They'd lose and then they'd have to work for him to pay him back. I guess he found someone who could cheat better than he did. When he didn't come back, I just thought he got lucky...in the physical sense, I mean." She shuddered as she recalled the night. "I slept in the alley with stray animals and huge rodents."

The driver's expression never changed.

"The next morning, I went to the cops and they told me someone had murdered Tyrus. They said the only thing found with the body was a crummy light pistol. A lot of good it did him. He went to the game with all of our money, our transport van, everything. I don't know if it was stolen or if he lost it in the game."

"Lost," the creature said. His eyes focused straight ahead.

"Then talk to the guy who won."

"Can't."

"Why?" she asked, not wanting to hear his answer.

"Dead."

"Then talk to the person who killed *him*."

"Tyrus."

"How could it be Tyrus? Witnesses said *he* died shortly after the game ended."

The being remained silent.

"Look, everyone and his slug are out to get me, and I've got zip."

"Perhaps." His tone evoked images of bamboo spikes up the fingernails.

Chandra shivered. "Maybe it would help if you told me what you want."

"Stones."

She took a breath. "What stone?"

He said no more; they rode in silence for some time.

Finally, Chandra asked, "What do you plan on doing with me?"

No answer. He seemed intent on his destination and unconcerned about her.

Chandra studied the com panel. It looked similar to the one on her old transport. Some of the readouts were unfamiliar, but she could make an educated guess about their purpose.

"So-uh-what do I have to do to get you to let me go?" she asked.

"The clear stone."

"Oh, bloody hell. I don't have your lousy rock. I've got nothing on me. I'm sure you've already checked."

He pulled his arm back to strike her. His demeanor changed from just menacing to deadly. Chandra shrank back, but his quickly moving hand still caught her on the cheek. She tried to block a second blow using her left arm as a shield. *I must sight him in,* she thought, targeting his nose for a bull's-eye with her personal protector. She pulled her right hand back as far as it would go, and then flicked her thumb forward, keeping his face in line with the pencil-fine barrel. A fine blue-white beam leaped from her sleeve, entering at the base of the skull and exited through his left central eye. He cried out and his log-sawing respiration ceased with a tremendous final gasp. Chandra fired the beam until it ran out of charge and then dropped her arm into her lap.

With a thunk, he slumped forward onto the cockpit panel, concealing the controls with his body and hood as if in revenge. The ship continued on its journey as if nothing had happened.

Trembling, Chandra gulped down air as a drowning man would gulp water. Her emerald eyes stared at him without seeing. In her phone company training she'd shot hundreds of paper targets and holograms before, but she'd never killed anything sentient. That was always Tyrus' job. And always in a self-defense-style shutout. Never just point and shoot. It seemed unfair, but still he HAD kidnapped her.

Calm down. Calm down! Breathe slowly. Then remembering the alien's own audibly regular breathing, she told herself, *Remember the saw. In, out. In, out.*

Screw 'em, she thought. *He was probably going to kill me.*

Suddenly, an alarm overrode the music. Ahead and approaching quickly, a nose-level grove of trees threatened to ruin an otherwise rotten night.

Chandra disconnected the alien's restraint harness and pushed him aside, while pulling up on the joystick. The Chariot lunged up just over the tops of the thicket, barely missing the upper branches. She increased her altitude, but returned the vessel to autopilot until she felt certain about all the controls. She checked the computer log and programmed it to backtrack to the spot where she had first encountered the mysterious alien.

The chariot pirouetted a graceful turn-about, lifted well above the trees and accelerated toward her stash of worthless treasure.

On the way back, Chandra hacked the security codes. She finally found his alarm, hatch codes and ignition codes. She reprogrammed her own lockout and security sequence and erased all taped log entries for the last eighteen minutes.

The music the late alien played had long since frayed her nerves; Chandra couldn't stand it any longer. She requested something a little more suitable. Nebula Amsterdam and the Forest Fighters Five filled the Chariot with wild interlocking phrases from hundreds of speakers.

"Yeah!" Chandra yelled. "Woooo hooooo! That's more like it! How could I think with all that quiet?"

Chandra had never felt the ecstasy of *real* flying before she confiscated this souped up rider. Mainly because Tyrus never trusted her behind the controls. Pushing the stick forward, she proceeded to strafe the area with the brilliant glow from the landing lights mounted on the speedster's underbelly. Eerie patterns formed behind the piles of the lifeless scrub across the barren ground. As she stared at the unreal shadows, images of the undead came to mind. And once again her thoughts turned to Ty.

If only Tyrus could see her in this hot number. She smiled, hoping that somewhere he had witnessed her "flawless" abduction of the Chariot. His chest would swell and he would poke that guy, Ranknard, in the ribs, saying, "See that? I taught her everything she knows, and a bunch of stuff she doesn't."

"I wish you were here," she yelled above the music. "You'd love this Chariot and the sound system, you'd just...die." She had certainly taken a giant step up from anything either one of them had ever owned...or stolen.

Off in the distance, she saw Bitter. With its plain white and yellow lights, it looked no more exciting at night than it had during the day. Just much more lonely.

She zeroed in on one of the twin moon's points, and pulled the stick lightly to the right while her foot pedaled to the left. In the forward window, a starlit sky replaced the darkness of dead ground. As the Chariot performed a slow easy roll, Chandra's stomach tightened. *I'm too low,* she thought yanking back on the controls.

The Chariot rolled with more ease than she ever imagined. Next, a snap roll. As the stars spun around her, Chandra's stomach took a dive of its own. With her head reeling, she turned the craft about and made another slow run over the scattered brush.

Then the panel registered one of the compounds she had

been looking for a few kilometers to the west. She pulled the stick hard about and went back.

Decelerating to the slowest possible speed and still managing to stay airborne, Chandra scoured the surface. There it came again. A tiny twinkling on the panel's map located her utility belt about fifty feet below her. She redirected her engines with the flip of a switch, and the craft descended lower and lower, until it hovered just a few feet above the ground. It settled to the surface as softly as a baby's burp.

Chandra jumped out. On her hands and knees she groped through the thicket of dense brush and high grass. A hand located the utility belt exactly where she had thrown it, safely concealed in the thick scrub. Locating it had been made easier by the fact that her seven level screwdriver contained iridium, a component that wasn't indigenous to Distress and was easily detected by the Chariot's sensors.

She grabbed the tool belt and slipped her fingers into one of the pockets where she felt the blue crystal. She sighed. In another compartment she was relieved to feel that cool smoothness she had so recently been introduced to...the mysterious Orb. Now it had a name. She shoved the orb back in its pouch in her tool belt and tossed them in the speedster. After she found her Harbinger along the trail and holstered it, she climbed back in the Chariot and headed for Bedlam. She'd only gone a few meters when she stopped the Chariot, opened the canopy and tossed out the iridium screwdriver. She started to push her companion to join the seven-level when she recalled something Tyrus had told her—advice she never dreamed she would have to use herself.

"Never ditch the body right away. And never dump it between towns. They always look for the body halfway between towns."

Instead of starting back toward Bedlam, she flew the Chariot off-course by a couple hundred kilometers to the east.

"I don't know how far I can go, cuz Buddy, you stink," she said to the corpse. "You know they make chemicals to help neutralize those pesky body odors."

After she'd backtracked all the way to Bitter, the Chariot veered off to the east of town, down a familiar alley. Using the Chariot's belly mounted landing light, she spied a pile of petron cables and debris from a rec cruiser.

After she set down, Chandra opened the hatch, climbed

out, then pulled the alien's body out onto the dirt. He hit the ground with a hollow 'thunk.'

Chandra grabbed him by the arms and drug him to the vacuum tube mounted just above the ground. Struggling with his dead weight, she worked his head into the tube. Nothing happened. She pushed the limp noodle a little farther into the orifice. Suddenly, she heard the sound of servos and wind. Chandra moved back and watched as the creature disappeared into the OK Packing Plant.

"I'll bet *he* tastes good."

She returned to the Chariot and pushed forward on the thrust lever and at the same time pulled back on the stick. The speedster shot straight up.

For the first time in days she felt happy.

After the starlit aerial romp, Chandra returned attention to her destination. She brought up the navicon on screen. Instead of having to go through those troublesome navigational computations she had always found so difficult on the old transport, all she had to do was indicate her destination of choice on the regional map and engage. The navicon would monitor all approaching traffic and take action to avoid potential collisions. Just outside of the Bedlam flight path, it would alert her to resume manual control.

In the meantime, she would try to formulate a plan for escaping from Distress.

Chapter Seven

It had been a long flight to Bedlam, so long that it took the balance of Distress's nine-hour night to reach it from Bitter.

High in the mackerel-cloud sky, two of Distress' three moons hung like seven-month-old half-eaten cheese, yellow-green and hardly appealing.

Chandra inhaled deeply. That breath told her Bedlam lay only minutes away. Nowhere else did town officials broadcast air pollution warnings based on the number of court cases scheduled. The unbreathability of the air related directly to the number of attorneys working on that particular day. Local weathercasters called it the CF, or Cologne Factor. The nearer to Bedlam she flew, the stronger the odor. Even the Chariot's sophisticated filtration system could not remove all the fragrance from the air.

Before long, Bedlam's famed two-story skyline appeared on the horizon.

Chandra parked her Chariot in a public garage and walked the rest of the way. Under the light of the car park the death-black Chariot hid discretely in its absolute lack of color, and its blackness accentuated the high polish of its trim. Chandra's instincts told her this cost more than an entire lifetime's pay, including bonuses. Far classier than any other craft flying around Bedlam, or anywhere else on the planet for that matter, this eyecatcher invited way too much attention. What better billboard to tell all interested parties she came from off world? She looked back when the Chariot had slipped almost out of sight. Too bad. Riding around in that speedster could have been fun, but not with the risk of being caught.

In town, residents of Bedlam kept their surroundings much cleaner than Bitter. Small broom-wielding robots scurried from corner to corner picking up trash and scolding litterbugs. Despite the superficial fastidiousness, the underside of the eaves wore a mold coating so thick that pharmaceutical houses were locked in bidding wars for the rare fungi. And cracked foundations marked the architectural rule rather than the exception. Most construction companies considered those buildings a wonder of modern architecture, since nothing built out of indigenous materials could stand for any period of time at all, much less survive twelve solar years in a row as these had. Needless to say, warranties on structures lasted only as long as it took to haul the heavy equipment out of the parking lot, and depending on the contractor, sometimes not that long.

InterGalactic Bell had good reason for picking this civilization-forsaken rock to install their ultra-long lines station. Executives claimed they based their decision on the strategic location. The system did offer an unimpeded path permitting re-transmission of signals around nebula interference to some heavily populated regions of the galaxy. Areas that at present were unnavigable in the travel sense due to high concentrations of space debris left by ships that prior to galactic green laws had used that area of space as a dumping ground. Now vast, frozen, uncharted chunks of coprolite waited to impale ships traveling at faster than light speed. This IGB rationale held some truth. But the real reason they chose Distress was economical—it came cheap.

IGB site selector Elkhed Perkins had won rights to the site on the planet when he kidnapped the Grand Rokum's third wife and held her for ransom. The Grand Rokum, delighted at his new semi-single status, not only gave Perkins exclusive site rights, knocking out the other communications conglomerate, he also paid the site locator a sizable loser's fee to keep his wife. Later, InterGalactic Bell returned to its previous semi-monopolistic status and accumulation of excessive profits following the galactic tribunal's decision that Terran anti-trust laws do not apply in space. IGB contended with token competition from Galactic Telephone Enterprises, a technologically inferior company, whose circuits went down every time there was a meteor shower.

Chandra did find it odd that the advance team in *this* installation consisted of only Tyrus and her. Usually she headed a team of twenty people whose skills ranged anywhere from corporate ambassador to heavy equipment operator, but this time everything appeared to be on the sly.

When she had asked her supervisor about the

unconventional procedures, he claimed that directives from above mandated a small advance team because of a sensitive political climate. Upon arriving, Chandra discovered that the planet had virtually *no* political climate, save that of the world leader Oylslik, who could not remember which lie he needed to remember at any particular hour or which of his fourteen personalities had control. Distress was the only world Chandra had seen with a world dictator constantly at war with himself. Had this installation been a more traditional setup with the entourage and redundant vehicles required by union labor, she wouldn't be in her present predicament.

She made her way among the aging buildings arranged in uneven rows like a battered smile, delineated by poorly maintained sidewalks. As she navigated the streets, Chandra discovered Bedlam had natural vegetation other than mold. Lying on every street corner, sleeping off binges in recesses of shops and businesses, and passing bottles back and forth among themselves, lay Distress's outcasts: attorneys.

Most of them tried to grab a few hours of repose before ambling back to their offices to lock horns over quagmire mining royalties and questions of whose client held the best box seats at the aquifer draining contest and who would win the two hundred year-old Galway Antitrust Case.

This is a dream. It's got to be. Any moment now, I'm going to wake up in St. Louis. "St. Louis," she whispered, remembering the sleek high-rise buildings, the famous arch, and the Mississippi River. "I'd trade Distress's two stars for Earth's one in a nanosecond."

As her mind slipped momentarily back to home, the first of Distress's suns, Rogan, peeked over a rise, exposing new aspects of the primitive Bedlam low-rise skyline. Barfude, the secondary star, would rise later in a different area of the horizon, travel a different path and shine as a small golden ball in the distance. Rogan provided the warmth, the light, but when the orbits and rotations were right, Barfude waxed throughout the night on an irregular schedule, totally disrupting the internal clock of every creature on Distress. When this happened, as it did for several months every few years, the inhabitants grew testy and litigious. Attorneys found themselves buried in work with no time for gambling on street corners.

Chandra dodged her way through the obstacle course of

intoxicated gownsmen arguing their cases in unintelligible legal mutterances to unseen juries. Mentally she thanked IGB for her extensive phone company physical fitness training and the agility that helped her leap drunks and avoid holes in the pavement. Today, it paid off in ways she never imagined.

At the end of the street, she read an unexpected but welcome sign. "Travel Agency?"

"Yeah. It just opened," one bum said. "They wanted to establish themselves before the phone company horned in on their business here. Guess they opened up just in time." He stared her straight in the logo.

Chandra placed her hand on her hard hat. She realized that it might attract unwanted attention with its distinctive design of nine planets tracing out their circular orbits around a bell, the galaxy's own Mother. But hiding the hard hat was pointless because Mother had also plastered the logo on her silvery flight suit breast pocket for the entire universe to see and identify. Anyone looking for either her, or the rocks, need only watch for the target patches. In fact, when she thought about it those orbiting planets on her suit looked every bit like a bull's-eye.

I might as well take out advertisements. Here's Chandra Solomon, the phone company flunky. Anyone interested, please, fire at will.

Worse still, no self-respecting travel agent, assuming that Distress boasted any, would sell a ticket to anyone who worked for the telephone company. For that matter, several years ago the phone company had forbid their employees to deal with travel agents or the travel industry, IGB's biggest competitor.

At one time, IGB could transmit a message from one point in the galaxy to another in far less time than it took to physically travel the distance. Sometimes they measured this lag in centuries, but it was still faster. Once faster-than-light-travel became commonplace, cruise liner rates plunged and a cutthroat price war ensued between the two industries.

Confined by not only the laws of physics but economic laws as well, IGB found itself left behind in the stardust. Light simply could not transmit faster than the speed-of-light. IGB scientists took a long look at the situation and immediately purchased stock in the Royal Sirian Cruise Line. Phone company futures plummeted and IGB purchased their own fleet of vehicles to drop off employees at their various assignments.

Chandra pulled her hard hat off and tucked it in her armpit. At least she could hide the bull's-eye plastered on her forehead.

"Thanks," she told the guzzling attorney. "I'll come back after I find some more appropriate traveling clothes."

"Look where you're going." One irate pleader looked up from his street-level card game. Around him sat five other resplendently clad men clutching shabby cards above the girth of their bellies.

She stopped and watched the entranced men for a while. "You playing Cryptic?"

One lawyer gathered his cards even closer. "What's it to you?"

"My partner taught me to play Cryptic. He always beat me, and he wasn't very good, I understand."

"He wasn't?" The one with the shortest pile of coins eyed her thoughtfully.

Chandra spread her hands. "That's what he told me. Of course, he was always better than I was, so who knows?"

"Do you have any credit?"

Chandra showed them the balance on the chip she found in the transport.

The suspicious one loosened his cards a bit. "Join us." He indicated a spot on the sidewalk with an open hairy palm.

"I couldn't intrude."

"No, really. There's always room for another. Tell you what, you can call the first game."

"Well, okay." She hesitated then giving them a slight smile, added, "Have you ever played strip Cryptic?"

Walking away from the game, Chandra rolled up the sleeves of her new size forty-eight-suit jacket to where she could finally see the tips of her fingers. At least the cumbersome pinstripe hid the lethal IGB symbol. Beneath the bulk of her new jersey-wool suit coat, she slid her hands into the pockets and smiled as she carefully fingered the hard edges of her recently acquired credit chips.

Chandra negotiated the maze of rumpled pinstriped sleepers sprawled along the sidewalks. Only now as Rogan rose high enough to shower a haze of light on Bedlam did the crop of lawyers come to life. One attorney in a three-piece suit rummaged through the pockets of a sleeping companion in quest of the funds he had lost the night before. Soon they would sleepily make their way to their offices, slap on a new layer of cologne, and engage in mortal combat with the same colleague, who not more than an hour ago drank out of the same bottle of cheap wine and lost all his money to the same card shark. And tonight when the suns set the ritual would begin all over again.

Just a little longer, she thought. All I have to do is make it to a travel agent...alive. Finally she wound her way down the street to the flashing neon-esque sign proclaiming that a thoroughly registered, licensed and practically reputable travel agent resided within.

Chandra listened outside the door of the establishment, and stared at the vagrants and humanoid debris staring back at her from across the street. Maybe she could find a way to convince them that she actually held the rank of Oylslik vice chancellor, and maybe they would let her book a trip off of Distress.

"Look, I've got to get off this planet." The well-dressed pleader's voice rang with desperation. "I can't take it any longer."

Behind the fortress of a desk cluttered with old Beutelguisian memorabilia, the agent shook her head. "All the transports from Distress for the next two years have been booked. If you want off now, you'll need to give me some incentive." She rubbed her thumb and forefinger together.

He produced a credit chip with what Chandra considered a very substantial balance on it, a balance that could have easily paid for the Chariot at list price. The woman took one look and erupted into uproarious laughter.

The attorney drew himself up. "Am I to understand that you require more than this just because my papers aren't in order?"

The woman's laughter went convulsive. She toppled out of her chair and lay howling until the lawyer left.

Chandra's shoulders slumped. So much for that way off the planet. On her way back to the Chariot she waded back through the maze of attorneys, taking special care to avoid the ones who looked like they might be personal injury lawyers.

Chapter Eight

Offworlders often described the traffic laws on Distress as "deviated." Tyrus tended to speak in more direct terms; he called them "perverted." He often said of most planets, "Traffic confound them, if the gods will not."

As a matter of habit Tyrus had always contended with intra-planetary transportation, allowing Chandra time to study the intricacies of their upcoming system design and read three year-old copies of *Beings Magazine*.

Tyrus also piloted because it kept him from peril at the hand of Chandra's dyslexia grande, which impeded her ability to tell her left hand from her right.

"Company doctors say I'm directionally challenged," she told Tyrus the first time she got them hopelessly lost.

Since Tyrus always navigated, *he* learned the vehicular regulations then gave Chandra a sixty second course in the more critical points, such as: on Distress rather than following the almost universally accepted custom that northbound traffic flies above southbound traffic, they flew on the same level and southbound traffic always yielded to northern bound traffic.

Chandra tore out of the car park, missing the parking attendant by only millimeters. He flattened on the ground, believing he felt the speedster plunging through his body, ripping him in half. But at the last instant Chandra pulled up fractionally leaving the terrified attendant safe to change his underwear at a more convenient time.

Caught up in a game of "Button, button, which one's the right button," Chandra lost track of the traffic around her. She worked the uncooperative controls with ever-mounting frustration. "You were a lot easier to fly when no one was around." She pulled back on the throttle, but while she reveled in that success, she didn't realize that she had veered into the path of several oncoming vehicles with the right of way.

At the edge of her vision flashed something fast and red. "Shit!"

The other speedster brushed against a wall and twisted into unnatural shapes. Outside, crimson metal groaned and wailed, protesting the abuse. Chandra clutched the stick and tightened every muscle she could without embarrassing herself. The speedster lurched to the right, and then settled to the ground like an ebony dancer finishing a leap.

The canopy opened. Sticking her head out and placing her hand over her face, she moaned a sound not unlike the metal's death throes seconds before. "Shit!"

"Are you crazy?" a male voice yelled from inside the wreck.

"Uhhh." It was the only word that came to mind.

He scrambled out of his gleaming new red Photon and dabbed a trickle of blood seeping from his cheek.

Chandra gaped at him. He towered above her by at least two heads. His well-tanned features could have been chiseled from a rock, but a perfect and unshaven rock, with dark eyes that looked capable of penetrating a steel wall. Dark brown hair, closely shorn to keep an unruly wave under control and a thick mustache framed a face like that of an old-time screen star. A look completed with dimples she could have drowned in.

He gaped at the remains of his vehicle. A hand leaped to grab his head, quickly joined by the other as he vented a primal scream. "Aaahhh!"

Chandra cringed. Who could blame him? Her stolen Chariot remained unscathed, but his speedster lay in a crumpled heap with the entire passenger's side imbedded in a wall. Nothing remained of the passenger's panel but a mass of tangled metal, not dissimilar to the condition of the late transport Tyrus had lost. His front panel had been smashed and the radar dome crushed. Only the driver's side compartment escaped damage.

"Look what you've done to my Photon!"

The impact-resistant glass fragments from the windscreen crunched beneath her feet. Chandra slowly turned her head to look at his shiny red Photon. *How could I have missed that?* "I'm sorry."

"You're *sorry?*" His head bobbed up and down as he took in every dent and wrinkle. His hand swept across the damage path. "You're *sorry!* Great! That makes everything all right! Look what at my speedster! I'm going to hear about this for the next six months. There's no way I can pay for it."

"It'll be okay. I'm sure the guy who owns the Chariot is insured."

His tan bleached white. "Oh, I see. He let an idiot like *you* borrow a flyer like this?"

"Of course, he did..." She paused, praying for inspiration. "That idiot was my father."

"My sympathy to him. Well, if he's got the capital to own a Chariot, he can afford to pay for that." As if to emphasize his words, the remaining part of the windscreen fell to the ground with a crash. "What's his name?"

"Uh, Dad doesn't live on Distress."

He didn't react to her statement. "All right. I'll call the police."

"No!" Chandra grabbed his arm. "Don't. Please. Get me to an ultra-long distance phone and my company's insurance will pay for your Photon and your injuries."

He studied her face thoughtfully.

A cop car flew up and hovered beside them. The man walked over and talked to him for a few minutes, shaking and nodding his head at intervals and using his hands to stress certain points. When the constabulary left, the man headed back to Chandra.

Her gut knotted. She swallowed. "Is he going to arrest me?"

"No." He kept an absent eye down the road. "He thinks you stopped to help me. I told him the speedster that did this drove on. He just called a wrecker."

Chandra exhaled slowly. God existed. "Thank you." She had never meant it more.

"Yeah," he said.

Staring at the piercing peroxide-bottle brown eyes and the distinctive mustache, Chandra said, "I don't mean to sound cliche, but, you do look familiar. Are you somehow associated with the phone company?"

He shrugged and turned away from her as a wrecker from Arnie's Aeronautic Automotive Association pulled up to the Photon. The cargo hold at the base of the wrecker opened and a tractor beam glowing like a humming street flair raised the Photon. Slowly, before it completely disappeared into the transport's hold, the back half crashed into the street.

The Photon man signed a computer work order and returned to Chandra. He handed her an ID card. Lance Goode, journalist with GNN (Galactic News Network)—The galaxy's eyes to the stars. Society correspondent.

"GNN?" She looked back at him. "That's it. I thought you were on the crime beat?" She paused and could not resist a smirk. "You're covering society, now?"

He yanked the card from her grasp. "Let's see your identification."

"Some guy robbed me," she lied. Stole it and my money. I'm Chandra Solomon...here on-uh-holiday."

"Holiday? You came to Distress on holiday? You jest."

She sighed. "It's...a long story."

"It must be. Perhaps you can tell me as you take me home." Lance extended a reluctant hand to hers.

She reached to meet his hand. "Do you know how to drive one of these things...in traffic?"

Lance flew the Chariot just outside of town to a large estate with rolling hills and a manicured landscape.

Chandra stared. "This is all yours?"

"No. I'm just a tenant. I stay over here." They landed beside a small bungalow.

Inside the cottage, the fragrance of herbs gave the place a welcome, homey atmosphere.

"How do you feel?" She took off her jacket and flung it on the overstuffed couch before joining it here.

Lance rubbed his neck. "Like someone ran over me."

She smiled wryly. "Someone did."

Lance sighed, then disappeared for a few minutes and returned with two ceramic cups, one rich with the aroma of coffee and the other full of a steaming clear liquid.

He offered her one of the cups. "Here, try some of this. It will calm your nerves a bit."

As she took a cautious sip, Chandra wrinkled her nose and curled her lips. "What are you trying to do? Poison me?" She restrained herself from spitting the vile liquid on his carpet.

A smile spread across his handsome face. "If you didn't look so miserable, I'd tell you I did it to get even for damaging my Photon. Now go ahead and finish it. It'll make you feel better."

She shook her head and set the cup down on a table. "I'm sorry about your Photon."

"I am, too. How can I reach Daddy so he can make me

mobile again?"

"Actually, Mother's the one you need to talk to. But I'm having trouble reaching her. Got anything to drink?"

"Would you care for some more herb tea?"

Chandra tried not to show her distaste. "No. I mean something to *drink.*"

While Lance rummaged through his cryo unit, Chandra inspected the bungalow. It sported antiques from many different planets and primitive art accenting the walls. Delicate leafy plants rested on white wire fern stands beside shuttered windows. One of the more luxuriant she recognized as a creation plant. The phone company mentioned it in its literature as illegal on many worlds and the use of the plant was not recommended except in cases when the IGB associate was forced to amputate his own leg without anesthesia. In addition to the plants, books of all colors and sizes lined the shelves with titles ranging from "Police Pharmacology" to "1001 Ways to Get Even with Anyone."

Chandra pulled "1001 Ways" from the shelf, opened it in the middle, and read the first entry that caught her eye: "Place a sexy personal ad in *Galactic Senior's Forum,* featuring the subject's direct and private communication address complete with physical home address and location. Include all conceivable perversions and fetishes your victim abhors." *What a waste! If I'd found it a few weeks earlier I could have done this to Tyrus!*

Lance popped his head around the corner. "I'll bet you're hungry. When did you eat last?"

"I don't remember." Although she did. *How could I forget my romantic dinner with Ranknard and all those yummy nutrition squares?*

Finally, Lance returned with some sandwiches on a plate in one hand and two glasses and a couple of ice-cold bottles of beer from the clear clean springs of central Australia gripped between the fingers of his other.

Chandra restrained herself as much as she could; she did not want to appear completely without manners. As delicately as she could, she finished the sandwich in four bites—too fast to notice what was in it. She closed her eyes and chugged down one-third of the contents of brew straight from the bottle. An intake of breath caught her attention. She opened her eyes to find Lance staring at her in fascination. "It's been a long time since I've had a good lager."

"So, is Chandra Solomon your real name?"

She stared back at him. "Of course it is."

He took a swig of his own beer. "All right, Chandra Solomon..."

"My friends call me Chani."

"Alright, Chani, why don't you tell me the *real* truth? What are you doing here on this backwater planet, and who are you running from?"

*What am I doing here? What are **you** doing here?*

Her heart raced and despite the ale, her mouth went dry. "The truth? What makes you think I'm not being truthful?"

He finished the lager in another two swallows. "You're a terrible liar. Not enough experience. Come on. Why don't you try telling me the truth? Consider it a novel approach. Besides, you never know; I might be able to help you."

"I don't think anyone can help me."

"Let me make a few guesses. You came here to do a job, and now you're stranded. The locals are trying to take advantage of your situation. I assume the phone company probably outfitted you properly before your assignment. You're part of IGB's advance team, aren't you?"

She held up her can as if to toast him. "Guilty. How do you know that?"

"It's no secret about IGB setting up a substation on Distress. Yesterday, I heard one of the crew was killed and the other disappeared. IGB employees are usually well equipped and well-staffed. I'm curious. People dressed in IGB flight suits don't usually need to steal speedsters."

"What makes you think I stole it?"

"Lucky hunch."

"If you believe that, then why didn't you turn me in?"

"I wanted to see if your company would pay for the damage to my friend's Photon. If it doesn't, I can always turn you in for vehicular theft. Maybe more. The authorities ought to pay a good bounty on you. Remember, the prisons here on Distress are not known for their amenities. Now, why don't you tell me the rest?"

Chandra held up her can. "You got another one of these?"

"Sure." He returned with two more cans of lager and stretched out in another chair. "Go on."

Tracing the outline of the can with her finger, she told him about Talisman's, the Totgarians and the packing plant, and recounted the attack by the stolid man in the Chariot. Conveniently, she forgot the part about the dream, the orb, and actually killing the alien.

"What happened to the rest of your team?"

"My team consisted of one guy, Tyrus Ratstall. He lost at Cryptic in a big way. The cops never told me all the details, but I think someone murdered him for cheating."

He polished off the rest of his brew. "Aren't you afraid the guy who owns the Chariot is going to come look for it?"

She pursed her lips and shook her head. "He won't. Some of his friends might, though." Chandra studied Lance's face. Under any other circumstances she would be more than happy to spend time with a man who could have made Michelangelo's David look like a geek. Now, she hesitated. His motives might indeed be only the desire to pay for the repair of his Photon. Or he, too, might be on the trail of the mysterious rocks. Chandra didn't think so. If he really wanted the things, he could have bashed her over the head when she first arrived. It would be months before Mother missed her. No, if he wanted the crystal and the orb, he would have just taken them. But he may have another motive—like maybe a story.

"Are you sure they didn't kill him for some other reason? If he cheats at cards he might be involved in other illegal activities."

She took a sip. "I'd rather describe him as unconventional. He always treated his workers fairly. Paid them generously and gave them bonuses for finishing early. I couldn't begin to guess what other reasons anyone might have. I *do* know they're after me, now. Maybe it's the travel agents. If you help me, I'm sure Mother will pay a significant fee to the person who solves the murder of Tyrus. They take a dim view of locals offing their personnel. I'm sure they'll show their gratitude in a tangible way." She rubbed her fingers and thumb together.

His eyes turned upward. "I could use the money."

"Why do you need the money? Look at how you live."

"None of this belongs to me. I've had an...economic setback. A friend I met while covering the society beat offered me a place to stay in exchange for good press. The Photon's his. Now, tell me about Tyrus."

"He always kept the things he did secret." She downed the last few drops from her second bottle of ale. "You might call him a bit of a daredevil, in a cowardly sort of way. He lost our speedster in that bloody game. He disappeared just after that and wound up dead. The nerve of him! He always said he wanted to go out with a winning hand. Well, he lost. Who'd have thought that his losing hand would've gotten him killed?"

"How did he die?"

"The cops said a professional hit man talked him to death," she said. "Tyrus had done a lot of things in his life. Most of them stupid. All of them insensitive. But none of them justified the cruelty that ended his miserable existence. The cops said they found him the next day with this really blank look on his face. The will to live drained from him, bored to death in the prime of his life."

Lance drew a long breath. "This is worse than I thought."

"Do you know who did it?"

"I know whose mode of operation it is."

"Well?"

"A guy called The Mouth. He's notorious. I heard of one time when he tortured this poor bloke droning on for over six hours with his war stories. The fellow chewed his leg off to get away. But it ruined him. Now he just sits around all day, rocking himself back and forth and begging someone who's not there to stop. He's the only one who's ever survived The Mouth's torture. Your friend never had a chance."

Chandra sighed. "This is the first time I've talked about him except with the police. I haven't even had a chance to think about all that's happened. I didn't realize how much I really miss him." She patted a tear. "I don't do this very often. I thought I learned Ty's lessons well, especially after all those years of his insensitivity training." Another tear welled up. When she closed her eyes, it slid down her cheek and fell onto her flight suit.

Lance handed her a tissue. "It won't do any good dwelling on his demise. Let's find out why they killed him and why they, whoever they are, want you now. Tell me about the man in the bar."

"The waiter called him Taglar Stagman. I'd never seen him before. He tried to chase the Corvian off but the Green Face roughed him up and sent him packing. Ironically, just a few minutes later that Corvian just fell apart."

"He couldn't handle the confrontation?"

"No," she answered. "He just fell apart. Flesh dropped off

of him like a salted slug, and then when I asked for my bill, the waiter told me that the Pictorian had already paid it." She paused, frowning. "You know, I think there's something strange going on at the phone company. I've never done an installation when we didn't have contact with ambassadors and a whole entourage in tow. Under normal circumstances this *never* could have happened. We should have had a fleet of transports with direct communications access to Mother. Someone there must be involved. Maybe they want both Ty and me dead. But why?"

"It sounds like you're in the way of whatever they want."

She stood up and paced the floor, glancing out the window. She moved like a hunted animal. She turned back to him and hesitated. "In the way of what, Lance? What is it they think I'm in the way of?"

"I don't know, Chandra. But if you'd like, maybe I can help you find out."

"How?"

"I have connections. Maybe we can get information from some of my sources."

"What sources would a society columnist have that could help me?"

"Don't forget," he said with a grimace, "I used to cover the crime beat. I might be able to tap some old sources."

"That's right! You were the one who broke the Watercress break-in/sex scandal story, weren't you?"

Lance nodded.

"Society beat on this dump is a long way from the Watercress. Whose wife did you get caught screwing to get a choice assignment like this?"

"Nobody's wife. I screwed myself. I ran a story about a powerful man, Lekkie Rongstuph. His grab for power over other conglomerates in his industry, his adversaries who disappeared. I even got an exclusive with his shrink, who feared for his own life. Rongstuph bought GNN after the story ran. Instead of firing me or having me killed—disposing of me mercifully like any normal vengeful tyrant—he did worse." He emphasized that point by slamming his fist into his palm. "He busted me down to the society beat on Distress."

"Why don't you go to another network?"

"I've been blackballed. All the other network execs tremble at the sound of his name. No one else will touch me."

"A few years ago, IGB sent me to set up communications link for the GNN news shoot. It involved Rongstuph's doctor. High security stuff. I had an armed officer watching my every move. That was you? You were really hot."

"Were. That's the operative word."

"He couldn't have sent you to a bigger sewer. I didn't think there was anything worth covering here on Distress."

"Believe it or not, many very wealthy people live here, trying to evade the limelight and taxes."

Lance walked over to his desk and entered a code into the computer. A three-dimensional image of the Pictorian appeared in front of her. "Is this the man?"

Chandra examined the rotating holograph depicting the Pictorian's image in miniature with such realism that it looked as though he might begin to carry on a conversation. "That's him. He's the one who paid my tab and tried to chase off the Corvian. I'd recognize those squinty little black eyes anywhere."

"Yes, that's Taglar Stagman. He works for Rithel Bartlemist, the head of the Blevins' Cartel."

"What's the Blevins' Cartel?"

"They deal in home and office furnishings."

"Furniture?"

"Certainly. The cartel controls furniture sales over half the galaxy. If he put a halt on trade, everyone in this sector would be sitting on bare floors. Bartlemist's assets include major warehousing on most industrially populated planets. He owns timber interests on Rigel, Alpha Centauri, and Helion. He's also cornered the galactic market on party goods to wealthy jet-setters."

Chandra smiled. "Party goods. You mean illegal drugs and paraphernalia."

"No. Party hats and noisemakers and exotic liquor. Rithel's company has been suffering some serious losses recently."

"What kind of losses?" Chandra asked.

"Most of his shipments are being hit by party pirates."

"Party pirates?"

Lance nodded. "They raid his freighters for his cargo, the food and elaborate decorations. No one knows what they're doing with the stuff. It hasn't turned up anywhere yet. No leads."

"What does this have to do with *my* problem?"

"Maybe they're connected somehow. Maybe that's an angle

worth looking into. They say he throws some of the best parties in this sector. As a matter of fact, I have an invitation to one of his affairs tonight. It might be interesting to see what old Rithel has been up to."

"Do you think Stagman or Bartlemist murdered Ty?"

"I don't know, Chandra. But I'll find out."

"You?" She frowned. "Don't you mean 'we'? I'm coming with you, and please, my friends call me Chani."

"No, Chani. I'm sorry. It might be dangerous."

"How do you know someone won't try to kill me while I'm here alone? If I'm with you, then you can keep an eye on me. Besides, you can't expect me to sit here while you a party."

He hesitated, then sighed. "All right."

Chandra's smile grew wide. "Nothing like crashing a good party."

"Do you have anything else to wear?" He eyed her flight suit disapprovingly.

She glanced at herself in the mirror. She did look a mess, and she smelled like a cattle car. Her teak-shaded hair frizzed in an uncontrollable confusion like the bride of Frankenstein, her cheeks lacked any color, and her kevlon flight suit hardly looked appropriate for a gala. "I'm afraid I left my real clothes, makeup, everything that helped me look human, in the transport. *This*," she said, sweeping her hand over her suit, "is my entire wardrobe." She held up the coat she won from the attorney. "And of course this lovely accessory."

"I have a friend who owns a dress shop in Bedlam. She can fix you up later this afternoon. In the meantime, feel free to take a walk along the beach. You can even go for a swim if you like."

"Thanks, Lance, but I'll pass. Mother warned us about swimming in the waters on Distress."

Lance smiled. "You don't have to worry about that here. This is a private lake. The owner went to great expense to install a system to filter out the pollution and caustic chemicals. It's even safe to drink it. You'll feel better after a refreshing dip."

Chandra took a sniff and raised her eyebrows. "What you're saying is that I *need* a refreshing dip."

He responded by not answering.

"Well," she said, "got some soap?"

Chandra dashed bare-footed along the edge of the beach, running in and out of the advancing and retreating waves. The wet GNN tee shirt she borrowed from Lance clung tightly to her body betraying more curves than she cared to show. Rogan stared down at her from its point in the center of the sky and Barfude from the west.

Skipping along, she scanned the beach. Not a being in sight, save a gullet bird flying overhead. This would be a good time to relieve herself of her treasures.

She trotted into the water, splashing drops high into the air with her hand and watching them land in the water like thousands of paratroopers, making a new series of tinier droplets. She waded deeper into the surf until the water reached her chest. Her bare feet rested lightly on the sandy floor. She balanced on her tiptoes until she found a large piece of coral securely planted in the sand. She dove under the water, then surfaced, shaking her head and sending small beads of water flying from her hair. Repeating her dive, she stayed down long enough to open her eyes and look at the coral. This would be the perfect hiding place. The local version of coral grew in a bush-like manner with a stem securely anchored in the course gray sand and then an inch or so above the floor branched out for several feet. She brushed away the silt and disturbed the floor, but did nothing more. As she broke the surface, her eyes burned from the water and air.

She swam farther out and repeated the procedure. Finally, satisfied that anyone watching would think her actions just the continuation of her frolic, she removed her treasure from her pockets and maneuvered them with her toes securely into their new home in the coral growth. Farther down the beach, she duplicated her ritual without the stones. Hopefully she left enough false hiding places that no one would be able to tell which one actually hid her rocks.

When she finally left the water, she jogged over to a pile of driftwood, stopping every few feet to peer around. She knelt and dug a hole beneath the pile, burying a few worthless stones she'd picked up earlier in the lake and hidden in her pocket. Only a new slightly obtrusive mound with recently patted sand hidden under the logs betrayed the location of the decoy rocks. If they want a treasure hunt, give them a treasure hunt.

Checking her chrono, Chandra headed back to the bungalow. Time to prepare for her trip into town. That little chore might take a while, she thought, pulling the wet hair out of her face.

Lance straightened his Antarian Eel jacket and walked to the Barhardy Clothiers. The doors opened automatically while a bugle-esque fanfare blasted in regal fashion through a loud speaker. Blue human-shaped androids paraded about modeling chic fashions Chandra would not bury an enemy in. An android with lavender skin, scantily clad in a sheer magenta drape, swished over to Lance and ran a supple hand across his face and over his left eye.

"Lance Goode," she crooned. "You have an account with topless credit and a triple Z rating."

"She means you have limitless credit," an alto Lauren Bacall voice said from an upper level. "Since she fell from the second floor last week, her programming hasn't been the same." The woman glided down the stairs with infinite class and into Lance's arms.

"Mona." Lance gave her a peck. "You look wonderful!"

"Hello, Lance, sweetie. It's been a long time." She smiled elegantly. Mona turned her head toward Chandra, taking her in hardhat to boots. "I see you're still picking up strays?"

Chandra stiffened.

Lance did not seem to notice. "Mona, this is Chandra Solomon. We've been invited to a cocktail party at the Bartlemist estate tonight. Chandra needs something more appropriate to wear."

She gave him a saccharine smile. "Lance, dear, you know we don't have a bargain basement."

Chandra shoved Lance behind her. "Mona, *sweetie*, I assure you, I can pay for any garment in this overpriced shop of seconds. Sapiens, I could buy the entire store, but I'm afraid the best I could do for it is tear it down and start all over. I've never seen such...unusual decor in my life. Oh, wait, yes I have. In the swampland whorehouses on Estes Seven. I did an installation there. Did you open a garment shop there too? Now, be a dear, will you, Mona, and find something nice for me to wear." She said the last through a smile every bit as saccharin as Mona's.

Mona laughed. "Why, Lance. Your friend is so...quaint. You must have found her in a litter box."

Chandra bared her teeth.

Lance stepped hurriedly between the women. "Mona, we're pressed for time."

Mona hesitated, then shrugged. "I'll do what I can, but you haven't given me much to work with.

"Varetta," she beckoned the somewhat confused android with a hand signal. "See what you can find for Miss Solomon."

Varetta wadded up the dress she was draping on a mannequin and threw it to the floor. Hips swaying, she sashayed past Lance into the back of the shop.

"Varetta do this. Varetta do that," she complained. "What does she think I am? Her slave?"

Mona turned her attention back to her customer. "So, Lance, you're going to the Bartlemist affair. I dare say, dear, you should find a more appropriate escort." She patted her hair.

"I'm doing a story on her."

"I hate to tell you, dear but she is no more material for your society column than a dead fish."

"Mona, I really need some help. This might be the story that will get me out of the wretched society section, no offense, and back onto the investigative beat. We think there's a link between the recent murder of an Earther and one of Bartlemist's employees, Taglar Stagman."

"Old Stagman involved in a murder?" She chuckled. "He might be, but if I were you, I'd check on Rithel's bodyguard. She's been known to take a gamble now and then. Remember?"

"Does she play Cryptic?" Chandra asked.

Mona sent Chandra a searing glance, then turned back to Lance. "She's quite good. People say she cheats."

Lance nodded knowingly.

"Here." The android tossed a gown at Chandra and pointed the way to the dressing room.

A few minutes later, Chandra returned in a shimmery blue and silver beaded gown with a long slit cut up the side and a low neckline. It fit perfectly, accentuating each nip and tuck of her trim frame.

"Not bad, Lance. She might prove to clean up nicely. Still, I don't believe she will fit in at the party."

Lance ignored Mona's remark. "Chandra, it's very attractive

on you."

"I'll take it," Chandra said to Mona. "And any accessories I need to go with it."

"Varetta, take care of the-uh-young lady."

Chandra dug through her tool belt for the credits she won from the street-corner attorneys. "Oh, yes, Mona, dear. I'm going to need something a little more comfortable than this old anti-grav suit to get around in."

Varetta nodded impatiently and stomped to the back of the store.

Chapter Nine

Far above the planet surface, a gaggle of clouds nestled around Rithel's summer home. Rogan had just ducked behind the horizon, while Barfude hovered lazily, waiting for its chance to rest. As the remaining sun set, the city's vaporous shroud of smog took on a reddish cast and bathed the mansion in the golden light of dusk.

Lance maneuvered the Chariot around the stalled traffic to the valet parking.

"Lance, do you think it's a good idea to let them park the Chariot? What if someone recognizes it? That guy might've been invited to this party."

Lance thought for a moment. "The sooner they move it to the car park, the less chance it'll be recognized."

A massive Draconian peered into the cockpit as Lance opened the canopy. A smile appeared beneath the creature's lengthy snout and his eyes gleamed as he examined the vehicle.

Gallantly rising from his seat, the reporter rushed to Chandra's side of the Chariot. Accepting his offered hand, she allowed him to help her out. Once on the ground Chandra straightened her gown and brushed her hair back with her hand. Confident that she appeared acceptable, she turned to Lance. "Let's party!"

Lance led her by the arm through the entrance of Rithel's house.

Thirty foot-high ceilings, three inch-deep carpet, and the most spectacular furniture she had ever seen; it took Chandra's breath away. Rare fabrics with distinctive trim made the draperies hanging from ceiling to floor a work of art. Brightly illuminated statues constructed entirely of lights and flowing glass lined the walls of the ballroom.

In the service of the phone company she had seen and stayed in the mansions of many a wealthy leader or entrepreneur. All that wealth paled in comparison to the

Bartlemist manor. Imagine, all this on Distress.

"If sir and madam would care to step into the main guest room, the butler will announce your presence."

"This isn't the main ballroom?" Chandra asked.

"Of course not, madam." Condescension tinged the servant's voice. "This is the entry hall."

As they walked through the massive entryway another servant approached them, offering to relieve them of their wraps. Reluctantly, Chandra relinquished her new cape of beautiful and rare blood silk, triple woven for warmth. If she let it out of her sight, would she ever see it again?

A different servant pointed them to another door leading into the main wing of the house. While similarly decorated, each room held treasures more spectacular and more costly than the last. Effigies cast from precious metals or carved from a single gemstone lined up sensuously. Intricate hand-woven rugs acted as protector for the luxurious carpeting beneath the serving tables.

And the food, colorfully displayed as one would exhibit any work of art, filled table after luscious table. Fountains flowed with liquor, but not just any fountains—glowing liquids cascaded from life-sized sculptures of winged and hoofed creatures running across a river of liquor. Where their hooves touched the liquid surface, small bits of spray arose, giving the illusion of splashing movement. Chandra found herself drawn to the fountains, not only for the alcoholic contents—although that, too—but the beauty of the beastly images.

Lance glanced across the room. "I see someone I want you to meet." He led her to a lanky young man with hair the color and texture of hay straw. Chandra moved away from the liquid refreshment reluctantly.

The man turned to greet them with a broad smile. "Lance. Hey, buddy." He slapped the reporter hard on the back. "Who's the babe?"

"Wright, I'd like you to meet Chandra Solomon. Chani, this is Wright Aulweighs, an old friend of mine."

Wright offered Chandra his hand. "I see Lance still maintains his high standards for beautiful women."

Heat rushed up Chandra's face, and her eyes found the floor. "Thank you. It's a pleasure meeting you, too."

Behind Wright, a sultry voice said, "Wright, baby doll, how are you?"

Spinning around, Wright lost himself in huge brown eyes and deadly curves.

"We'll talk to you later," Lance told Wright, who had stopped listening anyway. He looked down into Chandra's eyes. "You *do* look lovely, Chandra. Would you like to dance?"

She felt herself blushing again. "I'd love to."

Lance led her by the hand to the dance floor, pulled her close, and wrapped his arm around her bare back. A fifteen-piece Rigelian group played music that reminded Chandra of a twentieth-century big band. Resting her left cheek against Lance's chest, she closed her eyes. For the first time, in what seemed like ages, she felt safe. She wanted the moment to last forever. But just when she had melted comfortably into his arms, the bandleader announced a break.

Lance glanced around as they left the dance floor. "I don't see Rithel. He may not be here yet."

"He's late to his own party?"

"Always. So I've heard. He thinks it's fashionable. Sometimes he's so late he doesn't bother to show up."

"What about Bosson Corham?" She scanned the room for the bodyguard.

"That's her over there." He cocked his head the direction of a tall Erosian woman.

Chandra felt a chill sweep down her spine. The muscular black woman possessed almost hypnotic beauty, and hands that looked as though they could easily crush a brick. Bright red lip dressings dramatically offset her dark skin and bright eyes. She moved slowly, every motion deliberate and sensual. And Chandra knew her.

"That's the woman I saw a few nights ago. She called me by name, but I'd never seen her before. She's Rithel's bodyguard?" Chandra asked in a whisper.

"Yes, I am," a voice cold as a crypt said from behind Chandra.

Chandra spun around, finding herself looking up into the face of Bosson Corham. Bosson stared back with cold black eyes.

"You are what?"

"Rithel's bodyguard."

Bosson wrapped her willowy arms around Lance, in a lithe, snake-like manner. A wistful smile stretched across her lips, and his, too.

"Hello, Bosson; you look beautiful tonight."

Chandra rolled her eyes. *I've heard that before.*

"Gallant as always, my sweet Lancer. Let me get you a drink." Bosson left, but returned in a flash, bearing a strange looking concoction.

"Thank you." He gave his familiar, easy grin. Taking a sip, his smile grew broader. "Nobody can fix a drink quite like you. It's no wonder you work for the party goods potentate." He turned to Chandra. "She can fix one helluva a drink. Would you like one?"

Chandra shook her head.

"Lance, there's something I need to discuss with you..." Bosson eyed Chandra and added, "...in private."

Lance hesitated. "Bosson, it would be rude to abandon Chandra in a party full of people she doesn't know."

"Go ahead, Lance. I'll be fine."

Lance squeezed her hand. "We won't be long."

"Go for it." She ambled off in the direction of a lively looking drink fountain, but turned back to see the pair in a passionate embrace. "I didn't mean go for *that!*"

She stopped to listen to a group of Respirsian businessmen discuss shoptalk, and not even remotely interesting shoptalk. After a few minutes of their drivel, Chandra left in search of more stimulating conversation.

She found a few Dolimars arguing about sports and gambling, each one claiming his local team would win the finals. Every few minutes, the stakes escalated. Two characters bet their entire multi-world corporations on the outcome of EctoSuper, an upcoming kicker ball showdown.

One of the long-snouted creatures turned to Chandra. With each word, his nose wiggled and his nostrils expanded and contracted. "Who do you think will win the EctoSuper?"

She had no idea who would win, but she knew everyone at parties had to articulate an opinion on everything, so taking what she had learned from eavesdropping, she invented her own theory. The Dolimars listened carefully to each word Chandra said. A few nodded their shaggy heads in thoughtful agreement; the others argued vehemently against her. As they continued to haggle over the teams, Chandra glanced at her chronometer. Lance and Bosson had been gone for an inordinately long time. Politely, she excused herself from the Dolimars, who by this time had just about come to blows over the games.

As she trekked through Rithel's enormous home, she sampled a drink from each irresistible fountain. This one displayed statues of ancient mariners from different planets throughout the galaxy. They speeded around the tank toward approaching guests and dumped a rather potent-smelling red punch into a small drinking bucket via a rear-mounted bilge pump. After filling the bucket with a sufficient volume to last her half the night, Chandra scoured the rest of the mansion for Lance and the mysterious Bosson Corham.

Chandra examined room after magnificent room, still finding no evidence of the elusive pair. She wandered into the upper floor of a two-level room. When she looked down at the first floor, she spotted Bosson in the process of taking advantage of a supine obviously drugged Lance Goode. Chandra threw the bucket at Bosson, who ducked as the object flew past her head by only centimeters.

Quickly, Chandra adjusted her Personal Protection. "What the hell do you think you're doing, you galactic strumpet?" Under her breath, Chandra threatened the woman's existence, her mother, and a few other things most people consider sacred.

Before Chandra could heave a nearby antique vase at Bosson, the Erosian scaled the stairs and overtook her.

"I should kill you, now," Bosson hissed. She grabbed Chandra by the throat, picked her up off of the ground and slammed her into the wall.

Chandra clawed at Bosson's grip, but the more she struggled, the tighter those vise-fingers closed around her throat. Finally, after what seemed like years, Bosson released Chandra, letting her tumble to the floor. "You're no good to me dead."

Chandra gasped and wheezed, and tried to think as she bought time by rubbing her throat and coughing. She touched her Personal Protector beneath her long sleeves, switching it to "kill". Aiming the barrel just past the bodyguard, she fired a hole into a painting immediately beside Bosson.

Smoke rose from the portrait.

Bosson smiled, exposing perfect, white teeth. "Why, Solomon, from Tyrus' description I didn't know you had the fortitude."

Chandra leveled the weapon on Bosson's chest. "Try me.

Now what did you do to Lance? The same thing you did to Tyrus?"

Bosson laughed, a deep from the gut laugh. "I do not want Lance. I wanted to borrow him."

"I'll just bet you did," Chandra said.

Bosson looked down. A slight smile crossed her face, softening her fierce look. "I needed information, and he wouldn't talk. I gave him some help. It would have been to your advantage later."

Picking herself up from the cold floor, Chandra narrowed her eyes at her adversary and rubbed her throat with her free hand. "What kind of information?"

"Information about you."

"What do you want to know about me?"

Bosson down looked at Lance. "I thought Tyrus might have given you something he won from me."

"How is Lance involved?" Chandra emphasized her question with a motion of her hand.

"I don't know that he is. Since he helped you I thought you might have confided in him."

"There was nothing to confide except that I have a whole string of assholes on my tail wanting to kill me. I never saw Tyrus again after he left for the game. The cops said they found nothing on him except his Harbinger, which didn't do *him* one helluva lot of good. That slug abandoned me here with no money, no food..." Chandra recited her well-rehearsed speech, practiced over his grave and several other times since his death. "He even lost our transport vessel. Until last night, I hadn't eaten in two days. If someone hadn't already beaten me to it, *I'd* have killed Tyrus." Chandra stopped, glanced back at the partially conscious Lance and then glared at Bosson. "I'm sure that in his state Lance told you he searched my possessions and found nothing."

Bosson acknowledged with a nod.

"You killed my partner, didn't you?"

"I have done many things in my life, and I have killed many people, but I didn't kill Tyrus. I have observed, since I lost the crystals in that game of Cryptic, everyone involved in the game has died or disappeared.

"If you didn't, who did?"

Bosson shook her head. "I don't know. I played Cryptic with him that night, but I had no reason to kill him. Especially that night. Tyrus won some blaze crystal. Then some other Sagi toad cleaned us all. He won Tyrus' transport and another worthless piece of glass Rithel's chauffeur gave me to repay a debt. At the time, I did not realize that Taglar had stolen them from Bartlemist's private collection. Taglar has since disappeared; I do not want to be next. I must return them or the consequences will assuredly be most unpleasant. If I find them on you, Solomon, I'll kill you. Nothing personal. If you give them to me, I will provide you with passage home."

Lance moaned and tried to sit up. He reeled and fell forward like a person just out of a centrifuge. Chandra motioned Corham to descend the stairs and stand clear of the reporter.

"Lance," Chandra said. She touched him on the shoulder. "Are you all right?

"He will revive shortly."

A foolish grin crept across his face, giving his dimples a life of their own.

With Chandra's attention momentarily diverted Bosson charged Chandra again and threw her to the floor. "Now, Solomon. Tell me where you have hidden the orb."

Before she could answer, ear-shattering explosions thundered outside the door.

Bosson's ebony face faded to ashen. She rushed over to Lance. "Get up, Lancer. Get up!" She pulled him up by the arm, steadying him with her body. He tried to walk, but his legs refused to respond, buckling beneath him, a marionette with severed strings.

Outside the door, another explosive detonation. The house shook and Chandra stumbled back behind a heavy chest. *What I wouldn't give for my hardhat and kevlon, right now!*

The door blew open amid spewing smoke and a shower of wood splinters and metal door hardware.

Once again Lance tried to stand, but Bosson's weight slammed him to the floor. She filled the room with the shrill death scream of the elite warriors of Eros.

Chandra waited a moment and then ran over to where Lance and Bosson lay. She turned her head away from the bodyguard's wounds and lifeless eyes. After pulling Bosson off of Lance, she quickly checked him over. To her relief he had received no more than some minor cuts.

Footfalls tramped past the door, heavy, clunking footfalls made by large military-type boots weighted down by massive equipment. Chandra retreated back to her refuge behind the chest. A creature stamped in, scanned the room, and left. Within moments several more returned. One mercenary turned over Bosson's body. He drew in a deep breath then turned to face the man who had followed him into the room. "Master, she's dead. But she was with this human." He pointed at Lance. "I think he knows," he added hesitantly.

The man he called "Master," frowned. "You blew out the door?"

The man who had stormed in a few minutes before now cowered like a whipped puppy. He nodded meekly.

"You could not have simply opened the door?"

"I was trying to make a point."

Without another word, Master aimed his light pistol at his inferior and fired. The man crumpled to the floor a smelly mass of burned flesh.

"You!" Master screamed. "You behind the storage." Master pointed with his pistol at Chandra who wasn't as well concealed as she had thought. Another mercenary grabbed Chandra by the arm. She struggled, not wanting to leave the helpless Lance at their mercy. Her assailant yelled something at her in a dialect she could not understand. Tiring of her, the soldier pressed the two prongs on the barrel against her forehead. She saw bright lights, then fell to the floor, unable to move.

Funny. It didn't hurt. She remained conscious, but...disassociated from her body. She saw motion but no details or forms. Voices shouting, scraping and dragging. Then...silence.

Slowly, the world returned. Still lying on her back, Chandra moved her hand to her forehead, and winced. Her own touch felt sharp and painful, like an electric prod. She crawled to her hands and knees, and then slumped back to the floor. Curled into a fetal position, she cradled her head in her hands. The acrid odor of smoke and burning fabric did nothing to allay her disorientation. Finally, she gained her legs and lurched out the door.

Memory felt sketchy. Lance had disappeared, but Bosson's mangled body remained as a morbid reminder of the violence.

As Chandra staggered through Rithel's mansion, she found small fires and the bodies of the wounded and dead guests and servants. Everything and everybody seemed to come in pairs. Throughout the dwelling, security men assisted the injured and doused small fires. One pair of guests stuck their heads in fountains, both drinking punch without benefit of glasses.

Hobbling through the halls, she reeled to the floor. The floor had taken on a soft, comforting feel. Warm with two arms and hands that moved, rather too quickly and in a manner too familiar.

Through slightly less blurred eyes, she stared at the floors. They looked lean and lanky and blonde. Both seemed attractive and apparently uninjured.

"Hello," they said in perfect unison.

"Hi," she answered. "You're Lance's friend, and so are you."

"Yeah. Great party, huh?" they observed simultaneously, still gazing up at the bottom of the table.

"Yeah, great party. Are you okay?"

"Uh huh. Why? Shouldn't I be?"

She stared at them. Even for twins, their resemblance was uncanny and their movements as precise as a drill team. "Didn't you see those guys?"

They both tried to sit up, but watching them only made her dizzy.

"What guys?"

"You didn't see the guys with the blasters barge in here and blow all those people to Sirius and back?"

They swept their hands through their unkempt straw-colored thatch and gaped around incredulously. A pillar of smoke rose in gray curls only a few feet away. Wright and his twin raised their glasses to take a drink, but found them empty, the bottoms having been shot out of them.

"Wow! Must've been a better party than I thought!" He looked through the glass like a telescope.

"It *was* great, for a while." She pointed at Wright's double. "How 'bout him? What's his name?"

Wright raised his arched eyebrows. "Who?"

"Him." Chandra sat up and crawled out from under the table.

"Huh?"

The smoky haze overhead thickened, making breathing a strain.

"Look, Wright, we have to get out of here. If they didn't find what they were looking for, they may come back."

"But the party's just getting interesting."

"Fine. You guys can stay here. I'm partied out. Nice meeting you both. Maybe I'll see you again."

As Chandra made her way to the door, a woman with her head in a trash can said to no one in particular, "Ol' Rithel sure knows how to throw a party. I'll give him that."

A few bodies had been piled out in the garden, including one Chandra recognized as the creature who parked Lance's speedster.

"Who did this?" she asked one of the least injured men.

"The party pirates."

"Can you bring my speedster? It's a matter of life and death."

He motioned her toward an older model pocked by blaster fire.

"This isn't the one I came in," she said.

"Look, there are so many blown speedsters and dead guests, we can't match 'em up all perfect. Take it. I'm not going to get you another one."

"That's okay," a familiar voice behind her said. Chandra turned to find Wright. By this time her head had cleared and there was only one of him. "It's mine. You need a lift?"

She let out a deep breath. "Yeah, I'm headed for the Fomalhaut system. But, I'll be happy if you can take me as far as a shuttle station."

Chapter Ten

Chandra scanned Lance's cottage. "What a mess!" In a frenzied search, someone had scattered Lance's perfectly organized possessions, in broken pieces, everywhere. Even the couch had been ripped open, its stuffing tossed all over the floor, and the covers wadded up in the fireplace.

Sapiens! Would Lance Goode be pissed if he saw his immaculate home!

Wright followed her inside. "Hey, this is great. Just like home. Lance must have been *some* housekeeper."

"Yeah." Chandra shuddered. "Some housekeeper."

She dashed into the bedroom where she left her things, only to find it in similar shambles. Nothing had gone untouched. In seconds, Chandra slipped out of her evening gown and into her flight suit. She grabbed the casual clothes she had purchased at Bahardy and crammed them, along with her formal, in an overnight bag she found under a pile of mattress stuffing. A search of the floor finally turned up her empty tool belt, then the tools strewn about the room. They gave her power and a certain amount of safety. Quickly, she gathered them together and tossed them in the bag.

She raised her arms in triumph like a speedster race winner when she found Lance's creation plant. The stalk lay with its blue-green leaves bruised and its exposed roots drying in the air, estranged from its pot, soil spilled across the carpet. She scooped up the dirt, replacing it with all the care she could afford around Lance's prized plant. A little bit of Mr. Goode still lived in that plant and it would stay with her. Grabbing the plant and the bag, she rejoined Wright.

Wright blinked. "Hey, wow. A creation stalk. They're great. You wouldn't believe all the things you can do with those plants. I remember the time—"

She interrupted him. "I have most of my stuff. Let's get out of here." She took a last glance around Lance's house. "I'll be okay, Lance," she whispered, her vision blurring. "And thanks for everything."

She stopped when they reached Wright's speedster. "I need to go down to the beach."

"Don't you think this is a bad time to go for a swim?"

"I'll be right back. I left something very important down there."

She returned a few minutes later and climbed in his speedster, clutching the crystal and the orb, both beaded with moisture. Water dripped from her hair onto the upholstery.

"Take me to the shuttle station, Wright. Maybe I can get off this rock."

"Listen, Chandra, I've got to be on Rasalhague III in a five days. I can give you a lift that far."

"In *this* thing?"

Wright grinned. "Naw. This is just one of my heaps. I have a ship that will get us there."

"Heap" described it perfectly. Wright's old model Pegasus made Ty's speedster back home look just-off-the-assembly-line prime. The interior sported well-worn, slightly ripped upholstery, and splits in the Vyn-all around the instrument panel trussed together with silvery ventilation tape. A large crack crawled across the windscreen. On the instrument panel, a mummified half-eaten pastry rattled incessantly.

Chandra had her second and third thoughts about a trip with this guy. Five days of this would send her to a padded room—if she survived.

As they pulled up to the shuttle platform, Chandra gasped, "Oh, Sapiens!" Some might describe the transport as a classic vessel; she called it junk. "You fly in this? Wright, I doubt this thing can reach airspeed, much less reach escape velocity."

"Don't worry. This baby has almost two hundred light years on her."

"I believe it."

The tiny speedster settled to the ground just a few meters from the vessel.

"She's called *Blind Faith*."

"Why?" Chandra asked. "Are you a minister?"

"Naw. She's named that cuz my navigation equipment doesn't work all the time. But that's okay. I always get where I'm going."

"Always?" She tossed her bag over her shoulder.

"Almost always."

In the distance, Chandra heard speedsters, lots of them, approaching rapidly. She grabbed her possessions and trotted toward the ship. "Wright, let's get out of here!"

He straightened up and sniffed the air. "Aw, shit. Cops."

Chandra narrowed her eyes. "You can tell that by smelling the air?"

"Naw. I heard 'em talking on the police com frequency." He climbed out of the speedster and dashed past her.

Wright entered his security combination. The door hesitated, then struggled to open, finally stopping only partially up. Shrugging his shoulders with an embarrassed air, he stooped down and crawled under.

The police closed in; time was running out. She tossed her bag under the door, followed by the creation plant. She tried to scramble in behind it, but the door dropped, locking her out.

"Wright!" She banged her fist against the jammed door. "Let me in. They're right behind me!" Out of the corner of her eye, Chandra caught speedsters tearing through the underbrush and slamming to a stop. "Wright! They're here!"

On the other side of the door, stripped gears pounded and clanked.

One speedster took a few shots at her with the blaster mounted on the upper carriage. The shots missed her by only inches, close enough the heat from the blast almost seared her skin.

The old ship's engines powered up. "Wright, open that door! Wright!" *That bastard. He's got the rocks.*

The engine whine grew louder.

"Wright, please!"

Cop speedsters surrounded the shuttle. One officer dismounted his vehicle, and approached Chandra—his light pistol bearing down on her. "Drop."

She did.

Beside her, but too late, she heard the grinding of the door's servos as someone attempted to open it manually. With all that banging and gnashing of gears, it still opened only a foot or so.

It's hopeless.

A strong hand wrapped around her ankle and dragged her into the ship. Heat once again stung her as another blast sizzled past. The door slammed down in her face.

Wright left her lying face down on the floor and rushed over to the ship's controls.

She crawled to her knees, gulping air in relief. The deck of Wright's ship smelled like the inside of a thirty year-old garbage unit, not surprising in light of the mountainous stack of dirty dishes obviously forgotten on the floor beneath the control panel, and a pile of filthy clothes tossed in the copilot's chair.

"It's not as bad as it looks, and really, I didn't do it by myself." He shrugged and pointed to the heap of dirty clothes. "I had some help."

"Oh?"

He grinned. "Not a girl—Ivan."

"Ivan?"

From the center of the pile emerged a pair of amber eyes. They blinked and stared at her, intelligence disassociated from a body, assessing Chandra, the lower form of life. Slowly, a large chalk-white cat with auburn markings encircling both of his ears rose from the heap. His toothy yawn transformed into a smug grin as he glowered at Chandra. Ivan, Wright's feline companion and on-paper second-in-command, blinked, not at all thrilled that Wright had picked up yet another stray. Ivan hissed, leaped out of his pile of clothes, and padded off holding his auburn tail high in the air.

"We don't have much time," Wright reminded her. "The big guns'll be here soon. Stow the dishes and let's ditch."

That stack of plates would probably have brought a high price in the art market as abstract sculpture since the particular shade of green growing on a crust of gunk begat a totally new color. Artists across the galaxy would pay horrendously high tuition just to gaze upon the most significant artistic discovery in the past two thousand years.

"Stow them where?"

"In the trash unit. We gotta get out of here."

The ship shuddered from energy emitted from truck-mounted blasters. No problem for functioning shields, which remarkably happened to work on Wright's ship. "I think we just managed to piss them off."

With the crunching of the disposal, the galaxy lost the shade of green forever. Chandra dashed back to buckle into the copilot seat. Before she could, Wright slapped on his own safety strap and punched the thrust button. When the engines charged, Wright ignited the jets and they lifted off; Chandra found herself plastered to the bulkhead. She couldn't move a finger.

He was right. The ugly little ship did have get up and go. When he pulled back on the thrust, Chani fell from the wall into a pile of what she could only describe as "stuff."

"Great Sapiens, Wright. This ship belongs to you?"

"Yeah. Isn't it great!"

"It's...unique."

The ship looked worse than his speedster did. An inch-thick layer of dust coated the instruments. And the smell of a cat box permeated the ship. It might have been preferable to stay groundside and face the Tyrus' terrorists and the cops. She removed the pile of laundry in the copilot's seat and dropped it on the floor.

"Don't do that."

"Do what?"

"Ivan doesn't like it when someone moves his clothes."

She looked at the cat. "He'll live."

"He's not the one I'm worried about. The navigator post is free."

Chandra sighed, put the clothes back and plopped into the navigator's seat.

"Sorry about the mess," he said. "The maid couldn't come this week."

"You have a maid?"

"Yeah. She comes once a week, but she missed this week."

"You did all this in a week?"

"Yeah. It was a slow week."

She drew stick pictures in the dust. "Wright, just what is it you do?"

"I'm an architect."

Chandra took a dubious look around the vessel. "An architect? You're kidding. Wright, this ship looks terrible. How could you be an architect?"

"Yeah. Well, you've heard about the cobbler's kids?"

"How many kids do you have?"

"Huh? No, no. I don't have any kids. Aren't you from Earth? I mean the old Earth saying that cobbler's kids never have decent shoes. I can't stand to be around class for too long. It's like a disease."

"Uh huh."

"Really. Don't you wonder why Rithel invited *me* to his party?"

"Okay, Wright, I'll bite. Why?"

"I designed his house."

"Uh huh."

"No, really. That's why I have to be in Rasalhague in a five stellar days. The chancellor wants me to design a reverse pyramid for him."

Unconsciously, she began to draw an inverted triangle in her latest artistic medium. She wished for the lost green to add a hint of color. The creation took on a three-dimensional look as she used dots to give it depth. "That's absurd. Why would anyone want an upside down pyramid?"

He shrugged his shoulders. "Cuz the other architects and designers said it can't be done. So, I'm going to do it. Ever hear of the Haritian Spiral Dome?"

"Sure, I've heard of it. Everyone's heard of that. I studied it in my engineering design classes. It's a massive dome that's nothing but a huge spiral staircase. A big tourist attraction. The holos I've seen are pretty impressive, but it's not anything I'd go light years out of my way to see."

"You wouldn't?" His face fell.

"Well, if I had the time, I might go a few light years. But I'll never have the time. Why?"

His grin grew wide again and he sat up straight, sticking out his chin like a new father. "That was my project."

"You mean you worked there?" she asked.

"No, Chandra. That was *my* project."

She stared at the smut-covered ship and then at the frumpy architect. He looked hardly old enough to be designing backyard storage sheds, much less one of the Seventy-Five Wonders of the Galaxy.

"I don't understand. I studied the Haritian Dome back when I was in school. You couldn't have been more than...Oh, I get it." She laughed. "What a great joke." She stared. "Not a joke?"

A harsh red flush crawled across his face and he shook his head. "I'm older than I look. And a lot older than I act. Besides, I've been on vacation for a little while. I guess about forty-five years."

He punched a few codes into the computer. Up popped several images of different types of structures, each more bizarre than the previous one. These superstructures housed heads of governments.

"See that one?" He pointed to a massive corporate building that covered a quarter of the hemisphere.

She nodded.

"That one holds the body of the Rytheom ambassador, a well-known galactic swindler. No one knows this, but he's been cryogenically preserved in this chamber. He'll be brought back to life when the statute of limitations expires on all the crimes he's committed."

"You built all these?"

"Uh huh."

"And you're going to design a reverse pyramid on Rasalhague III?"

"Uh huh."

"What's it for? A sarcophagus?"

"Sort of. The chancellor's mother-in-laws. He wants me to design it with an entrance, but no exit."

Chandra glanced at the screen and noticed a few blips. The bogeys were a long way off, but they were gaining. "Wright, does that mean there's someone behind us?"

He armed his weapon system. "I bet they're cops." He pointed at the gunnery station behind him. "Ever used one of these?"

"Only in the arcades."

"That's all right. They're pretty bad shots, themselves. I guess you better go up there and shoot a few rounds at them. They'd be disappointed if we didn't." He scratched his head. "I don't understand what they want. I thought that warrant had already expired."

"What warrant?" she asked.

"Well, it wasn't much. You see there was this—"

Blind Faith began to rock and shake.

"Damn. They're really shooting at us! They're not supposed to do that."

The five ships on the screen closed in on their position.

"They're not cops. They're too accurate. Who are those guys?"

Just someone else who wants the rocks. I should toss the bloody things out the air lock.

"Chandra, get over there and man that gun," Wright yelled.

She charged over to the weapon center, and scaled the

ladder up to the turret.

Once again, a blast struck the ship. The concussion threw her against the tunnel wall. Chandra cried out as she lost her grip and tumbled to the deck below.

"Chandra, get your ass up there or we're going to be just so much space junk!"

She scrambled back up the ladder, plopped in the gunner's seat, and shook her head. The windows were so grimy she could barely see through them, but his expensive state-of-the-art weapons had all the latest bells and whistles. At least these targeting instruments seemed to work. Clenching her teeth, she placed her chin on the rest. Her eyes focused on a bull's-eye. "Targeting computer. Program sights."

"Targeting complete," the computer responded, allowing her to program her weapons to hit what she looked at.

Her fingers curled around the trigger and squeezed. Blasts of energy spirited from the weapon's barrel. As she fired, the entire turret vibrated, shaking her out of her seat and down the crawlway. Still, hands clinging tightly to the grips and her chin barely on the rest, she continued to fire.

They attacked too fast for her to focus her eyes to lock on the target, especially since Wright couldn't maintain an even keel.

Above her she heard a scream. Suddenly, something landed on her. Fur, teeth, claws in blurred motion. She screamed.

It screamed.

Wright screamed, "Keep firing until I can jump to hyperlight drive."

Chandra almost smiled. Just like the old days with Ty. Her life was back to normal.

Chapter Eleven

She kept firing. The intruders became more cautious after she began her barrage. The glass, frosted by her breath and countless layers of grime, lit up again with the glow of cannon fire. The return fire shook the ship and dashed her against the turret's padded walls. Still she kept after them.

One of the pursuing pilots inadvertently encroached on her visor cross hairs at the right time. She targeted his right exhaust port and fired. A small flare shot out the vent, glowing larger and larger until the vessel exploded into brilliant golden flames and quickly dissipated in the vacuum of space.

"Yes!" She waved her fist at the embers glowing in the darkness as her unknown assailant boiled away into nothingness. "That'll teach you to screw with me!"

Her gun swept to the right as she targeted another fighter. This one flew closer, but navigated more erratically than the other. His light burst shot harmlessly past *Blind Faith* and faded into the void. *He's probably just a rookie, like me. But that doesn't excuse his rude behavior, attacking us and all.*

This time, she took more deliberate aim. After several misses of her own she caught the poor dupe in the rudder. The ship spun into mad circles, tracing its uncontrolled route over and over again until Chandra could estimate the moment it passed her sights again. As she fired, a bright golden flash signaled the end of the wounded vessel's misery and one fewer item on her To Do list.

"Hang on." Wright's voice said faintly from below.

Between shots, she tightened her safety harness and braced herself.

Suddenly it felt like an invisible hand shoved her deep into her seat. The stars streaked into long bright colors and then disappeared in fiery specks. At the same time her nose tried to reach the back of the chair with a short cut through her skull. The chair had reached around to strangle her. And her stomach flipped twice.

When life and cognition returned, she realized that she was still firing. Bright strands of light from her cannon spurted at a no-longer-present enemy. Releasing the trigger, she slumped back into her chair. She felt like she needed a net to catch her breath. While scanning her scope for stray bogeys Chandra forced air out in a slow sigh.

Only the stars winked back at her.

"All clear," Wright yelled. "You can come on down."

Her legs behaved as though they belonged to someone else. After wrestling them back under control, she slid down the turret ladder to the main deck. Wright sat in the captain's chair toying with the navigation computer. He turned to her and pointed at the occupant of the copilot's station.

"Chandra, this is Ivan the Terrible."

"I'll say it is. This place is the pits."

"No, I mean my cat." He pointed at the cat sitting in the chair.

Well, it *had* been her chair. A pair of livid amber eyes stared back at her. "You're joking," Chandra said.

"No, I'm not joking. His name is Ivan the Terrible. He's my copilot."

"Move, fella," she ordered the pink-nosed copilot. He did not budge. Instead Ivan fixed her with an unblinking stare. She ignored it and gave him a gentle push.

Ivan rose to his feet like a vengeful god cast from his heaven. His muscles grew taunt and his eyes narrowed.

"Wright, the cat won't move."

"That's his chair," Wright said. "He gets a little upset when anyone else tries to sit there. You can sit at the navigator's station."

"His seat, my ass." Chandra swatted Ivan's rump.

Ears flattening, Ivan reached around and slapped her. Chandra jerked her stinging arm back. Three red lines crossed her hand. Lines that became thickened as blood beaded along them. In retaliation Chandra popped him on the top of the head, then retreated hastily.

"He scratched me!"

Wright beamed. "He likes you. He doesn't treat everyone that good."

Ivan shifted his weight and arched his back, his ears flattening even tighter against his head. His auburn tail lashed the shredded upholstery in rhythm with the drone of the engines, then giving her a glacial glare, Ivan circled the chair twice and settled back into a comfortable position inside his pile of clothes. He stared at Chandra daring her to move him.

Chandra held her bloody hand under Wright's nose. "Look what that little bastard did! Are you going to let him get away with it?"

"Don't worry; he's harmless."

Chandra snarled. "Harmless? He's about as harmless as a baby vice-adder."

Wright did not appear to hear her comment, but Ivan did. He tucked his head in a comfy position between his front paws and stared smugly at the intruder, clearly agreeing with her.

"Better be nice to him, Chandra."

"Call me Chani. Why should I be nice to him?"

"He's a Turkish Van."

Chandra raised a brow. "A Turkish what?"

"Turkish Van. It's a breed of cat from Turkey on Earth. They swim, they're big and they're real smart. I doubt he'll take too much crap from you."

"From *me*?" she asked. "*He's* the one who drew blood."

"I know that. But he's got a good memory and a twisted sense of humor. Better make peace or he'll make your life a living hell. I know. Try being nice to him. He'll respond to that."

"I'll just bet." Chandra rubbed her injured hand. "Don't you think you've spoiled him?"

"Naw." Wright swept his fingers through his hair. "He deserves whatever privileges he has. After all, Ivan puts up with *me*. Oh, yeah. Watch his nose."

"His *nose*?"

"Yeah. Some people call it the Vanometer."

He's insane, she thought.

"See how pretty and light pink it is?" He pointed to Ivan's shell pink schnoz. "When he gets mad, it changes color. The madder he is, the darker it gets. If it turns purple, clear out. Someone's going to lose body parts. And it won't be him."

Ivan glared at Chandra and began his bathing ritual, daring her to violate his fur. He extended his hind leg and stroked his fur with his tongue all the way down to his feet. Flexing rear claws, he massaged his pads and brushed the tufts of fur between his toes.

Wright leaned back in his chair, resting his feet on the console while absently displacing a cardboard carton that appeared to have once contained Chinese food. "So, Chani, why don't you tell me why all those guys are after you?"

She stared at him. "What makes you think they're after me? You said you had warrants out against you."

"I do, but I'm not worth *that* much trouble to anyone. Nothing I couldn't buy my way out of if I ever got caught. These guys are serious. What do they want?"

"How would I know?"

He glanced at his navicom. "Trouble seems to follow you. First the party. Then Lance's place. Now my ship. Nobody's ever been that impressed with me. You're in trouble. Just didn't know how much. So why don't you tell me what they want?"

She rubbed her hand across her perspiring forehead. "I don't know. Really."

He cocked his head. In the muted battle lighting of the cabin his pupils disappeared into the dark brown of his irises. Still they seemed to pierce to her soul.

She sighed. "All right, I know I'm in deep crap. But really, Wright, I don't know why."

Still he said nothing. The silence dragged on until she could stand it no longer.

"Really, I don't know *why*. But I guess I do know *what*." She hesitated. "If you knew I was in trouble, why did you help me?"

He shrugged. "I think you're cute. Okay. What do they want?"

Chandra hesitated, then reached into her bag and rummaged around pulling out items until she found the bluish crystal Ty had handed her. "This." She held it up with the reverence afforded a religious relic.

He took it from her and examined it. The transparent azure had eight equal sides, and uneven, broken ends. He punched the console and eased the lights off. Everything around him disappeared in the darkness except the crystal. Its cyanic glow filled the cabin with a soft blue light, giving everything an underwater look. The bright azure intensified in the darkness as if it held its own inner light source. The sensor readout indicated that it measured six centimeters long with edges cut so precisely its angles remained true to the eighth decimal place.

He looked up from the screen. "It's a Centaurian luminium crystal. They're real handy. They gather up whatever light's around it and project it. Where did you get it?"

She stuffed her belongings back in the bag. "My construction partner, Tyrus, gave it to me. He told me that he won it in a game of Cryptic. He said it was real important. Is it?"

"*Important?* Yeah, I heard someone stole it from Rithel Bartlemist's gem collection about three weeks ago. No wonder everyone's out to get you."

"How do you know?"

"It's been all over the news. I guess you haven't watched much video lately?"

She shook her head. "All that equipment was in the transport. Is the crystal valuable?"

"Worth a small fortune maybe, but...I don't think it's worth the trouble these guys're going to. Is that all?"

She rummaged to the bottom of her bag, pulling out the orb. "Tyrus told me to get this out of our old transport, but it's just a piece of glass." She handed it to Wright.

He ran his fingertips across the orb's cool surface.

"Nobody would want this bad enough to kill me. Best I can tell it's just a sphere of glass. There's nothing special about it. I assayed it. Just glass. They have to be after the luminium crystal. They killed my partner, and now they're after me. *He* did this to me."

"When did he tell you about the orb? Right after the game?"

"No. I never saw him again after he dropped me off at the maps and plats office," she said. "He came to me after he was murdered. How else would I know about the bloody orb in the first place?"

Wright gazed up from the orb to eye her dubiously. "How could he give you something after he died?"

She shrugged. "Ty always had a flair for the bizarre. He liked riddles, too. The pest," she grimaced. "He knew I'm no good at them and it's his way of getting even with me."

"Ever thought of spending a few months in a rehab center?" Wright asked.

"I'm not crazy!" Once more, Chandra repeated the episode of Tyrus and the card game. With each recounting, it had grown longer, partly because she had learned more, but mostly because this time she felt the need to level with Wright Aulweighs. She told him about the dream, about the crystal, and how she found the globe at the transport.

Wright examined it more closely. "It's a good grade of glass. Flawless. If we know what this is, we might figure out why they want it so badly. It doesn't appear to be an energy source. Can it be a component for a mechanism of some kind?"

Chandra shrugged. "I don't know. All Tyrus said is that it's my ticket to anywhere in the galaxy. Of course, you have to remember that Tyrus was always a little delusional. What he said and what he meant were usually two completely different things."

Wright pushed a button on the control panel revealing a small platform formed by thousands of tiny needles that wobbled and bobbed up and down. He placed the sphere on the stand, which molded around it, holding it securely. As a tiny needle ran across it, row of numbers ran across the screen in front of him in some form of script Chandra had never seen before.

"What's that?"

"It's analyzing the sphere."

"What's it made of?"

"I don't know. Chips, circuits and stuff. I'm not an engineer."

"No, Wright. I mean the orb. What is the orb made of?"

"Glass."

"Great. We're right where we started. A piece of glass and a Centaurian luminium crystal."

"Is there anything you're not telling me?"

"I've told you everything, Wright. I never meant to put you in danger, but I had to get out of there. I never thought it would go this far. They just keep following me."

In the copilot's chair, Ivan yawned with a squeak. The blue light gave him a ghostly appearance.

"I think he's telling us we're keeping him up."

"I'm so sorry, Ivan," she said. Slowly, Chandra reached over to pat him on the head. Without thinking she ran her hand down his back, just as Wright had done earlier. His fur felt like cashmere. Ivan responded with a lash of the tail. Rather than push it, Chandra retracted her already wounded hand.

Wright tossed the luminium crystal to her and switched

the lights back on. Everyone blinked in the glare of the sudden white light. "I've got it on autopilot. If any other ships show up on the screen, the computer will wake us up. We'll be in the Enuk system in about twenty hours. There's another bunk up the ladder next to your gun turret. You might want to get some sleep, too."

Chandra nodded and closed up her tote. Dragging the bag behind her, she climbed up the ladder to bed.

Chapter Twelve

Groggily, Chandra descended the ladder from her bunk to find Wright tending the creation plant. He'd re-potted the sagging stalk, and wiped the dust from the leaves.

"How far to Enuk?" She smoothed her hair back and straightened her civilian blue print jumpsuit.

Wright glanced over at Ivan, asleep at his assigned post, scanned his board, and shrugged his shoulders. "Be there in a few hours, I think."

"What do you mean, 'you think'? You don't know?"

He gave her a sheepish grin. "Well, sometimes the navicom doesn't work real good. I've been as much as one light year off. It's nothing to get concerned about. I always find my way back."

When he finished pampering the plant, Wright sat down at his pilot's chair.

Chandra gaped at him, then shook her head. "Sapiens? Wright, how can anyone brilliant enough to create those magnificent buildings have so little common sense?"

"When you're brilliant, it's dangerous to be responsible," with a boyish grin.

She took a moment to absorb that. "Really." *He's as mad as Tyrus,* she thought.

He nodded. "It's a curse. If you're responsible they expect too much of you. Take Ivan, for example. If he did too many useful things, then I'd expect him to do them all the time. As it is, he gets my ass out of a crack in an emergency every once and awhile. If he did it too often I'd expect it."

Chandra pointed at the cat, who had just finished his highly personal hygienic procedures. "How can *he* pull your ass out of a crack?"

"You'd be amazed." He reached over and scratched Ivan at the base of the tail.

Ivan closed his eyes, purred audibly and jacked up his rear end to further enjoy the attention.

"Hey, wanna drink?" he asked

She shook her head. "Too early." For a moment Chandra considered taking advantage of Ivan's more placid moment, and seizing the copilot's seat. But when she got within a few feet of his chair, Ivan cracked his eyelids long enough to make brief eye contact. Chandra stopped mid-step and returned to her navigator's station—Ivan returned to his Wright-induced nirvana.

"That's what I call "elevator butt," Wright said pointing at Ivan.

Wright placed a sherbet dish in the cup holder of the copilot's chair and poured something that looked like beer in the glass. Immediately, Ivan began to lap it up.

"Wright, I thought alcohol could kill a cat," Chandra said.

"It can. But this is no ordinary beer. This is GootenKatz."

"What?"

"I found Ivan drinking out of my beer glass one day. I tried to stop him, but he'd continue to sneak a drink. Hey, he's my best bud and I didn't want him getting sick, so I looked around, and in the Leo system I found this drink made of herbs. It's not real alcohol, but it has the same affect. It makes him happy and I don't have to pay vet bills. They make beer *and* wines, so we're covered. We may not have much food in here, but he and I can drink together. We have to be careful, though. After all, he's my designated driver."

Wright adjusted Ivan's collar as the cat polished off the cat beer in the bottom of his glass.

Giving up on the copilot's spot, Chandra grabbed her tote and returned to the navigator's far right seat—obviously lower rank. A quick search of the tote turned up no crystal. Frantically, she dumped its contents on the deck. "It's gone! Okay Wright, you Flebian scumball, what did you do with my crystal?"

Wright swiveled his chair around and smiled. "You're looking at it."

"Where's the damn crystal, Wright?" She stalked toward him, fist formed, ready to beat what few brains he possessed into mashed potatoes. "Look, damn you," she said, grabbing him by his lapel with her other hand. "I don't have a helluva lot. I don't know why it's so important, but it's worth money, and it's not going to be taken away from me. Not by you! Not by anyone!"

"Ow, shit!" She released him and spun around, grabbing her rear, to find Ivan perched on *his* chair flexing his razor claws. He had taken another piece out of her, and her new civies, too. Ivan wore a smug expression on his fuzzy little face, savoring his victory, while biting at his claws to remove the remnants of blue thread he had extracted from her jumpsuit. Chandra found her own scowl reflected in the eyes of her one foot-tall adversary.

Forget the cat. She turned her wrath back on Wright. "Where's the crystal?"

Playfully pushing her aside, Wright picked up Ivan and scratched up and down his plush white neck and behind his ears. Ivan reacted by holding his head up, exposing his throat for easier scratching access. "You're looking right at it. See?" He continued to rub.

"I don't see anything."

He nodded his head. "I don't think you'll have to worry about your crystal. It's in a safe place."

Deep down Chandra knew that Wright, in his own incoherent way, must be trying to tell her something significant. She peered closer at the cat. Fastened to Ivan's collar, and safely concealed beneath his dense mane-like ruff, was the crystal. Looking right at it, she still had not seen it.

"That's great! When did you do that?" She tried to take a closer look at the collar, but not too close.

"I borrowed your bag before you woke. I thought I'd better do something just in case we're boarded by one of your fans. Ivan's the perfect hiding place. He's so foul-tempered with strangers, nobody dares to come near enough to him to find it. You wouldn't believe the things he's smuggled for me."

"I'm sure I wouldn't."

"Customs won't touch him. They're always afraid they'll end up requiring major surgery. Believe it or not, he has quite a reputation across the galaxy."

"I believe it. Thank you, Ivan." Chandra reached forward to give him a friendly pat, but thought better of it. "I'm sorry, Wright. I just thought..."

"Naw. Don't apologize. If I were you right now I'd be horrendously paranoid, too." He thought for a moment. "Except I don't think it's paranoia when people're really shooting at you."

Wright called ahead to Enuk III's communication central station to clear landing instructions. Nobody responded. "No one's there."

Chandra's eyebrows furrowed. "Enuk's really a backward planet, but someone should be at the center." She'd returned to her IGB-issue flight suit and hardhat.

"You been there before?" he asked.

Chandra put her hand on the back of Ivan's chair...carefully, to avoid disturbing him. "Four years ago I did time here, in the employment sense of the word. Tyrus and I set up an ultra-long-lines complex down there. It was supposed to give the Enuk residents exposure to the rest of the cosmos. Why Mother picked this behind-the-times world for a state-of-the-art station like that, I never could guess. Other star systems that needed the com center were competing for it desperately, but Elkhed, the site locator, swore this planet would more aptly serve the company's purpose: to get the whole galaxy hooked on interstellar communication.

"Enuk's backward in its customs and in its technology. I suppose Mother figured that once the inhabitants became dependent on InterGalactic Bell communications, it would become a necessity not a luxury. As a bonus, an intergalactic substation would serve to extend use to the more difficult to reach sectors of the galaxy. It was all very simple. All the brass loved the idea.

"Enuk is really charming in its own way. It had charming little shops and charming little pubs and charming little people." She paused, remembering. "I especially liked the charming little pubs."

"It's sort of pretty from up here," Wright said. "You think they need an architecturally unique tomb or anything like that?"

"Maybe. While I try to reach Mother, maybe you could talk to some of the mucky mucks. I doubt they have much money, though."

Chandra climbed up the hill to the ultra-long lines complex. Looming high above her, the enormous dish reached for the hazy sky, soaking in all the signals and radiation that crossed its path. She trudged up the path, overgrown with grasses and shrubs. Downhill, lazy meadows of tall grasses and russet-colored farm crops surrounded the village of Shrunk. A slow stream wound its way through the center of town. Plush growths of stemmed algae shaded the stream shores with the most vibrant green Chandra had ever seen, even better than the mold on Wright's dishes. Off in the distance lay other towns equally as sleepy as Shrunk.

Chandra had missed Enuk and its slow pace. *Maybe someday I can come back here again.*

Topping the hill she found herself face to face with a heavily armed guard barring the entrance to the complex.

"I need to use the phone," she said to the sentry.

"Sorry. I cannot allow unauthorized personnel access to the complex," the geek wearing an IGB security uniform said.

"I'm not unauthorized. I work for IGB. I'm Chandra Solomon, senior installation supervisor, Planetary and Industrial Division."

"Where's your ID?" He held out his hand. He was from Ruckbah. She could tell. A large nostril peeked out through each of his cheeks. She cringed when she recalled meeting one suffering from a serious head cold.

She dug through all her pockets. It had disappeared. She must have lost it when those creeps ransacked Lance's house. Chandra thought. "I've had a terrible time. I must have lost it."

He folded his arms across his chest. "This place is off limits to all inhabitants of Enuk."

"Look at me. I'm not from Enuk." She fought back a scream. "I'm an employee of IGB. See." She pointed at the logo on her hard hat. "I don't have my ID on me. Mother needs to send me a new one. Just let me talk to engineering. Or call Elkhed Perkins. He'll straighten this out."

"No ID, no phone."

"Look, I'm wearing a company-issue flight suit. Why would I lie about being an employee?"

"I cannot let you use the system without proper identification."

"But I can't get ID if I don't talk to them."

He stared straight ahead.

Sapiens. What does it take to make him think? "I installed this damn system!" she yelled.

He still stared straight ahead.

"Look, this is a public station. I'll get the Enuk Grand Prefect to call them for me.

"Only if he comes armed with nuclear weapons."

"You can't prevent him from using his own station."

"If the Grand Prefect shows up, I have orders to arrest him on sight."

She gaped at him. "What!"

He motioned to the dish with the barrel of his weapon. "Their telephone service has been disconnected for non-payment."

"What?"

"If anyone from this planet threatens to enter the premises, I have orders to either arrest them or shoot to kill." He smiled. "I get to choose."

"Look-uh..." She glanced at the name patch on his jumpsuit. "Rancit, is it?"

He nodded.

"Okay. Look, Rancit, if you will call IGB and talk to Elkhed Perkins in the main office in St. Louis on Earth, you'll find out that I'm Chandra Solomon, the engineer in charge of the Distress installation in the Castor system. I installed this one with my partner about four years ago."

He stared at her, less than fascinated.

"A problem developed on Distress. Someone murdered my partner and stole all my equipment. They'll want to talk to me. If you don't notify them about me, when I get back to Earth, I'll give them your name and location and when they're done with you, the natives here will be able to use your chest as a bedpan. Do you understand?"

Rancit nodded his head; she had his attention now. "Alright, you stay here. I'll call them and if I get the approval, you can come in and talk to them. Until then, you stay here. If you touch the fence, it will incinerate you. Understand?"

She nodded.

A few minutes later Rancit returned, his nostrils undulating.

"Well, hurry and open this thing up," she said.

He resumed his armed-and-ready stance behind the gate.

"I said, open it."

"Go away!"

"What?"

"They don't know you."

"What?"

"They said you must have stolen the flight suit and they

are concerned about humans impersonating an IGB employee. If you try to gain access to this complex, they told me to kill you."

"What? Who did you talk to?"

A wide grin crossed his face. "Elkhed Perkins."

In a daze, Chandra wandered down to the Snark Sark, a pub where she and her team wasted hour upon intoxicated hour at the end of each workday. The first night, Tyrus had cheated a roomful of the natives at a game of cards. In typical fashion, rather than take their money, he encouraged them to pay off their debt by working for him. He hired plenty of good local workers, and he usually dismissed their gambling debts when the job ended, as a condition of their employment.

Alone in a familiar booth Chandra ran her fingers across the rough-hewn table. As always an elderly barkeeper kept the place so clean microscopic lifeforms dared not enter the door. The same old tapster from years before approached her spotless table, wiping it compulsively with his cloth. He looked like the average man on Enuk: a foot shorter than her, with something akin to a beer gut hanging over a loose skirt that resembled a kilt. He reminded her of one of Santa's elves in a dress.

"What's your need?" He picked at an invisible piece of dirt.

"Hemlock," she said.

His huge eyes rolled toward the ceiling. "Never heard of it."

"It's something fools and philosophers used to drink on Earth."

"And which are you?"

She grimaced at him. "I'm a fool."

"Would you like to try another choice?"

She nodded. "I don't think I want to be a philosopher."

"No, I mean would you like to choose another beverage?"

"How about some of your famous Snark Sark?"

He eyed her as though trying to place her face. "Not many beings off Enuk know about Snark Sark."

"Just a lucky guess," she said.

"It will cost you five credits."

"Okay."

He nodded and walked away.

While she waited for him to return with her drink, her

eyes ran over the familiar decor. Hand hewn timbers held up the walls and ceiling. Photos and holos of patrons who had been coming here for years littered the rough walls. Off to the side, in a hard-to-see corner, hung a holo of Chandra, Tyrus and their Enuk work crew, all forty-five of them. She smiled for a moment, then groaned and cradled her head in her hands.

"Here's your Snark."

"Thanks." She did not bother to look up. Chandra grabbed the multi-sided glass and clutched it in her hands like a child with a pacifier.

She nursed her drink for some time and then slugged the rest down in one hard swallow. A flush of warmth rose to her cheeks and a light-headed euphoria wrapped its fingers around her. But it only lasted a few minutes. It reminded her of the day at Talisman's in Bitter. She only *thought* herself alone then. She had not known what 'alone' meant. *Now, I'm really alone.* In Talisman's she thought reaching Mother would be her salvation and everything would be *fine*.

"Just fine," she said aloud.

Now even the apathetic arms of InterGalactic Bell had abandoned her. *Why did Perkins deny I work for him? Why is the Enuk system down? What the hell is going on?*

"You look like you need a friend," the old tapster said.

"I don't think a friend could help me much, unless that friend can put me in touch with my supervisor at InterGalactic Bell." She stared into the liquid residue in the bottom of her glass.

He seemed self-assured, yet timid. "I can't do that anymore, but at one time I had a calling card."

"So did I."

"Mine does not work anymore," he said.

"Neither does mine."

He eyed her hard hat and then turned to stare at the holo on the wall. "You were the engineer who spent all those credits here when they built that monstrosity."

Chandra took a deep breath. She tried to look up at the man, but could not meet his eyes. "Guilty. Yes, I set up that station."

The old man studied her face. "You put that station there?"

She nodded, still looking at her glass.

"That's a big station."

She cocked her head and glanced at him from the corner

of her eye. "One of the biggest I've ever designed. Why doesn't your card work?"

"They canceled it for non-payment. I always pay my bills."

"You paid your bill and they disconnected you anyway?"

"No, I did not pay my bill. When they put that station there, they taught us how to use it, but they didn't tell us that we would have to pay for it. We all thought they were giving it to us."

"They told you it was free?"

"No. But they didn't tell us how much it cost before we used it. Since they didn't tell us, we thought it was a gift. You should remember, the price is *always* discussed before the transaction as I did with you and your men. If no money is mentioned, then it is free."

"Crap! How much do you owe?"

He sat down in the chair opposite her. "Me, personally, or the planet?"

She blinked. "What do you mean 'the planet'?"

"IGB cut off the entire Enuk population. You want another one of those?"

She nodded.

"Ten credits."

"Okay."

He returned with her Snark refill.

This time she slugged this one down, but the warm feeling did not bring as much comfort as it had before. "You mean those bloodsuckers cut off the *whole planet*?"

"No. I mean those bloodsuckers *own* the entire planet."

Chandra choked on her Snark. "What? They really foreclosed on the whole planet?"

He nodded. "Some company called the Republic LoanStar Company came down and surveyed everything. Even my bar. Gave everybody fancy paperwork with hard to read writing, and said it belonged to them."

"I'm sorry."

"My brother worked on that project."

"I'm sorry," she repeated.

"Some fellow beat him at a game of Cryptic."

Chandra shifted in her chair. "Really?"

"Yep. Ol' Heppy had not worked in ages. Fed his family real good that year, he did."

"I've heard every black hole has a silver lining. I'm glad it worked out for Ol' Heppy and his family. It didn't do well for the rest of the planet."

The old man slapped Chandra on the back so hard she almost fell off of the stool. "Ha! That's where you're wrong. Here, have a drink on your old friend Tackle Halypath." He yelled across the room to the waitress, "Tager, a cup of our finest for..." He looked at her blankly. "What did I call you? Channa?"

"Chandra Solomon." *He never did get it right.*

"For Channa Solomon." Then, as an afterthought, he added, "And one for me, too."

"I'm sorry, Tackle. I thought the system would help you folks out. Instead, I got your planet repossessed. Gads, I wish I hadn't accepted that assignment."

"Before the phone company came, our world was depressed."

"Economically?"

"That, too, I guess. Nobody could afford anything. No work, no pay. You folks came and fed us real good. Got us going. I'm no worse than before except now InterGalactic Com owns the bar. They have to pay me to run it. I never got paid when *I* owned it. If they want things to run, they got to pay us. We eat and they own a beautiful chunk of rock they have to sink a lot of money in. Some day their accountants will figure out that it costs them too much to subsidize us and they will forgive the debt.

"In the meantime, we all eat. So, Channa Solomon, what brings you to our lonely little world now?"

"My partner and I were supposed to install an ultra-long-lines system like this one on Distress—I think you call it Castor—but he lost our ship and direct com link and then someone killed him. I came here cuz I thought I could make a call to Mother to come pick me up. And now that scrod-faced twit at the complex won't even let me make a call."

Tackle shook his head in sympathy. "A sad story indeed."

"Chani," Wright's voice said from behind her. She turned in her chair to face him. "I need to talk to you."

Tackle rose. "Want something to drink?" he asked Wright.

"Yeah. I'll have what she's having."

"Five credits."

"Put it on my tab, Tackle," Chandra said.

After the old Enuk left, Wright asked, "Do you know what

IGB did? They foreclosed on this whole damn planet for non-payment of their phone bill."

She shook her head sadly and rested her head in her hands again. "I know. How did you find out?"

"I talked to the Grand Prefect about designing a building that would enhance the natural beauty of the planet. He told me InterGalactic Bell must approve all construction. They own the planet. They stole it from a bunch of naive natives."

"I know. Wright, it's not that the natives are dumb. They aren't. The Enuk's monetary system is just different from our economic markets. They depend mainly on the barter system, and when Mother issued them a long distance bill for more than the world's ten-year budget, the people didn't know exactly what to do."

"Bastards," Wright said.

"Being the understanding sort of company it was, IGB said that was all right. They would just place a lien against the planet until the Enuks satisfied the exorbitant debt, plus interest. For the cost of a hyperinflated phone bill, Mother managed to acquire a planet, a substation, and all the labor it could utilize. And it's all my fault. I can't help thinking that this whole thing had to be premeditated."

"What did they say when you talked to IGB?"

She raised her head. "They told the guard to kill me if I tried to gain access to the complex. The site locator who sent me to Distress said he had never heard of me. My own company wants me dead. I just don't understand."

Wright dropped his glass. He shoved back his chair and grabbed hers. "Chani, let's get out of here. Now."

"Why?"

"You just drew them a map to where you are."

Chapter Thirteen

"Have something to eat. I've got some leftovers in here." Wright rummaged through the cryo unit. "Hey, this looks pretty good." He opened the carton and sniffed the contents. "Smells pretty bad, but looks pretty good. Well, maybe there's something else in here." He continued going through the unit, opening containers and then tossing them into the disposal.

"Thanks, Wright, but I'm not hungry...Aren't you worried about them attacking us?"

"Naw, they can't do anything to us while we're using the light drive," he said. "We've got plenty of time before we have to slow down."

"You know when I joined the phone company I just wanted to go into deep space to do a job, not find an adventure."

"Come on. You've got to eat something." He cracked another container. "Just not this. So, Chani, where're you from?"

She dodged a carton flying past her face toward the disposal. "I don't have a home right now. I grew up in Houston in the Independent Republic of Texas on Earth. My folks and my little brother still live there. But the last eight years I've lived out of a suitcase. What about you?"

Wright wiped slime off of his hands onto a towel, but from the look of the towel he was mostly wasting his time. "*Blind Faith.* She's my home."

Chandra scanned the architect's palatial surroundings, the dirty clothes piled at the copilot's station, heaps of nondescript stuff hidden in dark corners, and assorted food containers scattered on the deck where he had missed the opening to the disposal unit. "Wright, with all the money you make you could buy a luxurious cruiser with all kinds of conveniences. Why do you stay aboard a dump like this?"

Sadness crossed his face. "Because *this* is home. I get nervous when I'm around perfection for too long, even when it's my own perfection. I'm afraid I'll break something or get it dirty or ruin it. I can't ruin this ship, and I really have nowhere else to go. Ivan's my only family and one of my few real friends." He nodded at the red tail protruding from the mound of clothes in the copilot's chair.

"You're a misfit conformist," Chandra said.

"A what?"

"A misfit conformist. You know, someone who has all the intelligence resources and knowledge to conform, but can't quite fit."

He put his hand to his chest and mouthed, "Me?"

"Yes, you! Look at you! You're the best at what you do; no question about it. Sapiens, you designed one of the Seventy-Five Wonders of the Galaxy. You have an occupation that gives you status most people would kill for, and you scorn it. You could surround yourself with the finest things the galaxy has to offer. Instead, you live in squalor."

He heaved a container at the disposal. It bounced off, spewing a liquid that resembled tobacco spit across the floor.

"You have the most beautiful women in the universe clamoring to be with you; and you choose a foul-tempered cat for a companion. That's a misfit conformist."

"What are you?" he asked.

"Tyrus accused me of being the same thing."

His eyes eased upward as he pondered, not only what she had said, but also a sizable cobweb forming on the ceiling. "What makes you a misfit conformist? You seem perfectly normal to me."

"I couldn't work as closely with Tyrus as I did and still be 'normal'. No, I watch old movies, especially the really bad ones. I lose at the stock market. I've decided that my investing philosophy is, 'buy high, sell low, and live on the profits.' I study politics. I collect trading cards of past U.S. presidents. I'd give anything to have the Richard Nixon card. What a guy! I read only old magazines. You know the kind you find in doctors' offices, from a year and a half ago. For me it doesn't pay to keep current in anything but technology; things are always changing anyway. By the time I reach a place where whatever I read makes a difference, the situation has already changed, so I've worried about a lot of things for no reason at all. Does that make sense?"

With the sound of the garbage compressing in the background, he laughed. "I think so," he answered and stopped laughing, looking thoughtful.

"And so here you see me now. My world shot to hell by a Ty's non-stop talking hitman and a stolen light crystal. Life stinks, doesn't it?"

Wright took a deep breath. "Naw; I think I need to clean Ivan's box."

"Where did Ivan come from?"

Wright's face lit up. "I found him when he was just a kitten. We finished construction on a huge government building on Earth in the area they used to call Armenia. That little thing stood alone on the curb of a busy highway with speedsters and wheelers shooting past him. He just sat there, so tiny. I saw some jerk throw something at him, so I stopped and tried to catch him. Poor thing. He ran right in front of a wheeler. It almost hit him. Then one of them almost hit me. I thought he might get away, but I trapped him next to a fence. Ivan hissed and swatted, but I pulled him out anyway. When I held him next to me he trembled. I put him in some dirty clothes in my flyer. When we got to my hotel I fed him caviar. It was the closest thing room service had to cat food. We've been buds ever since."

In the background on the communications screen tuned to GNN, a smartly dressed correspondent droned on.

"Here." He handed her a spoon holding his latest find. "This one doesn't smell too bad."

She took it and smelled the contents of her spoon. "What is it?"

"Grilled quell."

Her stomach twisted when she remembered the Corvian and his delight in eating the live quell snacks in Talisman's.

"My own company wants me dead. I just can't believe it."

"Do you think Tyrus knew what was going on?" Wright asked.

She shook her head. "He wouldn't risk his neck for the likes of Elkhed Perkins. I think he must have inadvertently gotten involved in this deal and someone killed him in the crossfire. I've been doing this long enough. I should have known something was up when we didn't take a full team. I should have had at least one IGB ambassador."

Ivan stood next to Chandra sniffing the carton.

"Ivan you really don't want this," Chandra said.

Ivan continued to root around and paw at the box.

"Okay. Here." She offered him one of the quell on a piece

of paper she laid on the deck for him.

Ivan sniffed one side and then the other. He peered up at her.

"I told you."

He reached over the quell and pantomimed burying it with his paw.

"I know," she said. "It tastes like chicken. It's all right for me, but it's not good enough for you. I don't blame you." Chandra picked up the quell with her fingers and popped it in her mouth. Then she picked up the paper, wadded it up and tossed it toward the disposal unit. It hit the rim, and bounced off along the deck with the rest of the cartons.

Ivan dashed over to the paper, batted it with his paw a few times, and then picked it up with his mouth. He brought it back to Chandra and dropped it at her feet.

She scooped up the paper in amazement. "Wright, Ivan fetches?"

"Yeah. He does that all the time. I read that Turkish Vans love to fetch."

She threw the wad again. This time it flew across the cabin. Ivan pounced on it and returned to her with his tail raised like a battle standard.

"Thanks, Ivan." She patted his head. This time she felt no condescension, but almost affection. Once again, she threw the wad—with the same results.

"He'll last a lot longer than you will. It's that Vancat stamina."

She threw it again, and Ivan repeated his performance, swaggering to her with the now damp paper. Chandra took it from him and absently tossed it toward the copilot's seat.

She sighed deeply. "What do I do now?"

"When did he say you need to be at Fomalhaut?"

She thought for a moment. "He said to get it to the third planet in the Fomalhaut system before the Festival of the Fat Bore or something really awful would happen. I can't imagine anything more awful than what he's already put me through. According to my computer the Festival of the Fat Bore starts in about five Earth days."

"In about forty-eight hours we'll be on Rasalhague III. The chancellor is having an affair in my honor."

"Formal?" she asked.

Ivan dropped the paper at her feet again.

"No, it's an informal affair. He's having a state dinner too. I'll talk to him and see if he can't provide you safe passage to Fomalhaut. He really wants me to build that pyramid, so he'll probably help."

Chandra picked up the soggy paper wad. Suddenly she turned to the view screen. "What did he say?"

"Volume up one-eighth," Wright said in a loud clear voice. He, too, turned to the screen.

Instantly the volume on the newscast elevated. "...pirates have once again hit a freighter owned by Rithel Bartlemist. This is the third such attack the company has experienced this week. Blevins Cartel spokesman Pottican Rabelschtuff said they suffered significant losses, but declined to give specifics." The anchorthing had slightly damask skin and took deep breaths between sentences. "In a related story, the estate of Rithel Bartlemist received a serious blow this week when, during one of Bartlemist's well renown parties, a group of terrorists invaded the mansion. Our society correspondent Lance Goode reports on the latest development."

"He's still alive, Wright! Lance is alive."

Wright nodded and motioned her to quiet with his hand.

The screen switched to a well-worn Lance Goode attired in the tattered formalwear he had worn the night of the party. Even heavy theatrical makeup could not conceal the bruises on his face and hands. His voice sounded weary, unsteady, maybe even frightened. "I'm standing before the ruins of the Bartlemist estate, as it is. The tragedy inside, still an untold story. Fifteen beings died in the assault here last night."

"Fifteen people," Chandra repeated.

"Absent Rithel Bartlemist escaped injury," he continued. "But his bodyguard and companion Bosson Corham died in an explosion in one the mansion's drawing rooms."

Chandra nodded knowingly.

A holo of Chandra appeared on the screen and rotated, showing her head from every possible angle.

"Authorities suspect party pirates, but are also looking into possible involvement by an InterGalactic Bell communications employee, Chandra Marie Solomon."

"What?" she screamed. "That bastard!"

"Solomon was based on Castor VI, sometimes called Distress, to help assemble an ultra-long-lines deep space communications depot. Solomon is also a suspect in the murder of her IGB construction chief, Tyrus Ratstall of Earth."

Fury boiled up in her. "I'll kill him!" She flung the paper wad at the com screen.

"Shhh."

"IGB officials refuse to comment."

The screen switched to the Super-Ecto field.

Frustration and anger raced through her. "Lance knows I didn't do it. The Distress police said they thought the killer played cards with Tyrus that night! Lance probed me for information, but I thought he was just curious. Oh, Sapiens! I'll bet he's involved, too." Desperation chased out all other emotions. Her shoulders slumped. After a minute she looked up at him. "Wright, you're in terrible danger. You've got to get rid of me."

"Remember, the chancellor *will* help. He really wants that reverse pyramid. Imagine being able to get rid of all your mother-in-laws without having to kill them. Yeah, he'd commit the entire military for that."

"Why are you going to all this trouble for me? You barely know me."

"I'm a sucker for teak."

"Huh?"

"Teak. It's a wood on Earth."

"I know what it is. What's teak got to do with me?"

"It's the color of your hair. I can't resist a woman with teak hair."

Her face flushed. "You'd risk your ship and even your life for teak hair?"

"We'll..." He pulled another container out of the cryo. "Uh, gawd. What *is* that? You've got spunk. Don't worry, Chani. You'll be okay."

"Yeah. I've heard that before," she said. "Thanks, Wright. You're a great friend."

"I'm not that great. I want a cut of whatever it is Tyrus has you in for."

"Deal. We'll take equal cuts...Providing we survive."

Chapter Fourteen

In the old days, gazing at the view screen used to give Chandra a thrill. Just watching the star systems as they zipped past to later be replaced by brighter, more interesting, celestial objects had once made goose pimples leap up in anticipation. After so many deep space excursions, especially this one, the tedious collection of stars never seemed to move. Although she could pull up the chart and log their progress, it still seemed she was going nowhere — fast.

Bored, she ambled from the screen to the cryo unit. Supplies had dwindled dangerously low—not even so much as an order of underdone quell to fight over. Even recycled water was used at a premium.

Studying the chart, the X marking 'you are here' put her halfway between you-were-here and this-is-where-you-should-be. Between here and there offered little opportunity to replace provisions. Few of the planets in their path had life, even fewer carbon-based life, and still fewer possessed $H2O$ or a delta communications complex.

As sensors returned with unsatisfactory information, she requested longer range scans. These took much longer than the closer, less detailed sweeps. In the meantime, she tuned into some broadcasts from a system in the next sector.

The first signal she picked up seemed vaguely familiar. An old gray and white episode about a woman who worked in an archaic pie factory. Chandra had seen this particular show in 20th century retrospectives. As the conveyor inched forward, the woman sprayed oncoming pies with whipped cream, and then topped them each with a cherry, placing the finished pie in a box and moving it to a cart. At first everything moved smoothly and then the conveyor moved a little faster. It then raced so quickly that the woman could not keep up and pies soon covered the floor.

Chandra giggled as she watched the old broadcast.

"Scan complete," the computer said.

"Well?"

The computer gave its report. A planet orbiting an obscure red dwarf in the next quadrant seemed to have everything she needed.

"Eureka!" she called out.

Wright climbed down out of his cabin. His blonde bangs hid his eyes, still crusty with sleep. "What's the excitement about?"

"I found a planet in the Caroli system that's got both a delta class communication array *and* water. Thought we might drop in and use the phone."

He yawned in her face.

"Try to contain your excitement," she said. "I've been eavesdropping on some of their transmissions just to see what they're like. They've been re-broadcasting some old Earth signal. Ancient television."

"Anything else?" he asked.

"Not yet."

"What does the computer's tourist book say about them?"

"Give us all the poop on the planet orbiting the red dwarf Caroli," she told the computer.

"I have no information on the natives' elimination habits," the computer answered.

"Never mind," Chandra said. "Just tell us what you do know."

The computer projected a translucent hologram of a blue and white planet with large patches of green and brown landmasses. It revolved around a relatively small reddish star.

"Lucilla orbits the red dwarf Caroli," the computer said. "Technological development lags five-hundred years behind the Galactic Technological Standard. Their various societies are based on worship of deities that travel invisible through the air and materialize inside their homes. Their major landmasses are broken into twelve continents in varying sizes. Inhabitants of these societies worship vastly different deities.

"The most outgoing and friendly of the natives live in the southern hemisphere. While they tend to become cranky around religious holidays and during the mating season, for the most part they are non-belligerent. On the northern hemisphere, the natives tend to welcome visitors and often have them for dinner."

"As guests?" Wright asked.

"Usually as the main course," the computer answered. "The natives also have a fondness for Terran television signals."

"Where's that broadcast tower you told me about?" Wright asked Chandra.

She peered more closely at the topographical map. "The northern hemisphere."

Wright tried in vain to make his hair lie down but it sprang back out of place like a warped Slinky.

He yawned and started back for his cabin. "Great. I'll drop you off. Wake me up when you're finished."

"Not so fast, brave warrior." She threw a container holding a yellow ooze at the ladder above him. The ooze clung to the metal and slowly descended the handrail, then glopped to the deck in an undulating puddle. "While I'm working at the communications tower, you need to find us some water and food. That is if you can convince the natives we won't be all that tasty a meal ourselves."

"Can't you just use their system by remote?" he asked scratching his chest.

She shook her head. "It's too old. With all those analog components, it's going to take me physically flipping switches and pressing buttons."

Wright sniffed the goo dripping from the ladder and winced. "That's older than I am."

"Great." Chandra leaned back and propped her feet up on the console. "We should donate it to a museum. I think I'll check out some more of their transmissions. Computer, let's see what else they're receiving on inter-Lucilla broadcast frequencies."

Wright navigated *Blind Faith* through the Lucilla atmosphere. He set it down gently beside a lake just a few kilometers from the tower.

They left the ship and followed the graded path toward the distant tower. It stood big and burly, with thousands of steel arms crisscrossing like a giant metal pastry and its four supporting legs disappeared upward into the clouds. As puffy cumulus clouds billowed past, a hole opened up, exposing the power center mounted in a giant crow's nest at the top. Large as it was, from the ground it looked little larger than a thimble.

"There's an elevator." She played at the controls, but nothing happened. "The only way to use their systems is to climb up there." She checked her tool belt. "It shouldn't take me but a couple of hours."

Wright gazed up toward the top. "How high do you think it is?"

She placed a digital meter against one of the metal legs of the tower and waited a few seconds until it beeped softly. "It reads five hundred twenty eight meters." She sighed. "Well, I guess I'll sleep well tonight."

Wright stared where the top should have been, it was once again hidden behind the clouds. "Isn't there an easier way? Don't you think climbing that thing is kind of dangerous?"

She waved him off.

"You could be killed." He made a falling motion with his hands, which ended with his fist splatting into his open palm.

"Then you get the orb..."

"...and the string of thugs that go with it. Instead of you being the target of their affection, I'd turn into the guy with the bull's-eye painted on my head. You think I find that comforting?"

"Really, Wright, don't you think you're being just a bit melodramatic?" she said. "I'm only going to be gone a couple of hours. What do you think they give me all this safety equipment for? So it jangles smartly when I walk? It's designed just for this purpose. Remember, I do this all the time." She shifted her weight. "Look, if I can reach my old supervisor, then I can pay you for your trouble. You'll have some more pocket change; I'll be home. Why don't you go ahead and fill the water tanks?"

It was a ten-megawatt, forty-two terracycles, and at least a million gigablads transmitter. She found the gigablads dangling beneath an awning at the halfway point, those funny little gray flying rodents with a grumpy disposition and an appetite for the vital fluids of other living creatures. When sleeping, they looked as if they were covered with hundreds of little bumps, but as they took to the air, the bumps flattened and became tiny airfoils. They could sail and swoop effortlessly, but climbing required great amounts of energy, which just made them hungier and crankier.

A few of the little beasties tried to join Chandra on her climb, but reconsidered after she used her bug zapper on them. The others decided they wanted something a little smaller and without a bothersome energy field.

After climbing for an hour-and-a-half, her legs cramped each time she pulled herself up to the next rung. The rungs had been placed one-and-a-half times farther apart than the climbs she had trained for, making every step a painful stretch. She wrapped her belt around the girder, then snapped it securely. Although she had made it almost three-fourths of the way, she felt so weak and drained she could barely climb even one more rung. The last few days had taken their toll.

"Just ten more," she promised herself aloud as she pulled herself up the next step. "That's all. Just ten more."

Her arms quivered as she reached up for the next crossbar. She tried to ignore the cramps by remembering the near-deathblows she had dealt in countless hands of cards. She tried to recall the delicate microscopic circuits she had designed and repaired. None of that seemed to matter. Those gifted fingers had resigned their commission. They refused to close around the metal bars, and other times they cramped, stubbornly failing to open and reach for the next rung.

"Nine," she croaked. Her throat had grown dry and raspy as she panted between steps.

"Ten." She connected her belt to the tower. Leaning back, she shook her arms and flexed her fingers. "Almost there. Just ten more steps"

After a rest period that seemed all too short, though each had grown longer than the previous, she started on her next ten steps.

The rungs seemed to grow farther and farther apart.

Chandra groaned at the thought that she still had two more sets of ten to go before she reached the crow's nest at the top. She could almost hear Tyrus nag at her, "It's been longer than you thought. Boy, are you out of shape."

Ignoring that, she took a breath and looked down. From up there, everything below looked miniature, like a scene from an impressionistic painting. Oddly distorted mountains and a patchwork of fields spread out around her. A low-level cloud slipped quietly beneath her, hiding the ground for a few moments before it shimmied past.

She marveled at the fairy tale quality of everything on the ground. Some type of minute ground vehicles moved along a road only to disappear behind the horizon.

"Only three more rungs." She struggled for her next finger

hold.

This time her fingers refused to close around the crossbar. Her weight fell back, jarring the other rung out of her grip. Her left hand closed around the bar, but her foot slipped from its toehold.

"Sapiens," she screamed. "Wright!"

She hung from the bar with only four exhausted fingers between herself and a five hundred twenty eight-meter plunge. She reached for the rung, flailing, missing by millimeters. Her back arched; her fingers stretched. The cool metal brushed against her fingertips, but hovered just out of reach. She had slipped too far out to use the lower bar for a foothold.

All sensation had drained from her left hand, all the sensation except for the cramp that felt like someone had stuck her hand in a vise slowly and steadily closing around her flesh. Even so she gripped the bar tighter.

"Tyrus, you bastard. This is all your fault."

Red-faced and puffing for air, she struggled to maintain her grip.

"You're right," she heard a familiar voice just above her. "It is."

She raised her eyes a little higher to find a familiar form kneeling on the crow's nest just above her.

"I can't believe you've grown so careless," Tyrus chided.

She felt her fingers loosening their grip. Weak and cold, she could no longer hold on. Only three fingers remained between life and a fifteen-second plunge and a Chandra-made two-meter-deep crater.

His hand wrapped around her wrist. "You're never going to make it to Fomalhaut if you keep this up."

He pulled her up and dropped her to the metal grate floor.

Panting and trembling, she looked up. Backlit by Caroli she could only make out a silhouette, familiar though it was.

Chandra's hand spontaneously curled into a fist. "I can't believe you!"

The figure moved a few feet back, revealing the translucent face of Tyrus.

"You're welcome," he said.

"What?"

"I said, 'You're welcome,' for saving your life." He buffed his fingernails against his shirt.

"If it wasn't for you, I wouldn't be in this situation."

"It's good to see you, too, Chani. You look great. The weight loss is really attractive, except for those dark circles under your eyes."

She tried to pull up to her knees, but her legs failed to respond. "I lost weight because I've been starving to death. If you hadn't made off with my per diem I could have gotten a transport with a galley."

"Yeah, that's right. You've hooked up with that loser." He peered over the safety rail down at the ant-like movements on the ground. An audio aura of music and background noise seemed to surround him.

"Sapiens, Tyrus. You've got a lot of nerve calling someone else a loser."

He was just as she remembered him, a little overweight with an apple-round face and an almost perpetual smile that he wore even when pissed off. He knew it made people nervous.

"I just call 'em like I see 'em." He sat down beside her. "He's not what he appears to be, kiddo."

She brushed her static-straying hair out of her face. "What do you mean? He saved my life."

"Well, yeah. But, the talk is, he's an ailurophile."

From behind Tyrus, Chandra thought she heard a man ask for another drink.

"So?" she asked.

"I heard the guys talking about it."

"Yeah? What about it?"

She took a long drink of her remaining precious water supply. Her lips caught a vacuum on the mouthpiece and emitted a loud belch.

"Good one...That's what I heard. Sorry, Chani. He's a pervert."

"Sapiens, Tyrus, ailurophile just means he likes cats."

"Oh. It doesn't have anything to do with an auditory orifice?" Her stare could have congealed beer.

"You're too good for him, Chani," he warned.

"Tyrus, you're jealous." She reached down and rubbed her calves.

"Don't be stupid," he spat. "I just want to make sure you don't make any big mistakes."

"What kind of mistakes?"

"Like trying to get a hold of Mother."

She rubbed her palm with the thumb of her left hand, and

thought about the climb she'd just made. "Why the hell not?"

"I've heard there are a few tops there that have had their fingers in the wrong cookie jar. Most of the company is straight, but those guys think you stumbled into their soup. They'd just as soon see you under that Termagant tree next to me. Although I have to admit, it'd be just like old times." He pantomimed dealing a deck of cards. "That's why we didn't have our entourage and ambassadors and all. Elkhed Perkins didn't want us coming back. When I got involved in that Cryptic game, it was just a dream come true for him. Then when the players went after you, he offered a few virgins to whatever gods he worships. Chani, you can't go back. You can't trust them."

She slumped back against the corrugated metal shack.

"Are you telling me that not only are your pals after me for the orb, but Perkins and his cronies want me dead, too?"

"Dead engineers tell no tales," he quipped.

"You're dead and you're still here talking to me."

From nowhere someone screamed, "Ratstall, clean up that mess." He reconsidered her statement. "I don't count."

"Don't I know!"

"Look, kiddo, they didn't give me much time, so I better say my stuff and blow. Watch your back. You can't make it all the way with your pal down below."

"Screw you!"

"That's not what I mean. What I mean is that if you stay with him, you're going to get him killed."

"That's your opinion."

"No, Chani. That comes from a source in high places. They're going to keep after you. Dump him...for his own good. Besides, I don't trust him. He's a friend of Lance."

"Tyrus, I've had it! I'm just going to give the damn orb to someone. I can't do this anymore. I'm tired."

He sat down on the grate beside her. Taking her hand in his, he slowly wrapped his fingers around hers. He felt solid, but neither hot nor cold.

"You can't," he said with a ghostly softness.

"Like hell, I can't. This game is over, Tyrus. You gambled your life and lost. My life is more than just a game of craps."

He shrugged. "I suppose you can look at it that way, if you want. It doesn't change anything." With his free hand he took her chin, turning her face to meet his. His eyes glowed with a bloodshot cast from a lifetime of long nights at the card table with too much booze and too many smokers. "You have to do this, Chani. You have no idea what's at stake and I can't tell you. It's everything. Everything, I tell you. You've got to get that orb to Fomalhaut in time."

She froze. "That's ridiculous."

"For once, Chani, trust me. My time's just about out. Talk to your friend. You'll be interested to find out why he's taking you along for the ride. And, don't embarrass me."

"You?"

"Don't let yourself down, either. Oh, yeah. Why don't you take the elevator? It's a lot faster."

The metal in the elevator cage wore a crust of oxidation. As it descended, seemingly at an inch per minute, the cable creaked the mournful song of fatiguing metal. When an occasional heavy gust caught it, it banged up against the shaft and tossed Chandra to the floor. Chandra groaned, rubbing her bruised knees.

As the elevator eased down toward the ground, an especially enthusiastic blast caught it. Sparks flew from the control box, filling the cage with the look of the fireworks and the smell of burnt insulation. It slowed its descent and stopped suddenly, leaving the cage to bobble up and down as if attached to a rubber band.

Chandra fell on all fours. Her hard hat flew off, clanking against the cage wall.

"Shit!"

She punched the buttons but the only movement came from the swaying of the cage in the wind. She jiggled the wires, and finally kicked the control box with the same exasperating results. The controls had fused. Without replacement parts, it would be impossible to repair the elevator.

"Great! Just bloody great!"

The elevator had come to rest about eight meters above the ground. Below her, she could make out the top of Wright's head. Although she hadn't had a chance to pay attention to the activity before, she realized that several other figures accompanied him. They looked like little miniature people, too small to tell if they had weapons. Chances were, they were waiting for her to join them. They certainly did not appear to be interested in coming to her assistance.

The cage door squeaked as it opened.

"I say," she called down to the throng of twenty. "How do I get down?"

Wright traded words with a few of the natives.

"They'll have to send to town for a technician," he yelled through cupped hands. "Put your feet up. It could take a while."

"Never mind." She rolled her eyes. "How appropriate," she muttered, wrapping the fine synthetic spider silk rope from her belt around the rusty frame of the cage, "lowering myself into what might be a trap on the thread from a spider web."

She gave it a few test tugs. The electronic clamp held tight.

"That's probably Lance down there." Holding onto the silken rope she backed out the open door. "I'll bet they're in this together." She wiped her palms, then inched her way down toward the ground. "Wright must have told them where we were. That's how all those creeps have followed me. That bastard." Steadily the miniature winch inside her safety harness slowly released more of the tether. "No wonder he was so eager to help. If Elkhed found out where I was, it would save both Wright and Lance having to do me in. And they'd still get the orb and the crystal."

Below her, a group of natives surrounded Wright. "Serves him right. I hope they sauté him."

He waved up at her; Chandra smiled and returned the wave, but her other hand slipped its hold on the regulator and the winch surged. She sailed toward the ground, following her airborne hardhat. The weighty helmet made a solid thunking sound when it lodged six centimeters deep in the ground amidst a horde of scattering natives. Grappling with hands and feet, fingers and toes, and any other limb or digit she could, she wrapped the thread around her foot, stopping her descent abruptly like a yo-yo at the end of string. She found herself face to face with one of Wright's native friends. The problem being that one of them was upside down, and it wasn't the native.

"Hello." She reached out to shake his hand. "I'm Chandra Solomon. Nice to meet you." Her magnetic coiffeur hung down and spread out below her.

After the creature returned the greeting, she finished

lowering herself to the ground and released the winch. The thread-thin rope returned with a hiss to the harness like a tape measure to its coil.

Mustering what little dignity she could, she assumed an upright position and brushed the mud from her flight suit. "Wright, introduce me to your friends."

Standing erect, the natives rose to a good head taller than Wright. Instead of forcibly removing her intestines through her throat as she expected, the creatures circled her and fell prostrate on the ground.

"It *is* she!" exclaimed one of them dressed in baggy slacks and a white shirt. They had humanoid bodies with skin the same shade and texture as catfish. Where hair would grow on a human, they wore various splotches of blacks, whites and grays painted on their bald heads.

"She is the Great One," the other said. "And she came from the sky array just as the prophecies said."

The Great One glanced at Wright from the corner of her eye. He shrugged back as if to say, "I don't know."

"Just like the prophecies said, huh?" She brushed her hair out of her face but it continued to stick out and crackle when she touched it.

One of the females, who wore a black and white polka dot dress, wrinkled her nose at Wright. "Ricky's a little different than we expected him, but he's still kind of cute. Isn't he, Ethel?"

"Oh, yeah. He's really cute. Will you sing for us, Ricky?" the other begged.

Wright's eyes met Chandra's. She rolled hers and then turned back to the natives. "This is great, but do you think you might be able to sacrifice some food to me and then we'll just be on our way."

"Now, Lucy," Wright said. "You're not being very gracious to our hosts. They told me they would like to help us." His eyebrows peaked and he nodded slightly. "And we have come so far to be with them."

She smiled at the adoring throng who smiled in return.

"Okay. We'll stay a little longer," she told her admirers. "But..." She looked at Wright. "...Ricky, is it?"

He nodded. "I guess."

She turned back to the natives. "Ricky and I need to have a little talk." She glared at him and added, "In private."

"They're going to have a fight," one of the females tittered.

"We're not going to fight," she told the woman. "We're merely going to discuss trust and motivations in relationships. Aren't we, Ricky?"

"Whatever you say, Lucy," he answered.

They walked out of earshot of the growing crowd.

"What's all this Ricky and Great One crap?"

"I don't know. They just showed up, started calling me Ricky and blabbering about the Babaloo. They wanted to know where the Great One was. As a joke I pointed to you up there and they started going on to someone named Babaloo about you getting down safely. While you were hanging upside down they shouted over and over, 'She *is* the Great One.' I just went with it. Thought it was better than going to dinner with them."

She propped her hands on her hips and glared at him.

"Well, I was worried about you," Wright said. "Where have you been? It was almost four hours."

"Are we on a tight deadline, Wright? What's you're hurry? You got a hot date?"

"Huh?"

"Don't play stupid with me, Wright Aulweighs. Don't you think this Wright in shining armor routine has gone on long enough?"

He sniffed his hand and wiped the smut on his shirt.

"What are you talking about?"

"I found out that you and Lance have been in cahoots in this thing from the beginning. You're just waiting for the chance to crater my head and take the orb."

His eyebrows rose. "What *are* you talking about?"

"I should have known you weren't just being a nice guy. Well, I know about you now, and you're not going to get away with it."

He shook his head. "Raging hormones, Chani, what is wrong with you? Did you hit your head when you fell?"

"As if you didn't know. Come on. Admit it. You and Lance have been in it together all along."

"You *did* hit your head, didn't you? They're kinda weird, but I bet these people can help."

"Well, aren't you one helluva helpful guy?"

"What do you think I did?"

She stalked forward, forcing him to step backward even

farther away from the natives. "You and Lance planned all along to get the orb from me."

He stopped backing and took a step in her direction; she bumped into him and then began a slight retreat. "What the hell are you talking about?"

"Tyrus said you and Lance are after the orb."

"Tyrus? Isn't he dead?"

"See, you know. You were involved."

"I know? You told me that right after we left Distress. When did you see your dead partner this time? Before or after you fell?"

"A little while ago. On top of the tower."

"And what did he say?"

"He said he was murdered for the orb."

"And that's a surprise?" Wright closed his eyes for a second. He took a deep breath. "And what did he say about me?"

She thought about it, wanting to make certain she quoted him accurately. "He said you are a friend of Lance and that you had ulterior motives for helping me."

Wright grabbed her by the elbow, dragging her along until they had once again moved out of earshot of the advancing Lucillians. He stopped, turned around, and looked into her eyes. He licked his lips as if to stall, took a deep breath and shouted, "Of course I had ulterior motives! I never said I didn't! As a matter of fact, I believe you agreed to give me half of whatever you get from the orb. Didn't you?"

"Yes, but you didn't tell me you already knew about it."

"You didn't ask. You didn't care when those guys were shooting at you."

"No, I didn't."

"Don't you think if I'd wanted it that badly I could've just killed you once you were on the ship?"

She hesitated. "Well, yes."

"That's right. I could've. And yes, Tyrus was right about a couple of things, but I think you jumped to the wrong conclusion."

"What conclusion is that?"

"That Lance and I were friends and because of that I had something to do with Tyrus' murder."

"Well, yeah."

"We associated. We ran in the same circles cuz we both

had ties to Rithel Bartlemist. His tie was Bosson; mine was Rithel's mansion. The way I heard it, Bosson took something from Rithel, a couple of pieces from one of his mineral collections. She thought with all his stuff, he'd never notice. Well, he sure as hell did. Lance is the one that had your friend aced."

"How do you know?"

"I was at the game."

She lunged for his throat. "I knew it! You bastard. You're a dead man."

He pulled her hands away from his neck. "I didn't have anything to do with it. Lance's done a lot of that kind of work for Rithel. I just went to play a dishonest game of cards. If I'd known that half the table would've been dead in a couple of days, I sure as hell would've found another game. I'm not crazy; I want to keep my guts intact. I just happened to be there, just like Tyrus. A twist of fate and it could have been me buried in that unmarked grave. That was one game where the winners turned out to be the losers."

"Okay. What is it?" Chandra asked.

"What is what?"

"The orb. What is it?"

"Beats me," he answered. "I never understood what all the fuss was about. I just know there's a lot of bodies floating in its wake. I don't plan on mine being one of them, either. Let's just get off this rock and get rid of that hazardous waste you call an orb."

She broke eye contact with Wright to gaze at haze-heavy sky. Some gangly birds with a wide wingspan, long legs and stubby necks flew overhead. One started shrieking and then the others joined him. Soon they sounded like the victims in a Halloween haunted house. She looked back at Wright.

He said, "Some guy named Ranknard took us all to the cleaners. Wiped us clean and then rinsed us off. After the game, he and Tyrus went outside to talk, probably to work out a deal. Won everything your partner had on him except his clothes. The next day Ranknard wound up in some meat market after eating a tree the hard way and Tyrus was found on the edge of town. It looked like he had tried to rupture his own eardrum with a sharp object. Cops said he died of a brain hemorrhage. Probably too many hours of listening to The Mouth's war stories. That'll do it too. What a way to go! I'd rather be dropped in a vat of flatulent ripper bats than suffer through *those* stories."

Her face fell as she mentally pictured Tyrus's torturous end.

"I'm sorry, Chani. It wasn't a pretty sight. I guess Tyrus got the orb from Ranknard.'

"Tyrus never had the orb," she said quietly. "Ranknard wanted me to have it...or so Tyrus said. So why did you come to my rescue?"

"You want the truth?"

"Consider it a novel approach, Wright."

"I wanted to even the score with Lance."

"What?"

"Well, at least even it out a little. Every time I found a good-looking chick who liked me, old Lance would come over, turn on the charm and wham, I never saw her again. She made tracks for old sweet-talking Lance Goode so fast I always had tread marks across my face. When I saw you I thought just once I might be able to even the score. When you needed to leave so fast, I knew it was the perfect chance. It was just luck that you approached me for help at the party. In a way, I've more than evened the score. You've got the orb and I've got you."

"What does that mean?"

"Nothing. I just meant you've got the orb and you're with me. You can leave any time you want, and take that cursed crystal with you. Just let me know where the phone company wants me to send you and I'll bill you for my trouble."

She shook her head. "Let's just get our food and water and scram."

"I thought it was so important that you reach your old boss at the phone company."

She headed back toward the crowd. "Not anymore. After I deliver the orb, I need to straighten a few things out. Until then, calling home to Mother is as healthy as drinking antimatter bilge water. Somebody there has his own agenda. Our deaths would only fit into his plan like the last piece of a two thousand piece puzzle."

Wright trotted behind her. "Did I tell you about the fifty-nine story building that I designed to be put together like a giant puzzle? It had this..."

The Lucillians stood around waiting for the teak-haired deity to return. They chattered excitedly as the pair approached. "Here they come. Here they come," called a chorus of Lucillian women.

One of the women dashed up to Chandra. "Was it a good fight? I bet you let him have it."

She smiled tentatively. "I'm afraid we didn't have time to get into a really swell fight. We may have to postpone it for a while. But maybe we can come back and scream loud for you. I might even throw a pie at him or get my head stuck in a trophy for you."

"Oh, Lucy, if you don't want him, I'll take him," another bald woman offered.

"Maybe someday, ladies," Chandra said. "But not today."

"Is Fred still here?" Wright looked around the crowd.

"I'm here, Ricky." One of the Lucillian men stepped forward. He wore no paint on his head.

"Were you able to deliver that water?" Wright asked.

"Sure, Ricky," Fred answered eagerly. "It's waiting right down there just like you asked. If you'd like, Ethel and I can take you to your interesting airplane."

They all climbed into a vehicle that looked suspiciously like an old fashioned Chevrolet. Before they could leave a male Lucillian wearing a dark blue suit, a thin tie and a glued-on mustache ran up to the car.

"I just hear that SHE was here. Oh, Lucy, I can't tell you how long I've waited to meet you. My name is Theodore J. Mooney."

When he smiled his mustache twitched slightly.

"It's nice to meet you, Mr. Mooney," Chandra said. "I wish we could stay and talk, but I'm afraid we have a bit of a time crunch."

"Of course. Thank you. Thank you so much," he said.

As they drove away Wright asked, "Mr. Mooney was wearing a blue suit and everyone is wearing shades of black and white. Why is that?"

"Don't you know?" Ethel asked shocked.

"Sure we do," Chandra laughed. "We just wanted to hear your explanation. Sometimes things get so jumbled along the broadcast waves."

"Fred and I are Orthodox. Mr. Mooney and his lot who feel they need the color are reformed.

"Of course! That's right," Chandra said to Ethel, but shrugged her shoulders at Wright.

As they approached the *Blind Faith* she added, "Why don't you-uh-guys, drop me off at our..." Chandra stopped mid-sentence and looked at Wright.

"Car," Wright interjected.

"Yeah, that. And you and..."

"Ricky."

"Yeah, him. Can see to our supplies."

Chapter Fifteen

She walked onto the flight deck and plopped down into the copilot's seat. Immediately, she jumped up, expecting Ivan to own a portion of the bottom half of her flight suit again and extract an impressive quantity of her blood and flesh. She braced herself for the impact of the eighteen-pound furry mass, but it did not come.

Strange.

The cabin looked different, too. Cleaner. What happened to all the garbage Wright'd had stashed on the console? Someone had moved. Not Wright, obviously, Wright was with her. But then, maybe, because Wright was with her, the ship had spontaneously straightened itself up.

"Ivan," she called.

No Ivan.

She reached down to grab her light pistol, but a familiar voice behind the bulkhead stopped her.

"I wouldn't, Chani."

She froze. She scanned the panel for something to use as a weapon. Nothing.

She turned slowly, careful to keep her hands in view of the intruder.

"Hello, Lance," Chandra said evenly.

"Good to see you, Chani." The reporter looked as if he had stepped out of a fashion holo, attired in a striped double-breasted suit and yellow and turd-colored tie. A brown fedora dipped provocatively over his face, hiding his eyes. He wore a broad smile beneath his plush mustache. A couple of crimson lines on his face matched fresh wounds on his hand: Ivan's personal autograph.

"Back to dressing casually, are we?" he said.

Still pointing the pistol at the solar system on her chest, he walked over to her and pulled her Harbinger from the holster. "You won't need this." He stuffed the gun into his belt.

"What do you want, Lance?"

He ignored her question.

"Where's Wright?" he asked.

"You tell me. He's your friend." Again she glanced around but still found nothing.

"Lance, where's Ivan?" she asked.

"God, don't tell me you like that hairy razor blade?"

"Not really. But I can't believe you'd hurt a helpless animal."

"Ivan's not helpless and he's not an animal." He touched the newly forming scab on his cheek. "He's a torture chamber on paws."

Across the cabin, the hatch tried to slide open, but jammed midway. Wright's grunting accompanied the grinding of the hand crank he so often used.

Knocking and banging, then scraping of metal against metal, echoed throughout the cabin, then finally the door slid open wide enough for him to crawl under.

"Run, Wright!" Chandra yelled. "It's Lance!"

"Hey, Lance." Wright waved as he entered the cabin. "It's been a while." He sauntered over to the control panel.

"Wow, it sure looks different in here. D'you tidy up the place, Chani?"

She shook her head. "Didn't have time, but I would have if I'd known you were expecting company."

"Lance is always welcome on *Blind Faith*," he said absently. "Especially if he's going to pick up the place."

"You must have a helluva fast ship to catch up with us," Chandra said.

"Power skates could outrun this space-going atrocity."

Wright went through his take-off checklist. "D'you find what you were looking for?"

"Part of it," Lance answered.

"Hey, wanna drink? I think I've got some Bartlemist fizz rum in the locker. You know where it is."

Lance kept his weapon trained on Chandra.

"Bloggin' fell, Lance. Put that thing down," Wright said easily. "You might hurt someone. Relax, will you? You'll get it. So, Bud. What's the scoop?"

"Wright, your choice in women has taken an interesting turn." Lance gestured to Chandra with his weapon. "She's sober."

"She's all right."

Lance pointed his gun at Wright. "You don't need that hog leg."

Wright removed his holster and threw it on the deck. He brushed some dust about with his boot. "She scraped a few layers of crud from the bulkheads, but she can't even play a decent game of Cryptic." He moved a few steps away from her. "Hey, Bud, last time I saw you, you had an extra orifice or two."

Lance touched the brim of his hat with the barrel of his pistol like a mid-twentieth-century detective. "I'm a fast healer."

"You've got what you want, Lance. Why don't you leave us alone?" Chandra asked.

"Aw, come on, Chani. Are you telling me you don't know?"

"Maybe we can make a deal," she said.

"A deal?"

"Sure. I know where the orb is. I take it to the guy that's supposed to buy it from me. We split the profit."

"No deal. Too many cuts." Lance shook his head. He motioned again with the pistol. I've got another deal, Chani. I start by breaking your arms. Then, you tell me where the crystal is. You tell me soon enough and I'll only break one."

She ignored him. "Wright, he's got Ivan."

Wright motioned to the wounds on the society reporter's face. "Next time pick an opponent your own size. You'll fare better. Here." He reached into his liquor hold, grabbed a bottle and tossed it to Lance who caught it with his free hand. He turned to Chandra. "Why don't ya secure everything for lift off?"

She eyed Lance, who still had the gun trained on her. "I'm screwed."

Lance pitched the unopened bottle back to Wright. "You first."

Wright smiled, popped the cork and swigged a deep drink. "Hey, Bud, where's Ivan?" Again he tossed the bottle back to Lance.

"He's safe." Lance, too, took a deep drink. "Not bad. Where'd you get this?"

Wright grinned. "From the private stash you lifted from Rithel."

"Good choice. If I'd been you I'd have gone for Cavalier North Star Blanc. It's worth more."

"Yeah, but it doesn't have the same kick. I've been saving

it for a special occasion. So, where's Ivan?"

"He's on my ship. Probably tearing the stuffing from the upholstery as we speak." Lance answered in a more mellow voice. He threw the bottle back to Wright.

"Looks like he won that scrap."

"Damn cat. Why don't you drown him? He's got a worse disposition than that little blonde number I stole from you a while back."

"I tried. Afterwards I looked worse than you do. By the way, you sure did me a favor that time. Is everything okay?"

"The little blonde number?—sure."

"No. I mean Ivan. Is he okay?"

"He's fine. Better'n me." Lance slurred his words. "Give me the crystal and you can have him back." The reporter held up the orb. "You really should clean up around here more often, Wright. It's amazing what you find when you clean up."

Chandra walked back into the cabin. "Everything's stowed."

Lance pointed the pistol unsteadily at her. "Where's the crystal, Chani?" His voice rose as he ended the sentence. He laughed at the sound of his own voice.

Wright tried to stand up but fell to his knees. "Lance's got the orb and he'll leave us alone if you'll just give him the crystal. Tell him where the crystal is and he'll bring Ivan back from his ship. Oh, and bring me a bottle of the Elasian Tornado Whiskey. We're almost out." He rolled the bottle across the deck to Lance. "Really." Wright tried to sound serious, but laughed so hard he spit rum all over the floor.

"He's threatening to kill Ivan and you're drinking with him just like old times," she said.

"I didn't threaten to kill the cat," Lance giggled. "I threatened to kill you."

Wright nodded to Chandra, "Go ahead."

She rummaged through the liquor cabinet until she found a bottle of whiskey. Holding it up she said to Lance, "You've got it."

"That's not the right bottle," Wright said. "The Tornado Whiskey."

"Sapiens, Wright. Booze is booze." She turned to Lance. "Ivan has it."

"Ivan?" Lance echoed.

Wright giggled. "That's cheap stuff. On this occasion, only the best."

She found it in back of the cabinet. "It's on his collar." She slapped the bottle into Wright's hand, and said to Lance, "You already have it."

"I have?" He staggered toward the hatch.

Wright tried to open the new bottle, but couldn't make his fingers grip the stopper. "Here. Open it."

"Wright, we don't have time for this."

"There's always time for a drink with friends, Chani. This is important."

"That's what everybody says." She opened the bottle and handed it to him. Wright grabbed it and chugged down as much as he could without taking a breath.

Across the room Lance dropped his pistol. Chandra retrieved it. "You're both disgusting jerks."

He smiled broadly, producing those dimples she'd liked so much when she'd first met him. "Yeah, but *I'm* rich."

Chandra raised her eyebrows. "Really."

"...or I will be."

"Gawd, I feel sick," Wright said. "Barf bag."

She opened a compartment below the left seat and handed the bag to him. "I hope you're pleased with yourself. Now what?"

She was sorry she asked.

After he was finished, she asked again.

His eyes cleared a little, but his face grew a little paler. Wright took another drink and handed her the bottle. "Put this back exactly where you found it."

"You want me to put something away? Something on this ship has a place? This is something truly newsworthy. Lance should be conscious for this."

"It's an antidote for the drug in the first bottle." He staggered a bit and pointed at Lance. "He'll be out for a while."

"What now?" She stowed the bottle.

"Go get Ivan and I'll introduce Mr. Goode to our Lucillian friends."

"You want me to get Ivan? Why don't you get him?"

"You'll be okay. He'll be happy to see you. He's never cared much for Lance. He probably hates Lance's ship even more. He hates the smell of antiseptic."

She looked over at the semi-conscious Lance drooling on the floor. "Ivan's more intelligent than I thought."

As she walked out the door, Wright stopped her. "Here."

All the Marbles

He handed her the bottle of GootenKatz. "Give Ivan just a couple of laps of this. He likes it and it'll make him a little easier to handle."

A short time later she dropped Ivan into his copilot's seat. He rolled over and put a paw over his eyes.

"Is Ivan all right?"

Chandra nodded.

"Where's the crystal?"

"On his collar right where you put it."

"Yeah. When I got there, he was rearranging the decor of Mr. Goode's cabin. Now, it has that sort of a primitive-damaged look. You'd like it. Lance?"

Wright still looked a little wan and had to work at forming his words. "I told our friends out there that he's Mr. Mooney and he wanted to fire you. I had a feeling they were going to invite him for dinner."

Chapter Sixteen

Chandra sat on the deck a few meters from where Ivan laid.

His ruff encircled his face and shoulders, giving her the impression that she sat before a living miniature version of the Great Sphinx. The fact that Ivan and the Sphinx came from the same general region on Earth did not seem all that ironic.

She rolled the orb across the deck to him.

Ivan watched as it glided near him, and waited until it had almost rolled past him, then swatted it back to her. Once again, Chandra volleyed the sphere in his direction, and like a tennis pro, Ivan returned her serve. They fine-tuned the game, keeping it up for several minutes at a time. Finally, tiring of it, the Van trotted off, leaving the orb to roll past its target to the other side of the cabin.

At once, the orb and Chandra were momentarily airborne.

"What happened?" she asked.

Wright looked over the controls. "I think *Blind Faith* hiccuped."

"No. Really, what happened?"

"Really," he said. "She hiccuped."

Chandra rose to retrieve the orb, but fell to the deck nose-first. Ivan hissed and jumped into his new pile of somewhat more clean dirty clothes.

"Maybe it's more like she's surfing," Wright corrected himself.

"Surfing?"

"Yeah." He pointed at his screen. "Looks like some kind of shock waves are hitting us."

The ship lurched again.

Chandra made her way over to the control panel.

"Looks like we're in for a bunch more."

She reached over and adjusted the scanners to long range. A wavy line wobbled up and down from a source outside the screen's range. She pointed at the edge of the screen. "They're coming from beyond here. Sapiens, Wright, some of that turbulence is really strong. Don't you think we'd better try to find some place to land?"

"This is strange," he said.

"What's strange? Clean clothes?"

"Naw. Not t*hat* strange. These shock waves look a lot like earthquake aftershocks, rather than waves in space."

Another one hit the ship. This time *Blind Faith* rocked with so much urgency that the loose dirt on the deck bounced up in the air, did a short minuet and then found a landing pad across the cabin from its original home.

"I think you're right. We'd better find a place to land." He pulled up a chart. "There's a planet, Galway, not too far from here." He pointed at a blip that looked to be only a few centimeters off, but actually lay light years away.

He reprogrammed the navicom, and the "X" veered off in the direction of the planet.

Chandra pulled up Galway on her hand-held computer. "I don't know, Wright. The computer AAAA tour book says that it's been quarantined to off-world traffic. It doesn't really say why, but it says that galactic officials fear the aberrant behavior exhibited on the planet may spread to other systems. I don't know if I'm up to more aberrant behavior than we've already experienced." Another shock wave sent her reeling to the deck. "And then again, real aberrance might be refreshing."

Blind Faith struggled toward Galway, plagued every few minutes by an unseen hand slapping it with an invisible rocketball paddle.

"This is going to be tricky," Wright said. "I've never had this problem before."

"What is it?"

"The charcoal anti-matter suspension medium is breaking down. If it does, it could be pretty messy."

"You have a gift for understatement. We could be turned into so many disassociated molecules—atomic barbecue."

"If the charcoal holds together we still have a second chance at becoming star stuff when we enter the atmosphere with minimal power."

"Wright, you're such a comfort. You always know just the right thing to say."

He smiled. "That's me. I'm a silver tongued devil."

He struggled with the ship. He had all the control of a

deep-sea fisherman trying to reel in an orca on ten-pound test line. *Blind Faith* buffeted and the outer skin heated up as it breached the planet's atmosphere.

"It's a shame we don't have some mesquite wood." Wright wrestled with his joystick like a Begawan headed for neuter. "Automatic's out now."

"What would mesquite do? Help stabilize the charcoal?"

"Naw," he said. "But it sure makes a barbecue smell good."

"Great."

"Naw, wait a minute." He pulled back hard on the stick. "If I can adjust the angle maybe we can survive entry. Chani, enter this course change."

She did.

Within a few moments the ship broke through into the atmosphere.

He made some more minor adjustments with the stick. The ship leveled, buffeted, leveled, shuddered, and leveled again.

"We made it through the atmosphere," he said to nobody in particular.

"Great."

"Now, we'll just die in that sudden impact when we hit the ground. The heat burnt out the breaking system."

"What about the auxiliary front thrusters?" she asked. "Maybe we could make an auxiliary lift-wing landing assisted by the emergency drag chute."

"Drag chute?"

"Sure. It's GAA regs. All ships manufactured before the last century are required to have emergency drag chutes. When was the last time you had it inspected and repacked?"

He looked at her blankly. "What chute?"

"Never mind. At least it's a chance. The trick is dumping the chute at the right time. Too soon and it could burn up, too late and all they have to do is fill in the impact hole. Might be a good idea to strap in."

Wright relinquished the console to Chandra. Ivan burrowed deeper into his pile. Chandra said a quick prayer to Saint Icarus, the patron saint of all who enjoy the flight, but cease to enjoy that last half-inch at the end.

"Thirty-five hundred meters. Now!"

A sudden jolt rocked the ship. Everything that had any kind of resting place became airborne, flying across the cabin.

Molecules of grime, heretofore permanently attached to wall or floor surface, screamed through the room, making impact with other such molecules until huge wads of disgusting crud clung to walls and decks and Chandra's flight suit.

Suddenly, the pit of her stomach fell out the bottom of her feet. "The chute failed," she said watching the altimeter plunge.

Moments later, her stomach traveled from the soles of her feet through the top of her skull. All four legs flailing, Ivan raced to the bulkhead and fell to deck with a perfect, but hard, four-point landing.

Blind Faith had splashed in the middle of a marsh, then skipped across to the edge of a row of angular trees, dwarfing the vessel with their dense foliage, finally settling into the soft soil and crunched down into a pallet of leaves decaying in a bog.

After he caught his breath Wright emerged from the hatch, squinting to see through the bright, leaf-filtered light. "Come on." He motioned "all clear" to Chandra.

She limped down the gangplank to join him, also squinting.

"It looks like rotting vegetation cushioned the impact enough to keep *Blind Faith* from becoming scrap metal."

"This swamp smells the same way outside that it did inside the ship. And if we want to keep it intact, we'll need to stay on the ground until those shock waves stop; I guess another forty-eight hours," Wright said. "It's a shame I had to leave my speedster on Distress."

"We're cutting my deadline a little close, don't you think?" she said.

"Any suggestion on how to cut down some of that time?" he asked.

She shook her head. "Not really. Maybe we can lease a speedster somewhere. I've read ads from Marginal Rent-a-Wreck. There's always Acme..." She imitated the advertisement. "You know, a flash of dust and beep, beep."

Wright stared at her as if she had sprouted an extra head. "What?"

"They are supposed to be trans-galactic. Maybe they have a drop-off site here on Galway. We could just make a phone call and have them deliver it to us here, wherever *here* is.

"I wonder what the well-dressed Galwayans wear to parties these days?"

Wright climbed into the TransStar speedster that Marginal rented them. It had enough room to house three large families comfortably. Still, a used-car odor oozed from under the pilot's seat. He fumbled around under the pilot's seat and pulled out the remains of a petrified sandwich. After eyeing it for a moment he tossed it out the open door. "This is great; smells just like my old speedster."

Chandra adjusted the outside air vent to maximum. "Yeah. Aren't we lucky?"

Examining the control panel the architect said, "Some of these controls look familiar, but I'm not sure about these others. I think this one is the ignition." He punched one of the lighted buttons.

The entire panel went dark and the engine's slight whine wound down to silence.

He turned to Chandra.

She rolled her eyes and sighed. "Oh, Sapiens, Wright. That was the emergency kill circuit. You just cut everything off." Her royal blue and silver sequins and beads sparkled as she reached over and reprogrammed the console control. The panel flickered and then returned to full brightness.

She pointed to the line sketches etched beside each button, readout and gadget on the console. "These are universal symbols."

"Whose universe?"

"Why don't you let me fly?" she asked.

"Because you can't tell your left from your right, and you get lost going to the bathroom," he answered.

"Other than that?"

He ignored her, choosing instead to study the controls.

She referred to her own translator. "This one that looks like a ruptured eardrum is the radio." She pressed a button and a pulsating noise that sounded like the thousand decibel mating call of Altairian thunder beasts radiated from the speakers above the seat. Quickly she punched the button again. When the music stopped, she sighed, looked at Wright and said, "I don't think we should touch that one again."

"What?" He dug a finger in his ear as if the thunder beasts continued to trumpet and stampede inside his head.

"The configuration of this panel reminds me of a Betawan speedster. They run on low-grade radioactivity. Messy stuff, but they're supposed to be pretty fast."

After he flipped the power switch, a sultry female voice breezed through the speakers. "Your hatch is ajar."

He looked around for a second, then smiling, closed the door. "What a voice!"

Chandra stared at him. "You've got the hots for a *speedster*?"

"Your hatch is ajar," the speedster repeated.

"Thanks," he answered enthusiastically. "I could listen to her all day."

"Your hatch lock is unsecured."

"All *right!*"

"Please fasten your safety harness," the voice reminded him.

"I'd of gotten to it!" He shook his head. "We just met and she's already a nag."

He tried the power switch again, but nothing happened.

"The vehicle cannot operate with the vapor exhaust pollution control disabled," the sexy voice chided.

He let out a short sigh. "I think I used to be married to her," he told Chandra.

Chandra pointed to the button, which he punched.

He tried the power up switch again.

This time the whine of the engines rose to a roar and eased back down to a tolerable level.

The TransStar accelerated, but instead of easing forward smoothly, it lurched and bucked like an unbroken steed. Chandra fell forward, but her restraint stopped her short of smashing her head against the control panel.

She grabbed the sides of her seat and clenched her teeth. "Sapiens, Wright. Have you ever considered driving school?"

With a sheepish grin he readjusted the fuel valve and tried again. This time the speedster pressed forward like a rabbit, fast and bumpy. It rose high above the trees where he practiced some turns and a few hover landings.

Beneath them, pockets of glass-and-steel civilization spread out across the landscape, jutting through patches of tortoiseshell and peacock fields.

"What a beautiful town," she said.

They dropped down, easing through town, where well-attired people worked in street-side flower gardens. Occasionally, they passed freshly waxed speedsters parked on concrete landing pads being prepped for a jaunt to who-knew-where.

The TransStar flew over the industrial district, flying past billboards for soap and detergent.

"Where to?" He looked dashing in his double-breasted formalwear with unmatching shoes.

Chandra shrugged. "I don't know, exactly. Let's see if we can find a tipplorium in town. Once we've scoped out the place, we can make a better decision. Better still, let's find a party. On humanoid planets, Tyrus and I used to cruise around towns until we found a swanky home with lots of high-status speedsters parked outside. We'd go to the door, and then, when the host answered, we'd just walk right in and act like we've been invited. It's never failed. They don't recognize you, and they're too embarrassed to ask who the hell you are."

He nodded. "I like it."

"We've been to some killer parties that way. Some of them literally."

"Yeah," he said with a grin. "Like Rithel Bartlemist's."

"Something like that."

They flew past hazy clouds floating along the horizon behind tree-covered hills changing from gray to pink to orange and then red. Soon the natives would start their partying, as natives everywhere did, as the sun slid behind the horizon. Finally, they flew through a suburban residential development with larger homes and economically advantaged speedsters parked out front.

"Slow down," Chandra said.

The speedster stopped and dropped twelve inches to the pavement.

"Sapiens, Wright. I'm going to need spinal replacement before you figure out how to fly this thing."

"It doesn't fly like the old bomb I left on Distress."

Chandra thought about how he abandoned his treasured vehicular abomination to the cops on Distress, for her sake, and withheld further harassment.

"Ease up a bit. There are a bunch of speedsters parked outside that house a little farther up the block."

Wright pulled the rental up in front of a nice three-story home with two landing pads beside it. A herd of speedsters parked nearby matched the class of the house that screamed, "I want to impress you!"

"Let's stop here. I think this is the place."

Smiling, Chandra rang the door. She turned to Wright and sighed. "I need a drink."

Before long, a very nice looking Galwayan man appeared at the door. Chandra was amazed at how similar he looked to humans, just somewhat shorter, somewhat more pointed physical features. His conservative gray suit looked out of place with hair that stuck out in every possible compass direction. His face was so clean, he looked like a smiling bar of soap. He nodded at Wright, who returned the greeting. Then he turned and scanned Chandra, slowly, hair to sparkling shoes, smiling in recognition. "Why Don, Bubbles, please come in." He offered his home with an open arm.

At his invitation, they entered.

"I never dreamed you'd actually accept our humble invitation while you were in town. I'm Lyesope Scrubdell. Peria's going to be delighted."

Wright instinctively ambled into the main room, where he found refreshments being served. Chandra followed closely behind, but froze when she realized a gaggle of people had gathered around her, staring, mouths agape, as if she had begun a spontaneous striptease.

She looked at their dresses and then down at her own highly light-reflective gown. The women wore stylish, but unmemorable suits and dresses similar to what stuffy office executives wore. An apologetic look crossed her face and she bit her lip. "I'm sorry—I guess I'm a bit over-dressed."

She turned and whispered in Wright's ear, "Aw, gee, I didn't know I was supposed to wear something stupid."

"Oh, Bubbles," sighed a lady with big hair and a lapel so pointed it could have put out the eye of the person standing next to her had she turned around too quickly. "Your gown is breathtaking. We're so glad you could show us how the really successful distributors live."

"Of course," Chandra said. "I knew that."

"Maybe someday, if we work hard enough, we'll be able to afford to dress like you and Don," the host said. Peria eased closer to her husband and she slipped her arm around her husband's waist. "Won't we, my handsome soap dish?"

Another woman dashed up to Chandra.

"This is so exciting. I mean to finally get to meet a real 'Nova.' I mean—oh, I'm just so excited."

Chandra smiled nervously. She turned to Wright who had just popped a bluish something in his mouth. "What's she talking about?" she asked in a whisper.

Wright shrugged his shoulders and licked his fingers, winced, and walked toward the bar. "Looks like you've been mistaken for someone else again."

"I'm just glad we could make it," Chandra said to the woman. "We ran into a little trouble on the way here."

The woman nodded her head understandingly. "I've heard reports of terrorists capturing freighters out in open space. Every time my husband," –she glanced lovingly across the room at a Phadian— "has to take a trip, I worry so much. Since he is a citizen of Phad he's still permitted to travel freely. He's been traveling frequently to spread The Word. On his last trip, his ship was almost boarded by the Galactic Mental Health Department. Had his ship had a Galwayan registration, they'd have seized it and sent him to be reprogrammed. It's scary, but it's worth it. We recruited six new distributors. Someday we'll be Novas just like you!"

"We've had a few close calls, too," Chandra admitted.

More people began to flock around Chandra.

"I hear it's harder getting around the quarantine. But you've had to be determined to make it to Nova."

"You must travel a lot," one man observed.

"Yes, my job has taken me all over the galaxy."

"Our upline told us not to call it a job. We call it...an opportunity."

"Isn't that wonderful?" Peria oozed. "Even with our system quarantined Don and Bubbles can still expand the business across the galaxy."

"Hey, Bubbles, have you and Don been any place exciting lately?" squealed one young woman who looked excited enough to soil the floor.

"We did some time on Castor V," Chandra said.

"Do they need soap?"

Chandra recalled her week in hell on Distress and the legions of unwashed aliens whose assorted body odors reminded her of fresh dog droppings. "I think in some regions of Castor soap is illegal."

"That's all right. The company attorneys can handle that. We'll be cleaning up in no time!"

"I hope so," Chandra said. "One time I met a guy at a

perfumery called the Amazing Vern, Man of a Thousand Odors. If you could guess what the odor was, he gave you a bottle of cologne free. His most memorable was 'Medieval Peasant.'"

"We could make a fortune there…Would you like something to drink?" Peria offered.

"Would I! I could really use a drink."

"You poor thing. So thirsty."

Peria took off, leaving Chandra alone for a moment. It gave her a chance to scan the room. When she'd said she wanted to go to a party, she had something a little more lively in mind; but then, she'd been to requiems livelier than this. This party rated a minus three on her scale of one to thirty. Around her, the people pattered on mindlessly about products and sales, new presentations and holos. Another man chimed in about a sales conference he planned to attend on the other side of the planet.

"Where else have you been?" a woman asked Chandra.

"We just came from Enuk and Lucilla."

"I hear Enuk's a quaint little world," said an immaculately dressed man with the same silly haircut as the host. "Very clean."

"Yes. It's beautiful," Chandra admitted. "I've done business with the people there. They're hospitable…and trusting." Her own words made her wince. " Too trusting. I'm afraid my company screwed them."

"That's impossible. Customer service is our middle name," piped in a man who had kept quiet until then. "The company wants only what's best for us *and* our customers."

"You're just kidding yourself." Chandra shook her head sadly. "I found out I was just a pawn. You probably are, too. I've been thinking about changing companies. Going with an independent. I don't like the treatment I've been getting, lately."

Peria dropped her punch glass, splattering liquid the color, consistency and probably the approximate flavor of transmission fluid all over her white carpet.

Simultaneously, three distributors pulled sample bottles of cleaners and white clothes from their pockets and raced to clean the spot. Two collided, banged heads and fell unconscious, leaving remaining guest to attack the stain while reciting in a practiced voice, "Galway products clean thoroughly and naturally without caustic chemicals. See, I can even drink this safely…" She poised the bottle ready to take a sip.

Everyone not involved in cleaning the carpet stared at Chandra. Throughout the room the sound of conversation died away in unbelieving gasps of horror, followed by a silence so profound Chandra could have heard a dog whistle.

"Bubbles!" a horrified woman whispered. "I can't believe you'd say that. Why, that's...that's..."

"Blasphemy!" one shouted.

"Sacrilege," another gasped.

Lyesope finally closed his mouth. It was a few more seconds before he could speak. "You're...unhappy, too?"

"Sure," she answered. "The company's got me in more trouble lately than you'd believe."

Peria returned with a cup of punch in a pottery cup that gleamed like aluminum. Chandra hesitated, then slammed its contents down in one swallow. It had almost no flavor and about as much kick as a one-legged dancer. She peered into the cup. Forcing a smile she asked the hostess, "What's in here?"

Beaming, clearly thinking Chandra wanted her recipe, the woman spouted off the sizable list of ingredients. One important ingredient seemed to be missing.

"Oh," Chandra said with as much enthusiasm as she could muster. "It doesn't have any alcohol in it, does it?"

The hostess tittered. "Of course not. You know the company strongly discourages the serving of alcohol, especially at company functions."

"Yes," Chandra said. "Of course it does."

Wright wandered over to her and whispered in her ear, "I think we need to call a priest."

"Why?" she gasped.

"The punch is dead."

"I know," she whispered back.

"The hor d'oeuvres taste like swamp grass with car wax spread on them."

"I know."

As he walked away he slapped Chandra firmly on the back and said, "I've really got to hand it to you, Solomon; you really know how to choose a hot party."

"You'd leave...the company?" Lyesope asked Chandra.

"Hey, they're not the only phone company in town."

"Oh, yes they are," another insulted man said.

"Well, maybe so," she agreed reluctantly, "but there are

always alternatives."

"Like what?" he countered.

She thought for a second. "Like finding a new corporation on another planet. Why hell, why not start our own company?"

Relief washed across Lyesope's face. "We didn't realize there was dissatisfaction in the higher ranks. Who'd have thought the Novas were unhappy?"

Chandra sat down on something that looked like a couch with no legs. Her feet stuck out awkwardly in front of her. "You can bet I'm dissatisfied. My partner was killed cuz of the hazardous duty they put us on."

"Did you hear that," a woman gasped. "Don was killed."

"If Don was killed, who's he?" Peria asked.

"Wright Aulweighs, at your service, madam. I am Bubbles'...architect..."

"...cousin," Chandra corrected.

"Yes, that's it. I'm her...cousin...and her architect." He paused. "Her father sent me to care for her during her delicate mourning period."

"I thought your father was dead," one of the women said. "Ima Richman's book about successful organizations, that we had to pay eighty-seven credits for, told about how your father drowned bravely in a vat of liquid soap. You said, "It brings tears to my eyes every time I scrub the floor.""

"That's right." Chandra dabbed her eyes. "That was my other father."

"Poor Bubbles. First one of her fathers, now Don. How did it happen?"

Chandra brushed the back of her hand against her forehead. "...I just can't talk about it now." And she wished she'd chosen not to talk about anything at all.

Lyesope handed Chandra another drink that she poured into the pot of a nearby live green plant. After a few seconds the plant turned pale yellow and withered.

"Here in the trenches, things are going badly," Lyesope said sipping his drink. "There's simply no one else on this planet to recruit."

"That's right, Bubbles," Peria added. "Everyone is either a distributor or they work for the company—office employees, phone service, farming, manufacturing, satellites—and they can already buy the products at a discount. With the quarantine on the planet, there's nowhere to go. We're going broke."

"Other organizations are unhappy, too. If we break away, they'll join us."

"The shipping and handling charges are killing us."

"What if they find out what we're doing?"

"We'll take 'em," another shouted.

"I knew it would come to this someday," Lyesope said. He turned to Chandra. "You would really leave the company?"

"Sure," she said. "After everything that's happened, I have no reason to stay."

"We'll start up our own company," Lyesope shouted. "We can call it...uh..."

A very reserved woman who had been sitting on the couch taking in the whole frenzy leapt up waving her enormous arms. "We can call it Soakem Clean Company."

There chimed a chorus of, "I like that," and, "It does have a certain ring to it," and "Down with Galway."

"The planet?" Chandra asked.

"Not the planet, the company," Lyesope said.

"I'm confused," Chandra said. "Galway, what's that?"

Laughter echoed throughout the partygoers.

"That's great!" another one shouted. "That can be our new slogan."

"Will you head it for us?" the host asked.

"No," Chandra said. "Tomorrow I'm out of here. I've got to be across the galaxy in a four days." She pointed at Lyesope. "And why can't *you* head the new company? Of course, the parties will have to pick up a bit. But with practice, you'll learn. One thing I've learned: If you can host a good party, you can run a company. The first step is to get us something to drink with some kick to it."

Wright joined Chandra and whispered in her ear, "Chani, this party wouldn't pick up with a helium bag the size of Andromeda."

Suddenly, the mood shifted. The Galways began to celebrate as if released from generations of oppression; and they celebrated in the manner of a people who had not practiced the fine art of roof-raising. The transmission fluid punch was replace by a more appropriate and stronger version.

After several servings of revised punch, even the flavor of the food began to improve. As if by design, the music also improved and the conversation grew more interesting.

Discussions of the Ecto-Super replaced droll speeches on product superiority.

It had been several hours since Chandra had seen Wright. She finally found him resting comfortably under a table carrying on a conversation with the base of a floor lamp.

"We need to go." Chandra looked around. "We've been here too long. They might track us here."

He unwrapped his arm from around the lamp pole. "Chani, please. I think she likes me."

Chapter Seventeen

"Wright, let me drive. You're drunk."

"Naw, I'm fine, or rather I will be in a few minutes." He popped a beige pill in his mouth and swallowed it without benefit of water. "Aarrrggg. That's nasty."

"What is it?"

"It's called SobreX. It's an instant hangover without the fun, lingering effects of being drunk."

Back in the TransStar Wright plugged in the chart chip that displayed a holographic chart of the region and an electronic local yellow pages complete with electronic pages of yellow journalism.

Speedsters shot past them on the left and from underneath, both cutting in front of the Marginal rental. Bouncing and jostling, gnashing and rattling, the Marginal staggered along in the turbulence from the jet blast of the other speeding flyers.

On the screen inset on the control panel, tiny red blips swept past the green one that represented their own TransStar.

After a few minutes, he noticed that one blip lagged behind them consistently, veering hard left when he initiated the maneuver, and speeding up and slowing down, a perfect mimic of each change in their own course.

Another large transport zipped past them and Wright swung in behind them, catching the TransStar in its jet blast. The speedster buffeted and jiggled, helpless in the large jet's backwash.

"Wright, what the hell are you doing? You're going to get us killed!"

"Someone's following us. I can't get away from 'em," he said.

Wright pulled up on the joystick. The buffeting speedster clumsily responded, climbing out of the wake into more stable air. He accelerated, or tried to, but gained nothing above cruising speed.

"I'm sorry," said the sultry speedster voice. "You are attempting to violate the speed restrictions of this region. The speed limit is 650 kilometers per standard Galactic Hour."

"Damn. They've got a governor on the engine."

She motioned up with her index finger. "We'd better gain some altitude. I don't know how much more of this jerking back and forth I can take."

With her insides undulating, she eyed Wright whose face had turned the most particular shade of chartreuse. She assumed her complexion mimicked his.

On the screen, that same blip tagged constantly behind. "Did the phone company implant some kind of microchip in you when you went to work for them?"

Her eyes widened. "Oh, Sapiens. They could have done it at any time when they gave me my inoculations. It makes sense. How else could they have followed me all over the galaxy. How can I get away from them when they know my every move?"

Wright didn't answer. Instead he ordered, "Ask the screen for a menu."

She did.

"Tell it to put up a sectional of the area."

It did.

"Okay. Now a street map with buildings and landmarks."

Another transport sped past. The TransStar wobbled unsteadily.

Amber writing appeared on the status screen.

"What does it say?" he asked.

She tried to read it, but she did not recognize the symbols. She consulted her universal translator. "It's from the speedster that just passed us. According to my translator, it says it doesn't know which is smaller, your brain or your codpiece."

Another batch of hieroglyphics appeared on the screen.

Wright's eyebrow shot up. "Well?"

"The second one said, 'You're stupid as a storm drain'— Now, can I pilot?"

Another set of symbols appeared on the screen.

"Well?" He cocked his head in her direction.

She hesitated.

"Chani, what does it say?"

She bit her lip. "It says, give me what you have or I'll kill you."

He glanced at the screen, checking for additional messages and evidence of other tag-along traffic. Wright let out a startled "Oops" and then the Marginal plunged downward at spleen-rupturing speed. Just inches above the ground the speedster finally jarred to a sudden stop, but Chandra's stomach and intestines kept moving at near light speeds. So did her head; despite her restraints her head slammed against her padded instrument panel. She felt as if she was swimming in a pool of warm lard.

The canopy opened with a protesting whine.

Wright grabbed her hand. "Come on, Chani."

Her head still did breast strokes around her body and she was only vaguely aware of movement around her. She barely felt him pull her from the speedster.

Chapter Eighteen

"Come on. Come on," Wright urged.

He dragged her between buildings, and finally up a short flight of stairs into a busy lobby.

Four lines, red, blue, green and yellow, climbed the steps in their path, past an automatic door that flew open in their faces. The moving lines, slightly wider than a hand-width, diverged down different halls. One disappeared into a blank wall.

Wright stopped for a moment on the green line to let Chandra catch her breath, but he was actually the one panting. He threw her arm over his shoulder and took a step forward before he realized that the green line moved much faster than he could ever lug her.

The green line came to a stop in a room where three Galwayans huddled around a steel robocart. Bright lights beat down on them. Their attention focused, unshakably, on the center of the table. Not a centimeter of flesh showed beneath their full-face masks, gloves, and surgical scrubs.

Behind them, massive machines burped communicative beeps, and computerized diagrams flashed urgently, apparently directing attention to a critical problem.

One surgeon reached forward, making a deft, almost unseen, motion with his hand. The one facing Wright made another motion.

An alarm on the machine sounded, much the same as a klaxon sounding battle stations.

"Oh, damn, damn, damn," the first one cried. "I can't believe I made a mistake like that."

The third one, who up until then had remained silent, said, "Look, Eganmore, if you'd pay attention you wouldn't run into these problems. I think it's time to give up."

The one facing them straightened with a hearty laugh, threw his cards face up on the table and shouted, "This is

Cryptic, you bad dogs!" He scooped up some chips and collection Galway bottles, family-sized, into a large grouping right in front of him.

The one with its back to them swaggered a bit. He threw a few platinum chips and an industrial-sized bottle of Galway vitamins on the table with a clink. "Dummar, I'll give you the key to my summer lodge and these chips to cover your losses if you take the next case."

"Are you kidding, Mindwiper? Your summer lodge is right in the middle of a methane swamp." He pocketed the coins, then grabbed the cards, shuffling with casino-dealer expertise. He stopped. "Game's up. Our next case is here."

Wright stood on the end of the green line, holding a spaghetti-like Chandra by the waist.

"Chani." He shook her. "I don't think we're in Kansas anymore."

She answered him by straightening her back, staggering toward the table, and hurling into a brightly polished bowl mounted on the table between two of the doctors.

One of the creatures pulled its mask down exposing a Centaurian face with several vertical ridges along his cheeks. He had a thick shock of hair the texture of cotton candy and the color of old thirty-weight oil.

"Sorry." Wright trotted to where Chandra hung her head in the bowl. "She hasn't been the same since that last lobotomy."

She kicked him beneath the table, unseen by her audience.

"Ooww. Come on, Chani."

She dropped her head back into the bowl.

"Nice place," Wright said nervously. "Where are we?"

"Surgery," the formerly masked man said.

"At...?"

"Our Lady of Hope For the Best Hospital," a Centaurian answered. "My name is Poco Dummar. This is the universally renown neural/anal surgeon, Eganmore Mindwiper." He pointed to the being leaning against him emitting rude barnyard sounds.

Wright shook his head. "That's certainly convenient, especially if you have your head up your ass."

Dummar angled his head in the doctor's direction. "He could use a rectal lobotomy himself."

"What an interesting language he speaks," Wright

observed. "Where is he from?"

"Alpha Centauri, just like me, unfortunately." Dummar nudged the universally renowned doctor.

"And you," Wright said. "What kind of doctor are you?"

Dummar laughed. "Me? A doctor? You're kidding. I'm his bartender." He glanced over at Chani, who still had her head in the bowl. "And if you don't mind me saying so, I think your girlfriend has had a bit too much to drink herself. Don't be insulted. I'm a professional."

"Naw," Wright said. "Not this time. My flying made her sick."

"Drinking, flying, performing surgery, it's all the same. By the way, that's some guy's brain in that bowl. We just took it out for a cleaning."

Chandra pulled her green face out of the bowl. "Sorry. Send the phone company the cleaning bill."

"Dweezel," the barkeep said to the third card-playing being. "When our friend can vacate the bowl for more than a few seconds, why don't you take the brain back down to be cleaned again. Tell the floor to hold the patient for a few more hours. Until then, the substitute brain will just have to do." He looked at Wright. "He's using a Fyrud bog worm brain. It can be embarrassing to watch, but he'll never know the difference."

Dummar shrugged. "If he's not happy, he can go down the street to Our Lady of Perpetual Motion." He nudged the doctor, who had completely lost consciousness, sliding down to the floor. "Don't worry about this. He does this all the time. Now, when you put that laser scalpel in his hand he wakes right up."

"You say 'now'."

"In the old days, he used to have a problem: you know, tailgate parties."

"What's wrong with an occasional tailgate party?" Wright asked.

"Before the surgery?"

Wright listened thoughtfully. "I guess it's good anesthesia."

"That's why they call me an anesthesiologist. I put the surgeons under. I pass gas, too...usually after really spicy food."

Wright just nodded.

"I won't say he's a lush, but he's the only guy I know with a two liter shot glass."

"Do they still sell those?" Wright asked. "I'd love to have one."

"No problem. He got it from Leech Medical Supply, imported from offworld. I believe it's a subsidiary of the Bartlemist Party Supply. It's under specimen jars."

Dummar motioned to Wright with a long-stemmed glass. "Like a drink while we're waiting for the patient?"

Wright shifted Chandra's weight to his other arm and reached out for the glass. "Yeah. Hey, this is great. What is it?"

"It's a Sunrise Surprise." He listed the ingredients.

"Who would have ever thought all that together would be this good," Wright said. "You ever try a Big Bang?"

"What's that?" Dummar asked.

Wright described the flavor of a peppermint snowball with just a touch of heat from a small supernova, and the only slightly irreversible brain damage that occurs from drinking more than two in any given solar year. "Where's your bar? I'll throw one together."

With Chandra in tow, Wright followed Dummar to the green line and rode it until they reached the blue line. When it crossed the green and red plaid line they stepped off and entered an office.

"This is Mindwiper's office. And mine. He wants me close in case he needs an emergency consultation." He pointed to a monitor tuned to the operating room they had just left and then swept his hand to show off the well-stocked wet bar that took up an entire two-thirds of the room.

Wright dropped Chandra into a padded chair, then inspected the contents of the shelves.

Bottles of all shapes and sizes filled the shelves on the mirrored wall, like the gems in a well-organized jewelry box. One faceted bottle held an amber liquid, another clear container held something in glowing pink, and another clear decanter looked as if it held nothing at all. He recognized nebula water, which seemed to dance as it swirled around the bottle in a self-made current. A few very small containers could have held no more than a normal jigger.

"I've never seen such a vast selection of liquor," Wright said. "I'll bet this rivals anything ol' Rithel Bartlemist stocks."

Dummar's finger rose to his lips. "Don't say that too loud. If party pirates found out we had this kind of stash, they'd turn this hospital into a morgue real quick."

Wright put on an apron and fireproof gloves and went to work pouring and mixing. Before long, using a pair of long tongs, he handed Dummar a glass with glowing bubbles rising from the floor of the glass to the top, popping with a cracking sound, then disappearing.

As Dummar sipped his eyes grew wide and his pupils dilated until Wright could read the credit chips in them. "Wouldn't know where I could get that recipe, would you?"

"Might. But, it's got a universal copyright and an unbreakable patent lock."

"Any patent can be broken," Dummar said.

"Problem is, if you screw up this formula it will cause a chain reaction that could take out half a system. It's got to be just right. Maybe we could work out a deal." Wright stared at the monitor focused on the robocart card table/operating room table with the surgeon snoring on the operating room floor. "Can he operate like that?"

"No problem," Dummar said. "His last patient now has a mind that soaks up everything."

"His memory improved that much?" Wright asked.

"No, Mindwiper left a sponge in him when he closed up."

"Hey, Dummar, ol' bud, can I get someone else to take a look at her?" Wright pointed at Chandra. "She's got a bug, and it's giving her a hard time."

"A flu?"

"Naw, a microchip. An old boss put it in and I think it's going to kill her."

"Does she have Galway Health Care and Cleaning Insurance?"

"Naw, and she's as broke as a hand in a beginning martial arts class." He paused. "Maybe we could work out a trade. A chipectomy for a formula."

Dummar sipped his drink. Once his pupils contracted again, he said, "I think we've got some students who can handle it. You want Mindwiper to take a look at her head? I could wake him up. Looks like a pretty nasty bump."

Wright took a sip of his own Big Bang, shook his head and said, "Let's just get that bug out of there."

Chapter Nineteen

"Here's the little beggar." The student doctor dropped the microchip in Wright's hand.

It was slightly smaller than a grain of rice.

"Thank you, Doctor Duckworth." Wright examined the bug. Its multiple sharp edges bore tiny protrusions that acted as anchors to prevent it from migrating.

He rested his rump against the stretcher where Chandra dozed quietly.

She lay on her side, snoring noises that reminded him of a nuclear-powered chain saw. A small stream of drool rolled from the corner of her mouth. Teak peaks of hair poked out as if trying to take a look around; her bangs covered her bruised forehead.

The Pictorian intern climbed up on top of a box so he could look Wright in the eye.

"You were right, Mr. Aulweighs. It is a passive chip. It shouldn't be activated unless a specific scanner detects it. But, somehow it has been permanently activated—remotely somehow. Even so, I can't see that it can have caused her any trouble. But, you traveled with her; you would know."

"You wouldn't believe the trouble it's caused," Wright said.

"Well, it's still activated," Duckworth said. "I guess it could throw off some confusing signals if someone was looking for her. As they're not, you can just throw it away, and no harm done."

Wright rolled it around in his palm. "Yeah, no harm done."

He nodded in Chandra's direction. "Hey, Doc, how long will it take her to sleep that juice you gave her off?"

Chandra turned over and began to smack her lips.

"Oh, thirty or forty minutes at least."

"Good," Wright said. "Keep an eye on her. I'll be back in a little while. I have a little matter to take care of."

Chandra curled up in a fetal position from a gurney in the Neurology Department of Our Lady of Hope for the Best

Hospital. Dr. Duckworth placed his box next to her bed and climbed up to get a better look at his patient. He held up her wrist as if taking her pulse, instead he let go and her arm flopped down as if lifeless. He made a note on a chart and hung it back on her bed.

"Dr. Duckworth," a female Gawayan doctor popped her head through the door. "I need some help. I'm missing a patient, Mrs. Rounrump. She seems to have wandered away from her room."

Duckworth turned away from Chandra. "What does she look like?"

"She's tall, kind of heavy and has a bit of a hormonal problem." She placed a single finger above her top lip. "We gave her some medication before her surgery. It made her a little disoriented. She might even be argumentative."

"I'll keep an eye out for her." He returned his attention to Chandra.

"If you see her, just call security," she suggested, then disappeared.

The Pictorian doctor climbed down from his booster and left the room.

Chandra moaned, snorted and farted as she turned over. Then a long shadow fell across Chandra's sleeping form.

"What have we here?" asked Lance Goode. "Chandra Solomon. I knew you were nearby. My tracker indicated you were in this building. Then it quit working." He checked outside the open door to see if anyone was coming. Seeing no one, he closed the door and began rifling through the drawer mounted beneath her gurney. He found a blue beaded evening gown and a pair of matching shoes, but nothing else.

"Where's the damn orb?" he yelled at her.

Her only response was the loss of more drool.

Lance approached the bed, pulling the pillow out from under her head with his right hand and steadying it with the stub from his recently removed left arm. "I've had enough of you."

At the same time he placed the pillow over her face, the door opened. It was the female doctor who had been there earlier. "There you are!"

"I was just walking past this room and saw this pillow attacking her. I thought I'd try to help," he explained.

The doctor pulled a filled syringe out of her pocket, stormed over and gave Lance a poke right through his slacks.

"What the hell are you doing?" he demanded before his eyes glazed over.

"Don't worry Mrs. Rounrump. You'll be feeling fine in few a minutes. It's just a little operation. Nothing to worry about."

"What kind of operation?"

Before the doctor could answer, he slumped to the floor, unconscious.

The doctor removed the pillow from Chandra's face and called for an orderly.

When the orderly arrived she said, "Prep Mrs. Rounrump for her surgery. I'll be there in a few minutes."

Chandra opened her eyes. The room was unfamiliar and dark.

Her whole body protested as she struggled to prop herself up on her elbow. A sharp pain caught her between her shoulder blades. She lost her balance and fell back into the bed.

"Hi," a familiar voice said.

In the faint light creeping through the window, she could make out the Wright's face. His feet were propped up on a piece of medical equipment. In his hands he casually held a magazine as though he could actually read in the near dark. She thought she could make out a smile, though she was not sure.

"How'd you sleep?" he asked.

"Like a baby," she said.

"You cried all night and wet the bed?"

"No, I slept well, but I had a strange dream. Where are we?"

"We're safe," he said.

"Would you like to be a little more specific?" she said. "Where's safe?"

"Our Lady of Hope for the Best."

"Amen to that," she said.

"No, that's where we are. Our Lady of Hope for the Best Occasional Hospital and Soap Refinery on Galway."

Painfully she moved her shoulder. "Is there something you think you should tell me? I mean, anything really important?"

He dragged his chair over to the bed and sat down next to her. "You want something to drink?"

She nodded. "My mouth tastes like a wastewater tank."

He handed her one of Dummar's concoctions.

"Wright, what's going on? What am I doing here?"

"I don't think we'll have to worry about those guys following us anymore. They removed your microchip."

"Is that why I feel like a thunderbeast tiptoed across my back?"

"That, and you stopped the control panel in the TransStar with your head when I tried to land."

"I told you that you should have let me fly."

"Maybe I should have."

"Are you sure about that? I mean them not bothering us anymore?" she asked through a groggy haze.

"Yeah. I put the chip in the TransStar and crashed it into a wall. Great fireworks display. You should've seen it. Lots of colors and a fireball you wouldn't believe! I guess that means we won't get our deposit back. But at least they think you're dead."

She rested her head deeper into her pillow. "You did that for me?"

He shrugged. "Naw. I got tired of looking behind me all the time."

"If that were true, you could have left me any time you wanted."

"You kinda liven things up. Like a grenade with a lost pin. Ivan's good company and all, but it's not the same as having someone to talk to. Someone who talks back sometimes and yells at others. Someone who..." He paused to look at a scar on his hand. "...bites her fingernails. This is the first real excitement I've had in years.

"Now, get up. We've got to go rent a speedster."

Chapter Twenty

"Have you ever had the feeling you were being followed?" Chandra asked Wright.

"Naw," he answered. "Most of the time, I am being followed. You know, gorgeous women, rich. They want me for my body."

Chandra giggled. "No, really."

"Really."

"You're impossible to carry on a simple conversation with. I feel like we're still being followed."

It seemed as if they had walked for hours, though they had only trekked a few miles from the hospital when that feeling over took her.

"You're just paranoid," he said.

"Maybe," she said. "But, Wright, just cuz you're paranoid doesn't mean they're *not* out to get you."

After Chandra's left Our Lady of Hope for the Best, she had the stamina of a glabwort, allegedly the strongest pack animal in the galaxy, but with an average life span of eight years. Her glabwort must have just hit the twelve-year mark. She lagged farther and farther behind Wright.

"I can't keep up," she said. "I just need to rest for a while. Maybe a few days."

"You're running out of time on your deadline, remember, and I've a reverse pyramid gig and got a hot party I have to be at," he said. "We'll never make either one at this rate."

They ducked into a bar. The illuminated sign on the front was shaped like a bottle with fumes of some nature rising out of it. Next to the bottle read, "Good Spirits, a subsidiary of Galway Industries."

"You stay here," Wright ordered. "Have a drink, relax. I'm going to find a speedster. With that hole in your back, I can travel faster without you. I wonder if the insurance is going to cover the TransStar?"

Chandra pictured the two-meter deep crater he described at the point of impact. "You'd have to explain why you aren't dead. I think screwing up our credit is the least of our problems."

"Try to look inconspicuous," he told her as he dashed out the door of the darkened pub.

"Yeah, right," she answered.

How indiscreet could she look wearing a blue and gold beaded and sequined gown that announced either, 'I'm a hooker on a galactic scale,' or, 'I'm in trouble and in the wrong place'? Around her, Galwayans wore business casual, which meant they wore stuffy suits with the pointy lapels.

In the center of the bar a jukebox, with a three-D laser display, played a song by Betelgeuse Onion Repair, a group owning a beat where Gregorian chant met heavy metal.

"...Cheek to cheek," chanted the rocker, followed by a percussive boom bomp ba bom. Boom bomp ba baba.

"...They mooned at the dance..." Boom bomp ba bom. Boom bomp ba baba.

"...illigitimi non carborendum..." Boom bomp ba bom. Boom bomp ba baba.

A barmaid ambled over and took her drink order. Like the folks at the party, she looked as if she had just walked out of the board of director's conference room of a major corporation.

"Leonian brandy," Chandra said without looking up.

The waitress eyed at her outfit. "You must be the Nova that I heard was in town. You sure you want a brandy? It's a little rough for a person of your refined nature. Perhaps a two hundred year old Genteelberry wine?"

"I want something I can taste," she said. "Bring me the brandy."

"It's your taste buds."

Chandra stacked the empty brandy glasses, one on top of another. Dissatisfied, she ordered another. She dismantled her glass structure and transformed it into a train of sorts.

What's taking him so long? she wondered.

The music paused for a commercial.

"Are you bored? Do you miss all those fun tunes of yesteryear? Would you like to escape to the past without all the expense and health hazards involved in time travel? Turn on and tune in to all those tasteless ditties of the past with, 'Wretching to the Hits.' Just call and order today from Galway, where quality and high cost never go hand in hand."

Back to her glass sculpture, the train somehow evolved into airborne glass fighters dogfighting each other in the sky immediately above her table. Finally, just as Chandra ran out of imagination, a Galway woman sat down at the table across from her. A brightly colored do-rag bound her hair.

"I am Ratima," the woman said in a pseudo-mysterious voice. "This..." She paused for affect and waved her arm around the room. "...is my place."

Chandra tried to focus on the woman's badly mismatched outfit and the strands of shiny stones and crystal baubles dangling around her neck.

"Hey," Chandra answered, and waved with such force she nearly fell from her chair.

Ratima grabbed Chandra's hand with bony fingers and squeezed.

"Ow!" Chandra tried to pull her hand away, but the skinny old gypsy held fast.

"I see you're in trouble," the seer said. "Someone is after you."

"You can tell that by squeezing my hand?" Chandra gasped. She was really impressed.

"Pah, of course not," the old woman said. A fine spray of spittle accompanied her words.

"Then, how do you know that?" Chandra asked.

"Dat Telerite, over der." She pointed with a well-manicured nail. "He's got a light pistol pointed at your head. I can sell you some good luck crystals. They will protect you from harm."

Chandra spotted the Telerite from the corner of her eye. His eyes resembled a lion's, large and amber, staring straight through her.

"I doubt they'll stop that. People in my Galway down-line, you know—my underlings—would pay a sizable sum to assure my safety."

The old woman eased closer. "How much is "a sizable sum?"

"Ever heard of Bubbles Wizzinrite?"

Loose skin in her chin flapped as the woman nodded.

"I'm Bubbles."

"Yes, and I am Zomba, Queen of the Stars."

"I thought your name was Ratima."

"I am Ratima, but Bubbles Wizzinrite, you're not."

"Why do you say that?"

"Cuz I'm not Zomba...You want charms?"

"If I buy a charm, will you keep him occupied till I get out of here?"

"Two."

"Deal."

Ratima/Zomba slammed down a couple of shiny baubles and with the same motion picked up some credits and stuffed them down the front of her bustier. She waddled over to the next table where the armed Telerite waited, with his huge bear claw-feet propped up on the table.

"Get those things off my table!" Ratima popped his toes with one of her chains.

While the Telerite fought for his feet, Chandra took her two remaining full glasses and slipped out the door.

Hiding in the bushes would have been more interesting had she thought to bring along the snack dish.

She watched the speedsters arrive, but no one even remotely resembling Wright trotted up.

"Waiting for someone?"

She lurched around. "Wright." She glared at him. "Where's our transport?"

"You're standing on 'em," he said. "They won't rent me anything until I bring back the first one. We're going to have to use alternative transportation." He pointed at her feet.

When he pulled her upright, Chandra resembled a mime against the wind.

"How many drinks does that make?" he asked her.

She held up four fingers. "Three."

"At least one of us will be light on our feet," he said.

They walked and staggered for some time before they found a lot displaying a revolving sign that read, "Good Deal Used Speedsters." High above them, canned smoke puffed out of an exhaust port on the gutted flyer impaled on a rotating pole.

The salesman strode up to them chomping gum open-mouthed like a cow luxuriating over his cud. With orange and brown plaid suit and white-topped plastic shoes he looked the part of the used speedster salesman. His jacket emitted the same familiar odor she encountered on the streets of Bedlam back on Distress: the overwhelming scent of too much cheap after-shave, the aroma somewhere between Spanish cologne and three week-old dead fish. The cologne factor had skyrocketed.

Littering the lot were fifty or sixty speedsters in various stages of decrepitude. Many had aged far beyond Chandra's own twenty-seven years.

The salesman grabbed Wright's hand and pumped it up and down. He moved over to Chandra, shaking her hand with slightly sweaty palms. "Good afternoon. What a fine-looking couple you are. Searching for a nice mode of transportation? I'll bet we can find one for you. Lately's the name. Good to meet you. Good to meet you." He handed Chandra a holographic business card, but before she could pocket it, he snatched it from her fingers and dropped it back into his breast pocket, followed by a gentle pat of his hand. "What can I do for you? I'll bet you'd like to fly away with one of these fine babies."

Chandra turned to Wright and stuck her finger down her throat.

Wright   said, "We need dependable transportation—"

"Dependable? I've got just the thing," he interrupted. He pointed to a '57 TransStar with a rusty tail jet exhaust port. The odor of its fresh metallic blue paint job mingled with his whore-fish cologne.

"Just look at this baby. A Blitzen-Rogers 987 engine with dual log-rollers,...aannnddd." He paused for emphasis. "it's got..." He swung the door up and pressed a patch on the board. "...a vanity mirror for the lady."

A mirror rose out of the panel, automatically facing her direction.

"It's got a special sensor that seeks out only X chromosomes. What a feature!"

She glared at him. "You're divorced, aren't you?"

"Eighteen times," he answered proudly.

"I thought so."

"So what do you think?" he asked.

"How many hours are on the engine?" Chandra asked.

"Only about two-hundred since it was rebuilt. Won't be coming up on an annual for a few cycles." He glanced at his chrono.

"How many zeros go behind that two-hundred?" she asked warily.

"Only six," he said with slightly less zeal.

"What else you got?" she asked.

"It's really a fine speedster," he added.

"I want something with less time on it," she said.

"Oh, perhaps something a little more upscale?"

"Preferably something with no scales."

"I guess that means a Ziperoo Dragon is out of the question."

"You've got to be kidding!"

As they walked past the Dragon, Chandra whispered to Wright, "I've seen more ethical beings at a weasel convention."

Wright nodded in agreement.

"I know. I've got the perfect thing for you. How about an Egocentre Vortex? It's got heavy-duty jamrunners, reinforced farglers and a hyperspastic excelgarator. Just the thing to hop around the planet in." He bounded for a whitish speeder that resembled a flattened bullet slug.

"No. What about that one?" She pointed at a modest smaller model with a plaque on the back that read Taildragger.

"That one?"

"Yeah. That one."

The salesman sighed, walking over to the speedster in question. "It was flown by a little old lady who only went to the sacrifices on Chubsday."

"How often is Chubsday?"

"About every twelve Terran hours."

"Never mind."

"What are you looking for?"

"Something small that will fit in the hold of a Mammoth," Wright said.

"Why didn't you say so? I've got just the thing."

He led them to a speedster so small they could not cram themselves into it even if they had been greased down. "This is a Quark. Look at this paint job. Impressive isn't it?"

"Nice."

"Get a really good look. This is a special paint. The molecules are only point fifteen microns apart. Normal paint is point thirty microns."

As they leaned forward to inspect the metallic silver paint faded dull gray, he popped the gum out of his mouth and placed it on the back of a row of ceramic heat tiles.

"So?"

"What do you mean, 'so'?" He leaned his butt against the tiles, forcing them back into place.

Chandra squeezed into the crevice that allegedly held the pilot, looking rather like a megamammoth stuffed into a grandmother's rocking chair. When she settled in as deeply as she would fit, she asked, "What planet does it come from?"

"Pictorius."

"What..." Each time she spoke her teeth gouged her knees.

"Perfect fit," he gushed.

"Perfect fit? There's no room for Wright."

"It's got a nice little trunk."

"There's no room for him," she reiterated.

"If you decide to take it, I can have some of that equipment pulled out and have another seat installed. My, oh my, oh my. I didn't know if I could find anyone to buy it. This little beauty is a bit of a special interest flyer."

"What do you want for it?"

"Seventeen hundred credits..."

Wright started to say, 'sold,' but before he could, Lately yelled, "Down."

"Look." Chandra struggled to free herself from the cockpit. "I've got a credit chip worth fifteen hundred. Take it or leave."

"We can finance the rest," he offered. "All you need is a job. Your employment identification is your ticket to anywhere in the galaxy."

"I've heard that before," Chandra said to Lately. She shook her head. "Not worth it."

Wright grabbed a handful of evening gown and pulled hard to dislodge Chandra from the cockpit.

"Ow, Wright. That was me."

"Sorry." He readjusted his grip, pried some and then finally yanked her free.

Chandra slowly began unfolding her limbs as the feeling returned to her arms and legs.

"Sorry. That's a firm price. Can't go any lower. I've got more in it than that. You think about it. I'll be right back." He trotted over to a suit-clad Galwayan who stood looking over the Blitzen-Rogers enhanced TransStar, and picking at his teeth with a credit chip.

While Lately verbally twisted his new customer's arm, Chandra and Wright scouted around the lot. Wright trotted in one direction and she went in the other.

As she looked over a Nebula, she noticed a familiar Totgarian shuffling from flyer to flyer with a long-barrel weapon in hand. His head turned continuously back and forth like the head of a rotating fan.

"Damn!" She dropped to the ground and crawled back to

the Quark for cover. "It's Rigmar." She recalled her earlier episode with the Totgarian and his ill-fated BossCom.

Even without looking she knew his every move; with each step the medals chinked on his chest broadcasting his position. His own fruity smell grew stronger as the chinks grew louder. That, and the large spoon-shaped medals, made him a giant walking jelly kitchen.

Chandra crouched on the ground next to the base of the tiny speedster. Ca-chink. Ca-chink. The noise came from only a few rows away.

She held her breath. Then a second chinking began on the other side of the lot also headed her direction.

"Sapiens." She mouthed the words.

"Hey, Gragmar," bellowed the nearby Totgarian. "Get a look at this."

Both Totgarians approached Chandra's refuge from both sides. The Quark looked as though it could have been a roller skate for one of them. It came up to just above their knees and would only hold one Totgarian foot at a time.

"Look at this," the Totgar repeated, pointing at the speedster.

The jangle of medals joined in the chorus of their laughter.

"Hey, BossCom. This looks like one of those hypertops we played with as little Totties," Gragmar giggled.

BossCom hobbled over. "Fool. This thing won't spin like a hypertop. It's shaped wrong. See." He gave the nose a push.

It pitched to the left slightly, almost trapping Chandra under its belly.

She scrambled to the tail of the flyer, crouched, pulled her gown up to her knees—ready to move.

"Watch," Gragmar said. He gave the flyer a much harder shove.

It spun a quarter of a turn, but only under squeaking protest of metal grinding against concrete.

Chandra jumped back and then hugged what would have been the front passenger side of the nose, had the Quark had room enough for a passenger.

"Not bad," the new BossCom admitted. "I'll try again." He threw his arms back for a really big push.

From the other side of the lot the salesman came running, legs bouncing like a pogo stick, arms waving. "Just what the hell do you think you're doing?"

Wright followed close behind.

The Totgarian stopped in mid-push.

The aborted shove pushed Chandra back, pinning her between the Quark and the rust bucket parked to the left of it.

The salesman peered way up at the Totgarians. "Do you intend to buy this fine flying machine?" he asked.

They looked at each other and then at Lately. Their medals jangled as they shook their heads simultaneously.

"Then get your underpaid, overworked claws off of my valuable merchandise."

They stared down at him, two sizable Totgarian heads shorter than they, and laughed.

Not to be intimidated, he added. "And you owe me for the damage you caused to this piece of transportation excellence."

When they laughed all the harder Lately whistled across the lot.

Beneath Chandra the ground vibrated with low steady rumblings, small regulated earthquakes. Atop her the Quark quivered, too, as a small grayish mountain streaked past her and then moved around to the Totgarian side of the speedster.

"I'd like you to meet my accountant," Lately said.

This time it was the Totgarians who were looking up. The "accountant" stared down at them from above, grunting as he exhaled enough air to fill a blimp. He chewed nervously on his lip.

"He looks hungry," Gragmar said.

"He's extremely qualified. On a good day he can count to seven."

The Totgarians jingled as they backed away, quickly promising to send a few credit chips for the damage someone else must have caused to the Quark. Then they turned to make a hasty retreat, followed closely by the accountant, like a fox on the heels of squawking chickens.

I guess your girlfriend decided she didn't want the Quark." Lately looked around. "Damn. Lost another one that way. She'd have paid cash."

"I'm down here." Chandra half-squatted, was wedged like a sandwich meat between the two vehicles.

Lately and Wright struggled and managed to push the Quark enough to release Chandra. She fell to the ground.

"Is that the kind of riff-raff you attract at this lot?"

"Of course not."

Chandra reached back and rubbed gingerly between her shoulder blades with the tip of her thumb. She winced. "The cretins. You need better security."

"Are you hurt?" he asked. "Do you need a lawyer?"

"I'm not sure. Do you know a good lawyer?"

Once again, he retrieved his holo business card, flipped it over and handed it to her.

This time she took a step backward, and held the card closer to her. It read: "Binsuwd Lately, Attorney at Law. We get results. Certified in specialty in a Galactic Bar."

She took another sniff of the cologne-saturated air. "Sapiens. You're an attorney."

"I prefer to think I am a pleader of galactic justice for those with the need and enough money." He thought for a moment, then gave Chandra a slight push with his sausage fingers. "I could sue myself. It would be a tough case, but I think we could come out ahead. I only charge forty-nine percent for my services and another fifty-two for fees. In all, a decent profit for your lovely self."

"You're nuts!"

"So what you think of the Quark?" Lately asked. "You want me to write up that contract? With every speedster that leaves here I even throw in probating a will or a free medical malpractice suit. All I charge is a modest upkeep fee."

"Why don't you give me the flyer and we'll call it even?"

He shook his head. "Couldn't do that. Got too much in it."

"Have you ever played Cryptic?"

"How you doing in there?" she called to Wright through the ventilation system.

She and Lately had managed to cram him into the trunk with a Corvian-grade shoehorn and by dousing him in a gallon of cooking oil.

"It...isn't so...bad if...ah don't breathe," returned his muffled response.

"Hang tight," she said. "Here we go."

As she flew out of the parking lot, the entire fuselage shimmying beneath her, the gum holding the rack of ceramic tiles worked loose; the rack vibrated for a second, dangled for a few more moments and then hit the ground with a crash.

Chapter Twenty-One

"What a mess!" Chandra gasped as they entered *Blind Faith*.

Wright examined the trash scattered all over the deck. "I dunno. It kinda has that nice homey look to it again."

Padded panels had been ripped open and the stuffing removed. Wire hung out of control consoles like a spaghetti dinner gone awry. Holes had been gouged in the bulkheads.

"This isn't homey; this is obscene," she said. "Where's Ivan?"

Among all the tornadic remains, Ivan sat on his personal pile of Wright's dirty clothes in the copilot's seat.

"They might still be here," she said.

"Naw," he said. "If they were, he wouldn't be sitting here. He'd either be hiding or opening their arteries."

By the smug look on the Turkish Van's face, he probably already had.

Wright gave the Van a friendly scratch around his jowls. The cat responded by craning his neck for the most convenient access. "At least they didn't find the crystal," he said. "I wonder how they knew where the ship was?"

"That's the billion credit question." She continued to examine the damage. Every possible cranny in the cabin had been pried open and turned inside out.

She shifted her gown and removed the orb lodged securely between her breasts. "I feel like I have a third boob."

Wright lit up. "Really?"

She glared back.

Wright plopped down in the captain's seat, but flew out with just as much speed. The springs and struts that had laid dormant in the chair for so many years sprang to life beneath his unsuspecting derrière.

"Damn," he said. "They killed my chair."

"I think I need to examine this damage a little more closely." She climbed up into her loft to check on her instruments.

Her loft cabin had assumed the same new Italian food

Renaissance decor as the rest of the ship. The entire overhead had been disemboweled and bulkhead panels had been pulled down and laid out like cordwood piled in the center of the cabin. Her tool belt, though, remained apparently untouched in the locker beneath her bunk, all the tools neatly in their appropriate compartments awaiting their next calling. It looked just as it had, but for some reason, it did not. As a matter of fact, the belt looked a little too neat. She put it on over the waist of her beaded gown and fastened it.

In the bread-slice-sized mirror, as best she could tell, she looked like a character from theatre of the absurd. Her hair, formerly curled in a pristine up-do, now hung tired and cranky against her face. The leather tool belt looked all the more ridiculous against her sparkling evening dress.

One by one she removed each piece of equipment and inspected it, starting with her high-density material boring vaporizer. Nothing. Still, just a feeling. Something *felt* wrong. The long-range relativistic direction finder and distant measure was untouched. But, when she removed her laser cutter, it felt different, wrong, somehow. She returned it to its little pocket.

That's it!

She pulled it out again, switched it to test mode and turned it on. The little device buzzed and hummed like an out of sync school choir singing an off-key Christmas carol. The sound of real work and earning a living, not running and hiding and keeping out of sight. As she expected, she found nothing out of the ordinary, until she returned the cutter to its leather home. It had been seated all way into the pouch. She never did that. That particular instrument never quite fit right and it took more effort to seat correctly than it was worth.

Why had someone been careful to remove each item and then replace it to appear undisturbed, when the rest of the ship had been virtually destroyed?

One by one, she removed each tool and inspected it. Something was wrong; she just couldn't pinpoint it, yet. As she sent each contraption through its paces, it responded with its a hum or click or its own personal little read-out. The radiation flux transducer readings were high.

She fine-tuned its parameters but it still read higher than a goose step.

There's a bug in here.

Hidden inside the transducer was a tiny but powerful audio transmitter and tracking device on a specific frequency. Three guesses who put it there. All three guesses had the initials E.P.

"That bastard!" she said.

After she changed into her flight suit, she eased back down the crawl way with her tool belt in tow.

She found Wright on the floor with his head up the main control access.

"Wright," she said. "The phone company did this. Those lousy bastards."

"Well, that makes me feel a lot better," he said. "At least it's someone who likes us." He sounded like someone had just shot his best friend. "You're going to have to find another way to Fomalhaut. *Blind Faith* won't be flying again. At least, not this millennium. What do you bet they up my phone rates on top of that?"

"What do you mean, "Up your rates?" she asked.

"I have one of those personal semi-ultra-long line stations. You know the ones, for the busy executive or the teenager with a fast dialing finger," he said. "It hasn't worked in years, but that hasn't stopped them from charging me for it."

"Why didn't you tell me about it?" she asked.

"I didn't think about it until now," he said. "I must have had it for thirty or forty years. I bought it before light drive became affordable. It never worked right, but they had an iron-clad contract"

"Where is it?"

"I don't know," he answered. "I've never been very good at keeping track of paperwork."

"Not the contract. The dish."

"I've got it on ice somewhere in storage. Never got close enough to a phone mart to drop the damn thing off."

She crawled into the storage hold that had also recently enjoyed the ire of the phone company. Just as Wright had described, she found an old personal semi-ultra long line dish and its assorted accouterments scattered around the storage deck. She gathered up the wiring and the array mesh and went to work. Before long, she had the old dish working with marginal efficiency.

She dialed in a code and a touch-tone chimed through her handset.

"I'm sorry," said a computerized voice. "That code is invalid."

She tried again with the same results. As she expected, Tyrus' code had been disabled as well.

"All right, Elkhed, you want to play hard ball, this ball's going to have the density of a baby black hole—I'd like to make a collect call to Elkhed Perkins," she said.

"At the tone, please state your name," the mechanical operator said.

Chandra did.

The operator returned and said, "Elkhed Perkins is not accepting calls from Chandra Solomon."

"Operator, ask him if he is accepting calls from Rithel Bartlemist because ol' Rithel and I are real tight."

"Hello, Chandra," said the voice. "Good to hear from you again. Where are you?"

"Hi, Elkhed. I thought you already knew."

"Let's just say, I've been keeping tabs on you."

"So, I hear."

"You're in a galaxy of trouble, Chani." She could hear his smile in the tone of his voice. "We've had complaints ranging from petty theft to murder. And your old partner, too."

"Just one little thing, Elkhed..."

"What's that?"

"You'd better hope that nothing happens to me."

"Why is that?"

"Well, you see, Elkhed, I'm pretty good when it comes to hacking files. My attorney has all the evidence I've found linking you to everything you allege I've done. If I don't show up at my destination at the appointed time, an unabridged copy of those files will be sent to every official at IGB above the position of apprentice janitor."

"Nice bluff, but I don't believe you."

"Does a file 'Molten Desk Supply' mean anything to you?"

Mentally, she could visualize him: Elkhed Perkins, with a face that looked as if his mother had delivered him inside out, made all the more unattractive by his smug superiority.

"How'd you find that?"

"Does it matter? Maybe I should call my attorney and tell him to send copies to the Earth ambassador. And while he's at it he can send one to the ambassadors from about twenty other planets."

There was another pause so pregnant that she thought

he would give birth to triplets. She kept quiet and let him mull it over. For now, she would hold back her trump.

"Most of those ambassadors had full knowledge of my...activities."

"Of that I'm certain," she said. "But, what do you bet some of the governments and peasants might be real interested to know that their own representatives sold them out. I'd hate for the natives on Enuk to accidentally get hold of your personal communications code. I could give a copy of it to Rithel Bartlemist while I'm at it. He'd be real happy to hear from you. That could turn a little nasty, couldn't it?" She paused. "Your own hitmen would have you in their sights."

"I doubt you can cause much more than a stir, Chani," he said. "Besides, I think you're bluffing. I know more about your situation than you do, and you have nothing."

"But, there you're wrong, Elkhed," she said. "You'd better hope that nothing happens to me between here and Earth or your ass is going to be deader than mine. Does this mean anything to you?"

She sent a series of codes over the phone lines, account numbers and dates she had researched and accumulated since her brief jaunt on Enuk.

As she waited for his reply, she dropped the orb into the spare pouch in her tool belt, then began using one of her hand tools to sculpt a tyrannosaurus rex out of the wire that had been ripped from one of the controls. With enough alcohol one could almost make out a head and tail, but the legs were too small to support the body and it kept flopping over on its side.

"Chani, you know I have nothing but the greatest respect for your work," Elkhed said. "You have served the phone company adequately over the last few years."

"Adequately?"

"We have only the greatest concern for your safety."

"Uh huh."

"And just what do you want in return for my...cooperation?"

"First thing: I want to reimburse the pilot whose ship I chartered for expenses and damages."

"How do you propose I do that?"

"Ya know, Elkhed, that's your problem," she said. "I suggest you dig down deep in one of your hidden accounts. The third one down on my list ought to cover it. Now, that's the first condition."

"What are your other conditions?"

"Safe passage to my destination," she said. "I don't even expect a job when this is all over cuz I have a feeling that my name is in the dictionary somewhere between mud and shit."

Whispering and muffled voices echoed through the speaker.

"You wouldn't be trying to trace this, would you, Elkhed? I'd like our relationship to be based on trust again."

More whispering followed.

"I couldn't agree more," he said.

"I'm still on the ship that your cronies trashed, but I won't be for long. So here's the deal..."

Chapter Twenty-Two

A fully stuffed duffel bag flew out the loft that had been her cabin, hitting the deck with a solid "thwak." Holding on to the pot that held Lance's creation plant, Chandra climbed down the ladder to find one of the saddest sights she had ever seen.

Wright stood amidst a tangle of wire, welding a main support. Next to him Ivan, curled up in a coil of coax, yawned himself awake.

As he surveyed the damaged *Blind Faith* Wright looked as if he had just pronounced Last Rites for a dear friend. In a sense, he had. On the central control panel, lights failed to blink and the screens had ceased to read out unimportant information and meaningless trivia. Although she'd thought the egg crate of a ship was always "dust to dust" she now knew that it had also become ashes to ashes. C h a n d r a patted Wright on the back. "I don't think she's going to fly again," she said sadly.

Wright brushed his hand across the dead console, brought up a thick layer of dust, and blew it off. "We've been together a long time."

"I know," she said.

"We have history."

"I know."

"The dirt and I have history."

"I know."

"I had a history with the dirt before you were born."

"I know."

Ivan trotted over and curled up next to Wright. The architect idly scratched him under the chin. "We still need to get you to Fomalhaut."

"I think I can persuade the Galways to buy me passage on a cruise liner to a nearby system. From there I can try to book another transport to Fomalhaut. I've arranged for the phone company to pay you for damages to your ship, but I'm not

sure how long it's going to take. You might even be able to buy
a new ship. A clean ship."

He examined the silt of dust that coated his fingers. "It
wouldn't be the same."

"I guess not...Wright, I'm so sorry; this is all my fault."

He nodded. "You're on your own," he said glumly.

She scribbled something down on a piece of paper and
handed it to him. "Here's where you need to go to get your
money. I saw a bank in town."

He took the paper and shoved it in his pocket without
even looking at it.

"I guess I need you to retrieve the crystal from Ivan," she
said. "I don't think he'd just give it to me."

Wright unhooked the collar and reluctantly handed it to
her. The crystal glowed brightly among what little light *Blind
Faith* emitted itself. The azure glow made the ship's damage
all the more creepy.

Chandra stared at the bulkhead's warped casing and the
savagely ripped panels.   "I guess I'd better go," she said
quietly. "I have a few things to take care of before I catch the
cruise."

"You're leaving now?"

"Yes." She paused. She wanted to explain why she had to
go. She wanted to apologize without ceasing for all the damage
she had caused. She wanted to be somewhere else, now, she
wanted to stay.

Wright searched for a way to say good-bye, but settled for,
"What about my half?"

"If I make it to Fomalhaut, I'll send you half of whatever I
get. And if that doesn't work out, I'll wring more out of the
company somehow—if I live." She shoved the creation plant
pot in a compartment in the duffel bag, checked her tool belt
and placed her hard hat on her head with a pat. She headed
for the hatch, but hesitated for a moment.

"Thanks for everything." She kissed his cheek and then
left Wright and Ivan sitting on the deck amidst the rubble.

A moment later she reappeared through the hatch. "Wait
a minute," she said. "I have a better plan."

Chapter Twenty-Three

As the shuttle neared the docking platform, Chandra sighed. Almost there.

Through large portholes, the cruise ship loomed closer. An older vessel in style, it wore the scars of its many years of service: meteor pocks, hull patches and an occasional splotch where the paint had worn away. Even with its scars, still the ship looked relatively spaceworthy.

Chandra knew she was lucky to obtain last minute reservations, even as devoid of elegance as the ship was. Sector officials regulated travel in and out of Galway so closely that each passenger was usually scrutinized to prevent zealots from escaping into the general galactic population, and spreading their strange "disease."

She'd been surprised how easy it was to convince the Galways at the party to foot the bill for her cruise. After all, sporadic fighting had been reported and they wanted to protect their inspiration and possible future corporate leader. With more and more violence breaking out, they were all the more eager to move her out of harm's way, especially when she told them she had been robbed of her identification and credit chips. Before she could say "high-price detergent," she found herself in a shuttle armed with not only her Harbinger, but a forged passport, credit chips and paid passage aboard Royal Sirian Cruise Line. Sirian was only part of the name to make it sound swanky. The ship had no more association with Sirius than did Chandra's pet cat, Ree-u. This particular cruise liner was of Lucillian registry, *I.M.A. Redhead*.

After doing some research Chandra learned that the Lucillians had a fleet of ships purchased from more advanced races. They used them primarily as a tool to help convert other species to the Lucillian faith.

The moving gangplank drew Chandra and her cargo toward the opening of *Redhead*. Glistening chandeliers illuminated a massive lobby lined with portholes slightly larger than her

Quark speedster. At the entry a Galwayan woman greeted passengers, wishing them a pleasant voyage and handing them a free sample of soap. A Lucillian purser, who had a very loud announcer-quality voice and wore a top hat and sparkling coat with tails, gave Chandra her cabin assignment.

"Wizzinrite." He handed the porter her digital passport.

He shoved it in his hand-held manifest filer. A pointy finger followed the manifest until he came across the name. "Ah, yes. Bubbles Wizzinrite of Phad Alpha. How did you enjoy Galway?" he asked with a Cuban accent.

"It was…" She paused and thought. "…clean."

With a laser marker, he indicated Wizzinrite as "onboard," and returned her passport. "So I hear."

Beneath Chandra's arm, her tote bag hissed. She smiled at the purser and placed her hand on her stomach. "Sorry. Legumes always have that effect on me. Maybe I should hurry to my cabin."

The purser, fearing the worst, held his breath, and signaled to a porter to take Chandra's luggage.

The mountain of a porter wore what looked like sequined leotards and a matching undershirt. An entire topography of muscles bulged from beneath his tank top. He waddled over to the purser on legs the size of tree trunks and planted himself in front of them.

"The Great Mervik, please take Ms. Wizzinrite to her suite."

The porter reached for the squirming tote slung over Chandra's shoulder, but she pulled away and handed him the duffel. "I think I'll hang on to this one."

He threw the duffel she had been struggling with across his shoulder as effortlessly as if it was a purse.

"This way." He pointed with his free hand.

All her life Chandra had dreamed of going on a luxury cruise, to have hot and cold running servants offering her an endless supply of drinks decorated with colorful little do-dads and stupid miniature umbrellas. And when dinnertime came she would gracefully glide down a grand spiral staircase in the most breathtaking of gowns. Men from all over the ship would peer around doors and make unnecessary trips down corridors well out of their way just to glimpse the gorgeous Chandra Solomon. She'd spend hour upon hour in the casino surrounded by a covey of men, and she would win so much she'd have to hire a man, as big as the purser, to carry her heavy winnings. Her cruise would be perfect!

This wasn't it!

Narrow corridors wound like a maze through the deep innards of the ship. Some spaces were so narrow her escort had problems cramming himself through.

"In the brochure, the ship looked bigger," she observed.

He ducked as he sucked in his chest and squeezed through a doorway. "They shot photos for the brochures with a special wide angle lens that makes everything look bigger and they used midget Pictorian models."

"You're not the typical porter," Chandra observed. "You're a little more, uh, muscular than most."

The Great Mervik smiled broadly and flexed his pecs. "There was a strike at the cruise line. When they couldn't get anyone to work the cruise, they bought our circus cheap. They put us to work doing the jobs around the ship. I do an act in the Cabana Club tonight. You shouldn't miss it."

"I wouldn't dream of it."

They passed a poster touting the top-notch entertainment: Henny Youngman and Rodney Dangerfield. She stopped for a moment and stared at the one-sheet. "Cryonic Comedians Productions proudly presents the best of the Twentieth Century," the sign lied. "'Comedians on Ice.'"

She would check out the entertainment later. Now, if she didn't reach the cabin soon, her tote would sprout claws.

"You'll love the All-You-Can-Eat-Quell-Bar. They'll have quell loaf, quell spaghetti, fried quell, quell sushi, quell a-la-king, French quell, stir fried quell, quell chili, quell barbecue, Green Eggs and quell, and of course quell a la mode."

"Quell sushi?" she echoed.

"It could be worse," he told her as he motioned to the right. "It could be liver."

"Do you eat that much quell?" she asked.

"Aw, hell no," he said. "I eat with the crew. We bring sack lunches."

Rounding a corner, they came up on a door blocked off by yellow crime tape. The porter pulled it down and stuck it in his pocket. "You're staying in the Ricky Ricardo suite." He opened the door to her cabin, exposing a chalk outline drawn on the wall. Dropping her bag, he took a couple of sidesteps and came to rest in front of the outline.

"Lovely view." He pointed at a small blocked-off porthole

with a left lower hand. At the same time he spit on his right upper hand and started rubbing off the outline.

Chandra's eyebrows went up.

"Look at this," he said. "That wall is leaking that white stuff again. I'll send the maid right in to clean this up."

She pushed him aside and stared at the outline. "Someone was murdered in here?"

"Of course not," he said. "He died of natural causes."

"Heart attack?" she asked.

"No. Brain damage. It quit working when someone plunged a club down on top of it."

"What a shame."

"It was a painless death. See, there wasn't much gray matter to injure. But the club was torn up pretty bad." He gave the outline one last wipe and stuck out his chalk-covered hand for a tip.

Chandra handed him a credit chip and he left.

She let out a deep sigh. No, this wasn't exactly the cruise of her dreams. Neither was "suite" the word she would use to describe the room. Closet was more accurate, or walk-in closet with a minute closet of its own. She had seen crates for shipping animals that provided more room than this cabin. She half expected her closet was actually a standard room. Opposite the wall with the body outline, a fold-down bunk offered her a place to lay her tired body. She stowed her duffel bag, but the closet door would not close.

After locking the cabin door, Chandra loosened the cord on the moving bag. Slowly, like a Roman god, Ivan's figure rose from his prison. He scanned his surroundings, first left then right. Finally, he jumped out, whipped his tail about and scoped out his place on the bunk. On the way to the bed, passing the chalk outline he stopped for a moment, hissed and continued to his destination.

"I know how you feel," Chandra told her roommate. "This cabin gives me the creeps, too."

Dressed in sweats given her by one of the distributors, Chandra entered the exercise room. At first a couple of beings toyed at the equipment. One guy with four arms always had a pair of twenty-five pounders above his head as he went through his ritual.

She set her canvass bag down beside her and began a set

of warm up stretches.

Finally, the guy on the treadmill stopped his jogging. Panting and puffing, he wheezed his way out of the fitness center. Within a few minutes, the four-armed man left, too.

Knowing she had only seconds before someone else entered the room, she grabbed her bag and dashed over to the treadmill, popped the cover off and removed a small power transformer. She took a couple of objects from her bag and deposited them in a small void inside the machine. Quickly she replaced the cover and wrapped some yellow crime tape around it. As a finishing touch, she left a hand scribbled sign that said, "Out of Order" in five of the most common alien languages.

That done, she changed into something a little more presentable and left to enjoy the swimming deck.

The cruise director, Yazu M'Cule, had slightly scaly skin with purple pocks running along the side of his face. He drove a small hover cart around the deck of the ship. Along the way he stopped every few moments to chat with passengers. His reptilian face had a muzzle that came to a sharp point and lips that curled in a seemingly perpetual smile, his cylindrical teeth resembled miniature marshmallows. He eased his cart up to Chandra and stopped with a squeak of the breaks.

"Are you enjoying yourself, Mrs. Wizzinrite?" he asked. She nodded.

He blinked and turned his head. "That gentleman over there said he would like to meet you...discretely."

She looked in the direction that his nose pointed. A group of male creatures had gathered around a holovision and were jumping up and down as they rooted for their teams in the Ecto-Super. A human male shifted his gaze in her direction, smiled and gave Chandra a two-finger salute off his eyebrow. His forehead extended all the way to the back of his head and a dark mustache graced his upper lip. He smiled a smile that made Chandra cringe. She had never seen him before, but she had a feeling that she should be terrified of him.

Turning back to the cruise director, she said, "I don't think that's appropriate since my husband's not here."

"Very well, Madam," M'Kule said with a nod. "I will relay your message."

"Thank you, M'Kule. Did he say why he wanted to see

me?'

The creature looked Chandra up and down. His lips curled even more. "Madam, I would think as lovely a creature as yourself would find the answer obvious."

She sighed. "I'm afraid I do." Under her breath she added, "But not for the reasons you think."

After M'Kule rounded the corner on his cart, Chandra rose from her chair and headed toward the elevator. As she neared the exit, one pair of eyes tore away from the hololink, following her until she disappeared behind the doors.

The cabin looked somehow different, but the same. Her luggage waited in the same general area, but not the same. And Ivan was nowhere to be seen.

"Ivan," she called. "I brought you something to eat."

She pulled out a wadded up napkin with several slices of quell and opened it slowly, making certain the wrapping made plenty of noise. Within a few moments a pink nose poked out from under the bunk.

"Come on out you big coward," she said. "There's no one here but us."

Finally Ivan slid his head out into the open and then joined her on the bunk. Pawing at the package in her hand, he meowed and looked up impatiently.

"Have we had any visitors?" she asked as she handed him a chunk of the quell mixture.

As if to answer he stopped chewing and looked in the direction of the closet.

"Did you hear anything?" she asked.

He moved away from her.

"What's wrong, Ivan?"

He jumped back underneath the bunk.

"Nothing's wrong," a dignified male voice with an English accent answered as the closet door opened. "All is as it should be."

She reached for her Harbinger. Damn! She should have remembered the closet door hadn't been closed when she left.

"That wouldn't be very wise," he said. "Nor would your Personal Protection device."

Still managing to point his weapon, he squeezed out of the closet. He was the middle-aged human who'd tried to approach her through M'Kule. The most interesting thing about him was the Remington light pistol he fixed on her.

"That would be foolish; and Chandra Solomon, you're not a foolish person, or are you?"

"You tell me," she said.

He moved away from the opening and a very large humanoid crawled out. Not actually crawled as in an infant crawling along the floor; but more like being born, struggling to escape a too-small opening. Once free he began pulling stuff out of the closet.

As he did, the man continued to talk. "I believe you to be a wise woman. Wise enough to save your own life. All you have to do is answer one simple question: where are they?"

"Where are who?" she asked in a voice that did not simulate coy very well.

"Not "who," but "what." I want to know where you have hidden the rather plain sculptured pieces your late friend gave you."

"He never gave me anything. He died before he had the chance."

The associate dragged a briefcase out of the closet. It was no ordinary briefcase. It unfolded from a small box into quite a comfy looking slightly padded recliner with a few customized features like the loops around the arms and feet.

"Have a seat," he offered.

"No, thanks," she said. "I just got here a little while ago and I'm really tired of sitting."

"Standing is hardly the proper place for a woman in your position." He motioned to the chair.

"You mean *of* my position."

"No, I meant *in* your position. You see, you're in no position to negotiate or give orders."

With snake-like speed, he grabbed her wrist. With a simple and well-practiced motion he twisted her arm in such a way that she fell into his chair and into the bindings.

"We can make this simple and end all the hostility now." The associate handed him another briefcase. This one really was a briefcase filled with papers and stuff.

"How do you propose we do that?"

"You simply tell me what I want to know."

"I see, I give you what you want and then you just kill me. Right?"

"Chani, Chani," he said. "You don't mind if I call you Chani, do you? Or would you prefer I call you Ms. Solomon? I am a civilized man. Once I have what I came for, I will have no reason to *harm you further.*"

She struggled against the straps binding her to his chair. "I don't have what you want. I know you must have already searched the room. You know it's not here. One of those goons following me got it a long time ago."

"You'll tell me when you're ready. We'll see what kind of resistance you have."

"Who are you with? Are you one of Elkhed Perkin's cronies?"

"Who?" he asked. "Oh, heaven's no. I work for Rithel Bartlemist. Some lovely little items were stolen from his private collection by an employee. They aren't actually that valuable, mind you, but he does have a certain sentimental attachment to them. Mr. Bartlemist has a sizable reward out for his objects. Should you be the one to recover them for him, I am certain you would be impressed by his generosity."

"You're not with the phone company?" She sighed.

"No, of course not."

"If there's a reward for the return of his objects, why don't you get it?"

"My dear, I am on retainer. I am not eligible to benefit from Mr. Bartlemist's generosity. However, once they are recovered, I will receive quite a sizable bonus. You, however, could certainly benefit financially, as well as by simply having the opportunity to continue breathing tomorrow. It would take some time for you as a phone company engineer to accrue to the amount of funds you could earn by simply returning to Mr. Bartlemist that which is, by all rights, his." He paused. "It occurs to me that my manners are severely lacking. Let me introduce myself. I am Caron Kitilon, also called in some circles The Mouth, although I feel the moniker is a bit exaggerated. My worthy assistant here is Victor."

Victor waved Kitilon's weapon at her, since there was little room to do otherwise. He will be helping me, as necessary."

"You're the one who killed Tyrus."

"Let me correct you. I never actually touched your associate in a hostile manner. After a fashion he simply began to suffer from spontaneous brain hemorrhages. Not a pretty sight. And while you may have problems accepting my word as gospel, you may accept that in my vast experience as a procurer of information, I have never harmed anyone who willingly divulged complete and truthful information."

Kitilon settled into a small couch Victor had just assembled, examining an expensive cigar as he droned on. He leaned deep into the cushy back, crossed his legs, and paused for a moment to closely examine the chalk outline next to him.

Victor simply stood next to the door with his arms crossed.

With the two men, the new couch and padded recliner, there was virtually no room to move.

"Did I tell you I fought in the war?" he asked. "Yes, I did. I was captured by the Mirikians early in the conflict."

He paused to draw from the cigar and exhaled a parade of tiny smoke ringlets.

"Of course, I never would have joined the military had it not been for my father. He was quite a boor, as I recall. He was terribly uncivilized. I could never understand how my mother could continue to live with a man that drank Chardonnay with red meat.

"And his expectations were most unrealistic. He must have told me a thousand times about having to fly a thousand kilometers to school. You wouldn't believe the hardships that I, myself, was forced to endure.

"When I was growing up, my father was diplomat to a planet called Lepus Zeta. We lived there during most of my teenage years. They were terribly uncivilized people, but despite their primitive nature they were extremely clean. They bathed five or six times a day. It seems that they had been receiving some form of foreign aid from planets in the Galway system. The day I arrived they stripped me naked and threw me in a vat of soap."

As he spoke those words, a pink nose peeked out from under the bunk and then Ivan slowly emerged.

"What have we here?" Kitilon asked. "What a handsome creature. Let's see. Where was I? Oh, yes. They bathed five or six times a day, interestingly enough, much like a cat."

Ivan wandered next to Kitilon and rubbed back and forth against the cuffs of his pants. White fur clung to the sharply tailored fabric.

"He's going to get hair all over your clothes," Chandra warned.

"No matter. I used to have a cat when I was a boy," Kitilon said with a brush of the hand that Ivan took as an invitation. He jumped up in the assassin's lap, circled a few times and lay down facing Chandra.

"Some protector you are," she told the cat.

"Did I tell you about him?" Kitilon asked. "His name was Rover. I can't recall why we called him Rover except that he always came when my father whistled. He had short fur with black and brown stripes. He had this preoccupation with feet. Quite disgusting when you think about it, don't you think? Now, where was I?

"Oh, yes. They bathed frequently; not unlike a cat, eh, fellow?" He scratched Ivan's chin idly. "It was a relatively safe environment except occasionally, around their holidays, they had the unfortunate habit of sacrificing a number of visitors to their gods of the circle. I saw many a chap come and go, and many of them disappeared as a result of that most undignified ritual..."

After several hours, Chandra's eyes began to glaze over; her breathing shallowed.

How much more can I take? she wondered. And he hasn't even gotten to the war stories yet.

"I was sent to a school for alien boys. We devised a plan to steal a vessel and fly back to our various home worlds. It took us months to perfect the plan, but the scheme was foiled when one of our boys forgot to bathe and the boogers smelled him. Damn their noses, anyway..."

Suddenly, the cabin door flew open and crashed back against the bulkhead.

"I've got you now!" a familiar voice shouted.

Simultaneously Chandra, Kitilon and Victor all turned toward the noise.

Chandra yawned a number of times as she watched the show taking place in the doorway.

Elkhed Perkins stared at Chandra, a crazed expression worn into his face. Even through her Kitilon-induced dementia, he looked as he always had except for the dark crescents beneath his eyes and the worry ditches outlining his face. He held an IGB issue weapon that he moved from victim to victim.

"Young man," Kitilon chided, unruffled. "This is a private party. I'm afraid you'll have to seek your entertainment elsewhere."

"I don't want entertainment," he snarled. "I want her." He pointed at Chandra.

"Is that all?" Kitilon asked. "Well, if you'll just sit down and wait your turn, you can have her when I'm through."

"I want her now," Perkins said. He pointed the weapon at Kitilon. "You're going to hand her over to me and leave this room."

Victor, who had been standing quietly by the door, took Perkins' gun and tapped on his shoulder.

"I don't think so," Victor said.

Kitilon raised his eyebrows and motioned to the bunk. When he didn't move, Victor tapped him with his own gun and pointed at the bed. Reluctantly, Elkhed sat.

"Now, where was I before we were so rudely interrupted?" Kitilon asked. "Oh yes. The Mirikians captured me while I spied on their tribe for associates in Ubarea. Pitiless beings, with no feeling and treacherous torture techniques..."

Chandra began to cough.

Kitilon went into details about the war, his incarceration by the enemy, his flower garden. As he droned on the expression seeped away from her face and the will to live began to drain from her soul. The more he talked, the larger her eyes bulged.

He failed to neglect his tales of fighting against an aboriginal tribe on the armpit of Orion, Betelgeuse, and a fine bottle of wine he purchased at an auction on Antares.

Kitilon continued hour after endless hour.

After everything she had been through, this was how she would die. So close to her goal. Almost fulfilling Tyrus' final instructions.

While he droned on about the long marches the enemy forced him to endure, Chandra's thoughts turned to Tyrus in his final moments. Did he beg for mercy as she wanted to? Would he have given in had he only known where the coveted items were stashed?

"I built a space station made of toothpicks. It took me years to construct. It was five hundred to one scale. One day I was shocked to find that one of my employer's contractors had organized a party without my permission. By the time I finally discovered the soiree, they had dismantled five years' worth of work and used it to clean their teeth."

Chandra's eyes glazed and she started to develop an irregular tick in her left cheek.

Kitilon's incessant talking was starting to take its toll. Thrashing her head about, she coughed and struggled against the bindings.

Across the room Perkins, too, seemed to be affected by the assassin's incessant babble.

"This is ridiculous. I don't have time for this," Perkins sprang to his feet and waved his weapon at Kitilon. "Now, hand her over to me!"

Kitilon drew on his cigar. "Mr...?"

"Perkins," the phone company executive filled in the blank.

"Ah, yes, Mr. Perkins. You will just have to wait until I am finished with her. Then and only then, will you have the opportunity to air your disagreement with Ms. Solomon."

Chandra coughed a few times and smiled briefly at her co-worker.

"Now, Chandra, did I tell about the time..." He launched into another tale. "...she actually had a splendid sense of humor despite the extra nose..."

Chandra struggled with her restraints. "Noooo. No more. Please, no more. Maybe the others can take this, but I can't. You can have it!"

"Excuse me?"

"I'll tell you where it is. Just shut up."

He thought for a moment. "I haven't told you the story of my bout with Rigelian Hemorrhagic Fever or my long-time friend Miss Pristine Clipmouse."

"No, shut up. Shut up. Shut up. It's..." She stopped and looked at Perkins, who had begun to tremble uncontrollably. "But, I won't tell you if he's listening."

Kitilon carefully moved the sleeping Ivan to the bunk next to Perkins. The cat's ears flattened and he hissed.

Kitilon approached the recliner and leaned closer to Chandra. "Very well. Tell me quietly."

"It's in the exercise room. Look in bin marked body enhancements. But there's something else I think you should know."

"And what is that?"

"Remember that botched long-range communications satellite Rithel had installed recently?"

"I do. It was a most disappointing disaster."

"That's right. Without the boost of that satellite, his signals could never make it to our Ultra long lines."

"What's your point?"

"That he was forced to make do with substandard

communications. It took longer, cost more, and looked and sounded like shit through a strainer. Bartlemist had to resort to working with travel agents."

"Quite true. Rithel Bartlemist lost a fortune in lost revenues, delayed deliveries, and missed deadlines as a result. His own wholesale suppliers failed to deliver products. It devastated the party goods and office furniture divisions of Bartlemist, Ltd. The company had to find new supplies-uh-sources from which to fill orders at a substantially higher price. Costs have soared and stock prices plummeted into the galactic trash dumpster."

"Okay. You've got the idea." She nodded her head in Perkins direction. "Well, this is the guy responsible for that cheesy equipment and the poor engineering. See, I was supposed to do the Bartlemist installation myself and then begin the ultra-long-lines installation on Distress. He sent me to Bitter first just to line his own pockets."

Kitilon held out his hand toward his cohort. "Victor will check the accuracy of your revelation. Victor."

Victor continued to stare straight ahead mouthing words to himself. This time Kitilon increased the volume. His accomplice did not respond. Finally he threw a box of toothpicks at Victor.

"Huh?" Victor pulled the plug from his ear. "You want something?"

"She told us where the items are. I need you to retrieve them."

Kitilon handed the notepad to his aid.

Victor pulled the plug from his other ear as he rose from Chandra bunk. "Sure, boss." He tossed Kitilon the gun and sauntered out the door humming the ancient show tune, "I Enjoy Being a Girl."

"Ask him," she told Kitilon quietly. "He doesn't know who you are. I bet he'll even brag about it."

"Here you go," Victor tossed the orb to Kitilon. He caught it with his left hand.

The torturer examined it. "Plain. Isn't it? Who could imagine that anything so common-appearing could cost so much?"

"Here's the other one."

Kitilon caught it with his right despite the fact that it was two half-fingers short of being a full hand.

"You made me a promise," Chandra reminded him.

"So I did." He reached over and released the fasteners that held her in place. "You are free to go."

"Wait a minute. This is my cabin."

"You may have it back later. I am still in need of it for a while."

"What about Ivan." She pointed at the cat.

"He seems to be content here. And he is safe."

Chandra grabbed a book out of her tote and darted through the door with Perkins hot on her trail. Perkins' legs kept moving, but the rest of him came to a fast stop.

Victor's hand clamped down around his shoulder.

"Wait, Mr. Perkins," Kitilon said. "I'd like to talk to you for just a moment."

The Manhattan Project she ordered was dry, so dry she thought she could spit out sand. But it trickled down her throat stinging only mildly. The bartender set down a basket of munchies. Instinctively she reached for a tidbit, then hesitated.

"Does madam have a problem?"

"What's that?" She coughed a few times and then pulled a pair of sub-sonic plugs from her ears.

He pointed at the different finger foods. "This is the ship's specialty: Quell jambalaya and that's the customary quell."

"Oh, of course."

"Sautéed in a light wine sauce over a soft flame until the skin just barely crackles."

She could hear the tiny squeak of the quell the day this nightmare began. She could smell every disgusting molecule of stench in the Corvian's breath and cringed at the thought of the Pictorian who paid for her drink.

"Take them away. I'd like a hamburger."

He picked up a hand full of drink glasses and began to juggle them. "May I suggest a nice Quellburger with all the trimmings?"

"I don't think so."

"How about some nice Quellaroni?" Without missing a beat he grabbed one of the glasses he was juggling and balanced it on his nose.

She tried picturing the dish. "No, thank you. I enjoy a meal so much more when it stays down. "Let me guess: you were a juggler."

"What tipped you off?"

Finally the intergalactic version of her preferred meal arrived courtesy of the fastest growing chain food company ever. From the beginning the dish was suspect.

One bite reminded her why, when she had a choice between dining at McDonald-Douglas and Mom's greasy spoon, she almost quit eating food entirely and started with subcutaneous vitamin injections.

Across the room a gigantic slab of ice stood encased in a translucent box. Frozen inside was "Comedians on Ice," the best of Twentieth Century Earth's formerly live entertainer, Rodney Dangerfield, who had been around the galaxy one too many times.

From the speaker blared some jokes that Chandra had heard in some of the old television broadcasts she could sometimes intercept while working in space. "I don't get no respect," said a voice from a speaker attached to the box about the size of an antique phone booth.

"I hear it was hard to get the ice to freeze," the barman whispered so as not to interrupt the performer. "All that hot air escaping from the body kept melting it. By the way, Henny Youngman will be on in a few hours."

When the bus-thing came to pick up her uneaten dinner, the hamburger slid off the plate and onto the deck, causing a nasty dent in the floor.

"Sorry 'bout the noise," the thing said. "It was heavier than it looked."

"Just bring me another Manhattan Project and something semi-digestible."

"Sure thing."

Several times that afternoon Chandra tore herself away from the Cryo Comedians to make her way back to her cabin so she could feed Ivan, but the familiar drone of Kitilon crescendoed into an Aria of Perkins' tortured screams. Poor Ivan would just have to wait.

"Back again," the bartender asked. "Don't you ever sleep?"

"I can sleep any time," she said. "But this is a once in a lifetime chance. I want to experience every moment I can."

"On this cruise? You must be kidding? I've had more fun on the way to a cemetery."

Recalling her co-worker's screams she said, "Me, too. One last Manhattan Project, you know, for the hall."

"Sorry, three per day's the limit."

"Then bill it to my room."

"I can't."

"All right, here." She handed him her credit chip.

"No, with the galactic shortage each passenger is allotted only a certain number of drinks per day. Some cruise lines are stricter than that."

"Does this ship run on Galactic Central Time?"

"Sure does."

"Well, I work off of Earth Alcohol Time and there it's tomorrow already. So since its tomorrow now I'll have my yesterday's drink tomorrow. See?"

He looked at his watch. "Okay."

As he set her Manhattan Project down, she asked, "When is Youngman performing?"

"I just heard he's canceled the rest of his performances," the barkeep said sadly. "His compressor broke and he started to melt. But don't worry, Dangerfield will be back in about thirty minutes with an all-new show."

She grabbed her drink and commandeered a recliner at the far end of the room where a television hologram played to only an audience of bacteria.

It could have been only a few minutes, or she could have slept several hours. Chandra didn't know, but she awoke to the sound of explosions and the shock of discovery that the solid molecules that used to be her chair had suddenly turned to air and then instantly became hard deck.

The bar-thing rushed over to her.

"The word is the *Redhead* has been hijacked. You have to go to an escape pod."

He tried to lead her to a door on the other side of the bar, but she struggled against his firm grip.

"Not yet," she said. "There's something in my cabin I can't leave."

"You have to go to a pod. There's not enough room for everyone. If you don't go now, there may not be a pod left for you. Nothing is worth your life."

She wiggled free of his grip.

"Thanks, but it's really not so much what but who. I'll be okay. Promise."

He watched as she disappeared out the door.

Tortured screams could be heard all the way down the corridor. Elkhed was still paying for his transgressions.

Taking a deep breath, she opened the door and walked casually into the room.

"I hate to bother you guys, but I just have to grab a few things before the ship explodes."

Stuff flew through the air and miraculously much of it landed in the duffel bag. The creation plant and especially Ivan could prove to be more challenging.

"Why ever do you lug that plant and cat with you?" Kitilon asked.

"It's a religious observance," she said. "The plant reminds me of the beauty of creation and the blood the cat sheds from me reminds me of penance I must do for an evil life I've led."

She tried to stuff Ivan in the bag headfirst and then tailfirst, but found herself the recipient of enough penance to cover the next ten years. Through the shrieking ruckus he raised, Ivan also tried to verbally remind her that in his book, Chandra's rank fell somewhere between used kitty litter and a dried hairball.

After the tote successfully dropped over the irate Turkish Van, it turned into an animated lifeform of its own, like a loud, active giant amoeba.

Kitilon turned back to Perkins. "This reminds me of the time..."

Joining in on Ivan's chorus, Elkhed started to scream again.

"Aren't you leaving?" she asked Kitilon.

He checked his chrono. "Not yet. My ride is only just arriving."

With the writhing tote slung over her shoulder, she headed for the door.

There was only an eerie silence, save the hum of pumps maintaining the air locks. No being was around. Nothing remained but the empty pads outside the emergency exits.

Down the corridors, the sounds of fighting drew ever closer. Further along the docking bays even the small dinghies used for planetary excursions had already taken flight.

Staring at the empty rows of docking bays, she said to the angry tote bag, "So after all we've been through, this is how it's going to end. This is all *your* fault."

"Roooow," the sack screamed.

From behind, someone tapped on her shoulder. "Some people have no faith."

"Wright!" She swung around and hugged him.

"Let's get out of here." He took the thrashing and slashing bag from her and headed down the corridor. "These guys're in a real bad mood."

As she trailed behind him she asked, "How did you find me?"

"I knew you were still on the ship cuz I figured if you made the escape pod you would have been able to encrypt the emergency beacon."

Another tremor shook the vessel and the bulkheads at the end of the corridor began to buckle. *I.M.A. Redhead* creaked and moaned like the dying diva she had become.

"We gotta get out of here," Chandra said.

Wright pointed in the opposite direction of the hubbub. "The ship's just a few docking bay's in that direction." He took her duffel bag and picked up his pace.

The dock doors slid sluggishly open and she found herself greeted by a ship very similar to Wright's old *Blind Faith*. Same make and model, but this one looked newer. No meteor dings or space dust caked on the belly. It even sparkled in the artificial light.

Down the corridor the *Redhead's* shell groaned with stress. It wouldn't be long before the outer hull was compromised.

"Open," Wright told the ship.

It complied with his order; the hatch slid up with a quick whoosh and dropped shut smoothly once they were inside. The control panel had a polished, shiny-clean look. No thick layers of dust, not a single empty food container to be found, just a newly forming pile of dirty clothes in the copilot's seat. It even had that new ship smell.

"Nice ship." She plopped down at Ivan's copilot station and reached for the harness. "What do you call it?"

"*Blind Faith.*"

"You mean *Blind Faith II*?"

"No. I mean *Blind Faith*. I sold it to a junk dealer and by the time I got to the Good Deal Used Speedster lot they'd completely refurbished it. If I'd known they could do this with it I'd of trashed it years ago. Of course, it smells a little funny, but we'll have that back to normal in no time."

Chandra set down the wiggling tote bag and opened it up.

Ivan jumped out, stared at her and hissed his opinion of all the inconvenience and indignities she had put him through.

"Here." Wright handed her Ivan's collar and the orb. "Bet you'd like these back."

She replanted the orb in the creation plant pot, but she stopped short of restoring Ivan's collar to its rightful place. "I wonder how long it'll take them to figure out what I gave them came from that gypsy on Galway? If your plan hadn't worked you could have lost your best friend." She nodded at the cat.

Wright pushed a button that opened *Redhead's* bay doors by remote control. "Naw. If it hadn't worked I'd have lost my *two* best friends."

Before she could say anything the doors had yawned wide enough to give the ship clearance, and Wright punched the throttle. The ship lunged forward, out into the darkness of open space. He activated the pre-programmed coordinates in the navicom. "Next stop, Rasalhague."

Chapter Twenty-Four

The aromas of heavily spiced food mingled with the expensive perfumes of the Rasalhague elite in the crowded chamber. Of course, custom furniture and party decorations from the fine warehouses of Mr. Rithel Bartlemist adorned the hall.

Chandra, dressed in her beaded blue and gold gown, shadowed Wright's every movement.

Wright sported his smartly pressed day coat, strangely devoid of white cat hairs. Around his neck he wore several medals hanging by brightly-colored ribbons, decorations awarded for his achievements by numerous heads of planets, heads of state, and other talking heads.

"What kind of security do they have here?" Chandra asked.

"They have detectors that can sense a charge in a light pistol as well as numerous other weapons. You don't have anything to worry about. The chancellor's security is tops. Real pros. They don't like me a bit. So they must be good," Wright said.

"Why haven't I been arrested for having my Personal Protection?"

"They use a special screen that prevents energy bursts from working in the presence of the chancellor."

She tugged at her sleeve. "You're sure they won't arrest me?"

"Naw. You'll be fine."

Except I'm unarmed, she thought, but smiled and kept her reservations to herself.

"There's the chancellor and his two lovely wives. The others must have stayed home." He bowed deeply as Rasalhague III's leader strode by with his entourage of wives and security in tow. The chancellor wore an anatomically correct breastplate on the outside of his military uniform, with epaulets on the shoulder giving him a kind of ridiculous Roman/Italian look. His girth measured as wide as he stood tall and when he moved Chandra had difficulty telling if he was walking or rolling.

His wives were just smaller versions of the chancellor without the breastplate and epaulets. Their shimmery gowns flowed like foamy waves behind them as they motored through the ballroom. Beside the royal family marched the platoon of heavily armed guards, just begging an intruder to try to get through all that fat.

As the party passed them, Chandra bowed, but kept her eyes roving to monitor the other guests and their activities.

"Stay here," Wright ordered. "I'm going to have a private talk with the Chancellor about your situation. I bet we can have you on a heavily armed hyperlight cruiser bound for Fomalhaut before the end of the party. I'll be back in a few minutes."

She grabbed his arm as he tried to walk away. "Wright, don't leave me alone. I have a bad feeling."

He surveyed the room. "Come on. Chani, let me introduce you to a good friend of mine. The ambassador from Zubenelgenubi. Hey, Ramsbotm. How ya been, buddy?" With Chandra trailing closely behind him Wright walked over to the ambassador, who towered well above them both. His school bus-colored skin had a slight glow in the room's bright lights. No doubt a desired effect planned by Wright himself when he designed the room.

Ramsbotm gazed down at him. "Wright Aulweighs. It has been long since we have met."

"Yeah, a long time. How's the bomb shelter holding up?"

"I need to have the radioactivity screen purged. But I'm in no rush now. Right now we're not at war with anyone."

"Well, it's only a matter of time before you change that." Wright slapped him on the back. On many other creatures that would have been on the shoulder, but on Ramsbotm, Wright could reach no higher than the waist. "A few more years, and you'll be bombing the hell out of Zubenschamali. You'll be at full blown war and then both your economies will improve."

"We can only hope."

"Immenseness, I want you to meet a good friend of mine, Chandra Solomon. Chani, this is His Great Immenseness Ramsbotm ruler of all Zubenelgenubi. I know you've heard of him. Ramsbotm, keep an eye on her for me. She's a little nervous. Having a bad day and all. Ya' know, you might want to listen to her. She's a communications specialist. Might be able to help you with those Schamalis nuking your communications satellites."

"I see," Ramsbotm said. "What is your company?"

"Funny you should ask, Your Great Immenseness…"

Across the ballroom a Corvian refilled the lake-shaped punch bowl with the little bilge pumping boat. Like the other servants, he wore a white jacket, slightly too small but still in an extra, extra, extra large size. All night he had walked around with an empty hor d'oeuvres tray, waiting for his quarry to make her appearance. In the meantime, he pumped the potent refreshment into the miniature lake of punch and turned on a circulator to keep the liquor from settling to the bottom. Occasionally, he circled the ballroom to inventory the guests and offer drinks and petits four from a cart. Beneath a cloth covering the cart lay an old projectile-style pistol with a silencing muffler over the barrel. Its reputation portrayed it as having the accuracy and killing power of the Queen's Navy, although the manufacturers completely neglected to mention which queen or what navy.

Unobserved by the guests, the Corvian watched Chandra and Ramsbotm. Try as he might he couldn't get a clear shot. Every time he lined up Chandra in his sights, another guest inadvertently wandered past.

He watched like a vulture in the desert, who after days of waiting for carrion said, "Patience, hell. I'm going to kill something."

Suddenly he had a clear shot at his target. He grabbed the pistol and aimed.

"So, you think if I change the orbit of the Tester satellite, I'll get less interference from the radioactive emissions from the planet?" the ambassador asked.

"It won't completely eliminate it, but it should help," Chandra said.

"What wonderful news. May I bring you something to drink?" he asked.

He clapped his hands together, turning in front of her toward the lake of intoxication.

Pfft.

Ramsbotm cried out and toppled over backward. A stain of blood blossomed on his chest, spreading from a fist-sized point-of-entry to rapidly stain his entire shirtfront crimson.

"Your Great Immenseness? Ramsbotm?" She looked up in time to see the Corvian punch bowl attendant toss the weapon into the hands of a passerby and dash out the door. The surprised guest with dozens of medals, ribbons and sashes cluttering his military uniform, stared at the pistol, then gasped as other bystanders wrestled him to the ground.

A glance told Chandra that Ramsbotm was beyond help. She slipped out the front door.

"I need transportation," she said to the parking attendant. "I'm not feeling well and I can't find my escort." She jotted down a quick note on the back of the valet's log. "Please see to it that Wright Aulweighs gets this. It's very important." She handed him a credit.

An aristocratic speedster rolled up and the valet opened the side door for Chandra. She gave the driver his instructions and the long black speedster bolted out of sight.

Chapter Twenty-Five

Chandra opened the hatch to *Blind Faith* and ran onto the main deck as quickly as her evening gown permitted. Dropping into the captain's chair, she studied the control board. "Ivan, wherever you are, get ready," she yelled to the invisible cat. "We're taking off."

"Not yet," a voice behind her said.

"Shit." Chandra didn't have to look for him; she could smell him. When she turned around she found the Corvian mercenary with his pistol trained on her chest.

"You again?" she said. "Sapiens!"

"Where are they?"

She moved slowly, keeping her hands in view of the intruder. "I don't know. I gave them to Caron Kitilon a long time ago. Go talk to Rithel Bartlemist."

He grunted and motioned with the pistol. "That is why you are leaving?"

"No. I'm leaving cuz one of your friends just tried to kill me. Why won't you guys leave me alone?"

"You have the object." The Corvian stretched out his palm as if he was holding an invisible ball. "I want it. I have heard that Kitilon retrieved the wrong items. Rithel very angry."

"Did you ever think that Kitilon might have kept the real thing himself?"

"No. Not after Rithel got done with him—Rithel don't waste time talking."

Ivan jumped down from the turret onto the main deck with a *thunk*. The Corvian swung around to face the new intruder, his pistol seeking the source of the noise. Seeing only a cat, he spun back toward Chandra...and found her Personal Protection trained on him from under the sleeve of her evening gown.

"It's charged and set for kill," she said. "I don't want to have to use it. This place is finally quasi-clean and I don't want you stinking it up again. Now drop yours."

"I will gladly hand it to you." He took a step toward her, holding the weapon out in a submissive gesture.

"Drop it— there."

"The safety malfunctions. It might fire and damage the ship. Here, I will give it to you." He took another step toward her. It brought him too close for comfort, both safety-wise and nasally.

"Don't move at all. Put the weapon down right there." She pointed to the deck with her free hand.

During that instant he lunged toward her. She fired her protector at his leg. A pillar of smoke rose from the wound. He fell, but kept the pistol trained on Chandra.

"Where is it?" he demanded.

"All right." Sighing, she lowered her arm. "If you find it, will you leave me alone?"

"Yes. On my word as an officer in the Corvian Merchant Slag Fleet."

"I bet that's worth a lot. Okay. It's beside you," she said.

"Where?"

"On the cat's collar. It was the safest place I could find. Don't move. Just blow on the fur around his neck and you'll see it."

The Corvian curled his lips and blew his fetid breath at Ivan. Wisps of white coat lifted, exposing a small piece of the azure crystal. "It *is* there."

Ivan hissed and moved away from him.

"Yes," she said. "Just take the collar off of him and you can have it. But remember, you promised my safety."

He nodded readily and reached for Ivan, who took another step backward. The Corvian lunged forward, grabbing the cat by the scruff of the neck. Ivan screamed as he whipped around lashing and thrashing and removing chunks of the Corvian's face and uniform. The mercenary released the cat, but too late. Ivan had shredded his hands. He dropped his pistol.

Chandra dashed over and kicked the Corvian's pistol past Ivan, who sauntered a few steps away and began to bathe the Corvian smell off his immaculate coat. Tiny bits of dark thread from the Corvian's sleeve still remained caught in his claws.

Chandra steadied her weapon on her opponent. "Move to the door."

The Corvian blinked, and complied reluctantly, dragging his injured leg behind him. As his oversized feet shuffled for the hatch, his long toenails clicked against the deck.

"Open it."

He complied, but suddenly he spun back around to face her. Chandra fired her Personal Protection again. The beam hit the alien's upper arm, instantly the cabin filled with a horrific cry and the aroma of fricasseed Corvian.

Ivan hissed and ran back to the turret.

"Sapiens. The cat box smells bad enough, I'm not going to put up with you stinking up the place any more. Out," she commanded. "Get out, you bug-eating slug."

He stumbled to the door, a mass of blood and pain. As he left Chandra slammed the hatch, careful to lock it. She returned to the controls.

She programmed the nav computer. Now that it had been reconditioned she felt a little more confident of winding up at Fomalhaut.

She began her checklist. "Hydraulics, navigation—yeah, electronics, structure-right, communications, maneuvering systems—check." Everything appeared functional. "Engines fully charged. Oh, bloody, hell. No they're not. Sapiens. Wright turned the engines off." She reversed the charge on the outside hull to discourage intruders and initiated the power-up sequence. It would take a few minutes.

While she waited she ran up to the turret and changed back into her flight suit. She returned just in time to hear the buzzer tell her the sequence had been complete.

As quickly as she could Chandra strapped herself into the captain's chair. Glancing over her shoulder at Ivan, she said, "Ivan, you'd better go to your seat, cuz we can't wait for Wright."

Big amber eyes blinked at her.

"Don't worry. You'll see him again, I hope. Come on. Let's go."

As if he understood, Ivan hopped into Chandra's comfortable lap. He circled a few times and then settled down for a nap. A soft purr rose from his throat.

Chandra gave him a wary scratch behind the ears. She punched the ignition button. *Blind Faith's* engines roared beneath her. That was all. They just roared. She checked over the gauges. "Now what's wrong?"

An obnoxious buzzer went off. The perimeter alarm. Someone was approaching. Outside camera showed some heavily armed men she had never seen before.

Don't panic.

Carefully, Chandra readjusted the fuel allocator and reprogrammed the ignition sequence. The vessel's engines struggled.

The intruders drew closer. Whatever make of rifle they carried, it looked powerful enough to take out her entire power system.

She reset the system and started the checklist procedure once more. This time the engines sounded different. "Is that good or bad?"

Outside, the men aimed their weapons at the vulnerable power station underneath the fuselage.

She slapped the power on. For a moment Chandra held her breath. The ship shuddered violently as it struggled into the air. No more than ten meters off the ground, Chandra felt a warm sensation spread across her lap, accompanied by Ivan's frenzied yowl.

"Aw, Sapiens." She pushed the frightened cat off of her wet lap. "Ivan, how could you?"

Once they reached escape velocity, he settled down and jumped back into his own *dry* chair. Still, *Blind Faith* lurched painfully up against Rasalhague's gravity. The ship felt as though it were being ripped apart.

Chandra set the ship on autopilot, stood up, and scowled at the embarrassed feline. "You make one decent gesture and then you have to go and spoil it."

Ivan stared back at her defiantly and blinked once. He started to bathe the base of his tail.

"You could at least act a little apologetic."

He ignored her.

"Well you *did* save my life and you *did* protect the crystal. For that I'm grateful. But just remember, Ivan, I'll get you for this."

She grabbed one of Wright's dirty shirts and swabbed the cat pee from her flight suit and the deck.

When she had cleaned up, she returned to the navicom. "If I understand the navigation system, we're about three days from Fomalhaut...How do you feel about attending the Feast of Fat Bore?"

Ivan yawned.

"I guess you've got the right idea."

She finished entering the coordinates. "We're going to be

going into hyperlight in a few minutes. You can't sit on my lap again, so I suggest you get ready. Me, I find it bloody uncomfortable." She checked her safety harness fasteners. "Here goes!"

Chapter Twenty-Six

After his conversation with the Chancellor, Wright grabbed a drink and then ambled back into the main ballroom where he found the chancellor watching some commotion. His Great Immenseness Ramsbotm laid sprawled on the floor, stone dead, though he appeared so life-like that he might have jumped up and complained that the drinks tasted watered down. Not much chance of that, though, with that hole in his chest nicely showcasing the elegant stone floor beneath him. His fingers remained wrapped around the stem of the glass and a stain of liquor spoiled the sleeve of what had been an immaculate royal uniform.

"Wright, old fellow." The chancellor beckoned to him. "Pity you didn't get to visit with the old boy again. Nice sort. Have you seen your lady lately?"

Wright shook his head and looked around. "I don't see her. As I told you, she's a bit jittery these days."

"My security chief wants to have a little chat with her. It seems that she and His Great Immenseness were involved in a conversation when this rather nasty event occurred."

Wright cringed. "She was?" He pretended to be shocked.

"It seems so. We have a good idea Ambassador Ripenall from Zubenschmali may have been the culprit, but Miss Solomon appears to be the only eyewitness. It's rather imperative we speak with her."

"Well then, Chancellor, we may have a problem. I don't see Chani anywhere. I'm afraid whoever offed ol' Ramsbotm may have snatched her."

"Pity," the chancellor said. "She sounded like a charming engineer." He cupped his hands in front of his chest. "Nice integrated circuits." Glancing at one of his servants wearing a low-cut uniform partially revealing the tops of three breasts, he said, "Though not quite enough circuits for my taste."

Wright stared at the Zubenschmali ambassador, who griped loudly about the lack of quality in the chancellor's party. "You think you could torture old Ripenall into telling us what he did with Chani?"

"Well, Aulweighs, that depends. What are your plans for the pyramid?"

"You find Chani and I'll build it."

"Supreme. Very well, we will see what we can do about extracting some information from him." The pair approached the swarm of officers surrounding the Zubenschmali ambassador.

"I didn't kill him," Ripenall protested. "If I had, I would have chosen a far more painful death. He would have lingered in agony for weeks. He got off far easier than that dog deserved."

Five soldiers surrounded the ambassador with high-powered light rifles with exaggeratedly long barrels. The commanding officer grabbed the ambassador by his collar. "If you didn't do it, then who did?"

"I don't know. A servant ran past me and handed me the weapon. I'd never seen him before. Ugly and green. Funny eyes. Bad smell. Go find him. It is time you cease this silliness and release me." The ambassador folded his arms across his chest.

"Where is he?" A very tall and equally broad woman in resplendent regal vesture stormed through the ballroom door, fists clenched.

A soldier pointed at Ramsbotm's body.

She stared at it for a few moments. "Ramsbotm, you've never looked better." Her Grandness Pyrobloya turned to the guard, who backed a safe distance from her. "Where is the Ambassador Ripenall?"

This time the soldier used his rifle to point at the circle of guards.

She nodded, and walked away in long business-like strides.

The soldier hurried after her, scrambling to keep from being entangled in the acres of red fabric billowing behind her. "I am sorry, Your Grandness," he said timidly. Her size and dress made her resemble an active volcano with legs. "No one is permitted to talk to the accused until we finish interrogating him. You'll have to wait."

She stared down at the guard. "By Jock's belches, I'm not waiting!" She pushed the muzzle of his rifle to the floor and confronted the accused. "Ripenall of Zubenschmali, as you have committed the aggrieved act of inflicting holes in our most tolerated leader My Royal Payne Ramsbotm, without the expressed permission of our ruling counsel or from me, which you would have had, had you only asked, I must conclude this is an act of war. Therefore, I will piss on your grave with both barrels as soon as I can arrange it."

Ripenall threw up his hands, which encouraged the guards to train their weapons with more intensity. "Your Grandness, while back on my world I would enjoy nothing more than the acclaim I would receive for cleaning up my sector by disposing of Your Royal Payne Ramsbotm, I fear the honor is not mine but some Corvian fed up with the activities of your most undistinguished race."

"What quarrel have Corvians with Ramsbotm?"

Standing a full head below her, Ripenall shook his head.

"Good Ambassador Ripenall, you have done the worlds of this galaxy a supreme favor by your action. For in murdering my poor beloved Ramsbotm, may scavengers starve on his tiny brains, you have guaranteed the destruction of your own unsavory world." She sent a glance at the highest-ranking guard. "Release him."

"What? We can't release him. He killed your husband and leader."

"I did not."

"I insist that he be returned to his own planet where our weapons will sauté the inhabitants into fondue for our farm animals." She turned to the ambassador. "This is a formal declaration of war. I expect you to inform your government. May you die only after many long hours of pain. Have a good day, Ambassador."

She departed the room in a last billowing of red fabric.

"Sir Aulweighs." One of the servants approached Wright. "Your young lady departed some time ago, just after the commotion broke out. She asked me to give you this. She said it was vital you receive it." He handed Wright a folded piece of paper containing a hand-scrawled note and held his hand out awaiting compensation.

Wright opened the letter and read it.

Dear Wright,
  I see that these dangers will follow me until I am

either dead or have delivered the products. My main concern is for you. I cannot allow all your kindness to be repaid with a light beam in the ribs. You will be safe in the company of the chancellor if I am not around. You will be safe nowhere if I stay.

I am not a thief but I must borrow Blind Faith. If I live, she will be returned to you. If not, then you have the right to litigious action against IGB. They are responsible for my actions, especially since they choose to deny me transportation. In this note you have proof that as an employee of IGC I have taken your vessel.

I wish I'd had a chance to get to know you better. I don't want anything to happen to you. I don't think I'd be very good for your health. People who hang around me tend to have short life spans. I guess I'm worse than cholesterol.

Thanks for all your help and your kindness. I'll never forget you.

Watch your back.
Chani

He reread it. She had gone. She took his ship and left him. What about Ivan? The note neglected to mention him.

Maybe I still have time to stop them!

He ran out the door toward the parking lot.

The air on Rasalhague III held less oxygen than he needed for a marathon run across the compound. But despite feeling winded and light-headed, he pushed on. When he arrived at the parking lot he puffed like a steam engine.

"I'm looking for *Blind Faith*," he gasped to the attendant.

"*Blind Faith*?" The old fellow scanned his log. "She lifted off twelve minutes ago. The lady said she had an emergency. Gave me all the right codes."

"I'll bet she did."

"She left something behind. It's alive but just barely."

His gut knotted. *Oh, no.* "Where is he?"

"It's over behind the shack." The guard pointed at a well-landscaped building barely large enough to hold Ivan much less the guard himself.

He dashed to the back of the shed. Only to find a bloody and fried Corvian moaning and breathing heavily.

"Is this it?" he asked. "Didn't she leave me anything else? A cat or a box with air holes?"

"Huh uh. Nothing else. Ditched ya, did she? Happens to me all the time."

"I'll bet it does," Wright said.

"The last one took my twenty year-old speedster and all my credit chips. Strange woman. You know she had breath that could curdle beer..."

The attendant continued to speak but Wright heard nothing. No voice, no words.

"She's gone," he whispered. "She didn't even say good-bye."

Chapter Twenty-Seven

Although only ten hours had passed, but it seemed like ten years. *Blind Faith* lacked the amenities that the telephone company transports had: entertainment facilities, relaxation facilities, exercise facilities. At least the refurbished *Blind Faith* included one comfort she craved: a working shower.

She unzipped her flight suit, which had taken on the penetrating aroma of cat pee. "Ivan, I'm going to take a shower. You take left seat until I get back. Okay?"

Ivan lay in his chair and lifted his head when he heard her voice. Seeing that she planned to offer him neither food or amusement, he dropped his head back onto his paws and closed his eyes.

Chandra checked the panel before she left. Everything looked right. Buttons and monitors that had never worked before, or at least not since she had begun to serve time aboard the ship, flashed and gave the appearance of functioning properly. The Sentinel, an old feature, stood watch among the rest of the components on the control panel. It scanned for any object that entered within 632,000 kilometers, the distance between the Earth and the moon, it would sound an alert. If anything came too close the ship would tell her.

Before jumping in the shower, herself, Chandra hosed the cat piss from her flight suit and hung it next to the electronic towel to dry. The towel was a wall of vents that blew warm air. It had the duel job of warming the room and blow-drying the person after the shower.

Chandra climbed into the shower and adjusted the water to as hot as she could stand. As showers went, it was not the Ritz, and it did not rank with the exclusive resorts in which she stayed while on phone company assignments. The medium-grade tile was covered with a clear sealant, and the floor coated with abrasive Slip-not tile. The drain emptied into a standard water reclamation unit that took all non-toxic liquid, filtered it, and returned it for non-consumption use.

The heat of the water streaming across her body made her feel safe; or at least gave her the illusion of safety. As the droplets massaged her, they rinsed away all the grime and grubbiness she had felt since Ivan's "accident." But like Lady MacBeth, the blood that vicariously stained her hands only faded with water, and the aroma of cat piss seemed to only diminish faintly.

Time melted away; had it been five minutes or two hours? She could not remember, nor for now did she care.

Suddenly something touched Chandra's foot. "Sapiens!"

She stumbled backward slamming against the wall and saved herself from falling only by grabbing the water spigot and nearly ripping it from the wall.

From outside the stall, Ivan reached in and pawed at the stream of water.

"Ivan, you almost gave me a heart attack. What are you doing here?"

He looked up and blinked at her as if to say, "What's your problem, lady?"

Convinced he had told her off, the Van returned his attention to his newly discovered wet toy. As he bit at the streams of water, tiny droplets collected on his whiskers. The tips of his fur gleamed like jewels in the heat lights above.

Chandra stepped out of the stall and dried off. "You can stay if you want. I'll program it to run for a few more minutes."

He continued to bite and swat at his liquid prey, stopping just long enough to bid her good-bye.

It had almost been a day since she left Wright behind. A long day with nothing to do and no one but Ivan to talk to. Chandra stared at the stark bulkhead.

"I can't stand it anymore," she told Ivan. "What does Aulweighs do when he's between places?"

Moving only his eyelids, Ivan eyed her momentarily, then returned to a hard-earned slumber. Underneath his paw one of Wright's unwashed socks stuck rigidly out of the pile.

Chandra kicked at it to see how much force was required to make it bend. It gave only slightly, then sprang back into place like a fabric tongue giving her the raspberry

"Maybe we can watch some tube," she suggested, halfway expecting an answer from her feline companion.

"Computer," she said. At her voice the computer screen

illuminated for a moment, then reverted to a star field. "Entertainment. Scan for anything exciting."

For most of the day "entertainment" took the form of holographic static, black and white fuzz dancing in a tornadic vortex around the flight deck. The static disappeared, but instead of being replaced by another hologram, the computer screen lit up. A ridiculous representation of a duck on a spring dropped down to the center of the screen. It held a sign that read: "complimentary."

"You just said today's magic word," said an odd-looking character wearing Groucho Marx nose and glasses. What a great disguise. If she had a pair of those, no one would ever recognize her, maybe. The man's own disguise was so good, she could hardly tell it was a get-up.

"Computer, is there a problem with the holographic projector?" she asked. "Why is this going to the screen?"

"This program does not contain holographic encoding," the computer told her in a normal computer voice devoid of personality or accent. "This broadcast is a direct feed from Earth."

At the speed of light that meant that the show had aired on Earth over two-hundred-and-twenty years ago. He was not wearing a Groucho disguise. He was Groucho.

"Computer, you got any new feeds or signals. I want to see what's happening now."

Soon the signal faded and once the center of the cabin displayed a three-dimensional image of a handsome man with perfect hair and perfect teeth having an argument with a woman, also with perfectly styled hair and teeth, wearing a very expensive dress. Next to them lay the man's dying lover. It was easy to tell she was dying. In addition to having perfect hair and teeth and wearing a beautifully fitting hospital gown, her face glowed and her makeup—perfect. She looked the picture of health; she must be dying.

"*As the Universe Turns*" will return after a message from our sponsors," said a sexy male voice.

"Mute!" Chandra yelled.

The commercial continued to spew across the deck.

"I said mute."

"The advertiser has a mute override," the computer explained. "This volume may not be lowered."

"Then change channels. Let's see what else is on. Bring

up the schedule."

On the screen appeared a schedule of the shows and rerun times and frequencies: *One After Life to Live, Fazer of Our Lives, Another Planet, The Guiding Quasar, Edge of Flight,* and *All My Pictorians.*

One title caught her eye. *The Young and the Weightless.* Soaps had never interested Chandra much, but there was nothing else to do. Even mindless entertainment was better than watching the light years click away on the nav panel.

"Hmmm. In a few minutes, *The Young and the Weightless* will be on. Either that or maybe *The Edge of Flight.* I know. How about *Orion's Hope*?"

A beautiful woman with immaculately styled hair and recently applied makeup and wearing a skimpy, perfectly pressed dress, gazed at a man who looked every bit as rugged and striking as Lance Goode. A tear trickled down her cheek without her mascara running. Breasts heaving, she rushed into his arms.

"My darling. I missed you so," she said.

"Did they harm you?" he asked

"Oh, Rush. It was dreadful."

"We thought you were dead," he said to her, so close and with such velocity his breath flowed through her ears and rippled the curtains just the other side of her face.

The well-endowed woman turned and faced the screen with a distraught expression. "When they weren't watching me I slipped out of their hideout. I lived in the caves with rats and ate maggots." She touched her perfectly painted lips.

"My precious, you've been through so much."

"Isn't there anything else on?" Chandra asked the computer.

Instead, the computer switched to *Galactic Hospital* where Lake and Lowra found themselves cornered by an angry mob of department store managers and were being flogged to death with marked down designer ties. Of course, this was the end of that episode. If she wanted to find out what happened to Lake and Lowra, she would have to tune in tomorrow, same time, same frequency.

Fat chance.

"Anything else on?"

The frequency changed to GNN. Monte Crandavelius, who

was momentarily interrupted by a network identification that bragged that Galactic News Network was not only the eyes and ears of the galaxy, but the feelers, too, droned on about the latest galactic catastrophes.

"...Scientists continue to be stumped by the unprecedented cases of space folding into itself in the far reaches of the universe. If the phenomena continues at its current rate of expansion it will begin to affect our galaxy later in the year.

"In other news, Galway, a planet long known for its soap-based economy has been thrust into turmoil by a planet-wide rebellion. As most sentient beings know, the planet's entire economic system depends on the sale of detergent and the recruitment of other salesthings. In recent years, the economy has grown stagnant due to the fact that everyone on the planet had been recruited into Galway as an independent sales contractor or worked directly for the corporation in the manufacturing division. Their problems were further compounded when surrounding star systems voted to quarantine Galway to prevent the spread of mental, social and economic disease.

"For unexplained reasons recently some Galwayans in the southern hemisphere threw down their sales pads and refused to attend any more meetings of indoctrination. From there the insurrections have grown to planetary proportions. Angry Galwayans buried the corporate office in a mountain of soap foam. We have a report live from the scene by Lance Goode."

Chandra's spine stiffened at the mention of the traitor's name. A spasm between her shoulders followed like a stab in the back.

How did he escape the Lucillians? she wondered.

Crandavelius's face faded, replaced by the strong jaw line and rugged features of Lance Goode. He had changed; the bruises and swollen eye miraculously had disappeared. So had his left arm. In its place there was an obviously prosthetic limb in a lavender hue with three stubby fingers and an opposable thumb. He had two other features that stood out: two enormous knockers. He tried to button his jacket, but the bulges couldn't be concealed.

"Shit!" the microphone picked up.

He stood up straight, folded his arms across his chest and said, "I'm standing outside the galactic headquarters of Galway. Just moments ago, rescue workers discovered one of the corporation's founders in the penthouse, dead. He had been cleaned to death by an angry mob armed with toilet bowl brushes.

"It seems that the rescue effort was hampered by the fact that the relief workers from a neighboring system refused to enter the planet's atmosphere until Galway officials signed an agreement not to try recruiting them or selling them soap. Once the safety of the rescuers was assured, they bravely landed on the planet to attempt to save as many they could.

"As you know, Monte, the Galway system has been quarantined for many years for fear that the direct-sales dementia might spread to other systems."

"Bastard!" Chandra yelled, looking for something to throw.

"The uprising has resulted in the loss of many Galwayans lives and the cleansing of the entire planet. Military reinforcements have been requested by the Galway Corporation, but like the rescuers, their safety must be assured before they will be permitted to enter orbit."

"Well, Lance, what does this mean to the people of the planet Galway?" Crandavelius asked.

"It means the loss of their dual deities. It may also mean an extensive rehabilitation of the economic structure of the entire planet. Only in those isolated pockets selling or trading off-world products on the black market will there be an immediate recovery. These sites may well become the new economic centers of the planet. With that in mind, nearby worlds may consider withholding military aid."

Behind him rescue workers set up a giant fan. They turned it on. It revolved slowly at first, then built up speed until it spun so rapidly the blades seemed to melt into the blue sky. Enormous clumps of soap foam released their grip on the building and lifted into the air. Once airborne, a gust of wind caught the bubble airship and carried it away. The camera remained focused on the bubbly clumps until they disappeared into the distance.

The camera returned to Lance, who was speaking to a longhaired local teenage girl. He brushed his hand across her cheek and oozed something about what he would like to show her.

"Live mike, you asshole," someone off-camera yelled.

Lance shoved the girl off screen, snapped erect, and straightened his jacket. "After the team has evaluated the extent of the damage, we will return with another update. Back to you, Monte."

"Thanks, Lance," Monte said.

Although the camera switched to Crandavelius, Goode's voice in the background yelled, "What the hell is wrong with you? Don't you know you're supposed to warn me before we come back to a live shot...You could have caught me picking my nose...What do you mean, the mike's still hot..."

Despite the fact that she had actually caused the trouble on Galway and she wanted to drop Lance Goode in a vat of Galway Vinyl-New, a product to make plastic personalities new, she ebbed in and out of sleep.

"Sapiens. Any music available?"

A familiar three-D laser display writhed on the deck accompanied by the unforgettable tune of Betelgeuse Onion Repair and their heavy metal Gregorian chant.

"...Cheek to cheek," chanted the rocker followed by a percussive boom bomp ba bom. Boom bomp ba baba.

"...They mooned at the dance..." Boom bomp ba bom. Boom bomp ba baba.

"...illigitimi non carborendum..." Boom bomp ba bom. Boom bomp ba baba."

"Geeze, again!" Chandra complained. "Got anything else?"

A different image appeared on the floor. A guy with perfect hair and a tool belt just like Chandra's stood high atop a transmission tower singing, "...and Galactic lineman, is still on the liiinnnneeeee."

"That's better."

Chandra put her feet on the console, humming along to the voyeuristic exploits of a fellow deep space telephone company lineman. "I know I need a small vaa-caaation..." she sang almost on pitch with the holographic crooner. "But working here's a real paaiin. And if that meteor shower hits, lines'll never sta-and the straaiin..."

"Sing it again, baby," she said. "I've been there, too."

About that time Ivan padded up to his chair. Only the ends of his fur were damp. He jumped up into the copilot's post and shook the water droplets from his coat.

"...And I need you more than want yoouu. And I want you at warp niiinnne."

Ivan held his head up and glared at her.

"...and Galactic lineman, is still on the liiinnnneeeee."

Smiling at Ivan, Chandra wailed louder and intentionally even more out of tune.

With that Ivan jumped and trotted to the turret ladder, scaling it to the top with little effort.

"Payback's a bitch, ain't it," she called to him. "Everyone's a critic...It wasn't *that* bad." Humming the tune to herself, she stopped. "Maybe it was."

Chandra took a deep breath. "Sapiens, this place stinks. I'll bet Wright hasn't bothered to clean your box since he moved back into the ship?"

The answer hung in the air.

"I know what I could do," she said to Ivan who listened from above with ever-increasing disinterest. "I could clean out your box. You'd be happier." She took another deep breath. "I'd be happier."

In a closet, she found a pair of protective gloves that went to the deep space suit in the storage closet. Since the custom gloves had been made to fit Wright they were slightly too large for Chandra but they would still serve the purpose. She put them on, walking with hands held up in front of her like a doctor in a B-grade horror flick prepped for surgery. She followed her nose to a closet with the door jammed open. When Wright moved the litter box into the "new" ship, he'd apparently moved the cat box as it was...poop, pee and all.

"Sapiens, Ivan. How do you stand this? This is awful. No wonder this place still stinks."

Ivan trotted over to watch her.

"Really. You should have trained Wright better than this."

She pried the hardened litter out of the box. It fell in one solid chunk denting the deck. "When was the last time he changed it? This century?"

He thumped his tail and sat down a few feet away to supervise the event in silence.

Chandra placed the mass in the trash unit and programmed it to transfer it to the external tank until she could eject it into a dump unit later. Rummaging through the closet she found three unmatched shoes, carbon crystals for the water filtration system, and a sack of petrified garbage Wright must have saved. By the looks of it some archeologist would have killed to rummage through that eclectic pile. With all the amazing assortment of stuff stowed around the ship, she found no fresh litter. She looked to Ivan. "What are we going to do now?"

Ivan sat silently and pounded his tail as if to say, "What do you mean, we?"

"Well there's no litter. Maybe some of these carbon filter crystals will work."

After she scrubbed the box with a disinfectant she refilled the kitty commode with the filter crystals. As she scooped the crystals into the box Ivan inched closer.

"Ah ha! I finally get a reaction out of you."

Before she could even finish, he pushed his way past her, jumping in and digging through the crystals with the exuberance of a successful gold miner. Bits of carbon flew out the back of the box collecting in tiny piles on the deck.

"I go to all that trouble for you and you just clutter the floor. Some gratitude." She headed back to the main deck to give the anxious cat a small amount of privacy.

As she reached the captain's chair GNN's Monte Crandavelius' three-dimensional image once again droned on boring details about other significant news events of the galactic day.

"Once again space pirates targeted the Blevins Cartel shipments. The freighter had scheduled supply deliveries on the outer realms of the known galaxy which is suffering from a critical shortage of furnishings and party goods."

Crandavelius paused and took a breath. "War has once again broken out between the systems of Zubenelgenubi and Zubenschmali. Both sides are mounting massive invasion efforts. Officials expect the combined casualties to mount into the trillions. The row occurred over the recent murder of Genubi ruler His Great Immenseness Ramsbotm allegedly by Sedgway Ripenall, Zubenschmali ambassador to Rasalhague. Previously tensions between the two systems had been mounting over the fact that both of the planet's First Females wore the same dress to an earlier Rasalhague party. With the political conditions in the sector so tense over the dress fiasco, the murder of Ramsbotm only exacerbated the situation to the point of ignition."

The camera panned around the chancellor's main ballroom. There stood the Chancellor staring down at Ramsbotm, whose body had been forgotten in the melee. In the background next to the lake of liquor the victim's bereaved widow swigged punch directly from the little boat's bilge pump.

The reporter stood next to the Chancellor. "Chancellor, would you care to make a statement about this most unfortunate situation."

The chancellor paused for a moment searching the ceiling for inspiration. "I am pleased to say that after the unfortunate incident at today's reception, my neighbors to the south can no longer accuse me of throwing dull parties. However, to prevent future wars I am requiring at upcoming soirees that all female guests register their apparel in advance."

As he rambled, someone familiar in a day coat ambled across the camera field past the chancellor and joined Her Grandness Pyrobloya at the lake.

"Wright!" In the few seconds he had appeared on camera Chandra could see that he looked unhappy, miserable actually. His shoulders slumped. "Poor Wright."

Crandavelius continued. "The situation has been further complicated by the disappearance of a guest, Chandra Solomon. Solomon disappeared shortly after the murder. It is uncertain whether she was an accomplice or a victim of the Schmali plot to overtake its long-time adversary."

The chancellor looked over at Wright who, when he came back into the frame, was by that time drinking directly from the lake. "Oh, we're not at all convinced that the young woman left of her own volition. Not at all."

The holo returned to Monte. "In other news, scientists have found new pockets of instability in outer realms of the galaxy. Scientists theorize that in some areas the fabric of space have unwoven and have initiated the search for a new tailor. Other sections of the universe have simply vanished leaving huge unpaid bond debts. An estimated seven trillion, four hundred sixty billion, nine hundred three million and a few hundred thousand sentient beings were killed as a result. Scientists are at a loss to explain this interesting phenomena..."

"Oh, shut up," Chandra said.

She leaned closer to the fuzzy holo.

Monte's holographic form disappeared but was instantly replaced by a cloud of fuzzy gray static, accompanied by the irritating dead air.

"Still better," Chandra said, then added, "Computer replay the news article involving Rasalhague."

Once again, Crandavelius appeared before her just as it

had earlier.

"Okay, go to the beginning of the chancellor's statement."

"I am pleased to say..."

"Kill the volume."

The three-D chancellor continued his speech without benefit of his voice.

"Zoom in on the refreshment fountain in the background. Especially the man drinking out of the fountain."

Wright's face replaced the other objects.

"Cheer up, Wright, at least you got to finish the party," she said. "Computer, is there any audio for this person?"

"Certainly," the computer said.

"Start this section over again and play only the audio of the person drinking out of the lake."

Wright's lips moved but the sound was unintelligible.

"Can you clean it up and intensify it?"

"Certainly."

"Great. Do that and replay."

On his knees Wright slurped directly from the fountain. "I can't believe she left; I thought she liked me."

Chandra reached for the holo. "Oh, Wright, I do."

She asked the computer to play the segment over again and again until she couldn't stand it any longer.

She was alone again, and this time it was her own doing. She should have given those damn rocks up. Let them have that junk. Look at all the people who have died because of her, because of the crystal and the orb. An entire system was going to war because the Corvian shot missed killing her. Galwayans were smothering each other in vats of suds because of her. A small innocent planet full of gentle people became indentured servants because of her.

Chandra sighed.

She rummaged through Wright's liquor cabinet and dug out a half-full bottle. She pulled the cork and took a long drink. It felt warm as it slid down her throat. She sat cross-legged on the deck and took another sip. "Computer, continue to replay that last news segment until I say otherwise."

After all, you shouldn't drink alone.

Space travel wasn't hard work. Except when things were shooting at her, the hardest part was doing nothing during those long periods between spaceports.

Even in her old Bell Transport it seemed to take forever, but in this antique former rust monger it really would! She didn't have forever, a little over two galactic days.

She stared at the stars, betting against herself how long it would take to get to the next one. Somehow, she always lost. Finally, a yellow main sequence star came into view with twelve or so satellites orbiting around it.

A few of them looked interesting.

With the blessed silent spell after the racket of Chandra's singing, Ivan sauntered back to his station and settled back into his pile.

"I'm afraid that Wright left us a little low on fuel and supplies. What you say Ivan? Want to stop for a while? Not long, after all, we're running out of time."

Ivan burrowed deeper into the pile of Wright's dirty clothes and drifted off to sleep.

"*Blind Faith*, this is Rasalgheti B planetary traffic assistance. Give us your code and we will bring you in for a controlled landing at the public pad."

"Understood traffic assistance. Just a minute, Rasalgheti," she said as she reprogrammed a temporary code into the computer. "The code is four, zero, two, four, X-ray, Tango."

"Confirm code four, zero, two, four, X-ray, Tango."

"Affirmative traffic control. I'm handing control over to you — now."

"We confirm control *Blind Faith*. Will bring you down for a baby-soft landing at pad Foxtrot two-three-seven. Enjoy your stay on Rasalgheti B.

"Two-three-seven," Chandra echoed. "Thanks, traffic assistance. You guys know where I can get something decent to eat around here? Got nothing to eat but green leftovers. I need to get some fuel and supplies, too."

"*Blind Faith*, you might want to try Hambog's House of Quell. Good quell."

Chandra winced at the suggestion. "Thanks assistance, but I'm afraid I'm about quelled out. Any *other* suggestions?"

"There's a place called the Supply Stall. They have anything the poorly-equipped traveler could use. "

"That sounds good. Thanks."

"Standby *Blind Faith* and I'll send directions to Supply Stall."

"Thanks assistance. Appreciate the help. *Blind Faith* clear."

"That's why they call us traffic assistance. By the way, is this the *Blind Faith* that used to belong to Wright Aulweighs?"

Chandra froze. "How do you know Wright?" she asked tentatively.

"Royal hormones. It *is* his ship. Wright and I go back, oh, I guess at least a hundred years."

She tried to steady her voice. "Really?"

"Is he there? Let me talk to that slob."

"Sorry to disappoint you, traffic assistance, but he's not here."

"You his wife?"

"A friend. I'm borrowing the ship while he builds a reverse pyramid for the Chancellor of Rasalhague."

"How 'bout that. The chancellor finally got him to build that thing. He's been putting that one off forever. In my business you get to know a lot of the characters that travel this area a lot. He still have that mangy cat? Wretched, wasn't it?"

"You mean Ivan?"

"That's it. Ivan. He still got him?"

"I'm taking care of him for a spell while Wright's busy with that job."

"Hey, those folks at Supply Stall probably still have an account for Wright," assistance said. "I got an idea. Why don't I come by and pick you up? I'll take you where you need to go. I can get caught up on Wright. Next time he flies that flea trap in here, I'll have some poop on him."

"Thanks traffic assistance, but that's too much trouble. I couldn't ask you to do that."

"Who's asking? I insist."

"Great." She gritted her teeth as if enduring torture. "Who could resist such a generous offer?"

"I'll be there in a short. By the way, the name's Begel."

"I'm Chandra. You'll know me by..."

"I know, by your teak hair." The transmission shut down.

Chapter Twenty-Eight

She touched her hair. "My teak hair. Nobody but Wright ever called my hair 'teak'." She turned to the cat. "Oh shit. Ivan, we're in big trouble."

Ivan lashed his tail against the chair seat as if to say, 'What do you mean, we?'

Chandra squared herself in front of the command panel. She entered the ignition sequence and completed the checklist as required by the ship's manufacturer, who by the age of this ship had died long ago.

Nothing happened.

She tried again with the same results. Absolutely nothing. The vessel did not even attempt to power up.

Chandra laid her head on the console and covered it as if trying to bury herself. "He's shut us down."

Trying to rally herself, she programmed a back door. She entered a sequence. "This should disable his code." She tried to power up again. *Blind Faith* just sat there—hibernating.

She ran up to the turret and grabbed her bag and tool belt. After descending the ladder she headed for the hatch. "Well I'm not sticking around to see what this guy's going to do to me. Manacles, bread and water." She paused. "Actually that sounds better than what's available to eat on *Blind Faith.*"

She flipped a few switches and punched the button that instructed the hydraulic locks to release and free her from the scow. No response.

"We're dead," she said.

Ivan, lying in his pile of clothes at the copilot's station, yawned.

"All right. I'm dead. You're supposed to be here. You think you could plead my case for me? You know him."

Ivan's eyes closed, reflecting the utter lack of concern he felt over her plight. Within seconds his whiskers flicked and his paws twitched irregularly.

"You're probably dreaming about what will happen to me.

Well, old boy, I guess I'd better get ready." She adjusted the hand that held her Personal Protection trigger. "If this guy's a friend of Wright's I don't want to use it, but I will if I have to."

The hatch began making grinding noises, the same sounds she had heard the night Wright had to drag her into the ship by the ankle.

She backed away from the door.

Before she had a chance to hide the hatch had opened. A Gheti entered and shut the door behind him. He had narrow eyes, which naturally gave him the look of a thing with an agenda. His smooth skin glistened of jaundice, although all Ghetis looked as if their livers were past useful life. He leaned back against the bulkhead and then pulled away quickly, inspecting the back of his uniform. His stubby fingers tested the fabric and seemed surprised to find it free of unidentifiable sticky substances.

He was unarmed and seemed unconcerned about Chandra's threatening presence. She aimed her Personal Protection at him. "Don't move," she said. "I don't want to hurt you."

"I don't want you to, either," he said. "It's clean?" Confused, he held up clean fingers.

She moved her arm so he could see her weapon but that did not seem to affect him. Begel smiled. "Oh, come on, Chani. I'm not going to hurt you. Put that thing down. It doesn't work, anyway."

She held her arm steady. "You're bluffing."

"Okay. Try it. Aim right here." He pointed at his chest and then to his head. "Or here."

He was too sure of himself. Chandra dropped her arm.

"How'd you disable everything?" she asked.

"Standard operating procedures," he said still testing his fingers and his back. "We get tough sorts in here all the time. Once they land we can surround their vessel with a charge that temporarily drains all the energy from their systems. It keeps them from tearing the place up."

She nodded. "What are you going to do with me?"

"That depends."

"On what?"

"Where's Ivan?"

She pointed to the white mound of fur hidden within the

pile of clothes.

He walked over to the copilot seat. "Hey, Ivan." He kept a safe distance.

Ivan opened his eyes and glared at Begel. He burrowed a little deeper and fell back to sleep.

"He's all right," Begel said.

"Of course, he's all right. What did you expect?"

He said nothing.

"You thought I did something to the cat? Sapiens, no. Why don't you take a look at my hands or my butt." She held out her wrists, still decorated with fading tributaries of cat scratches. "He's injured me more than a few times. Actually, we've come to a working arrangement. I feed him what little food we have here and he bleeds me only occasionally."

Begel held out his own hand, exposing a thin scar running from the knuckle to his wrist. "Ivan and I go way back, too." He walked toward the hatch. "Okay. Let's go."

"Where?"

"Where I said I'd take you. The Supply Stall."

She grabbed her bag, which held the remains of the creation plant, and joined him at the hatch.

"You need to leave everything here," he told her.

"What?"

"Those are Wright's instructions."

Panicked she looked at her bag. "Everything?"

"Except your weapon. You can bring that. I'll even activate it when we get into town. You have to promise you won't use it on me until after we've had a chance to talk."

"So talk."

He shook his head. "Not here. Don't worry. I'll seal the ship with priority security. Anybody trying to gain access will wind up in intensive care. Whatever you have will be safe."

His speedster was an economy model, a Pyxis with few options inside and an ugly ecru exterior paint job, the kind of color that made it easy to spot in a crowded parking lot. It ran well and Begel appeared to keep it clean, very clean compared to Wright Aulweighs standards.

They had been traveling in silence. "When did you talk to Wright?" she finally asked.

"Earlier today," he said.

"Are you going to have me arrested?"

"No."

"What are you going to do with me?"

"I'm taking you to the Supply Stall so you can stock up. Oh, yeah. Wright wanted me to remind you to get cat food and some GootenKatz."

"I planned on it," then as an afterthought, "and cat litter."

Rasalgheti was a beautifully vegetated planet, at least in this region. Massive trees with blue-green serrated leaves. Dainty vines with yellow and fuchsia flowers danced in and out of the branches. As the speeder gained altitude the tall amber grasses that seemed to grow everywhere filled thousands of kilometers like a quilt spun of golden thread.

She stared silently out the window. She felt trapped without a cage. Threatened without a threat.

"How's Wright?" she finally asked.

"He's upset and worried."

She nodded knowingly. "About Ivan."

"Yeah," Begel said. After a silence a few minutes long he finally added, "He's worried about you, too."

Her eyes tore away from the landscape to stare at Begel. "He's worried about me? I stole his ship. You must know that."

"Yeah. He told me."

"I'm surprised he hasn't asked you to take me off and have me killed."

A smile crept across Begel's face and broke into a laugh deep from the gut. "Wright have someone killed? Only if they hurt Ivan."

"I guess he wants me to go back to Rasalhague."

"No. He wants you to go to Fomalhaut. Whatever you're doing, he must think it's pretty important." He tore his eyes away from her to the windscreen just in time to miss the planetary control tower. "He also wants you to reach there alive."

Her shoulders slumped. She looked out the window not wanting to meet the occasional glances of Wright's friend.

"Chani, the reason he contacted me was because he thinks someone planted another transponder in the ship. Maybe even a listening device."

"I got a clean sweep on it when I checked it."

"When did you last check it?"

"I cleaned it out on Galway. Before he sold it, and it was

rebuilt."

"He thinks that it was reinfested it with bugs after it was refurbished," he said. "That's why whoever it is keeps following you. Theoretically, any listening devices went inoperable when I disabled the ship, but just in case, I didn't want them to hear what I told you. They probably know you're here so we have to make this quick and send you on your way."

Off in the distance a community of homes emerged like a box of multi-colored jellybeans. Below them, the center of the town wore a belt of businesses that leaped into the sky with multi-story buildings. As the speedster hovered closer to the streets, Chandra could see people moving like ants in and out of the structures.

"You came at a good time," Begel said. "It's market day."

Chandra and Begel entered the shop. Beings from across the galaxy stood around the counter impatiently waiting for service. In the corner near the entrance a frazzled clerk took computer chips encoded with the day's order and fed it into the computer. He, like Begel, looked as if he suffered from the advanced stages of liver disease.

"Will there be anything else?" she asked.

The Pictorian customer standing before him scratched his rear with his furry hand and thought for a moment. "You have any of those the little purple things?"

"What?" He squinted her eyes behind a clear visor. "Your order will be ready as written in fifteen minutes around the dock outside. If you are more than five minutes late, it will be returned and we will charge your account a restocking fine."

As the Pictorian grumbled and walked away, Chandra stepped into the line. "I feel like everyone's staring at me."

Begel looked at the assortment of beings waiting for their provisions. "By the looks of them I'd say it's because they haven't seen a female of any species in a long time."

She shivered. "Thanks Begel. I certainly find that thought comforting."

"Any time."

When her time came Chandra realized she didn't have a chip. "I need six cases of standard number two rations, a case of Gassy Nebula Beer, a six pack of GootenKatz and six cases of cat supplement...oh, and some cat litter."

Begel gave the clerk the billing instructions.

"Why is Wright paying for this?" Chandra asked.

"He said you have some kind of deal. He expects you to keep your part of the agreement even if he isn't here to help."

"I will."

"He also said he's a sucker for teak."

"So I've heard."

"Yeah. That and Ivan's tired of his cooking."

Chandra's stomach flip-flopped recalling the leftovers in the ship's cryo. "Begel, Wright couldn't cook his way out of a poly-styrene bag with a blow torch in each hand."

Chandra watched the activity throughout the warehouse. Big-boned Corvians and other large species loaded bundles of supplies onto a conveyor.

"Thanks for all your help Begel."

"I did it as a favor for Wright," Begel said. "But I have to admit, I understand why he's a sucker for teak."

"Begel," she said hesitantly. "I want you to know why I left Wright on Rasalhague."

The Gheti man threw up his arms. "It's none of my business."

"Maybe. But, I think you should know. And if you talk to Wright I'd like you to tell him. There had been so many near-hits on me, I was afraid he would be caught in the crossfire. Tyrus warned me that Wright would die if he stayed with me. My phone company flight suit has a giant target on it, and as long as he was anywhere near me, he was wearing a huge skull and cross bones on his own head. Wright's different in a nice, strange way. I couldn't bear it if something happened to him cuz of me. I hope he'll forgive me."

"He will. As long as he gets Ivan back."

Finally, the supplies fell down the chute. The lot had been marked with Chandra's order number and had a manifest of products in the box. "One case assorted prepared meals distributed by OK Manufacturing, Castor. Oh, Sapiens. I can't eat this stuff. What about the cat food?"

"What about it?" asked the Corvian dockworker.

"What's it made of?"

"I don't know. Dead stuff."

"I know it's dead stuff. Is the cat supplement from OK, too?"

"Sure."

She turned to the Corvian warehouse attendant. "Don't

you have products from somewhere else?"

"Yeah, but that's the best tasting stuff we got. There a problem?"

"I've been in one of their plants. I didn't like the sanitary conditions."

"One plant's no different from the rest."

"I don't care. Get me supplies from someplace else, preferably Earth. The cat food, too."

The warehouse worker shrugged and kicked away one of the cartons. He returned shortly. "This comes from some place called Delicious Foods from a place called El Paso."

"Great. I'll take it."

"This will cost you more than the other."

"Fine."

Once again he left and returned a few minutes later.

"Put the containers in the Pyxis," Begel told the Corvian. "And could you push it. We're in a rush."

"Yeah, yeah," the dockworker said. "Everyone's in a rush."

Chapter Twenty-Nine

After hours of taking measurements and entering meticulously figured computations, Chandra reprogrammed her current position and destination. She checked and rechecked and re-rechecked, and everything seemed to be in order.

As she entered the last set of digits she turned to Ivan and said, "Ivan, now that I finished setting our course, can you tell me where those creeps planted the bug."

His ears perked forward at the mention of his name, but he failed to betray her pursuers secret. She searched every nook and cranny of the visible ship with her meter. Chances were it was somewhere near the engines where the different magnetic and radioactive fields would deceive the meter.

"I'm going to bed," she finally told Ivan. "Hopefully I have enough of a head start to keep me safe for now. I'll have to continue my search after I've had some sleep."

He responded with his usual concern; he yawned.

She crawled up the ladder and climbed into her bunk.

It wouldn't be much longer. Fomalhaut lay just around the galactic corner and once there she could deliver her coveted cargo and lose tons of ugly fat in the form of thugs, thieves and murderers. Once she had the reward in her hands, she would take Ivan back to Wright and get on with her life.

Hopefully tomorrow she'd unload Wright's ship and his antisocial cat.

As she tried to imagine what her life would be like when she returned home Chandra drifted off into a restless sleep.

In a cloud-filled ballroom Chandra found herself in Wright's arms, dancing around the floor with the grace of Cinderella and Prince Charming. She wore a new gown, a long emerald satin dress foaming and flowing like soft waves as they wheeled around in airy circles. Then he kissed her tenderly on the cheek. But, it did not feel as expected. It felt...sharp.

"Ivan!" she shouted as she tried to sit upright in the bunk. That attempt failed. The cat stood on her chest licking her face—raw. Her cheek smarted as if flayed. "What are you doing?"

He jumped off the bunk and then leapt down the ladder to the flight deck. Chandra staggered to the ladder and stared down at the cat. Immediately below her Ivan stopped, looked up, then paced in a circle and stared up again.

This was more activity than Chandra had seen out of him during the entire voyage.

"What's wrong? You want me to come down there, don't you?" Chandra asked.

He continued to gaze up at her in the cabin as if to say, *Who do think I am—Lassie?*

"All right. All right." Through sleepy eyes she groped for the rungs.

If this isn't important, I'll kill him, she thought.

She stumbled down the ladder. The flight deck looked normal, but something about the way it sounded and felt was all wrong. Unfamiliar noises seemed to come from outside the ship, but she knew that sound could not travel through the vacuum of space.

Plopping down into the pilot's seat she checked the computer. The sensors indicated that something outside the vessel was creating stress on a small area of the hull. Was it a meteor or asteroid impact, maybe space debris. Or was it another ship? Whatever it was, why didn't it trigger the alert system?

"Sapiens," she said to Ivan. "Someone's got a tractor beam on us! Look at the stress it's putting on the aft section."

She watched as the pressure continued to rise. If she didn't cut back on the engines, they'd be damaged beyond the point of spaceworthiness. Just kiss Fomalhaut good-bye. She backed off the power and the vessel gained on them.

"Great. You realize they're going to board us, don't you? You can stay out here in the open," she told Ivan. "But I'm not going to!"

She grabbed her Harbinger and Personal Protection and dove into a recently accumulated pile of Wright's dirty clothes as well as some sheet and blankets she'd dumped there awaiting for wash day or the end of time, whichever came first. Clutching the weapon tightly to her breast, she held her breath.

With a metal fatiguing groan, the hatch slid open. Through

a tiny opening among the folds of the fabric, she watched a slouching Corvian carrying a high-powered rifle ease past her hiding place. Several other beings followed him, not all of them Corvian. Their voices barked, barely audible through the layers of clothes.

Why did I hide here? she wondered. *This is the first place they'll look.*

Her finger tightened around the trigger of the light pistol. She held her breath. As the Corvian drew closer to the pile she lost sight of him, then his voice grew fainter with each clodding step. A few minutes later he returned. With his gun barrel, he probed the pile of clothes as though checking a roast for doneness. Then finally he came just too damn close. She fired her Harbinger.

The lovely fragrance of smoldering Corvian made its way through the fabric filter of her clothing camouflage, smelling somewhere between week old dead fish and an over-cooked casserole forgotten in the cryo for six months. A slightly fresher scent mingled with fish casserole. Something like...smoldering dirty clothes.

Damn!

"Good shot," she heard a familiar voice from outside her view. "Now, Chandra, be a good sport; drop your weapon and come out of there before you turn into baked Texan. Don't try anything. You'll be dead before I can even give the order to kill you."

She tossed the weapon to the deck and leapt out of the smoldering heap. Coughing and hacking, she slapped herself to kill the flaming fabric still clinging to her legs. The remaining pile rose to a nice campfire-sized flame as another Corvian dashed over to stomp it out.

Chandra turned around and looked up in to the face of her old friend.

"Hello, Lance. What brings you out this way?"

"Chandra Solomon, you're a tough person to catch. A tough one to kill, too." He smiled.

"How'd you get this far out so quickly?" she asked.

"I leased a much faster ship than this bucket. I could have ridden a hobby horse and still caught up with you."

"Lavender's a good color on you." She nodded to the prosthetic arm. "It's interesting that you can't seem to hold your wrist straight any more. You got a problem?"

He slid his hand in his pocket.

"I get it," she said. "You traded your arm for a nice set of boobs."

"Your little prank with the Lucillians cost me my arm. I got a replacement on Galway. Unfortunately, they didn't have one in stock for my species. I tried to pay you a courtesy visit when you were in the hospital, but while I was there, someone stuck me in the ass with a sedative. When I woke up, I had these." He slapped his chest, rather breast.

She tried not to smile.

"You can laugh all you want, Chandra, because you're a dead woman walking."

"What do you want?" She knew it was a dumb question. Like asking a man in a body cast how he felt.

"You have something of mine." A smile crossed Lance's rugged face. Without the GNN theatrical makeup, his black eye and some cuts and bruises gave him that capable-of-cutting-your-throat-cuz-it's-fun look. "Come on, now. Let's not play games. I know you have the my rocks."

"Sorry, Lance. Truth is, I gave it to some crazy guy with a big mouth a few days back on a Lucillian cruise liner."

"What you gave Kitilon was not the crystal." He held out the impostor. "I should have killed you and taken it when I first met you, but I wasn't certain you had it. I am now. So, why don't you save me a lot of trouble and you a lot of pain and give me what was stolen from me."

"Lance, I've told you before, I didn't see Tyrus' body until after the cops had gone over him with a magnifying glass. If he had anything of value on him, they kept it. They denied he even had the Harbinger," she lied.

"I know. The only thing on him was the gun," he finished. "Don't forget. I've heard that speech before. I didn't believe it then, and I certainly don't believe it now." He turned to the men accompanying him. "Search the ship."

Lance turned back to Chandra. "Chani, I really like you. You have guts. I don't want these guys to do the kind of things they do to get information out of people. They have a different method from Kitilon. By the way, you're the only one to survive interrogation by Kitilon and still maintain most of your sanity. Congratulations. I can guarantee you won't be as fortunate this time. If you live, you'll never look quite the same. Why don't you just tell me where the pieces from my collection are?"

"Lance, I gave Kitilon all I ever had. What can I do to convince you?"

The Corvian with the highest rank and the worst body odor looked at Goode. With a slight nod from their boss the pirates began to tear the ship apart panel by panel once again.

Systematically, the henchmen ripped walls apart, pulled up flooring, tore open newly replaced upholstery of the seats. One of them noticed Ivan lounging in his copilot's seat watching the action around him. He grabbed the cat by the scruff of the neck, but Ivan unsheathed his claws, and carved his signature into the Corvian's wrist and forearm.

"It's not on the cat," Lance announced quickly, rubbing at his still healing wrist with the purplish artificial hand. "Keep looking," he ordered.

They did, noisily and with great ceremony. He then turned to her. "Where is it Chani?"

"Lance, I guess you'll need to talk to your dead girlfriend. Why can't you understand? You searched the house. You searched the ship. I have nothing for you to find."

"Search her," he ordered.

They did.

"I don't want to hurt you," he reminded her grimly. "I only want what is mine."

"I don't have your damn crystal. How many times do I have to tell you that?"

"Until I find it, or until you're dead."

Chandra swallowed hard. "You keep saying that they're yours. I thought it belonged to Rithel Bartlemist."

His brows peaked. "It does."

"You mean you're Rithel?"

"Surprised?"

She nodded.

"Yeah. That's the joke. None of those idiots had any idea that I was watching them the whole time."

He bent down, nose to nose. "Things were going just fine until you came into my life. Your company screwed up my communication contract and then I had delivery delays. Then I had to start robbing my own freighters just to serve my customers."

"Great scam. So you were able to create an artificial shortage and crank up the prices on furniture and party supplies," she said. "That way your losses on paper went up and your taxes dropped, and your profits increased. But why the alter ego? Why Lance Goode, the fallen network society reporter? But wait a minute, you reported real news on Galway."

He smiled. It wasn't Lance's smile. It belonged to someone else, someone with a lot of power. "I gave myself a temporary promotion. Insurance in case my little Chandra finders quit working or were discovered. As a society reporter I could report poor Rithel Bartlemist as the victim of circumstances. Besides, I grew tired of the crime beat. Too many people get mad and want to get even. In society I could do the same thing and asked the same questions of the same people without the risk. No one ever suspected I wanted anything except a story. I even set up the Rongstuph fiasco so I would buy the network under his name. It was such a shame he died so shortly after that. When you own the network, you can have yourself transferred to any beat you want, any time you want. I put myself in a good place. I was getting ready to cash in the rock when one of my amoeba-brained employees had to raid my private collection because he heard he could clean up at the Cryptic game with your partner."

"Why do you think I have it?" she asked.

Lance eased over to the navicom and pulled up her programmed course. "I know you have it because a legend that accompanies that piece of junk says that the person who takes it to Vega will be rewarded with great riches. If I'm not mistaken you have set a course in that direction."

"What do you mean—Vega?" she gasped. "He told me Fomal..."

"Sir..." the commanding Corvian interrupted as he plodded up to Lance. "It's not here."

Lance glared at Chandra. "Take her to the airlock. We've wasted enough time."

One of the armed Corvian's grabbed her by the elbow with his free hand, and started walking. She planted her feet firmly on the deck, but her slight weight was hardly an anchor. He dragged her like downed prey toward the hatch. She grabbed at hatch holds, anything that would slow him down.

"Lance, please don't. I'd tell you if I knew."

"Sorry, Chandra. That sounds like a personal problem to me. If you tell me where it is, we'll drop you off at the first star system that has communications with your company."

She continued to struggle. The guards laughed as they watched the octopus sideshow she was putting on.

Chandra stopped struggling and fell limp to the deck. "All right. All right. I'll tell you where it is. Please, don't hurt me anymore."

The Corvian yanked her up by the collar. As he did, she stamped on his foot. He dropped his gun and grabbed his foot. Taking that moment, her very last chance to escape alive, she pushed him with all her strength. Off balance, he stumbled. She seized the gun, and clubbed the guard across the temple. Then spinning, she caught two of the other pirates in the weapon's deadly beam. Their smoldering remains crackled and popped on the floor by Lance's feet.

Glancing down at the power gauge, she found to her dismay that the weapon was almost depleted. Hardly enough charge left to even stun a man. Lance saw that, too.

"You never give up," he said.

"Neither do you." She aimed the pistol at him.

He walked toward her. "You don't have enough juice to give me a headache."

"You can't blame me for trying." She pulled the trigger. The beam shot past Lance and hit the sad-looking creation plant wilting in a pot behind him. It smoldered and smoked, but Lance remained untouched.

"You missed," he said. By then he had drawn his own weapon and was bearing down on her.

Chandra took a deep breath and held it.

"You thought you could outsmart *me*?" he asked. "Well, you didn't, Chandra. And now, things become a little unpleasant. I'm going to enjoy this part. You are going to tell me where it is."

Without a word, she gave him a reluctant nod.

"Well, where is it?"

She pointed at Ivan.

"The cat has it?"

She nodded yes.

"Of course." He clapped his hands together. "That's right. Ivan has it!"

With his weapon still aimed at her chest, he started for the copilot's seat. But he began to stagger, his steps unsteady. He reached for Ivan, who took an energetic swipe at him. Lance stumbled back, his breath quickening. His eyes glazed over and he began to giggle. The giggle grew into a laugh and he fell to his knees, red-faced and gasping for breath between guffaws.

Chandra eased over to the port side of the cabin and picking up one of the filtration masks lying on the ground next to the fire extinguishers, placed it over her face.

Lance dropped his weapon and turned back to Chandra. The scowl had turned to a silly grin. "I don't think he likes me."

Chandra smiled back. "That's okay, Lance. He doesn't like anyone."

"I feel funny," he complained.

"I feel with my hands."

He wavered. "Why are you spinning around?"

"Am I?"

He nodded. "So is he." He pointed at Ivan, who had stopped pounding his tail. Even from across the room, Chandra could hear the purr that had erupted from the throat of the Turkish Van. He rolled back over on his back, offering his underside for a good old-fashioned tummy rub.

"Touch your belly? Not on your life," she said. "That's a Venus Flytrap if I've ever seen one."

Chandra walked over to the smoldering plant and reaching into the pot, and dug through the dirt until she found her prize, the glass orb. She stashed it in her jumpsuit pocket. She ran and grabbed her duffel bag and walked back to Lance.

He slid to the ground.

She could not resist the urge to pat him on the head as she reached down to retrieve his light pistol. It was freshly charged.

"How many men are still on your ship?" she asked him sweetly.

"Oh...just two," he answered just as sweetly. "It's on autopilot. With that computer, I don't need a crew. I don't trust people."

As he spoke, she scooped up Ivan, who by now hung as limp over her arm as a wet rag.

"Well, good luck, Lance, "she said as she opened the docking bay to the freighter.

The airtight door slid shut behind her, leaving Lance to vegetate for the next eight hours in the smoke of the creation plant.

She placed Ivan, who rolled over into his give-me-a-belly-rub-and-I'll-give-you-stitches position, on the deck.

"Later."

He did not move a muscle. No, Ivan fixed his vision on the light above and stared. His mouth parted and his pink tongue lolled out the side.

"My protector," she said with a laugh.

Still giggling, she dropped Ivan into her duffel bag.

Then her moment passed. It was time to go hunting.

Chapter Thirty

She opened the door to the cargo hold. It seemed to go on forever, rows on rows of crates reaching to the overhead, crates of glasses, designer foods, snacks, decorations, and liquors of every conceivable type and brand: Leonian brandy, but only the best; nebula waters, champagnes from some of the known systems and a few so obscure Chandra had never heard of them, ales and wines and a few crates labeled just: "good booze."

A partygoer's paradise. More food and drink than she could consume in a thousand lifetimes. What an awesome prospect. She could almost taste the expensive whiskey slithering down her throat and stopping to dance a minuet in her belly.

"In a little while," she promised herself. "I just have to rid myself of the unnecessary cargo."

Treading softly, Chandra made her way to the bridge. Just outside the door she recalibrated the setting on her Harbinger for "delayed motion" and balanced it along a ridge in the bulkhead.

On the bridge she found two somethings she did not recognize playing a hologame. The holographic characters were obviously chosen with this species in mind, because they resembled the pilot and navigator in every way except size. One translucent game thing covered with spikes had just received a foot-at least she thought it was a foot-to what was most likely the groin by a creature that resembled a hyperactive snowball with a thyroid problem. The movements of the animated figures were accompanied by screaming and gnashing of fangs and toenails not unlike that of their counterselves in the command chairs.

A dozen arms popped out of the snowball's fur, bashing the spike thing's head from two sides. Spike thing whipped around, producing a sword from nowhere, and spun. The outcome looked like a curlicue fry without the aroma of stale oil.

The curlicue had begun to grow back together when Chandra breathlessly ran just inside the bridge, planted her hands on her hip and yelled, "Bartlemist is hurt. He's down the corridor. They said he quit breathing. One of the Corvians said that you'd know what to do."

The snowball laughed, but it sounded more like breaking wind. "We know what to do." More snowball farts. "We do nothing; we get ship."

"The Corvian said that you'd say that. He also said that Rithel, or whatever his name is, set the ship for a silent self-destruct if it took off without his code. I guess that was just in case you clowns decided to leave without him, which I know you'd never do."

"Self-destruct?" echoed the spiky thing. "He would do that?"

The two dashed out the door and into range of the awaiting Harbinger. The sound of the light beam hitting them was not unlike that of a bug zapper on an Arkansas Saturday night. Sizzling, they exploded.

Checking her chrono, she decided she had better wait another minute or so just to be certain the Harbinger's autosensor delay had timed out. She stepped back into the corridor she found only two piles of cinders beneath a layer of rising smoke which resembled tiny thunderstorm clouds.

Putting her hand over her nose she said, "Maybe incinerate was a little overkill."

It would take more than a thunderstorm though, to kill the carrion odor of the fried aliens.

"Sorry for the misunderstanding, guys." She ran down the corridor, grabbed the bag and returned to the bridge.

Chandra opened the duffel bag and dropped Ivan into his new copilot's seat, sans the dirty clothes, and plopped herself down at the captain's station. It took only a few moments to find the docking bay door release and eject the disabled *Blind Faith*. The little ship shot out from beneath the larger freighter and lagged behind until it faded from the rear screen.

Chandra studied the star charts.

Even with the sophisticated navigation equipment on this tub, she still could not figure out her location. Tyrus tried time and time again to teach her the finer points of astro-navigation, but try as he might, he couldn't relay the knowledge in a form Chandra could grasp.

As a student in interstellar engineering, she was required to take several semesters of navigation. But she was never very good at it and always bribed someone else to take her exams. And during the semesters that emphasized star charts and map reading, she paid some guy to attend class, write the papers, and take the finals. It cost her big bucks, at least in the perspective of a college student. *What a stupid thing to do!* If only she'd read even one of those papers she'd paid so dearly for. If only she'd asked Tyrus more questions and paid attention when he programmed the navicom.

Planetary maps were tough enough, but these stellar maps were a real bitch. She had to face the truth, hard as that was: she was lost. As best she could tell, the corsair was on course to a completely different sector than she entered into the navicom. Try as she might, even between the computer, the maps, and her own eyes, she couldn't make sense of any of them.

"Damn." Her arms fell into her lap, crumpling the chart. She gazed over at Ivan, who lay napping after his tough day of sleeping. "One of the best equipped ships in the galaxy and I can't make the navicom work. We're lost. All the work I did and all Wright's coordinates are in *Blind Faith's* computer. I don't know if I could even find *it*."

Ivan responded by flexing claws, and then by beginning to bathe the spaces between his pads. When he finished his ablutions, he yawned, emitting a tiny squeak, and laid his head back on his paws. It was her problem.

"You're not even decent company," Chandra complained.

He responded by pounding his tail on the seat of the chair, as if to say, "How's that?"

Chandra checked the navicom, but the current coordinates in the computer didn't match the star charts. The longer she waited the farther off course they drifted.

From her own computations, it looked as though they were heading toward an uninhabited area of space. By the time she could find a transportation alternative, she would miss the Festival of the Fat Bore.

Frustrated, Chandra struggled to at least locate her position on the course Lance's crew had set. She entered a few courses in the Navicom. If she understood, and she wasn't sure she did, then the new course would send her to the nearest civilized planet in the Fomalhaut system. Her current problem solved, for now, she leaned back, propped up her feet and drifted off into a troubled sleep.

After hours, the freighter's alarm rudely woke her.

The ship was still on autopilot, but stress to the outer hull had risen to a dangerously high level.

"I hate reruns."

A quick check of her instruments showed that the vessel was caught in an extremely high gravitational field. One so strong, she could not pull free of it even with the vast reserves of available power.

Chandra re-computed her position.

"We're not at all where we should be," she told the sleeping Ivan. "I don't understand this. Some behemoth of a gravity field is pulling us off course. We could try to break away, but all that will do is burn up our power. Then we'd just drift."

Star charts littered the control panel like beer cans after a rock festival. Pulling out chart after chart, she compared it to the course the ship followed.

"Unless I'm wrong," she told Ivan, "and for once I don't think I am, it looks like we're heading straight for a black hole. How could I be so far off course that we're caught up by a singularity?"

She wadded the map up and threw it across the room. "Damn you, Tyrus. Why didn't you take more time to teach me to navigate?"

She turned to Ivan, who was using his claws to properly break-in the copilot's chair, not an easy job without the pile of comfy dirty clothes. "I guess it's just you and me till the end." She checked her chrono. "And I don't think that will be too long now." Reaching over she gave the cat a playful scratch behind the ears.

Something felt wrong.

She knelt beside him and examined his collar.

It was gone! The crystal she had risked her life for, that she had been chased half-way across the galaxy for, that people, including Tyrus, had died for, was gone.

"It's gone! I can't believe you lost it!"

Ivan held his head up and pounded his tail in a rebuttal of her accusation.

She could almost read his mind, and if he was thinking what she thought he was, he was right. It wasn't his fault.

"Lance must have gotten it after all. I guess since we can't make it to Fomalhaut, it doesn't matter anyway."

Chandra cradled her aching head in her hands. "I can't believe this could happen to me."

Her eyes scanned the instruments frantically. There has to be a way out! There just had to be. She hadn't come this far to be defeated by a black hole, a cat who was smarter than she was, and her own carelessness.

She ran her calculations until she came up with the same coordinates twice in a row, then set a new course. A course back to *Blind Faith*. "By Sapiens, that's *my* crystal. Lance isn't going to get it that easy."

Once she had laid in the heading, she tried to execute it. The freighter struggled and strained. Its massive engines protested her pointless commands with a high-pitched whine. She went to full power. The ship beneath her felt as if it were being ripped apart. Indeed, she knew the engines would implode, if she continued to fight the gravitational pull.

"Warning," the computer said. "Engines will explode in five minutes."

"I don't want to die," she confided to the cat. She eased off and the ship returned to its original course without any help from her. By then, the black hole was visible—not the black hole, but the debris flowing into it on a spiral course. The ship itself had begun a wide swing in a circular course towards it.

She could feel the gravity begin to work on her body. Her movements became slower and more laborious. If an answer existed, she'd better come up with it quick, before long the oppressive force made it impossible to even move.

She ran the problem through the computer, several times, always with the same discouraging news: The ship was hopelessly caught in the gravitational whirlpool of the approaching event horizon.

She called up the cargo manifest. A vast list of goodies came up, a list so long it would take a lifetime to consume. What a waste! The remainder of her lifetime was measured in mere minutes. She placed an order for some easily available items and turned to the cat.

"Ivan," she said. "We're on a freighter full of party paraphernalia. It's just you and me."

Ivan looked up, stretched a front leg and yawned.

"Well, fella, we're going to party."

She went down to the cargo hold and grabbed four bottles of the most expensive champagne she could find, a handful of permacold chem-ice crystals and a carton of the most intriguing cookies, tidbits and munchies she could find. She also took a large jar of Phadian caviar for Ivan and a bottle of his special GootenKatz.

As she walked back on the bridge, she held up her find and emptied the contents of her duffel bag on the deck. She held her evening gown against her body, checking to see if it would still fit. "Ivan, if we're going to die, we're going to do it in style."

Decked out in her favorite and only party dress, Chandra poured herself a glass of Blue Moon Champagne for herself and a safe brew, GootenKatz, in a sherbet glass for Ivan. Immediately, he joined her in a drink. She propped up her bare feet on the instrument panel.

As she sipped her drink she examined the champagne glass etched with astronomical images, nebulas and spiral galaxies. After polishing off her first glass, Chandra began sipping straight from the bottle. "This is good stuff," she observed, holding the bottle up.

Glancing up at the viewer, she found the black hole alarmingly near. Its ominous presence overwhelmed the entire screen. By now, it was a struggle to bring the champagne glass to her lips.

"Won't be long, now," she told Ivan as she gave the gauges a quick glance. "Just a few more minutes."

She fought against the ever-increasing gravity to pour a little more GootenKatz in Ivan's glass and top off her own. "We may as well finish it up. A little more of this and we'll never feel a thing. Besides, you're a lot more pleasant when you're drunk."

A single lash of his tail and his ears flattened against his head, Ivan gave Chandra the impression that he may not have understood every word she said, but he did know when he had been insulted.

"I'm sorry. I didn't mean it. What a shame I didn't get to know you better. You're actually pretty good company. We could've become drinking buddies. Wright was lucky to have a friend like you. I'm sorry I've done this to you."

Chandra stared at the screen where the abyss loomed

even larger. It was hypnotic. She thought of hundreds of things she wished she had done, of many places she wanted to go, and worst of all, of many things left undone. She listed Wright at the top of *that* list.

Ivan licked up the last few drops of champagne. She opened another bottle and poured him a last glass. "Last call, Ivan. Here's to us," she toasted as her bottle clanked against the cat's glass. "We gave it one helluva shot."

They both took a last slug before everything went black.

Chapter Thirty-One

At first, Chandra only heard muffled conversation, the kind she would expect to hear at a restaurant or a party. "I think she'll be all right," said a male voice.

"Oooohhh." She did not know whether to clutch her head or her gut, which both expanded and contracted at the same time. She didn't remember drinking enough to feel this hung over!

Slightly cracking her eyes, she found herself nose to trunk with an elephant. "Sapiens, I'm still drunk. At least you're not pink."

"Hello. You're finally awake," the elephant creature said with an Eastern Indian accent. "I am Ganesa; I welcome you." He paused. "Waiter, would you get her a Gleoppen? I imagine she could use a touch."

Ganesa offered one of his four hands to help Chandra up from the plush lounge on which she had slept. In another hand he clutched a flower, while he fumbled through his breast pocket for something with still another. His second set of arms fell idly at his side.

"It would have been a shame for you to die now, after coming so far," Ganesa said. "You should have worn your safety harness. You wouldn't have that headache now, if you had."

"You sound like my mother. Why bother to strap myself in for a one-way ride through a black hole?" Chandra pressed her hand against her aching head. "I'm dead anyway, aren't I?"

"They're always so disoriented when they first arrive," Ganesa said to someone Chandra could not see. "She'll get over that soon enough."

A few minutes later, the elephant handed her a glass of bubbling amber liquid in one of his four hands. The fluid boiled, but the glass felt cold to the touch, so she held it to her tender jaw for a moment, then sipped it tentatively. As a kid when her mother gave her concoctions intended to make her feel better, they usually left the aftertaste of drainage-trap grease, but this tasted like a cross between apricot brandy and an Alka Seltzer.

As soon as she had drained the glass, a frosty pain relief began to spread down through her throat and into her stomach. Within a few moments her body parts had begun to settle down. At least they had quit jumping up and dancing.

"Thank God. There's liquor in Heaven." Again she placed a tentative hand on her bruised face.

Ganesa smiled beneath his trunk. "You're welcome, sort of. But, this is not exactly Heaven, not in the way you usually think of it when you think of Heaven."

Holding up her empty glass, he said, "I call that Gleoppen. It's my own creation. I don't drink it myself, but I've been told it eases at least some of the discomfort people feel when they first arrive."

"Would you like a drink, madam?" a familiar voice asked.

She turned to see a human, elegantly attired in a tuxedo, balancing a tray of drinks above him in his right hand.

"Tyrus!" She jumped up and embraced him, toppling the tray and sending drink glasses and dip flying. One Phadian threw himself across a woman wearing a Roman toga to protect her from airborne hors d'oeuvres. Seconds later Chandra returned to her senses when clips of her life over the last two-and-a-half weeks flashed through her mind. She'd longed for this moment since the Corvian grabbed her face, since she found the body in the packing plant, since her former confidence disintegrated into rabbit-like fear of shadows.

She pulled away and decked him with a firm right cross. "You bastard! Do you have any idea what you put me through? I could just kill you!"

"Gads, Chani. Where'd you get that punch? He rubbed his jaw, then moved it from side to side. "But look at you! You won! You came through."

"I won? You're crazy," she yelled. "I've lost everything. I've lost my job. I've lost someone very special to me. I've lost my life; and it's all your fault!"

She squeezed her eyes shut as if to block a hideous sight. "Eternity with Tyrus Ratstall." She tested the words. "Ganesa was right. This definitely is *not* Heaven. *This* is Hell."

Tyrus set down the empty tray and stooped to retrieve the glasses she had helped him break. With an apple-round face framing his perpetual grin and double chin, he looked as he always had, except a little more dignified in his butler's tuxedo. "Why would you think just because I'm dead and you're here, that this is Hell?"

Feeling just a little guilty for the ambush, Chandra joined him on the floor to help. As she gathered the large shards, the floor itself commanded her attention. Cold as stone. Was it black onyx? It was so oddly translucent. Millions of brightly glimmering diamonds studded the tiles. In some places accumulations of diamond dust collected in a hurricane pattern.

Her attention returned to Tyrus and the reality of her situation.

"You're here," she said. "If this isn't Hell, where else could it be?"

Ganesa's trunk gently tapped her on the shoulder. "Come now, Chandra. You needn't bother yourself with menial tasks." He curled his trunk around her arm, pulling her away from Tyrus and his mess.

She stopped as she rose. "Where's Ivan? Where's my cat?"

"Ivan's fine," Ganesa said. "He's found a girlfriend already. I shall find something for you to eat. I'm afraid the menu options will be few, for now. Perhaps you like curry?" He kissed two fingers. "The others have taken a break from the game while you are recovering. It's also giving them a chance to unload your freighter. Let me show you to your room." Touching her back lightly with his trunk, he lead her through what looked like a game room with the same onyx/diamond motif.

They passed an assortment of beings milling in what appeared to be a vast space dome dotted with stars and nebulas and galaxies. A few appeared to be from Corvus, but they didn't smell. One Phadian laughed loudly and slapped a human on the back. In the center of the room a few characters surrounded a table embellished with a brilliant spacescape.

Across the dome she spied a polycranial alien with multiple arms. Three of the heads were arguing with each other in Hindu while the other kept the attention of a Phadian. He shuffled two decks of cards simultaneously.

"That's Vishnu," Ganesa said. "He fancies himself a magician. Just a warning: don't ever bet against him on anything. You can't win. Watch his heads. Those three start an argument and distract the mark. While his victim pays attention to them, all those arms can get away with outrageous things. I won't tell you how many times I had to pay off before I caught on."

He pointed at a door with his trunk. "When you're up to it you can join us and we can start up again. There's no rush. If you need anything, just ask."

"Who should I ask?"

"Just ask."

"Where am I?" she asked.

"You are at your final destination."

The décor in Chandra's chamber made Rithel Bartlemist's rooms look like a slumlord's flophouse. Like the other rooms, tiny points of light peppered the rounded walls and floor of black velvet. A rotating spiral chandelier illuminated the room from above.

The furniture was fashioned of Rare Centauri knotted wood. In the corner a huge canopy bed draped with a cover of spun gold caught her attention. The dresser held a snack tray of crackers and cheese and a carafe of white wine. Quickly she downed the food and polished off the wine.

Like the modest snacks among the splendor, Chandra, in her tattered gown, felt out of place. That layer of grime on her skin only further separated her from her surroundings. She kicked off her shoes and sank deep into the bed.

This must be what a cloud feels like.

Later Chandra awoke to soft rhythmic snoring next to her and a hairy head resting on her shoulder. She bolted upright with a start. Next to her Ivan slept on his back, his legs splayed in every possible direction. His head fell back onto the pillow and the snoring stopped.

"You scared me!"

Cracking his eyelids ever so slightly, Ivan rolled to his side and curled his front paws, giving him the appearance of a puppy begging for food. His eyes followed Chandra and his auburn tail whipped about impatiently.

She scratched his throat. "I wish I knew where we are and what's going on. Do you know?"

He answered by sitting up, raising his hind leg and licking

his breeches from hip to toe. After a moment he paused as if waiting for her to say something brilliant. When she remained silent, he continued with a more personal bath. He stopped mid-lick to the sound of a rapping at the door.

"Yes," Chandra said.

The door opened and Tyrus appeared. "I thought you might like some coffee." He offered her a porcelain cup so thin she could see through it. "I know how cranky you get without it."

"Thanks." She sipped slowly. What flavor! The coffee tasted so mellow, so smooth. It bore no resemblance to the battery acid she'd endured in IGB construction shacks across the galaxy. She must still be dreaming all of this.

Within moments Ivan brought reality crashing back up her nostrils with the subtle fragrance of a very recently used litter box that someone had thoughtfully placed nearby.

She put down the cup and covered her nose. "Sapiens, Ivan. Don't you know how to cover it?" Then after a moment thought, *Cat shit still stinks! What sort of Heaven is this?*

Tyrus also grimaced at the odor, but continued to place something on the bed. "I thought you might like something clean to wear, too. A few of the others would probably appreciate it, too."

She pressed her face against the fabric and inhaled the lingering absence of body odor, momentarily blocking the lingering odor of Ivan's litter box.

Tyrus flopped down on the bed, bouncing a little as if to test the mattress for a later purchase. "Hey, this is comfy. You ought to see what *we* get. Want to trade?"

"Get off my bed!"

He slid off. "Aren't we learning fast!" He frowned. But then his mood lightened. "You did it, Chani!" he almost sang. "I didn't really think you had it in you, but you did it. Of course, with some well-considered advice from me."

"What did I do?

"You won the round." His smile was as big as the sun.

"All right, let's pretend I know what you're talking about. What do you get out of it?" she asked.

"Not a damn thing."

"Tyrus, you've never done anything in your entire life that didn't benefit you in some way or another."

"I'm a changed man."

She laughed out loud.

"I had nothing to gain, but I had nothing to lose either. Besides, it was the only chance you had for getting out alive," he said. "I owed you that."

"For all the good that did me."

Another knock came from the door.

"Yes."

"It's your breakfast, Ma'am."

A Bulivarian entered the room wheeling a cart filled with a colorful feast of a breakfast.

"Ah," Tyrus said. "This is Ranknard. You know, the guy that's responsible for you being here."

"You did this to me?" She stalked toward him ready to grab him by the lapel and make someone else's breakfast out of him. She stopped, recalling his mangled body at the OK Packing plant; *that* had already happened. She retreated to the bed where Ivan waited in anticipation of his breakfast.

"Hi, Ranknard," she said. "You look much better than you did last time I saw you."

"Thanks. So do you," he said. He no longer wore the cuts and bruises he'd acquired before their rendezvous at the packing plant.

"Thanks. How good can I look? I'm dead," she said weakly. "I'll never see Wright again."

"There's a down side to that?" Tyrus asked. "Think positively: You'll never eat quell again, either."

"Get out of here!" she screamed.

"Wait, Chani," Tyrus said. "There are a few things you need to know."

"Get out, both of you. Get your worm-ridden carcasses out of my sight." She grabbed the closest thing to her, which happened to be a bowl holding something with the disgusting consistency of tapioca. Taking aim she threw it at Tyrus. The spinning bowl missed, but the contents hit a perfect bullseye, or rather a Tyrus eye.

As the men scrambled for the door, Tyrus said, "Bastet wants to meet with you after you've eaten. She said, "Bring the cat.""

When she had calmed down Chandra scooped out a spoonful of pâté for Ivan and then prepared a plate for herself. Exactly what she munched on, she did not know, but it tasted better than anything in recent memory.

She slipped into the change of clothing that Tyrus left her, a more comfortable and silkier version of her old flight suit.

She grimaced as she looked in the mirror. It told all, and this reflection revealed a horror story. Even a platoon of stylists could not save her hair. She ignored it. Dead people weren't expected to have great hair any way, at least not until after they were embalmed.

Outside her door a woman, sort of, waited. Tall, lithe and beautiful, she towered above Chandra. She gazed down at Chandra with the striking emerald eyes of a tabby cat, and a face to match, but she walked upright on two legs like a woman. Ivan stared up at her, hopelessly in love.

She ran her hand across his back down to the tip of his tail. "Hello, Ivan. How did you sleep?"

He answered by rubbing his cheek along her legs. His message read: "She belongs to me!"

Finally she turned to Chandra. "I am Bastet. Will you two join me?"

"This is our destination," Bastet pointed to a door similar to countless others they passed.

Chandra did not expect what she found. After all the spectacular chambers, this one looked like a closet, a shabby one at that. It was nothing but an oversized construction shack, not unlike hundreds she had whiled away the hours in, cramped and utilitarian. A Mount Everest of rolled up plans completely obscured a corner drafting table. Above it, T-squares, triangles, a compass and other drafting tools hung from pegs mounted on the walls. Several sealed cartons of erasers waited to undo even the most horrendous error.

Some of the people in the room looked vaguely familiar, others simply looked odd, like the many alien species that she encountered every day in her job—or rather former job.

Several beings crowded around a table cluttered with blueprints, line drawings and star charts. It had once been a beautiful conference table. Although well made, it bore the scars of many years of indifferent abuse. The finish had dulled from use and lack of care. Water rings pocked the finish like craters on the moon. Off to the side a couple of half-consumed cups of coffee waited to be refreshed or tossed out.

One human with black pompadour hair stopped mid-sentence when Chandra, Ivan and Bastet entered. "Thank you, thank you very much...

"Are you the sweet young thing who just joined us?" the pompadour guy asked her. His white polyester cape draped down around an alabaster jumpsuit gaudily adorned with more sequins than Chandra's evening gown.

Chandra nodded.

When a drop of sweat trickled down his cheek, he wiped it away with a snowy scarf and handed it to Chandra. She cringed and held it away from her, suspended only by the very tips of her fingers.

"Did you bring any fried peanut butter and banana sandwiches?" he asked expectantly. "It's been centuries since I've had one."

"Sorry," Chandra said. "I don't remember seeing that on the ship's manifest."

His face fell. "I had faith in you, girl. I believed in you and you let me down. No fried peanut butter and banana sandwiches. How will I go on?"

"I'm sorry," she said.

"Did you bring me any Moon Pies?"

She shook her head. "No."

"RC Cola?"

"Huh uh."

"What about country fried chicken? Butter beans? Grits? Blueberry pancakes? Turnip greens simmered in pork lard?"

"I think I saw something about Scandinavian roe," she offered.

"You let me down, girl. You really did." He yanked the scarf out of her hand.

"Excuse me." Bastet pulled Chandra away from the man. "I reserved the conference room. We just have a few little issues to clear up and then you can all ask Chandra whatever you would like."

When he had ambled out of earshot Chandra said, "Thanks Bastet, I thought I was stuck." Chandra nodded to the pompadour guy.

"Oh, it's Elvis," Bastet said. "He wants everyone to call him, 'The King.' Just ignore him."

"Do you mind, Bast?" interrupted a burly red-haired man. "We're working on something here. Can't you come back later?"

"Finish up, Thor," Bastet said curtly. "I scheduled the room."

Thor shook his head. His helmet and its horns, shook with bewilderment. "I never understood why those dumb Egyptians ever worshipped you."

She did not respond, but Ivan hissed at the clean-shaven Viking who used his hammer, Mjolnir, as a pointer.

He held up his hand with his fingers spread. "Just five more minutes." Then he turned back to the blueprint. "I say if we set the charge right here— " he motioned with the hammer, "—we can have a habitable world in just a few thousand years."

"That's ridiculous," scoffed a real old guy with a long beard. "You can't set off a charge there. It will have absolutely no affect. You need to go back and take Demolition 101."

"Come on, God. It's not only a charge—it's a reaction," Thor said. "Try a Boilermaker with a mag detonator instead of just that series of weenie charges you want to use. It'll get the job done in a tenth of the time your plan will take. Before you know it, we'll have lifeforms. Not the ones that look like moldy green peppers—something that will eventually get a handle on the deity thing."

"Dad's right," a younger bearded man said. "It won't work. I think we should put a standard detonation right here." He, too, pointed at the drawing, except he pointed with his middle and forefinger.

"This is impossible," Thor said. Using the hammer he pointed at Jesus. "*He* likes Earth." Then he pointed at a warm glow hovering just above the younger deity's head. "*He* wants something with a lot of fire." He pointed at God. "And He just wants a lot of everything and at below cost. Even Trinity can't agree on what they want. How can the rest of us expect to?"

Chandra noted those present. Most of them she recognized as deities: Thor, the Trinity, Ganesa, Vishnu and Bastet. She stood in pretty impressive company!

Thor wheeled around and pointed Mjolnir at Chandra. "We are so glad you made it. When Elvis came he only brought those damned fried peanut butter and banana sandwiches." He shuddered. "Disgusting!"

"—All right guys, you're five minutes are up—Out." Bastet commanded the horde gathered around the drafting table.

"We're a bit busy here, Bast," Thor protested. "Can't you take her somewhere else?

"Thor, if you don't move, I'll make an anatomical alteration using your own hammer," Bastet said.

Thor laughed at her. "You mean, "astronomical," he corrected. "You said anatomical."

"I know what I said. Do you want me to draw you some plans?"

Thor's Nordic features paled. "You wouldn't believe what she did with my hammer one other time."

He shuffled from side to side and then backed away from her until he had moved out of her reach. As he sidled past Chandra he whispered, "Watch out for her; she's mean."

After the crowd thinned, Chandra joined Bastet and Ganesa at the conference table. A handful of the original crowd continued to mingle just out of hearing range.

Close up, she could see that graffiti had been carved into the table.

Bastet watched Chandra read the different inscriptions. Bastet hissed when the engineer came to the one scribbled immediately under her own hands. "Bast loves Elvis."

Bastet hissed. "Thor is so immature."

Chandra tried to imagine the dignified Bastet and the one who handed her the sweaty scarf in midst of a steamy romantic encounter. It was too absurd to even consider. "Nobody would ever believe it, would they?"

"Of course not," Bastet said. "Elvis is a dog person."

While they waited for more privacy, Tyrus popped his head into the room. "Someone said you need me."

"Tyrus, get your friend some refreshment, and one for me—no octane," Ganesa said. "And a couple of milks."

"Do you know who I am?" the elephant guy asked his guest.

"You said you're Ganesa." Chandra said.

"Does that mean anything to you?"

"As best I can remember, it's the same name as a Hindu god," she said.

"Mostly correct," he said. "But I *am* Genesa." He polished the nails of his lower hand against his silky jacket.

"*The* Ganesa?"

"The very same." His Eastern Indian accent grew thicker for emphasis. He paused to let Chandra think about it.

During the silence, Tyrus returned to the room with a drink for Chandra, Ganesa, Bastet and Ivan.

"Let's see; non-alcoholic for Ganesa, milk for the felines, and rotgut for the lady," Tyrus said to himself. "I did it right this time."

Ivan jumped up on the table between Chandra and Bastet. After sniffing his cup to assure quality, he dunked his paw in the cup like a donut, and then licked the milk clinging to the fur tufts between his pads. Bastet lapped her drink more delicately, directly from her personal extra wide cup. Soft purrs escaped her throat.

Before Tryus could sneak out the door, Bastet yelled, "Not so fast, Ratstall. Sit."

Reluctantly he complied.

Bastet looked at Tyrus and then to Chandra. "While we discourage interaction between the players and the help, I think some of Mr. Ratstall's input could be useful until Chandra fully comprehends her position here—and his."

Pointing at Ganesa, Chandra said, "If he's a god and you're a god—" Chandra stared at the Egyptian goddess then spun around to face Tyrus, "Are you telling me that *he's* a god?"

"Ratstall, answer her," Bastet ordered.

"Chani, I'm not a god; I'm just dead. Do you think they'd make *me* a god?" He looked at Ivan, who had fallen asleep on the table. "Hey, that's a nice looking cat."

Chandra gulped down the rest of her drink. She felt as low as she had when the Corvian first approached her in Talisman's Bar, what seemed like years ago. "So, that's it. I'm dead, too." Her head dropped into her hands.

"Of course you're not dead," Bastet said. "You're one of us now. You have won the hand for your player and you've earned the right to become a player yourself."

"What do you mean—player?" Chandra asked. "Do you mean a god? Me? Right!"

"You could say that. Actually that's what many of the races across the universe think we are."

"And what do *you* say?"

Bastet glanced sideways at Ganesa who said, "We're really not "gods" in the sense that humans think. We play a game that sometimes affects other events throughout the universe. Any other questions?"

"Where am I, and how did I get here?"

"She's a little slow sometimes," Tyrus said apologetically to Bastet.

Ganesa held an old star chart and pointed dead center with his trunk. "At this very moment you are here—in the very middle of the universe."

"But how did I get here?"

"You delivered the special piece to where it was supposed to go," Tyrus said.

"I hate to disappoint all of you, but I didn't make it anywhere near the coordinates Tyrus gave me. I sure didn't get there before the Feast of the Fat Bore, and, on top of everything else, I lost the crystal piece. Tyrus, I blew it."

"Not really. I changed the coordinates," Tyrus confessed. "If I hadn't, as dyslexic as you are, you wouldn't have found it in a million years. Kiddo, I know how lost you get. You make the very same mistakes every time. Remember all the times I tried to teach you to navigate?"

"That variable singularity permits travel in and out of our space," Ganesa said. "It moves. Another hour and there would have been no way to transport you and your ship here. That's why the strict deadline; pardon the pun. Since the singularity moves, it permits beings from all over the universe to take a chance. That's how Richard Nixon got here. He sent the orb with the Apollo Eleven crew to the moon. Rumor has it that he found it hidden in one of Kennedy's secret compartments in the Oval Office."

Chandra quietly mulled over the new revelations.

Thor returned waiting quietly for a moment.

"Excuse me." He finally broke the silence. "I'm sorry we got off on the wrong foot. I want to welcome you to our little group." He reached out to shake her hand, and Chandra returned the gesture. The silence between the sentences grew deafening. "Hey—that's some cat," Thor said uncertainly.

Almost as if he had been trained to act on a signal, Ivan rolled over on his back, curling his paws and giving Thor an innocent 'come hither' look. Chandra gave Bastet and Ganesa a quick glance, smiled diplomatically and said, "Yes, he is.

"No problem, Thor. And just to show you there are no hard feelings, you want to pet my cat?"

Moments later, the Viking god was seen fleeing the room, his forearm bleeding profusely. A few of the others heard him complain something about implementing a "no pets policy."

Once Chandra and the audience encircling her quit laughing, she confessed, "I hate to disappoint you, but I left the piece somewhere on the other ship. Rithel Bartlemist or Lance Goode, or whoever he is must have it now."

Her audience kept quiet.

"Wright mounted the crystal on Ivan's collar. It fell off. Just look."

Bastet ran her fingers around the cat's throat. As Chandra had promised, she could feel the small mounting device built into the collar, but it held nothing.

"Crystal?" Bastet dropped her head to allow Ivan to give her a few gentle head-butts. "Believe me, you still have it. The orb—that is."

Chandra almost knocked over her empty glass. "The orb? Why, that's worthless glass."

"Let me put it another way," Ganesa said. "Did you ever play Monopoly?"

"Sure."

"What game piece did you always use?"

It had been so long since she had played the game, she had to think about it for a while. Last time she had played was with her younger brother, and he cheated.

"I liked the wheelbarrow. That way I'd always have a place to put all the money I won."

"Chandra, the orb is the same as the wheelbarrow. The lead piece, itself, costs just a few microcredits, but as a Monopoly piece it could be worth an imaginary fortune. The orb, by itself, could bring a couple of credits as a trinket. While in your possession, you too, become the game piece. The possessor also tends to become a focal point of pivotal events. Wars start around you, revolutions, and murders. Go back and look at the last nine days. You'll be amazed at everything that you inadvertently caused."

"It was never the crystal?"

"Hell, no," Tyrus said. "I knew you'd be afraid of losing it if it was too valuable. I won the crystal in the game from that Bartlemist chump. It's valuable, sure—I gave it to you to light your way, literally—just a flashlight."

"You survived your trip through the black singularity, Chandra," Bastet said. "That could happen only if you have the orb. As you drew nearer to the black hole's sector, the orb resonated at a frequency that protected your ship from the crushing gravity. Both you and Ivan are quite alive."

"Without the orb that black hole would have squashed you like a bug," Tyrus said.

"Chandra," Bastet said, "Some people are born great, some

have it thrust upon them."

"And some stumbled onto it like a blind pig," Tyrus said. "Congratulations, Porky."

"Thanks, Ty," Chandra said.

Chandra looked around at the beings milling around in the corner. She asked Tyrus, "If you're dead, why don't I see a lot of other dead people?"

"They go somewhere else," Bastet said. "You can visit them if you like."

"But if Tyrus and Ranknard didn't make it here with the orb, why are they here?"

"Ratstall and Ranknard both died in possession of the orb, and no one else knew where to find it. With the stakes so high in this particular round, the other players agreed to give you a hint. Compare it to drawing a Community Chest card in Monopoly. Once our happy helpers—" she nodded at Tyrus, "—had told you where to find it, we couldn't very well kill them again. That wouldn't be very sporting or godlike. So we put them to work in the kitchen."

"Tyrus told me that something terrible would happen if I failed."

"No," Tyrus said. "I said something awful would happen to everyone."

Tyrus glanced at Bastet, then clammed up.

"I'm afraid we underestimated the shortages caused by those freighter hijackings," Bastet said. "We may be "gods" but we still eat. That's why you found the less than elegant meal of cheese and crackers when you first arrived. Even for that, we had to scrape the bottom of the cracker barrel.

"It had already started. Some of our less patient members had started folding up the board. So, when you took the Bartlemist ship and ambled into our black hole, you brought new life and a hefty supply of refreshments to a very old and tired bunch of players," Bastet said. "Had the other players retired in earnest, they would have folded up the entire board and closed the game."

"What did you mean, you were going to fold up the board and leave?" Chandra asked.

"In a real-life game your Milky Way galaxy is just one square on the board. Other galaxies make up other squares on the board. When they folded the portions of board those squares disappeared—forever. A few galaxies have already suffered a tremendous loss of life."

"Indirectly Rithel Bartlemist is responsible for that loss of life," Chandra said. "He orchestrated the freighter hijackings to defraud his insurance companies and create the pretense of a shortage."

Bastet straightened herself to full height. "He did, did he? How do you know this?"

"He confessed to me when he thought he was going to kill me," Chandra said.

Bastet looked to Ganesa. "This must be addressed."

The elephant nodded in agreement.

"So what would've happened if they folded up the entire board?"

"The end of time," Ganesa said. "Time as most lower beings know it."

"All those beings just snuffed out for all eternity?" Chandra gasped.

"Their lives would be recycled," Ganesa said. "But by their finite frame of reference it would be an eternity before they were. After, creation of a new universe takes a while. But now, we'll be able to play for at least another billion years or so."

"It's a big freighter, but how can it feed all these people for that long?"

"You wouldn't believe how Jesus can stretch out a meal," Ganesa said.

"So we just stand around for all eternity at a party playing a dumb game," Chandra said. "Isn't that awfully boring?"

"It's much more than that."

"Come, look at this." Bastet led them to another room.

The room appeared to be a workshop of some sort. Heavy-duty saws, grinders, drills and an assortment of other construction equipment filled the room.

"This is what we do," said the old man from Team Trinity. "This is our workshop."

He pointed at a slowly rotating spiral galaxy suspended by a bar of stars running through its center. Chandra could make out individual stars as they swept past her. It looked familiar and strangely foreign at the same time. "Is that the Milky Way?"

"Very good," he said. "You're looking at it from a different angle than you've seen before. Even the holos taken by probes have never shown this perspective. Stunning, isn't it?"

"It's breathtaking. You made all this?"

God sighed. "I'm afraid I had help. Too much help."

Behind him someone hidden beneath a welder's helmet struck a spark and ignited a torch. "How 'bout I just close up this little gap here," called Thor.

"Thor, move over a few billion kilometers that direction." God pointed at the plans and rolled his eyes. "Idiot, that area's inhabited."

That dense mass of tiny diamond-like suns obscured Chandra's view of home, the Earth.

Suddenly she felt very alone and homesick.

"We create new universes," Bastet said. "We seed worlds with new life. Sometimes, if we feel like it, we go visit the places."

"I'm not stuck here forever?"

"We have some logistical problems to work out. Lately, we've had difficulties getting in and out. But once those have been corrected you can come and go at will."

Bastet nodded at the galaxy. "That Team Trinity—they're masters of creation. They do some nice work, don't they?"

"Take Thor for example," God said. "And when we're finished, please take him. He went to Earth around 1200 BC. He returned later and inspired a late twentieth century television show about an inept builder. The show's character captured Thor's true character and ineptitude—you've heard of the Big Bang?"

Chandra nodded.

"That was Thor's fault," God explained. "We wanted to set the charges in different places so we would have a nice distribution of life-bearing worlds. You know, spread things out. He decided to improvise. He set off a massive central explosion instead—the Big Bang."

"We've had problems since the beginning," Bastet added.

"What kind of problems?" Chandra asked.

"When we take leave from the Game for whatever reason, we're having problems with the communications from here to here." Bastet pointed at the chart with a very sharp claw.

"Here's your problem," Chandra said. "This asteroid belt blocks signals every fifteen years. But even when the asteroids have moved out of range then you have to contend with this orbiting system blocking it intermittently. No wonder communications are such a mess!"

"Another thing, these two galaxies are colliding." God pointed at the Whirlpool Galaxy and a much smaller galaxy plunging right into it. "You humans call this mess M51." He pointed at four points of light. "Those planets are inhabited. If we don't do something we're going to lose them. And any charge big enough to separate the galaxies will kill most of the life. It took so long to grow them. We figure if we add a galactic whirlpool right here, the spinning will correct the problem in about thirty-million years."

"What you need is an architect," Chandra said. "I have a friend who could correct these plans and make them workable. You've heard of the Haritian Spiral Dome, one of the Seventy-five Wonders of the Galaxy? Well, Wright Aulweighs built it. He's the one that Ivan really belongs to."

"You can't just bring him here anymore than we could bring you here," God said. "But if you think he could help, you could guide him here as your playing piece in the same way your player guided you here, with a little help from Ratstall."

"Who was my player?"

"I was—" said a gravelly woman's voice. It belonged to a redhead, or rather, The Redhead. She approached the circle and laughed, the guffaw Chandra had heard when she intercepted the old Earth broadcast transmissions as she traveled between assignments.

"You're the god the Lucillians worshipped," Chandra exclaimed.

Lucy touched her hair. "They're great people," Lucy said. "Some of them will never get past that orthodox and reform problem of the black and white series versus color.

"Bastet, don't you think we should send Chandra and Ivan out for a little reconnaissance mission?" Lucy asked.

"Can I leave here?"

"Not now," God said. "The entrance is misaligned. The black hole is the only way in and out. Occasionally, when the singularity is lined up just right we can make a short call.

"You could go back and have a quick conversation with your friend, but you can't stay long. With all the interference, you can't make a connection for more than a few minutes."

"Before you go, how about a quick snack," God suggested. "Would the cat like some caviar?"

Chapter Thirty-Two

Wright sat alone under the stars, staring at the constellation of the garbage freighter. With his eyes fixed on a distant star, he sighed.

Although he had not known her very long, he had become very fond of Chandra. Something had happened to her. He just knew it.

"Hi, Wright," a familiar voice spoke behind him.

He looked around.

"Hi, Chani!"

"No, Wright, I want to *get* high.

"Sorry, fresh out, but...you're alive!"

"Yeah, I'm fine." She reached over and handed Ivan to him.

"Where have you been?"

"Listen, Wright, I don't have much time..."

Acknowledgments

I never would have been able to write this book without the support, knowledge and skill of an army of wonderful people. Thank you to my husband, Weems Smith Hutto—your very presence made it possible. I love you.

Thanks to my mentors, Lee Killough, for leading me through the publishing process, Selina Rosen, for looking at my proposal even when she had a tower of other manuscripts on her desk, Lynn Stranathan for all her hard work, Carole Nelson Douglas for advice and encouragement, Martha Schipul and Sondra Tyler for their encouragement, and Joanne Avant - you were a great first editor in junior high school.

Also David Lee Anderson, your cover is awesome.

And my most sincere thanks to my top sergeant with a red pen, Dorothy Wilkinson, for being the proofreader's proofreader; to Margaret Rainbolt, Bobb and Debbie Waller for being honest even when it hurt; to Peggy Dee and Mary Hamilton, who didn't tell me to go to hell *too* often. Thank you Ruthanne Brockway, for gently showing me the basics of journalism; Ruth McClure for technical assistance and also had to listen to "what-if" scenarios; to Chani and Wretched, who taught me how wonderful cats really are; and Karen Hooker and the real IVan the Terrible, brainstormers Sally Bahner, Pat Chapman. And finally, a special thanks to my proofreaders: Fran Pennock Shaw, Allison Owen, Lynn and Connie Crites and Andrea Albright.

You're all wonderful!

About the Author

Dusty Rainbolt is an award-winning freelance cat writer, and a fifth-generation Texan. She and her husband, Weems Hutto, live in the Dallas Metroplex with their cats, including three Turkish Vans. It's been reported that she hangs out in cemeteries and haunted buildings with a loaded camera. Dusty's book *Kittens for Dummies* (Wiley Publishing, Inc.) will be released in mid-December, 2003. She is working on a paranormal mystery, *Death Under the Crescent Moon* and a sequel to *All the Marbles*.

About the Artist

David Lee Anderson illustrates science fiction and fantasy for publication in paperback books, magazines, games and game cards. He's shown paintings at more than 350 convention art shows, and has been the artist Guest of Honor at twenty conventions since first showing art in 1980. First published in 1985, he's done work for TOR and Baen Books, Tomorrow SF, Isaac Asimov's SF, Mayfair Games, Bethesda Softworks and currently Yard Dog Press, among others. He directed the Art Programming track for LA Con II, the 1984 Worldcon, and the 1985 World Fantasy Con, taught art at grade school to middle school level part-time, and was an adjunct professor at Oklahoma City University teaching illustration. He was President of the Association of Science Fiction and Fantasy Artists (ASFA) from 1990-92. He is known in fandom as an an accomplished MC, former DJ at convention dances, rock and roll singer, guitarist and songwriter, and all-around party professional.

Yard Dog Press Titles As Of This Print Date

The Four Redheads: The Wrath of Satan, Linda L. Donahue, Rhonda Eudaly, Julia S. Mandala, & Dusty Rainbolt

The Garden In Bloom, Jeffrey Turner

The Geometries of Love: Poetry by Robin Wayne Bailey

The Golems Of Laramie County, Ken Rand

The Green Women, Laura J. Underwood

The Guardians, Lynn Abbey

Hammer Town, Selina Rosen

The Happiness Box, Beverly A. Hale

The Host Series: The Host, Fright Eater, Gang Approval, Selina Rosen

Houston, We've Got Bubbas!, Edited by Selina Rosen

How I Spent the Apocolypse, Selina Rosen

I Didn't Quite Make It To Oz, Edited by Selina Rosen

I Should Have Stayed In Oz, Edited by Selina Rosen

In the Shadows, Bradley H. Sinor

International House of Bubbas, Edited by Selina Rosen

It's the Great Bumpkin, Cletus Brown!, Katherine A. Turski

Judas Gene, Gary Moreau

The Killswitch Review, Steven-Elliot Altman & Diane DeKelb-Rittenhouse

The Leopard's Daughter, Lee Killough

The Lightning Horse, John Moore

The Logic of Departure, Mark W. Tiedemann

The Long, Cold Walk To Mars, Jeffrey Turner

Marking the Signs and Other Tales Of Mischief, Laura J. Underwood

Material Things, Selina Rosen

Medieval Misfits: Renaissance Rejects, Tracy S. Morris

Mirror Images, Susan Satterfield

Mirror, Mirror and Other Reflections, James K. Burk

More Stories That Won't Make Your Parents Hurl, Edited by Selina Rosen

Music for Four Hands, Louis Antonelli & Edward Morris

My Life with Geeks and Freaks, Claudia Christian

The Necronomicrap: A Guide To Your Horoooscope, Tim Frayser

Of Two Minds: Location Shoot, It's a Miracle, and Other Strange Stories, Bradley H & Sue P. Sinor

The Pinnacle, Gary Moreau

Playing With Secrets, Bradley H & Sue P. Sinor

Redheads In Love, Linda L. Donahue, Rhonda Eudaly, Julia S. Mandala, & Dusty Rainbolt

Reruns, Selina Rosen

Rock 'n' Roll Universe, Ken Rand

Shadows In Green, Richard Dansky

Stories That Won't Make Your Parents Hurl, Edited by Selina

Rosen

Tales from Keltora, Laura J. Underwood
Tales Of the Lucky Nickel Saloon, Second Ave., Laramie, Wyoming, U S of A, Ken Rand
Tarbox Station, Rhonda Eudaly
Texistani: Indo-Pak Food From A Texas Kitchen, Beverly A. Hale
That's All Folks, J. F. Gonzalez
Through Wyoming Eyes, Ken Rand
Turn Left to Tomorrow, Robin Wayne Bailey
The Twins, Selina Rosen
The Undead Ate My Head, Ethan Nahté
Wandering Lark, Laura J. Underwood
Weirdough, Inc., Selina Rosen & Sherri Dean
Wings of Morning, Katharine Eliska Kimbriel
Zombies In Oz and Other Undead Musings, Robin Wayne Bailey

Double Dog (A YDP Imprint):

#1:
Of Stars & Shadows,
Mark W. Tiedemann
This Instance Of Me,
Jeffrey Turner

#2:
Gods and Other Children,
Bill D. Allen
Tranquility, Tracy Morris

#3:
Home Is the Hunter,
James K. Burk
Farstep Station,
Lazette Gifford

#4:
Sabre Dance,
Melanie Fletcher
The Lunari Mask,
Laura J. Underwood

#5:
House of Doors,
Julia Mandala
Jaguar Moon,
Linda A. Donahue

Just Cause (A YDP Imprint):

The Bitter End
Selina Rosen

Death Under the Crescent Moon
Dusty Rainbolt

Duckrt Escapes from Jail
Zeb Rosenzweig

Duckrt: Mystery at the Museum
Zeb Rosenzweig

Getting It Real
Selina Rosen

The Ghost Writer
Selina Rosen

It's Not Rocket Science: Spirituality for the Working-Class Soul
Selina Rosen

Meditations of a Hoarder
Melinda LaFevers

Not My Life
Selina Rosen

The Pit
Selina Rosen

Plots and Protagonists: A Reference Guide for Writers
Mel. White

Vanishing Fame
Selina Rosen

**Fantasy Writers Asylum
(A YDP Imprint):**

Blood Songs
Julia Mandala

Gateway to Corimar
Julia Mandala & Linda L Donahue

Tale of the Black Heart
Linda L. Donahue

Non-YDP titles we distribute:

Chains of Freedom
Chains of Destruction
Jabone's Sword
Queen of Denial
Recycled
Strange Robby
Sword Masters
Selina Rosen

Three Ways to Order:

1. Write us a letter telling us what you want, then send it along with your check or money order (made payable to Yard Dog Press) to: Yard Dog Press, 710 W. Redbud Lane, Alma, AR 72921-7247

2. Use selinarosen@cox.net or lynnstran@cox.net to contact us and place your order. Then send your check or money order to the address above. *This has the advantage of allowing you to check on the availability of short-stock items such as T-shirts and back-issues of Yard Dog Comics.*

3. Contact us as in #1 or #2 above and pay with a credit card or by debit from your checking account. Either give us the credit card information in your letter/Email/phone call, or go to our website and use our shopping carts. If you send us your information, please include your name as it appears on the card, your credit card number, the expiration date, and the 3 or 4-digit security code after your signature on the back (CVV). Please remember that we will include media rate (minimum $3.00) S/H for mailing in the lower 48 states.

*Watch our website at
www.yarddogpress.com
for news of upcoming projects
and new titles!!*

A Note to Our Readers

We at Yard Dog Press understand that many people buy used books because they simply can't afford new ones. That said, and understanding that not everyone is made of money, we'd like you to know something that you may not have realized. Writers only make money on new books that sell. At the big houses a writer's entire future can hinge on the number of books they sell. While this isn't the case at Yard Dog Press, the honest truth is that when you sell or trade your book or let many people read it, the writer and the publishing house aren't making any money.

As much as we'd all like to believe that we can exist on love and sweet potato pie, the truth is we all need money to buy the things essential to our daily lives. Writers and publishers are no different.

We realize that these "freebies" and cheap books often turn people on to new writers and books that they wouldn't otherwise read. However we hope that you will reconsider selling your copy, and that if you trade it or let your friends borrow it, you also pass on the information that if they really like the author's work they should consider buying one of their books at full price sometime so that the writer can afford to continue to write work that entertains you.

We appreciate all our readers and *depend* upon their support.

Thanks,
The Editorial Staff
Yard Dog Press

PS – Please note that "used" books without covers have, in most cases, been stolen. Neither the author nor the publisher has made any money on these books because they were supposed to be pulped for lack of sales.

Please do not purchase books without covers.